When a Stranger Comes...

Karen S. Bell

A KSB Press Publication
Copyright © 2017 Karen S. Bell
Cover Design by Karen S. Bell

To find out more about this author's work, please visit www.karensbell.com.

ISBN-10: 1549772325
ISBN-13: 978-1549772320

Printed September 2017

Acknowledgements

The final version of this work is the result of many hours of review and support by Julia Bell. Her keen eye and instincts improved the narrative tenfold.

Thanks also are extended to my beta readers: Jenafer Bell, Nan Honig, and Carol Willingham.

Special thanks to Beth Isaacs for her time, patience, and excellent copyediting skills.

For Tim, as always.

When a Stranger Comes...

Karen S. Bell

"Greed is good," *Gordon Gekko from the movie*
Wall Street

The devil is in the details—Anonymous

Prologue

When she opened her eyes, it had taken Jodie a moment to realize she was lying on the living room floor. Automatically checking her wristwatch that now had a cracked plastic face, she saw that she had been unconscious for about 20 minutes. She was alone. That was good. There was blood all around her. That was not good. It had been difficult to get up and walk, but she needed to see the damage and tend to her wounds. Shuffling over to the front door, she engaged the deadbolt just in case he decided to come back. Usually, after one of these brutal fights, he stayed away for several hours getting so drunk that his rage turned into remorse.

She turned on the bright florescent lights and looked in the bathroom mirror. What she saw was so shocking that she stared at her image in disbelief. Her left eye was swollen shut and the surrounding skin was dark purple. Her bruised and battered lips were swollen, cracked, and caked in blood. Two teeth were missing right in front giving her face the frightening hint of the homeless beggars she saw sleeping in the alleyways and picking through garbage. It hurt to keep her pummeled mouth open but her broken nose made breathing difficult. The metallic taste of blood oozing on her tongue and dripping down her throat made her gag. Her chafed skin, where his fists pounded on her chest and neck, was achy and throbbing. Gaping sores, almost to the bone on her arms and legs, were from where he kicked her with his heavy work boots after he knocked her down. Their exposure to the air or where they contacted her torn clothing stung as if touched by a hot poker. Ugly, chilling mementos of his snarling, wild-eyed mania as he bashed her again and again.

With shaky hands, she turned on the water and noticed her swollen black and blue knuckles most likely from when she punched him hard in his face. She moistened a hand towel and carefully brought it to her eyes. The warm compress felt good and she stood like that for several minutes until a wave of nausea hit her. She grabbed for the sink feeling dizzy and broke out in a cold sweat. *You fucking bastard, I hope I punctured your eye and scratched all the skin off your face!* For a split second the horror of that fight gripped her again and she swallowed hard, her bloody saliva choking her. Trying to take deep breaths was excruciating, so she took quick shallow puffs of air in an effort to calm herself, but her heart was racing and pounding like a drumbeat in her chest. Focusing on her wounds, she tried to regain her composure as she gingerly washed the blood off her face and body but kept dropping the wet towel in the sink.

And then the doorbell rang.

She froze, as a spontaneous paralyzing fear shot through her. Quickly, she turned off the water silencing any noise. Maybe whoever was there would go away if they thought she wasn't home. *No one can see me like this.* Then the banging started and for one frightening second she thought he had come back, angry that she bolted the door. "I know you're in there." It was Kerry, her next door neighbor. She hadn't realized she was holding her breath until she started breathing again. "Are you okay?" Kerry yelled. "I almost called the police. Open the door and let me in. You might need to go to the hospital. Jodie? ...Jodie?" Then she got annoyed. "Suit yourself." And the yelling, banging, and doorbell ringing stopped.

Waiting a few minutes until she thought it was safe, Jodie came out of the bathroom and sat on her bed. She looked at her packed suitcase, the empty threat that had started this most recent vicious confrontation. No more. Now she was certain. She had to leave. To get out of there. Right now. He used his fists on her...again. He had kicked her...hard. Next time he might kill her. Beaten to death. Another homicide in this godforsaken white trash part of town. *Why am I so stupid? Why have I stayed with this guy? I thought we had something, a future. Said he was so sorry the last time. Said he loved me. Said he'd never hurt me again. Lying scumbag!*

She left without so much as a goodbye note. *Why would he care anyway? The prick.* But before she walked out, her wounds opening anew, her blood dripping on everything, and her hands trembling, she poured the remaining whiskey in the 2-liter bottle on the crappy sofa. Her rampage gaining momentum, she bashed the flat-screen-52-inch-TV with the empty bottle knocking it off its stand, causing it to crack in several places. Nearly passing out again, she managed to smash all five bottles of his precious booze on the cheap linoleum floor. Shattered glass flew everywhere making the whole room a minefield for bare feet. *Good! I hope he comes home in the dark and walks on this in the morning.*

Her frenzy in full froth, she wobbled into the kitchen. Every dish crashed to the floor. Wine glasses. Crash. The pretty porcelain candlesticks they bought at the fair. Crash. Holding on to the kitchen counter to gain some strength before she grabbed her suitcase still on the bed, she found scissors in one of the drawers. Stumbling over to his closet and then his dresser, she cut up his shirts and pullovers, scissored the pant legs off his jeans, and clogged their bathroom toilet with his underwear. As an afterthought, she slashed the mattress, gouged the feathers from the comforter, cut the foam in the pillows into wedges. With a final relish, and gathering up all her remaining might and power, she slammed his laptop against the wall.

Then she hobbled as fast as she could. Threw her suitcase out the door and onto the pavement, it being too awkward to carry in her condition while negotiating the few stairs. Luckily, her car was parked close. Easing herself into the driver's seat, her lacerations making her wince, she stepped on the gas and left town, calming down only slightly when the trailer park was out of range of her rear view mirror. She did not speed. She did not want to get pulled over looking like someone's punching bag. At least she could see okay out of her good eye. Driving carefully, she took the highway heading north. Anywhere but here. Any town but this. Another ending, another lonely drive to nowhere…and then a sliver of hope. Always that sliver of hope. A new beginning. A fresh start. *I'll figure things out. Be smarter. And finally get it right. Yeah, this time, I'll get it right. Find a decent guy with a good job. Find a guy who doesn't drink. Find the life I've always wanted.*

The End

Chapter One

Thanking the cosmos

It had been a hard few days of long hours and late nights writing and rewriting. I'm glad to be done finally with this first draft of the manuscript and enjoy a quiet afternoon reveling in my accomplishment. I had just finished writing the last sentence, typed the "d" in end, and was about to quiet my mind, giving humble thanks to unseen energies, when the phone rang. *Damn it!* A most unwelcome disturbance interrupting my moment-of-silence ritual. "Stop that incessant ringing," I yell at the phone. It's either Margaret, my copy editor and friend, or my publisher. I'm not in the mood right now for either of them or any conversation, for that matter. This final book in the trilogy was charged with emotion and left me worn out. After finishing each novel, and this was my tenth, I thank the cosmos for my gifts and pay homage to the blessings afforded me in this life. Hard to believe, I had written ten books in four years. I let the machine pick up.

"Alexa, are you there? Lex, pick up, I have some interesting ideas about marketing your trilogy, especially, *Darkside*. Pick up. C'mon. I know you're there. All right then, I'm coming over to tell you in person." Click.

Margaret. Of course, it's her. She's more than excited with these new works and can't wait until they're published. But I just need to unwind right now and will have to temper her enthusiasm after she gets here. Multilayered novels with psychological overtones concerning female empowerment are themes that form my work, messages in sort of a code that either you get right away or if you don't you can still enjoy the work at face value. When I started writing this trilogy using the same woman, Jodie, as the main character, I knew that one of the books would be difficult. In the first two books, Jodie follows the universal female progression from young maid to nurturer. But in the last one, Jodie is stuck in-between these two archetypes never fully experiencing either.

Brightside, the first book, is a coming-of-age story set at a university. We are introduced to Jodie as a college freshman who distances herself from her nerdy high school image by consciously reinventing who she is through deceit and guile. Ultimately reconciling her contrivances with her true self, Jodie comes to realize that being sincere in all things brings a spiritual richness to one's life. Personal growth, identity crises, and sexual tension form the narrative. A happy ending heralds a bright future.

Inside/Outside is a journey of self-discovery where our Jodie is challenged in her marriage and parenting skills. Learning to compromise in her relationship, coming to terms with her child's shortcomings as well as talents, Jodie realizes the unique tapestry of our lives is uneven at best and the way we spend our time each day shapes, although haphazardly, our singular journey. The narrative is filled with plenty of emotional stress and a semi-happy ending that rings true as Jodie's inner turmoil finally surfaces so that she is more present, mindful, and can make desperately needed changes.

Darkside, the last book in the trilogy, is about a dysfunctional Jodie and a departure from my usual ideal of the feminine divine. A cautionary tale about the importance of choices. Jodie lives her life on automatic pilot not having the skills or self-awareness to see that she is attracted to violent men. The story is wrapped in the psychological tension brought on by the continuous loop these scenarios play in her life's path. Jodie, as an older single, suffers from borderline personality disorder, a consequence of her troubled childhood, so she compulsively seeks abusive, dangerous partners. Men who will eventually cause her physical harm.

Never learning from her mistakes, Jodie is like a hamster running on a wheel to nowhere. To make this point, except for changing the name of the neighbor, I repeat the opening paragraphs at the end of the book. This ploy helps readers understand the hopelessness and helplessness of Jodie's inability to change. To give them pause to reflect on their own choices and think about their own hamster wheels. Why do we deny ourselves happiness? Why are we so insecure that we choose a suboptimal existence? And why is it mostly women that behave this way?

Although it was a rough go to write, all my work not only sends messages to my readers but also teaches me something about myself as well. *Darkside* was no different. I don't know where these strange thoughts come from. Perhaps part of me, in my subconscious mind, is like Jodie in this book. With my own peculiar hamster wheel. My own continuous loop of worry and obsessiveness. Maybe…

Now, ignoring Margaret's interruption, I can savor having typed that last period in that last sentence. Another book finished. I have to pinch myself sometimes at my good fortune. Being paid handsomely for what I love doing. How many of us actually get to do that and not worry about how to pay the rent? Illogically, however, whenever I finish a project, a sense of impending doom, a fear of the unanimous dislike of the work from readers, nags its way into my conscious space. And as always, in my moment of silence, besides being thankful, I also ask the cosmos to send *Darkside* into the hearts and minds of the populace. To bless it and give it wide appeal. To make it a blockbuster, sell in the stratosphere, like my first book several years ago… a lifetime ago. I hold that wish in my heart. And every time I've made that wish after completing my books, I think of the wise old adage, *be careful what you wish for*, and laugh at myself.

I look at my watch. I have at least 40 minutes before Margaret gets here. The city is always mobbed, and going anywhere from point A to point B takes at least 40 minutes, so even though she lives relatively close, she probably won't get here before 1:40 pm, perhaps later. I pour myself a glass of Shiraz and walk over to the floor-to-ceiling windows and stand there feeling exhilarated at the height. Mountaintop omnipotence. My silly mind game, where I command all within my view. I love looking down at the continuous flow of busy, tiny dots of anonymous people and then looking out at the other buildings touching the sky.

Clear skies today. Bright sunshine. Another day of blazing hot sun with nary a wisp of clouds, our new normal. The daily weather is now controlled by our never-ending drought. I yearn for the familiar rainy day that brings a cozy feeling as I sit in front of the computer. But these blue skies at least afford me an awesome view of an average workday in the city. Little ant-people scurrying around, bumper-to-bumper toy cars inching forward. The outside world, for me, is like watching a silent movie with no plot. Soundproof windows and insulated walls make my loft peaceful and serene.

I know full well that down there is a cacophony of noise because it startles me whenever I emerge from my quiet paradise and walk the streets. Horns honk, brakes squeak, car doors slam, and people shout. Background talking noise flows out of every alley and crossing, the random beat of feet hitting pavement assaults the ear. A profusion of sound by the street philharmonic. The spectacle and clamor of the moving mob. As I look down, I remember a dream I once had where everyone walking on the street below looked up in unison and could see me at this very window. I was naked from the shower and they were waving and jumping up and down. Naked skin. Naked soul. Naked fear. That dream haunts me still, especially because I had it before my book deal and well before I bought this place. A premonition of the intrusion into one's privacy when celebrity and fame take over your life.

"The view alone is worth several million dollars," said the realtor when she showed me this Battery Park loft. I sucked in my breath in shock because of the déjà vu moment seeing this exact loft window and precise view from my dream. Premonitions, dreams of possible portending events, they are a quirk for both me and my mother.

"Yes, it's quite outstanding," she said misinterpreting my reaction and already pocketing her commission.

Standing here sometimes, because of the paranoia evoked by that vivid dream, I imagine one of the minuscule people separating from the crowd, a face illuminated by the sun like a spotlight, turned upward staring…at me. Ridiculous. This building, adjacent to two others of similar height, has these walls of glass, but no one can see inside because of some new technology that provides privacy day and night. Especially important for nighttime when the loft is lit up inside, but the glass can also be darkened during the day if the sun is too bright. Having windows such as these was an important selling point, because New York City is notorious for having voyeurs with Peeping Tom telescopes aimed at the ample supply of neighboring apartments to pursue their peccadilloes.

Being on the penthouse floor, I could see both rivers and a glimpse of the Statue of Liberty. I loved being downtown where Manhattan island narrows, and the West Side and East Side become a short distance from each other. This part of town affords a more peaceful lifestyle in the evenings and on weekends and is a refreshing change from the hustle bustle of midtown neighborhoods. It's also less expensive at the moment than uptown neighborhoods, such as Riverside Drive and Sutton Place. One can have a quiet stroll on a Sunday in the Wall Street financial district when crowds are scant, enjoy fine dining around South Street Seaport, and just be a stone's throw from trendy TriBeCa. Also appealing is this loft's close proximity to Chelsea Piers, a multi-faceted sports village. I take tennis lessons at their indoor courts whenever I need to break away from the computer and this apartment to enjoy the clever banter of my Columbian instructor who was well trained in Bogota.

This home, my sanctuary, is the epitome of the spoils of success that came at full speed when it finally happened. Never quite believing my good fortune, it always felt as if I were lifted by an unseen hand from my mundane, underpaid existence as a blogger and feel-lance writer to be plopped down into someone else's life. Like I'd shed my old skin and put on a new one. The snake analogy is perfect because achieving your life's dream, the good part, can be like slithering into the bright sunshine of recognition only to have certain aspects, the bad part, become so repugnant that it morphs into trying to find a rock to hide under. The realization of the underlying shallowness of instant fame. A fickle audience created by constant exposure.

The good part had its perks. The award ceremonies and galas. Invitations to dinner parties. Weekend getaways at private residences from the Caribbean to Maine. Private jets. The best tables at the best restaurants. The in-demand darling of talk shows because of my reasonably good looks, my ease and playfulness in front of the camera, and my first book an epic success. Also, because I was so young, I became the personification of *you can do it too.*

That started the bad part. A whirlwind of attention. My face plastered on advertising billboards, made-up stories in gossip magazines fueled by the nonstop television appearances orchestrated at first by my publicist but then developing its own momentum. My unappreciated cherished privacy vanished in a flash. A flash of cameras everywhere. A flash mob of adoring crowds…anywhere. The horror of losing my privacy. Not a moment's peace. Just doing my daily routine became stressful.

Paradoxically, when the flurry of celebrity subsides dissipating into nothingness, and crowds no longer gather, invitations no longer extended, and the talk shows have moved on, there's a dearth of self-esteem and looming depression. A shocking realization given my former disgust of the shallowness of fame. Fading adoration has turned my everyday life into the boring ordinariness that once I craved and now loathe. What remains is the unsettling disquiet of a debasing hunger and obsessive need for fawning masses that can't be explained. This has become the unfortunate iteration of myself living on the downside of world acclaim and notoriety. However, there's one positive outcome. I no longer fear paparazzi when I go about my business, which makes my current anonymity bearable at some level.

Writing my debut novel didn't come quickly. It took years to get it right in my mind before I sent it off to agents. Online tarot cards were my obsession on a weekly basis. These virtual cards told me a bright future was near at hand, to stay the course. I became a "new age" acolyte believing that we create our own reality with our thoughts, and thus envisioned my novel in bookstore windows, a bestseller, maybe even winning the Pulitzer. Fancied what I would do with the money when the royalties rolled in. I was driven and persevered, illogically feeling there was a guardian angel watching over me, never letting me quit.

I also tried to keep myself balanced, reminding myself that the process is the journey and that it's all about being creative, all about the craft of writing, and the fun of it. Not about monetary rewards.

Keeping this mindset was challenging because I lived in a roach-infested fourth-floor walk-up in Inwood, a section of the city that's way uptown. Daydreams of vast amounts of money from imaginary book sales could not be squelched, no matter how Zen I tried to be about my existence. To practice becoming mindful and pull myself into the present, I would find ways to count my blessings. Hands down it was that my online writing gigs let me work from home, so I rarely got crushed in the subway mobs during rush hour and could work on my novel in-between my paying gigs. These episodes of being grateful were only a pause, could not override, my cravings for success.

To feed my lust for money and fame, I was addicted to reading all the out-of-the-blue success stories about obscure self-published authors selling millions of their ebooks that got them six-figure deals with major New York publishing houses. My jealously toward those authors notwithstanding, I gained an insight into the new world of modern-day publishing. Indie publishing was an option, if I couldn't interest an agent or a traditional publishing house. It was somewhat of a relief to know that no matter what, my book would be published, even if I did it myself. I tried to feel empowered by that alternative but knew deep down that self-publishing reduced my calling to a hobby. Earnings in pennies. However, there were those million-to-one success stories that might be me.

Pushing through the doubts that invariably surfaced to sabotage my visions of success, I had given a few chapters to my mother in hopes of receiving some emotional nourishment and possibly evoke some premonitions concerning its path to being published. She said it was a budding "masterpiece." A quite minimal response and rather disappointing in its brevity. No predictions about its future...my future. It still felt good, though, to hear her call it a *masterpiece*, not there yet, but perhaps becoming one. So I slogged away, blogging and writing marketing pieces, and the like, to pay the rent. And then back to the work, nodding off to sleep at the computer and waking up when nearly falling off the chair.

It was tempting to enter the domain of young adult novels about romantic escapades with vampires, or a world full of zombies, polish off a quickly written dystopian fantasy, or plunge into erotica bordering on porn. Topics with a proven insatiable audience. But I couldn't do it, wouldn't be true to myself, if I pandered to the masses. I had read the greats as an English literature/creative writing major at Smith, so that was my yardstick. Old habits from required research papers, erudite discussions about the writing masters, and fiction projects red-penciled by my peers.

My definition of writer was hard wired from that experience, and so I never rested from the task. I was consumed with plot, characters, and obsessed with choosing just the right word for the cadence of the sentence. Hungered for the poetically written phrase. Writing, rewriting, crossing off chapter milestones from the "to-do" list, until after years of being in the throes of creativity, the final period was cast in the final sentence. The hypnotic and ravishing madness of that process. A cherished memory that now being obligated in a multiple-book contract subsumes with its deadlines and editorial teams.

It took months, nearly a year, to find an agent that said, "yes." Gloria Arnold of the Arnold Agency is legitimate and important. Her agency is a member of the Association of Authors Representatives with a list of bestselling authors. She loved the premise of *A Foregone Conclusion*. She instinctively knew it was written at just the right time for the evolving collective attitude toward single mothers. A Cinderella story without the prince, the novel is about an unwed teenager and high school dropout who manages to make a very successful go of her life. Her success flies in the face of conventional wisdom and the foregone conclusion that a woman in her predicament is doomed.

Luanne, who is trapped in poverty and surrounded by unsavory people, becomes resourceful and purposeful when her daughter develops life-threatening allergies. Inventing a natural, non-toxic, non-allergic household-cleaning product that skyrockets into a multi-million-dollar corporation, she not only saves her daughter but also saves herself. Although Luanne is sabotaged at every turn, defeated and undermined by disloyal and jealous cohorts, she remains determined, sassy, vulnerable, and ultimately a winner by anyone's standards.

I didn't have to delve very deeply to get the inspiration of that particular tale and my feminist ideals. My number one idol and role model is my amazing mother. She emigrated from mother Russia, still the Soviet Union at the time, having the sense to give birth to me on American soil. Under the guise of religious persecution, she sought asylum in the United States. The real reason being she was six-months pregnant and had been kicked out of her family for the shame of being an unwed mother. Thanks to her courage and ingenuity, I count myself extremely lucky to be a natural-born citizen.

Gloria's enthusiasm for *Forgone* and offer of a contract was a magical new world. Overnight, there was the wow-factor bidding war. The sums of money being bandied about were heart stopping, rare, and amazingly happening to me. I hovered as an observer to my changing reality. It was hard to grasp this wasn't some fiction I created. Luanne's story would resonate with women of all ages, all nationalities. *A Foregone Conclusion* became a blockbuster in the US and international bestseller translated into several languages. It garnered rave reviews from Kirkus, Publisher's Weekly, and the New York Times. Critics described the work as, *A literary triumph, Prose as poetry, A love letter to and for women,* and it set me up for life.

I became quite comfortable. No private jets, no entourage to do my bidding, but enough money to relax. I'm a writer, following my bliss and, at that time, in a three-book deal, so my writing continued. Titles started coming faster and the contract was renewed. I was not as prolific as some authors, and not selling in the stratosphere like the debut, but always selling well and making the bestseller list, albeit not in the top 10. Enough to keep my agent and publisher more than happy. But I had yet to match the success of *Foregone.* Once you taste the achievement of international acclaim, it's a heady experience, cherished, and continuously sought after...by me. I was addicted to the rush of it, more than the accompanying wealth. But, I couldn't quite get there again.

Reviewers were harsh saying that they were always disappointed by my not hitting the mark as flawlessly as the first. They compared every new work to my "masterpiece" as they called it, validating my mother's initial assessment. Their dismissal became my motivation to do better. I would rewrite until the world got fuzzy. *Foregone* had stayed at number one on the bestseller list for one year and in the top ten for another year. So, now, I keep polishing my writing hoping to repeat my brilliance. Striving to hit number one on the list again has driven me to self-induced torture.

My whole being has become a wellspring of characters and plots, wisdom, and perspective. Maybe this book will do it! No, maybe that one! Writing projects crowd out my dreams. Prey on me insidiously. But this time, unlike when I was writing *Foregone,* fear keeps me going instead of the thrill of writing. I'm petrified of writer's block and my contract being canceled. I have to keep working on a new book, like an actor who's afraid there won't be a next gig and says, "yes" to obviously lousy projects. Selling out to the production line instead of quality.

Neuroses have overtaken rational behavior. My fan mail assures me that I have loyal followers, but I have to keep testing it. Afraid if I don't keep the pipeline of books humming, they will disappear and I will become the dreaded mid-list author, ultimately dropped by Jameson Publishing. My paranoid behavior is my agent and publisher's gain. Only Margaret knows that my desperation to once again dominate the literary scene is the motivation for churning out titles and not the contracts. Even my mother doesn't know about my warped psyche. My joy of being a writer has been slowly turning into my agony. I know I need to take a break. I know that I'm *about* to break.

So as soon as I finished the last sentence for *Darkside* and immediately after I took that all-too-short meditative moment before the phone rang, fear replaced the satisfaction of a completed project. Except that this time, there's a whiff of a feeling that the Jodie trilogy will bring me back to international acclaim. This trilogy has a real chance of being a hit because trilogies are popular. Trilogies are the new family sagas. Trilogies are the new cliffhanger chapter serials of old. So, these stories just might do it for me. Hope. The tarot cards support this win. I really need it, or I'm going to lose my mind and wind up in a straitjacket at Bellevue Hospital. Logically, I know I'm head and shoulders more successful than most writers slogging out their ignored work. So why do I need more? I know. I know. Get real. Enjoy the journey. Enjoy this view. This fantastic view. But I'd do anything for just one more chance at the stratosphere of success.

Just then, a bolt out of the blue, a startling flash of bizarre heat lightning with long scary tentacles bursts across the sky. It forks to the now strangely empty sidewalk accompanied by an extremely loud explosion of thunder. Boom! Like a bomb going off, boom, another round of thunder rumbles through the loft. I barely recover from the instinctive rush of adrenalin brought on by a sudden unexpected noise, when the sound of the doorbell buzzer makes me jump again with fright and I nearly spill my wine. Oh...right. Margaret. Pulse back to normal. I look at my watch, 1:40. Forty minutes exactly.

Chapter Two

The stranger

Margaret is on my permanent access list with the concierge and I gave her a key for my private elevator. She can just come up without the concierge notifying me. When I configured this condo loft space, I opted to put in a small, enclosed lobby so that the elevator didn't land right in my living room. The wooden door with etched glass insert added an elegant touch and was rarely locked but Margaret always knew better than to barge in without ringing the doorbell buzzer. It's a purposely-harsh sound that I can hear when lost in thought in my study at the other end of my loft. Finishing the wine in one gulp, I open the door.

I greet Margaret with forced enthusiasm. I still wasn't in the mood for company, but it was worse than that. She was not alone. I sigh and brace myself for another hanger-on trying to get into our inner circle. At least he's better looking than some of Margaret's other sycophants. Adoring fans wanting me to sign their books is one thing. People wanting to invade my space to gawk right here in my loft, well that's entirely another matter. Invasions of that sort still annoy me, especially when I'm unprepared mentally to receive anyone. But then, I guess it means my mojo is still working to some degree.

"Hey, how's it going?" I say smiling slightly as I let them in.

"Lex...Alexa, I'd like you to meet my cousin, Alex. How funny is that?"

A cousin this time. How tiresome.

"Nice to meet you," he says while nodding and shaking my hand. "That Chinese Emperor in plastic in your anti-room there is quite…"

"Lucite, not plastic," I interrupt.

"Yes, of course, wearing those beautiful red-silk robes. It's quite a lovely piece and that porcelain umbrella stand almost too pretty for an umbrella."

What is he a decorator?

"The emperor was a present from one of her Asian…" Margaret adds before I interrupt again.

"It was sent to me through my agent by a loyal Asian-American fan and is one of my prized possessions. The umbrella stand was bought at the big flea market in Paris. The mahogany console that the emperor sits on is a valued antique and the Art Deco octagon-shaped beveled wall mirror I found in SoHo. So, you're a designer, interested in that sort of thing, I guess? I wasn't forewarned that Margaret was bringing someone, but I'm in no need of a designer just now."

I give Margaret my blank stare of annoyance. Then I study her cousin and immediately become transfixed. Something…odd. He doesn't seem to notice my scrutiny. Walks right past me into the living room. Something about this guy is not right. Something…is…very weird. I get a rush of a nervous feeling. An awful creeping premonition of strangeness. Unsettling. *What is it? Hmm.* He reminds me of someone.

But who?

"Didn't I tell you this was a fabulous place?" Margaret asks Alex as she drags him over to see the view. "Nice, huh?"

He nods slowly, like he's impressed.

"Can I get you something? Water, coffee, tea?" I ask being polite but actually becoming increasingly irritated along with feeling rattled at this intrusion. Margaret should know better than surprising me with a guest. I'm not that vain, but come on. She knows what I look like when I'm working. No make-up. Greasy hair. Comfortable sweats. It would have been nice for a heads up. Plus, I'm in no mood to be social after working almost all night with just a few hours cat nap. Maybe if I yawn, they'll leave soon. I yawn. No reaction. But then I remember, she has some important news for me. Oh well. Better make the best of this.

"Some ice water would be great," he says.

"I'll get it," says Margaret and runs into the kitchen slamming cabinet doors and getting ice water from the fridge dispenser. "Wait," she yells, "Do you want sparkling water or plain?"

"Great, I'll have some Pellegrino," he says in a strong, deep voice with no discernible accent.

"No, it's straight from the fridge, one of those fancy-schmancy kind that serves sparkling from the dispenser," she calls to us. "How about you, Lex?"

"Sure, fizzy sounds good."

I direct him to have a seat and he walks with a slight limp over to my cushy cream-colored leather, L-shaped sectional sofa, puts his briefcase on the floor and sits down resting his arms on the back. The body language of being in charge. I sit opposite in my club chair from my old apartment. This well-worn greenish, suedeish recliner, a garbage night found treasure, is a constant reminder of how far I'd come and stands out as an oddity in my well-furnished home. It's also my talisman for chasing away writer's block. Sit in the chair and ideas being to flow. I don't understand how it works, it just does. I'd had a lot of need for its remedy in the last few years.

Cousin Alex sits looking at me and then around at the loft and back to the view offered by my wall of glass, like he's making a mental calculation of the cost of my lifestyle. The rather large sofa that he's sitting on is dwarfed by the 15 ft. ceilings and more than ample square footage of the open floor plan. Soft, soothing earth tones are the color palate for my walls, pillows and throws, offset by the large, woolen antique Oriental rug in opulent blues, reds, and greens over my dark, bamboo floors. I see him eye my wildly colorful and quite costly Chihuly hand-blown glass bowl, the perfect complement to the glass coffee table designed by Piero Lissoni, where it is placed for optimum enjoyment. While he studies the surroundings, I study him boldly in the silence before Margaret comes in with the drinks. He wasn't much of a talker and I wasn't feeling like making small talk myself, which afforded me the opportunity to continue observing him quite intensely until I knew why he seemed familiar.

Stonily observing every detail of his face, it suddenly became clear to me in a rush, that Alex was actually someone I knew very well. It was so startling that I almost gasped audibly at the shock when I realized he was a character from one of my books sprung to life. Not in name, of course, but in every other way. A dark-haired, blue-eyed handsome lad that is the consistent image in my mind when I write the villain or the love interest. With his chiseled features, thick black hair, lightly tanned skin, sexy stubble of facial hair, Alex is the manifestation of the exact words used to describe the good guy in my debut.

And he is right here in this room. Right here in the flesh. Alive. Sitting on my sofa. I know that description is not like looking at a photo and readers can come up with their own mental image. But here's the thing, his face, Alex's face is what I saw in my mind when I wrote his character, Rick, in *Foregone*. The first romantic hero that I pictured and the basic model for all the others that came later. His exact face. A knot forms in my stomach. *How does one deal with absurdity?*

"Okay, here we are," says Margaret, as she sets the tray of drinks on the coffee table and joins Alex on the sofa. "Let me give you some background here. Alex just moved here from LA. He's the creative director and set designer for Off Street Films, a newly formed but apparently well-funded production company in TriBeCa that's looking for new projects. I gave him the first two manuscripts of your trilogy and told him about *Darkside.*" *Now it makes sense why he's been scoping out my apartment. A set designer.*

"Let me take over here, Peggy." *Peggy?* I ask her with my eyes and she just shrugs.

"I love the concept of these books," Alex continues, "the different dimensions of the female psyche manipulated by life's challenges, molded by unique circumstances. From what Peggy tells me, *Darkside* is kind of a modern day *Looking for Mr. Goodbar* meets *Sons of Anarchy*. So I was thinking of combining all those stories into one. Have a tragedy happen just after Jodie gets married when she graduates college, and before any kids, throwing her into the Jodie of *Darkside*. That version of Jodie and her terrible choices becomes the main plot of the movie."

This angers me. "Whoa. Stop right there," I say in a tone of displeasure. "Is this the interesting marketing idea you mentioned when you called me, Margaret?" She looks at me perplexed. Then to Alex, "You sound as if there's an imminent deal. There's no imminent deal. This is the first time I've heard about this. Did Margaret tell you she spoke to me and I was interested? If she did, she was deceptive. She knows how strongly I feel about this.

"I swore I would never allow any of books to be made into a film again after my horrible experience with A *Foregone Conclusion.* I felt violated. The story was in tatters, the movie was a bomb and probably led to my subsequent work not selling as well, now that I think about it. Right off the bat, you brazenly tell me how you *intentionally* want to destroy the integrity of the trilogy. No-no. Emphatically, no. I don't even know the movie you mentioned, the mister candy and the other...sons...whatever you are referring to."

I stand up to signal the end of this meeting. My eyes send daggers to Margaret and I have already fired her in my mind. She knows she's in trouble when she catches my look.

"It's *Looking for Mr. Goodbar*, a financial and critical success, I might add, and the other was a recent hit TV show about a biker gang."

"I don't care. Not interested. Sorry. I'm busy just now and exhausted. I need to rest before taking care of important business. If you'll excuse me. You can show yourselves out."

"Wait, Lex! Hear him out. This is different," says Margaret jumping up and looking petrified as if she just saw a spider. *She definitely caught the meaning of my look.*

"No, I'm done. As I said, not interested. Good day." I walk into the hallway to my bedroom and shut the door firmly. I hear murmuring in the living room for about two minutes and then the front door clicks shut.

I'm furious and run the water for a bath to calm myself. Half undressed, I decide another glass of wine is warranted and walk out to get one. I stop short and let out a startled scream.

"Oh, I'm so sorry," he says, as I run back to get a robe and turn off the bath before coming back out.

"What in the hell are you still doing in my loft? Look, Alex, mister, whoever you are," I say calmly trying to recover some decorum by acting in control, the mature and successful woman who's no longer half-naked. "I could have you arrested for being here uninvited. When I asked you to leave, I meant it. Margaret's cousin or not. I don't know you. And actually, I don't care to. So please leave. At once." And I walk toward the door.

"At least read the offer," he says as he pulls a packet out of his briefcase and puts it on the coffee table before walking over to the door. "Read the offer and then come out with me for dinner tonight. Make reservations at your favorite and most expensive restaurant. I'll come back here at 8:00. Even if you're still not interested in working on this project, I'd like to take you to dinner." He leans in as if to kiss me and his alluring, strong, masculine scent, a mix of the freshness of a pine-tree forest, wood fires burning, worn leather, and the wind-whipped sea knocks me back and arouses me. My unexpected reaction confuses me, as he hands me his business card instead of a kiss.

"Oh," I say awkwardly after snapping my head back before realizing what he's really doing. I look at his card. "What? What is this? Your name is Wainwright? Alex Wainwright? This is a joke, right? And not funny at all, I might add."

"One of life's strange coincidences," he says playfully. Before I can say any more, he's out the door and jumps in the elevator. I'm more than shocked. A coincidence? He being a ringer for Rick? Having the same name as me? Well, not really my name. Of course, Alexa Wainwright is a made-up perfect pen name that I changed legally.

Gladys Lipschitz, my real name, a major misstep on the part of my mother, was a name that belonged embroidered on the shirt of a pink waitress uniform. Gladys evokes an image of a woman who wears a hairnet and keeps a small lead pencil tucked behind her ear and an order pad shoved into her skirt pocket. She works the late shift serving greasy food at a dive luncheonette on the upper far West Side under the elevated trains. That Gladys personified my obsessive fear of being a failure as a writer. I wanted to get as far away from her as I could. Alexa connoted sexy and sophisticated. Wainwright sounded snooty, British, non-ethnic.

I also played with the idea of calling myself Alex instead of Alexa, but I really didn't want any gender confusion. I was proud of being female and wrote mainly for a female audience. If I had done that, though, Alex Wainwright and I would have the exact same name. Odd, so odd. Also odd is his lingering scent. From that quick close encounter when he leaned in and his masculine aroma filled my nostrils, I now smell it everywhere. It has taken over my loft. I spray Pledge on my furniture and mop the floors. Pour my favorite perfume all over me after I take that bath. Spray it into the rooms. No good. His scent is in my nose. In my being. Leaves me restless and uneasy and doesn't go away. I'm edgy, unsettled, fearful that I'm being marked for something. A spider web of intrigue is ensnaring me. Pulling me closer to its center where I can't escape. First it's his scent that I can't get rid of.

What's next?

The packet stays untouched on my table for several days. Not interested. *Why bother reading it?* Finally, I grab it and throw it in the trash. Sitting down in my club chair with my morning coffee the next day, I pick up one of my gossip magazines that's sometimes on that table with the mail, a guilty pleasure. Actually, it's more of a compulsion, checking to see if there are any articles about me. Of course not. Not anymore. But wait. *What the...?* It's not a magazine. It's that damn proposal. Shape shifting into a magazine and then back again to mock me. I drop it in horror on the table and then throw out the rest of my magazines. The packet gives me the willies, but I won't touch it again. Trying to bring logic into the equation and rekindle the memory of throwing it out, I recreate the steps. Envision the garbage can and try and feel the packet in my hands. Can't completely remember doing it. I don't know, maybe I really didn't throw it out. Still creepy, though.

Margaret repeatedly calls and I won't answer. She texts me incessantly and I don't respond. She knows better than to just show up here when I'm angry at her, afraid of my reaction. Afraid I might actually fire her. She's learned that it's best to give me a cooling off period when I've outright threatened to fire her in the past or just have given her that look she's come to know. It has worked before but not now. I'm so livid with her presumptuousness. A movie deal! When she knows full well how I feel. Then I just go for it. "You're fired," I finally text her at a random moment on a random day.

I had already begun busying myself with editing and copyediting *Darkside* and, although boring, it was important. By now, I was pretty good at catching wrong words that spellcheck didn't catch, "faze" instead of "phase" and the like, and missing periods at the end of sentences. So...who needs Margaret? Saved me money and her bothersome obsequiousness. The editors at Jameson would go over it again, so no real worries about missing something.

However, there's one aspect of Margaret's help that I will miss, but oh well. She gives my writing a brightness that sometimes gets lost in the complicated story lines. Tightens the narrative. Fills in the plot holes. Sharpens the tone. Her instincts are genius. She's the perfect collaborator. I found her on a jobs website for editors and she polished up *Foregone* for not much money. She was probably responsible for Gloria, saying "yes" and then Jameson House offering that three-book deal and hefty advance. Yeah, she was a real find and was also company. A welcome disruption from the intrinsic isolation of being a writer. I admit, I'll miss her spontaneity, her easy laugh, and her off-beat style. But I'm stubborn and she crossed the line. No regrets. Well, maybe. Firing her in a text was a chicken shit thing to do. I feel better about myself after I mail her a large severance package.

Done.

Not done.

I forgot to take her off the easy access list and to lock my front door, which I rarely ever do because my private elevator needs a key. Margaret still has a key, an unfortunate oversight on my part.

"Please Alexa, don't do this," she says hysterically crying as she rushes into my study unexpectedly and makes me burn my tongue on a hot sip of coffee. "I'm sorry I brought him here. He's not really my cousin. I just met him at a script-writing seminar. He was giving one of the classes…"

"Wait. Thstop," I say, my sore tongue making it hard to speak for a moment. "What? You brought some jerk that you didn't even know up here to my home? You know what, Margaret, you're still fired…and moreover fired again! Now get out and don't come back." And I turn back to my computer screen and cool off my tongue with a sip of bottled water.

"Alexa, please listen. He's not some jerk. He can do what he says. Okay, the cousin thing was stupid. But when I saw your face as you opened the door, I had to think of something fast, so you would let us in. Please just listen. This could be big for you. Put you back in the spotlight."

I turn around slowly. "*Peggy*," I say sarcastically, "you are not in charge of my career. You cannot create any spotlights for me. You and your fake cousin Alex Wainwright do not have the magic. I make my own magic. I alone. Now get out."

"Wait. What? His name is Alex Wainwright?"

"He didn't tell you his name?"

"Well, I knew it was Alex, but I never really paid attention to the seminar materials listing the leaders. They just called him by his first name and only mentioned his title as the creative director of the production company holding the seminar. And it never came up at dinner."

"You went out with this guy?"

"Well, yes. He asked me after the lecture when I mentioned to the group that I worked for you. He wanted to know if you were working on the third book of the trilogy. When I told him you were, he took me out to dinner to discuss it."

"This makes me angry on so many levels. The book hasn't been published yet and you're discussing the plot with him before it's officially out, and worse yet, giving him manuscripts, which probably violates something in my publishing contract." I shake my head in disgust. "I should probably sue you, but I know you're broke."

"Except for my severance pay. Do you want it back?" she asks sheepishly.

"You're fired. It's yours. Go away. But first tell me how did he know anything about my first two books of the trilogy? That there even *is* a trilogy. Jameson is waiting to begin a big marketing push and until then keeping things very secretive. No one knows, outside of my editorial team."

"I'm not sure. I didn't tell him anything because he already knew. All I did was mention that I work with you, as I said. Maybe he knows someone at Jameson? Or possibly, Gloria? I'll try and find out. But let's look at the bright side, pun intended. The trilogy is already creating some buzz."

Bingo. She said the exact right words to bring me around.

"Anyway, as I was leaving that afternoon to come here, he called and asked to join me. To have me introduce you to him. We met in the coffee shop and he showed me the offer."

"Wait, so you called me before you met him? What were the marketing ideas *you* had that you wanted to tell me about?"

"What? I called? I never…"

Just then the phone rings. "Hello…hello?" No one there. No caller ID.

"So, what did you think of it?" she continues forgetting our conversation thread, as did I. "The offer. You can't be upset about the offer. It's mind boggling."

"I haven't looked at it."

"No *wonder* you're so angry. It's an amazing offer. You have to look at it." She sees me contemplating what she's just said and senses the fight is out of me. At least toward her. "How about I make us some fresh coffee and those grilled cheese sandwiches that you love so much, and you come into the living room and read the proposal packet, okay? By the way, your place smells nice. Have you installed an air freshener?"

I just look at her not knowing what to say. I haven't left the apartment, so I don't smell him anymore. Gotten used to it, I guess. It's too weird to explain, so I just nod my head "yes" and she goes happily into the kitchen. I sigh. You just can't get rid of some people. And really deep down, I don't want to. I've been quite lonely during this altercation and missed her...a lot. I've also been missing my mom. Right now, she's probably sleeping off an all night observation after gazing at the stars somewhere for a well-funded research project. I've become accustomed to her absences as a professor in Theoretical Astrophysics, but there are times I really need her.

And I need her right now. Need to be in her presence. Need a hug. Being overwhelmed by the emptiness and fear when I complete a new book project can be assuaged by a little mother/daughter time. Her remarkably inquisitive mind and nurturing attention has the power to soothe and the sweet scent of her signature lavender perfume always calms me. I also want to know if she thinks *Darkside* will be my big comeback. Being desperate for positive feedback and assurances borders on the ridiculous and is embarrassing. But I'm trapped by these hated insecurities. I know she's proud of me. Proud of my accomplishments thus far. Just then the phone rings, again.

"Hi, my darling."

"Mom! Hi! Where are you?"

"Well, I can't really tell you. Top secret location and all that," she says laughing. "I tried to call a few minutes ago but couldn't get through. Bad signal. Damn cell phones."

"Is the research going well?"

"Better than expected. The additional funding has been approved and I get to stay and play for a few more weeks, maybe longer. I must say, the work here is so exciting. We're finding some very interesting things about dark matter. All of us are psyched about making major advances in this field. Might solve all the mysteries of the universe," she says laughing, "but we have to do it before the funding runs out. What a crazy business. And how about you? I'm glad you finally finished that book. I know it was a hard one for you. Emotionally, that is."

"How'd you know I finished it? I haven't spoken to you in a while."

"You know, one of my silly dreams. I see big things with this one darling. But be careful."

"Be careful? Why be careful?"

"Not quite sure. Just a feeling. Big successes sometimes come with drawbacks, as you are well aware. Anyway," she laughs again, "you've been warned, so be alert. By the way, has Jerry called you?"

"No."

"Well, if he does, tell him I'll call him in the next few days and send him kisses. Gotta go now, darling. I'll call soon. Love you. And remember, just be careful."

Jerry was my mother's most recent beau. No one can call *her* because of security. Also, due to the delicate aspect and precision of the work, none of the scientists wanted to be disturbed by ringing phones. When she wasn't at the observatory she was asleep. So *she* made all the calls and everyone respected that, even me. This latest project was top secret because it was funded by NASA, the results solely owned by the agency. It was kind of fun thinking of my mother as a NASA scientist involved in a high stakes game.

Maybe she was really at Area 51 interviewing aliens. I pictured the aliens looking at my *mother* with awe and wonder. She's tiny, only about 5 feet, like the grays, those big-eyed aliens of myth and legend, but she wears dangerously high heels to disguise her height. Her blazing red hair is cropped short and her enormous blue eyes, aided by colored contacts, are mesmerizing and make her appear touched by the gods. She's a curvy size 6 with ample breasts and can pull off wearing body conscious clothing of tight jeans and boob hugging tops. No stodgy scientist attire for her even at her age, which she won't tell me.

I assume she's at least in her late-40's or early-50's because I'm 31. Sometime ago, I found a hard to read birth certificate but she told me it was fake. So her exact age remains a mystery. With limitless energy and a magnetic personality, she attracts all within her purview. In articles written about her, she has been described as a fireball, a force to be reckoned with, a dynamo, and so on. I've tried to capture her essence, her vitality, to own it for myself, but alas, I never could. The genetic pool of my DNA must favor my father, whom I have never met or even seen in photos. I would have loved to be a red head and have her coloring, but my hair is nearly black and so are my eyes. No one would describe me as petite at 5 feet 7 inches and although I'm slender, I can't get my butt into her jeans or walk for very long on the circus clown stilts that she calls heels and wears even when home.

"Coffee and sandwiches are ready," Margaret calls from the kitchen.

I waddle into the kitchen, still in my bathrobe and slippers and grab a sandwich and almost swallow it whole without chewing. I realize that I haven't eaten since yesterday, my absorption into grammar, style, and usage being my sole focus. It will be a relief to hand it off to Margaret. Even with her *meshugas*, Yiddish for craziness, her input will be invaluable. Margaret watches me wolf down the food and sits down with me at the kitchen table in the breakfast nook of my chef's kitchen. The kitchen has all the current trends in design with its concrete countertops, stainless steel Miele appliances, and multi-colored mosaic glass tile backsplash. The rage. It opens to the living room/dining room combo where the untouched packet can be seen still on the coffee table from the week before and it still looks…sinister.

Margaret takes dainty bites of her sandwich, her table manners the result of good breeding. She's a card-carrying member of the New York social elite getting an education of what it's like to be among ethnics like me. She's a pixie, a ringer for Peter Pan, all wide eyes, snub nose, short hair, tiny waist, and as short as my mom. Eventually, she will marry well and move to New Canaan, Connecticut. I motion to her that I'd like half of her sandwich. She happily gives it to me and we eat in silence.

Then we both start talking at once.

"You first," I say.

"No you."

"Okay, what were you thinking, leaving him here alone? You didn't warn me that he was still here. That was really not cool. I was nearly half naked when he surprised me in the living room as I was getting a glass of wine after undressing for my bath."

"He stayed here? He said he would be right down, that he just wanted to make a note on the packet and leave it. The elevator was right there, so I took it. I wasn't thinking straight because I was afraid you would fire me for the zumpteenth time."

"Well, another stupid decision on your part. Tell me, is there something else going on? Are you into him or something? Hoping he'll hook up with you? Or have you already done it?"

"No! Well…yes. No to having had sex and, yes, he is quite the looker. But he has shown no interest in me. Only used me to get to you, I realize that now. He hasn't called me since…or taken my calls."

"I see. Using his wiles on you. By now, I thought you'd be immune, Margaret, to all the people trying to get to me through you. When will you learn? Having some notoriety and money brings out the sharks and wannabes. But this pursuit. This is different. I don't get it. He invited me to dinner. Told me to make reservations at my favorite expensive restaurant. Harvey, the night concierge, told me there was a car and driver waiting for me at 8:00. A car and driver. How pretentious. I told Harvey to tell him to get lost."

"You didn't go?"

"I just told you that."

"And you didn't read the offer? Read it now."

I just look at her annoyed and sigh. She gets up and grabs the packet from the living room and brings it to me. I shrink away in horror and tell her about the weird shape-shifting thing and that I think it's possessed.

"Don't be ridiculous. You probably just forgot. You're always forgetting things when lost in work. Don't you remember how you thought I had brought some of your clothes to Goodwill when you never actually gave them to me? I found them still in your closet. So...read this. Now!"

With trepidation, I open the folder and shuffle through the papers. There's a lot of reading. A lot of contracts to sign. A lot of really big numbers. Nervous anxiety rushes through me.

"I have no patience to read this. You seem to know what's in here. So tell me."

"Let me pour us another cup of coffee."

Coffee in hand, we move to be comfortably seated in the living room, and she fills me in. She tells me that Off Street Films is part of a conglomerate made up of many different companies in all aspects of communication. The holding company is known as Trinity of Sixes Communications. There's an ad agency, a PR firm, a boutique book marketing and publishing company, a talent management agency, a literary management company, a music label, a theater production company that owns two Broadway theater venues, a film marketing and distribution company...*and* the movie production company, Off Street Films, soon to be renamed Trinity of Sixes Productions.

Right now they're in negotiations with a streaming video company that has branched out into original scripted material. They say it will put Netflix out of business because of their clout to get distribution of films while they're still in theaters. The holding company is also considering starting a cable network and their publishing company is thinking of acquiring a large, traditional book publisher.

Margaret doesn't know how they have been able to sign so many diverse companies in all facets of communication so quickly but this conglomerate came on the scene like a flash of lightning. They have a pulse on the zeitgeist of popular culture and big money behind it to fund all these entities. International money. Oil billionaires. Casino owners. Tech giants. They are cornering the market. Big name talent signed in all sectors with very generous offers.

Bottom line, they know that I'm in negotiations about the trilogy and my publisher is planning to release them simultaneously. They will buy out whatever is existing in the contract with Jameson House including the rights to *Foregone* and the rest of my backlist. That number is negotiable, so it doesn't appear in the contract, but it will be a very lucrative deal for Jameson, as well as prudent, because their bestselling authors are managed now by Trinity of Sixes literary management.

The publishing arm will pay me a $20 million advance for the trilogy. She repeats for emphasis, $20 *million*. They will give me a $5 million advance for a two book contract to be fulfilled within two years and after that a book every other year for a duration decided by Trinity of Sixes Publishing. They will buy the movie rights to all three books in the trilogy for $15 million and pay me another $5 million to write the script and give me five points on the back end, quite lucrative because in the film industry that means a percentage of the total gross. With the *Forgone* film, there were no points offered. The only drawback for this deal is that I must be exclusive to them on everything. No more Gloria.

"First of all why is a film company making book deals?"

"Alex says all the subsidiaries work very closely together and projects overlap, that's why there are all those contracts to sign. The CEO and Chairman is very hands on, treats the organization like one big family. Anyway, that's according to Alex. He's extremely excited to be part of this media phenom. Because Alex wanted the film rights of the trilogy, the CEO decided to add you to their author's list of their publishing arm. They uniformly love your work."

"I see. Okay. Flattering, I must admit. So, let me reiterate, you said fifteen million for the movie rights, five million to write the script, and a percentage of the film? Twenty million for the trilogy. Well... that's...nuts! Why? Why such an over-the-top deal?"

My mind races and I think out loud. "Not just over-the-top. Obscene. Except for *Foregone* my books right now top out at around ten million before everybody's cut, so I don't get it. What do they really want? Who are they? Trinity of Sixes...Trinity of Sixes...*hmm*...really strange... funny name. Wait, wait a minute is that code for triple sixes? Isn't six, six, six, the sign of the Devil?" I laugh but nervously. "Sounds absurd but is this a Faustian deal?" I ask Margaret. "I never believed in that stuff, hell and such, but this feels weird. Is glamour boy...your fake cousin...the Devil? And also, why is his name the same as mine? How can that be? It's so strange. More than strange. I don't know. This doesn't feel right. I have to think it over. And you, Margaret, where do you fit in?"

"Let's not go overboard with the Faustian worries. Trinity of Sixes is a legitimate company, Lex. They already have some lucrative deals. *The Monarch* with Wes Adams. You know it, right?" I nod. "That's one of their hit movies. Alex said there's one right now in postproduction starring a really popular husband and wife team to be released next Thanksgiving, really hush-hush. And as far as what I get, well, to be perfectly honest, I get a finder's fee for making the introduction. But other than that, it's up to you. We can work together, just like we do now with me as your employee or in whatever capacity you think is fair. I'm really excited about this. I tell you, even if this is a deal with the Devil; it's a no brainer, Alexa. I'd take it in a second," she laughs.

"Seriously, Lex," she continues, "Trinity of Sixes has the entire supply chain sewed up to basically guarantee success. They have the marketing budget, production budget, and mega stars that are signed on to their talent management agency to make *Darkside* a cinematic blockbuster. Alex thinks it could gross more than three hundred million not counting the video release. And that will only increase book sales. The trilogy and your next two books, if you sign the contract, are practically guaranteed to be bestsellers with all their advertising and marketing campaigns. Becoming number one again, think about it. Every new book you write making the top ten and the buzz flowing over to sell your backlist as well."

"Oh boy," I sigh. "Let me really think about this. Now I must actually read the contracts. I hate to give up Gloria. She believed in me and made me who I am today. I wouldn't even know how to tell her. As far as the money, I'm in pretty good shape financially but this deal trumps everything. This is huge. Legacy money. More money than I could spend in my lifetime. Money to leave to my future generations, my future children and their children and so on. I could set up foundations. Make a difference in this world. Do some good. I still don't get why they think I'm worth all that money and that's very, very troubling."

"Lex, you're a money making machine. All your books sell well. You have a following. A giant marketing budget would put you back in the number one position that has eluded you since your debut. No more number nineteen on the bestseller list. How about being number one again?"

"Yes, I know, it's very tempting, more than tempting, really. This offer hits right to the core of my obsession to be at the top again. An obsession of which I'm not proud. An obsession that has taken over my ability to enjoy my craft. But I want it to happen organically, not because there's a giant marketing budget to make it happen. Like mind control of the masses. We'll talk again later. I'll send you *Darkside* to edit and I want to go the gym. I haven't been in several days, actually it's been a week, and I need to think and unwind. But first, on another disturbing note, did you notice how Alex looks like he could have jumped out of *Forgone*? A ringer for Rick?"

"Like *Rick*? Well, I guess. Now that I think about it, oh yeah, okay. But Lex, get a grip, your description of Rick could be like a million guys."

"Yeah, I know. But that's how I pictured him in my head. And he has a slight limp. The same slight limp."

"Oh," she frowns. "Well..."

"Forget it. I can't process this strangeness. I gotta get to the gym. We'll talk later."

The full service gym is on the penthouse floor of the other tower of this complex. I take my private elevator down one floor to the connector bridge between the towers and head for the women's private lockers to grab my gym clothes. All the while my mind is racing. *How did these people get into my brain?* Over and over I ask myself the same question. Like they knew my infantile obsession. My torment. I get on the treadmill, slow run to fast run. Breathing light. Breathe, breathe, breathe, rhythm breath. *It's like they knew just how to get me, deep inhales getting to my stride, like they knew I needed to rekindle that explosion of acceptance into the popular culture that came with Foregone. My Achilles heel.* Breath stabilizing, smoother breathing. In the zone. Running, running, running. *The safety of knowing, of guarantees. No worries of the mid-list waste land or what to do next.* Breathing. The lure of wealth beyond anything I have seen thus far. *Should I do it? Be careful. Big things, but be careful. How can I be careful? And why? Mom? What do you know?* Cool down. Slow down. Walking now.

Pumped up, I get off the treadmill and go to the universal.

Be careful. Lift. *Big things.* Pull. *So much money.* Arms. *Write a script.* Legs. *Could be fun. See that Alex guy again.* MY NAME! Hmm. *So weird. Be careful.* Release. *And let go! Whew. Good workout. Done!*

I grab a towel to wipe the perspiration off my face. *Damn! How did his scent get on this?* Vigorously, I throw it into the hamper. *He's hounding me...somehow.* Once in my loft, I soak in my Jacuzzi with the constant refrain swirling in my head.

Be careful.

Big things.

I spend a very restless night. My workout did not relax me at all because Alex is on my mind. He's not only gotten into my nostrils; he's gotten under my skin. Never before has someone inundated my senses like that. Suddenly, I realize that I feel like a schoolgirl with a crush. And why wouldn't I? Alex is Rick. The perfect male in form and substance. *My* perfect male. The one I created in my mind and with my words. He's also my second shot at number one. Alex Wainwright...Alexa and Alex Wainwright.

Bizarre!

Freaky!

Wacko!

Chapter Three

The meeting

Over the course of several days, my thoughts run to the deal. The deal that would practically guarantee the rekindled success that my lusting after has turned into my personal demon. Like the stranger offering candy to a child, it beckons dangerously. *Don't take candy from a stranger,* says your protective parent. *Be careful,* says my mother. But in the end there are always those who take the candy and follow the stranger, and it is their undoing. Will this be mine, if I sign? And how will I be undone? And this Alex Wainwright is he...*what* is he? *Who* is he?

More than strange that he has my name. Outlandish and a little terrifying. But I can't stop going there. Where did he come from? Oh yeah, California...Los Angeles, Margaret told me. And again curious still, I keep going over that he looks exactly as I had written him. *Exactly!* Margaret blew that off. But he's Rick, for sure, the Rick in *Foregone,* just the way I pictured him in my mind. One of the good guys. And...oh my god...he was also from LA! Oh, I'm getting ill. Let's see. *What else?* He drove a black Porsche 911 Targa 4S. Loved to wear sneakers and jeans, like a uniform, no matter where he went. Even to fancy dinner parties but then he added a sport jacket. Oh no! That's what Alex was wearing, sneakers and jeans! Stop! Get a grip. That's what most guys wear.

But...the way he looks. I keep thinking, ad nauseam, *it's exactly how I pictured Rick.* So now this weird thought starts spinning in my head. *Did I conjure him?* Did I create Rick in the flesh by writing his character? My stomach tightens and I gag. *Enough!* This is ridiculous. But could I have? Is that even possible? *Could I have conjured him?*

I don't venture out for several days and wander around my loft aimlessly. I need my mother to call. I am disturbed and frazzled. I feel like I just slipped into an alternate universe. A universe where if you think it, it manifests. So now I'm afraid to think. Will I bump into Jodie's mean boyfriends? I watch the news and it depresses me further.

The big news today is that the drought in New York is becoming severe. High temperatures with no humidity add to the increased danger for wild fires. We've not had the necessary rainfall for more than a year now. This winter also had very little snow, so melt is minimal. Our reservoirs are shrinking...coming up next is the climatologist H.G. Davis who will explain our dire situation. Stay tuned... I flip through the news stations, same headline story. The weather is oppressive. Relentless sun beating down, or overcast days, smog days, with no rain. Really hot temperatures and this is only the beginning of May. It adds to my nervous state of mind. I drink copious amounts of wine to numb myself. I pass out each night and don't dream. No premonitions. The phone finally rings.

"*Mom!* Thank goodness! I've been really needing you to call."

"Excuse me, is this Ms. Wainwright?"

"Oh, sorry, I thought...yes, this is she."

"I'm calling on behalf of Trinity of Sixes Communications and Off Street Films. We would like you to come to our offices tomorrow at eleven a.m., if you are available. We are located at six-two-six East Sixty-Fifth between Park and Lexington on the corner. It's a private residence and also our offices."

"Wait, excuse me, did you just say six-six-six?" My voice catches in my throat, my pulse races.

"No, six-two-six between Park..."

"Oh...ok," I interrupt. *Whew!* "Look, I don't mean to be rude but how did you get this number? I don't give it out."

"I don't know, I was just told to call. If this is a bad time..."

I interrupt again, "Well, you can just tell *Mr.* Wainwright that I don't appreciate this invasion of my privacy."

"I'm sorry, if I didn't make myself clear. Mr. King Blakemore is the one requesting this meeting. He's the CEO and chairman of Trinity of Sixes Communications. Please let me know if eleven tomorrow morning, Thursday, the sixth is convenient. We can send a car and driver, if you don't have your own."

"Please tell Mr. Blakemore that I am still considering his offer. I haven't made up my mind and I need to send the contract to my lawyer."

"I've been instructed to tell you that this is just a get-to-know-each-other meeting. No signing of contracts. No pressure. Can I send a car?"

"Well...okay. Sure. Eleven a.m., you said?"

"Yes. Wonderful, I'll tell him. He'll be overjoyed. The car will be waiting outside your building."

"Thank you, Ms..."

"Blakemore. Jewel Blakemore. I'm his eldest daughter."

"Oh...well...thank you, Miss Blakemore."

"Please call me Jewel. We all go by first names here."

"Okay, thanks Jewel."

"See you tomorrow."

The day and evening pass in their typical way when there's a lot on my mind. I think about breaking the rules and calling my mother, but I can't bring myself to embarrass her. I pace the loft. I pace my large terrace off the kitchen but it's too hot. I go for a swim in the pool on the amenities level to clear my mind and grab a salad at the gym cafe. The swim doesn't relax me in my present state, so I decide to watch an old Keanu Reeves movie I stumble upon while surfing channels in my media room. Big mistake. It's about demons, angels, and the Devil! I medicate myself with sleeping pills and go to bed early.

In the morning after my drugged sleep, I groggily take a piping hot shower and dress carefully. I drink several shots of espresso to snap out of my fog and start to get enthused about this meeting. I haven't put make-up on in weeks. Blowing my hair dry reminds me that I need a haircut but it still looks pretty good with bouncy and full layers to my shoulders. It's uplifting to not look like a slob. I feel clean, beautiful, and powerful.

I choose my plum stiletto Louboutin heels (for occasions such as this) that match my Dolce and Gabbana summer weight suit in dark plum, a color I look great in. Brings out my dark eyes. I love a monotone look so I choose the matching silk shell. I change my purse to my Louis Vuitton that *nearly* matches. Just getting out and putting on my designer clothing is thrilling after all these weeks, months even, plugging at my computer in my sweats. Devil or no. Maybe I'll have Margaret meet me for lunch. Maybe I should plan a vacation. I'm bubbling over. The espresso is definitely working. Giving me a real buzz. But I *am* excited. That amazing deal is real. *Hmm*…got the shoes on. These are killer shoes, really sexy but extremely hard to walk in gracefully and I need a bit of practice. My mother is *nuts*. A few turns around my living room and my gait becomes more natural, sensual.

Go for it girl!

Ready.

Maybe.

I turn my ankle while walking to the door and almost fall down. *Shit!* Why are these tortuous contraptions so popular? Why did I buy them? Flats probably come in purple. Slowly, walk slowly. If I walk slowly, maybe I won't look like such a dork. And I'm quite tall in these shoes, tall equals powerful. Use it. *Hmm*, anyway, I'm sure this meeting will be conducted sitting down.

Getting downstairs without tripping, I hand William, the daytime concierge, my contract packet and tell him to please make a copy and message it to my lawyer, Jeff Roseman. Wonderful perks living in this building. After William called to tell me the car was here, I scrambled to find all the pieces to the contract that I had spread all over the place. Better get it to my lawyer right away. "There's your ride, Ms. Wainwright," says William, as he nods with a wide-eyed smirk toward the car parked right outside that I can see when I look through the glass double doors of the lobby.

And then I get the meaning of the look. A sight to behold. A chauffeur dressed in full livery is standing next to a purple and gray Rolls Royce Phantom. Definitely the way to get a girl's attention, especially a superficial, money-grubbing yuppie girl like me anyway. Jeeves, or whatever his name is, opens the door for me very formally. "Watch your step, Miss Wainwright," he says with a British accent. "My name is Reginald, Miss, and if there is anything I can do to make this trip a little more pleasant for you, please let me know. There is bottled water in the holder in the seat. Please avail yourself, if you so choose." I thank him politely.

Although Reginald could have been sent over from Central Casting, and the car could be leased just for this meeting, it's quite entertaining. Heads turn looking at the car. People peer in to see who the passenger might be when we get to a light. Quite fun, really. I text Margaret. *Going to a meeting at Trinity of Sixes. Not pleased that you gave out my number. Sitting in the back of a Rolls right now with a driver in full livery. We can discuss over lunch.* She texts back immediately that she never gives out my phone number. But she can't make lunch today, too busy with *Darkside*. She wants to have lunch tomorrow to show me her edits.

Disappointed that my dynamite-looking self will have to dine alone after the meeting, I busy myself with checking my make-up and reapplying my lipstick. When I'm satisfied, I lean back and try and relax, but *wham!* We're there. Traffic was unusually light, so the trip uptown was super fast. Looking out the window, I see the fully detached brownstone mansion. Huge. It takes up a good deal of the block. Very impressive and a rare type of residence in this city of row houses and skyscraper apartments.

The driver pulls into a cordoned off spot right in front. *How much did that cost in pay offs?* He escorts me inside and the cold blast almost makes me gasp. There's an elevator, he tells me, to take me to the second floor. Dozens of people are rushing about the quite roomy ground-floor offices. Clusters of people are outside in the lush, landscaped garden visible through the glass-paned French doors. I'm slightly perplexed as to why I'm going upstairs. As soon as the elevator door opens on the second floor, I'm greeted by a tall, slender blonde with a perfect thick, bouncy, bob cut, aristocratic cheekbones, and a small straight nose.

"Hello, Alexa, I'm Jewel, so nice to meet you. Please follow me." Older than she sounded on the phone, she's a head turner, even at her age. She leads me to a a formidable room with breathtaking proportions and lavishly decorated. She asks me to wait a moment at the entrance while King, I assume, King, is talking to someone. My eyes dart back and forth sweeping the room. The focal point of the geometric, gold paneled ceiling is a trompe l'oeil painted center illustrating a blue sky with puffy clouds and looks real enough to be a hole in the roof.

Hanging from a vintage-looking plaster medallion placed among the clouds is a magnificent and imposing gold candelabra chandelier that grabs the eye. Carved and painted columns form a cozy, corner seating alcove tucked away from the main area. The rest of the room is not at all intimate with various armchairs and sofas in clusters and looks like a receiving room for the aptly named King. An impressive collection of museum quality portraits, landscapes, and contemporary art in elaborate gold frames hang on walls covered in gold leaf something or other. In fact, gold accents dominate throughout. My eyes land on gold filigree-adorned porcelain vases, gold threads forming the tufts for seat cushions, and gold-painted antique chairs covered in pale blue and white silk fabric.

Luxurious, colorful Persian rugs stand out against the high sheen of the polished dark wood floor. Colorfully painted cabinets, end tables, porcelain lamps of all sizes, and numerous objets d'art finish out the grand reception room. A flawless representation of the great Rococo palaces of Europe. Distracted by the opulence, at first, I don't notice the heady scent of flowers filling the room. Aware now of the pleasant aroma, I see there are several large vases containing elaborate arrangements of exotic blossoms from deepest Africa or South America. Certainly a room to make one gasp in its extravagance and flaunting of wealth by its owner. This type of decor looks unbelievably tacky when it's the choice of today's nouveau riche, but here it works. As if this house, and especially this room, were in an Eighteenth Century time warp. The person talking to King is finished and Jewel signals that we may now enter the room.

Getting up from a high-backed chair placed so that it has a position of prominence is an extremely tall, older gentleman who towers over me even in these heels. He's elegantly dressed in a black suit of fine fabric and black silk shirt with a bright-red silk scarf tied flamboyantly about his neck. Peeking out from his jacket pocket is a matching red silk pocket square. This is undoubtedly the man fittingly named, King. At first look, his eyes knock me back, as if looking into yellow glowing eyes with vertical pupils like an ancient beast of lore. But then, when I blink they immediately transform and become normal looking but dark and hidden.

I'm also nonplussed by his uncanny resemblance to the evil characters played by Vincent Price in classic horror films my mother watched obsessively when I was growing up. I always thought it peculiar, but she told me it was a way for her to relax from her studies. So, yes, this guy could easily be a vampire or the Devil himself, with his goatee, pencil-thin mustache and slicked-back black hair the color of shoe polish. He extends his hand in welcome and his ice-cold touch sends shivers up and down my spine. Strangely, as he holds my hand for a moment, a calming, relaxing warmth circulates through me.

"Please…sit, sit, Alexa," he says in an indefinable cultured sounding manner with the hint of a British accent and shows me to a quite comfortable-looking armchair in a conversation arrangement with two other armchairs. The chair gives me a sensation like I'm floating on air as we three sit facing each other, King, Jewel, and I. Although there are comforting sensations pulsing through me, I am also on high alert feeling at a disadvantage in this stranger's domain.

These opposing feelings throw me off-kilter. Here I sit in his personal space to which I am now privy, as if I were among his intimates, yet I am a total stranger. I would have preferred an office meeting, something more sterile, businesslike. But at least I'm sitting…*damn shoes!* King crosses his legs and reveals he's wearing matching red socks and red sneakers. What an odd fellow. Wealthy, but odd.

"I'm so pleased you agreed to come today," he says in a very friendly manner. "I have followed your work from the beginning of your first success, and I must say I'm a huge fan. Your use of language, attention to detail in describing the world and characters you create are nothing short of brilliant. And your storytelling, your plot development is so engaging. How it all fits together in the end is akin to Dickens, in my opinion. Quite remarkable. I daresay, few writers have this gift in this day and age. The skill of writing is disappearing. Tweeting is an abomination to communication.

"Snippets replace sentences, acronyms replace words. The art of letter writing has been replaced by quickly written emails. Books are written for grade-school-level readers. I think even Dickens would have had trouble getting a following today.

"But there are still, thankfully, sophisticated readers as well as brilliant writers who startle you with their intellect and command attention. Like you, my dear girl, who have remained true to the great literary traditions, despite the obstacles. Welty, Fitzgerald, Kafka, Steinbeck, these writers didn't face the demand for mediocrity or the onslaught of trash. A writer, such as yourself, must be nurtured, given incentives to continue her craft. There are so few left. You have shown that good writing will out, but even you, lately, are having difficulty achieving your rightful place. Personal computers and e-books have made it easy and inexpensive for anyone to enter the market. Great writers are being drowned by a tidal wave of garbage."

Whoa! Who is he kidding? What a load of crap. Dickens? Steinbeck? But…these words hit me right at the crux of my obsession, my pathetic neediness. Stroke my damned ego. Flattery, unfortunately, works with me, even if I sense it's disingenuous. Nevertheless, this guy is a pro and I'm such an easy mark…a sucker. But still…

"Thank you," I say humbly and with some difficulty because an unexplained stupefying numbness takes over me. I can actually see my breath when I say this, it being so incredibly cold in this house. I'm glad I'm wearing a suit jacket. Still on my guard, but taking everything in, I sit back and listen as he explains the vision of Trinity of Sixes and the origin of the name. The sound of his voice is mesmerizing and relaxes me like a dose of Xanax. So far, everything about this meeting has had a quieting, almost drugged-out effect on me. His touch, his voice, this chair. My nervousness slips away and my mood elevates. A sudden surge of positive feelings lightens my spirit. I haven't felt this euphoric in a while. Happy. Just happy. Most welcome.

Enjoying my mood, I casually survey my surroundings again and my companions. When my eyes land on Jewel, I get irrationally giddy. I try to control laughing out loud and put my hand over my mouth, but can't seem to quiet the urge. The others seem aware of my strange behavior but act politely indifferent. The thing is, she's another one! Jewel. I didn't notice it before because I was gobsmacked by the ambiance of this place. But she's another one of my characters come to life. From my third novel, *The Lucky Ones*. Jessica Warren, a blue-blood, born into the wealthy elite.

I thought she looked familiar because that's exactly how I pictured her. High cheekbones, thick, shiny platinum blonde hair styled in a sleek bob. And the way she tosses it when she turns head, just like she does in the book. And all in white. Her signature look. A closet full of white everything. I wrote *her*. Created *her*. This is too much. This feeling of euphoria is wrapped around me like a cocoon and hard to shake, but my confusion over this strangeness grows stronger until abject fear pushes through. My held-in laugh erupts into a gag and I start to cough. Can't catch my breath. *I've got to get out of here!*

"Oh dear, are you alright Alexa? You've gone quite pale. Eugenie," King calls out, "bring Alexa some water, quickly! Are you too cold? I know I keep this house quite cold. I hate the heat," he says. *Did I hear him growl just then? Like an animal?*

Someone scurries in and hands me a glass. A few swallows and breathing through my nose allows me to contain myself and I manage to say hollowly, "I'm okay now. Thanks. I'm fine." *Gotta take control.* If I calm myself, I can figure out how to GET OUT OF HERE. "I'm sorry, Mr. Blake...er King, I missed what you just said because of the coughing... so umm...well...oh my...is...that a Vermeer, next to a Picasso?"

"You're quite the art scholar. Very impressive. Yes, it certainly is. Vermeer was not a very prolific painter. We're lucky to have one. It came to me through my family. The Blakemores have been around for centuries and a distant relative lived in Delft at the time. Probably got it for a basket of vegetables or some such nonsense. Vermeer was not well off. Clever of us to keep it and to pass it on until his work became fashionable and in demand. Now it's worth millions."

His family dates back centuries? Transylvania like Dracula? No, he said Delft. The Netherlands. Dutch. Like Vermeer. I feel light headed again.

"And as for the Picasso? Well, Pablo was such a rake. He was quite fond of my Aunt Justine, my dear departed mother's second cousin who we called aunt out of respect for her high status in society and because," he laughs, "she demanded it. Made her feel closer to us. Never having married, she bequeathed it to me her only living relative."

Okay. At least he had a mother. But bad feelings about these people still nag at me. Jewel looking exactly like Jessica Warren. Just like that guy Alex looks like Rick. I'm more than creeped out. I need to get out of here and assess what's going on in the safety of my home.

"I'm so sorry, but I'm feeling a little dizzy. Perhaps, we can reschedule?" I say starting to get up.

"Nonsense! I think some lunch will be just the thing. Come, let's go into the dining room. Philippe, my chef, has prepared a fabulous repast. He's a culinary artist of world renown. I managed to entice him to come work for me creating the most fanciful delights for my pleasure. Please, take my arm. We'll walk slowly. I'm sure you'll feel much better after you've eaten."

Stuck. This pretense of not feeling well isn't having the desired effect. Nothing I can do right now. At least his arm helps me balance in these ridiculous shoes. Why am I here again? Oh yeah, Margaret... she started all this. Soooo angry at her. I should fire her. Oh right...I did...but...We cross the massive living room. It's hard to believe this huge mansion is right here in the city and not on the North Shore. Must be worth...a lot. And so arm-in-arm we make our way to the dining room.

The spacious dining room could be a royal dining room of a French palace during the Baroque period. The fleur-de-lis crystal chandelier is glorious, the silk wallpaper is a delicate hue in the cream family, and the dining table could easily seat 50 people and is most likely Louis XVI. Plush, wide chairs with arm rests reduce the seating to half that amount and we three sit at one end together, intimate. The china is Royal Doulton, the vintage sterling silver flatware is Buccellati, and the stemware is Baccarat. I know because I sneakily check the labels. King Blakemore definitely has cash and loves the finer things in life. What more could he want? *And why me?*

A bell is rung and lunch is served. The food is a festival of flavors in my mouth. The cabernet is velvety and full-bodied. There are several courses. The fish course is sweet and tangy; the lamb roast is so tender it dissolves on the tongue. My inhibitions disappear and my mood shifts once more to elation and an overwhelming sense of goodwill soars through me. I needed a good meal and this meal is certainly fabulous, a culinary extravaganza. Perhaps I was mistaken about Jewel. How could I have created her? She's his daughter and practically a stereotype. Probably a former debutante. A poster girl for inherited wealth. *Humph!* She's a dime a dozen. A clone of every member of the Colony Club. *Get a grip silly girl. But...she looks...nothing like her dad.*

During the meal, King politely asks me, if I would like him to tell me again about how he chose Trinity of Sixes as the perfect name for his company.

"I'm not sure you heard me because that's when you had your coughing fit."

"Yes, please. I'm sorry, yes, you're right, I didn't hear what you said and I'm quite interested." So he tells me about the play on words. Trinity represents basic Christian values. And Sixes? Well, the Lord created the world in six days. So the meaning has to do with being a moral organization while having dynamic creativity. A perfect melding of concept and action. The member companies are in all aspects of the creative space of business. "Yes, I knew that," I tell him trying to focus and starting to feel slightly buzzed from the wine.

When the last glass of wine is poured, he says, "Let's retire to the parlor room and take our coffee and dessert in there." Utterly serene and now quite lethargic, I manage to get up but very slowly. Taking small steps to keep my balance while pretending to be perfectly fine, I nearly fall down anyway when we're back in the parlor, his name for the room we were in before.

"Alex, there you are. Glad you could finally make it."

Originally, I assumed he would be here, but then forgot about it. Alex Wainwright. Right. The movie deal needs to be discussed, I guess. But I'm off my game right now. Not really ready and I have to hear back from my attorney. Alex gets up from a love seat sofa next to where we were sitting before lunch and walks over and shakes King's hand, politely kisses Jewel, who has been oddly mum all during lunch, and smiles warmly at me.

"So glad to see you again and looking quite lovely, I might add."

This comment reminds me of my half-naked self being shocked by his presence in my loft when I thought he had left with Margaret. I acknowledge him with a slight nod to deflect my embarrassment. Jewel walks over to where Alex was sitting and sits down. He turns and joins her. She leans close. *Hmm.* So they're a couple? She's a little old for him. Well...come to think of it, Jessica in *The Lucky Ones* had a penchant for younger men, a tendency toward being the cougar.

This thought brings me back to the preposterous notion that she's another one of my characters given the breath of life. She whispers something in his ear and they laugh. *Arrgh.* I don't like watching them. It makes me uncomfortable because I realize, I'm a little...jealous. Of *her?* Stop it. I created her! Dessert is brought in and put on little tables placed close to each of our seats. A confection beyond delicious. Each bite feels like a shot of love.

As if this day couldn't get any weirder, my reality starts to shift. *What the...?* All of a sudden, I'm out of my body hovering near the ceiling watching the goings on below happening in slow motion. King says something to Jewel and it sounds like a record playing at the wrong speed, stretched out, garbled, with a low rumbling timbre. She laughs in a distorted manner, as if singing an aria in the wrong key and musical notes sail out of her mouth. I pop back in my body and hear her say something to me using a weird sounding voice and speaking a peculiar language that doesn't make any sense. I answer her in the same strange language not knowing what I'm saying. We speak in this foreign tongue for several minutes.

Alex hands me a piece of paper. It turns into a bird and flies away. I follow it out the window and soar above the skyscrapers. A delightful rush of ecstasy pulses through my veins as a force pulls me ever higher until I touch the stars. A brilliant blue marble, the Earth, captivates the eye as I twirl and spin in outer space. Frolicking in Orion's Belt, I grab a speeding rock and propel myself to the center of the universe. Eerie, beautiful, spellbinding, and wrapped in utter silence until someone calls my name. And *thwack!* I'm back sitting in the parlor. Dizzy and disoriented, and as if in a freeze-frame, I'm holding up my dessert spoon ready to swallow its contents.

The last drop of this splendiferous dessert melts in my mouth, as the chef slowly glides in on dancing feet and bows in stages, as if choreographed. "Alexa, meet our amazing chef, Philippe LaFrere," says King in his strange wrong speed voice. We all applaud in slow motion and the sound of the applause is faster than our hands and out of sync and ridiculous. King makes a big fuss, all in stop-action sequences. I find myself laughing out loud. Not only at the silly spectacle unfolding before me but because another character from one of my books has sprung to life.

"He's...not...Philippe," I shout slurring my words but somehow managing to slowly move my mouth. "He's...Henry...Olmsted...from... my third...novel, *The...Pushover*. Hi Henry. Swindle...any poor old...ladies lately? Scam...any...unsuspecting widows? How'd you...like prison?"

Henry/Philippe looks horrified and embarrassed and turns bright red, a slow progression on his cheeks. *That's strange, he never got embarrassed in the book. Oh wait, yes, when the female judge called him out in the courtroom. I had fun with that.* Jewel drifts over to me.

"Here sweetheart," she says in that crazy voice but now in English and pours me a large cup of coffee. It takes forever to fill up the cup. "You must have had one too many glasses of wine. Finish this coffee and then drink this cold glass of water," she says. I take several sips with her help.

Slo-mo is gone immediately after finishing the coffee. Reality takes over and I feel like a crazy fool. But I'm also frightened and still dazed from my out-of-body experience. Something is definitely wrong with these people. With this place. My survival instinct kicks in. *I've got to get out of here.* Take control of myself and get sober. King and Alex are making plans about something and then Alex tells me he'll take me home. I meekly protest but my legs are like rubber. I kick off these stupid shoes and manage to hold onto the walls, as I make my way to the elevator. It's a closet door and not the elevator! Alex tries to usher me to the right door and I swing at him and miss and fall down.

"All of you people keep away from me," I say as Alex tries to help me up. "Something's not right here. And listen carefully," I say sternly looking ridiculous still on the floor. "I'm not signing any goddamn contract. Moral and ethical? Christian values? What BS! You think you can just drug me to get your way, but I'm not signing anything. Ya hear me?" Now, I'm screaming. "YA HEAR ME?"

King is quietly looking at me now back in his throne-chair. He is stoic. From the look on Jewel's face, she seems concerned about me but makes no move. King nods at Alex and he picks me up as if I weigh nothing. Next thing I know, we're downstairs and he's placing me carefully in his car parked close to the building. Of course, it's a black Porsche, but I'm too ill to say or do anything. I don't remember how we got up to my loft, but I have a vague understanding of being brought into my bedroom and placed on my bed.

The room is spinning.

The bed feels good.

I'm home.

Safe.

Chapter Four

Alex

Floating in and out of consciousness for several hours or perhaps days, I slowly become aware of someone's warm breath on my neck. There's a scent of pine and leather. Cocooned in my mindless state, wakefulness comes in spurts and finally emerges solidly through touch. Masterful fingertips play gently on my skin and begin to switch on my suppressed passion. Lips touching mine, at first lightly and then deep, complete, and strong. Lost in his mouth on mine, a sweet taste, there's a yearning for more, the emergence of my raging sexuality.

I run my hands over his naked taut and muscular chest. His skin is soft. I grab his thick hair and pull him close when he moves slightly away. I'm ignited. On fire. We lustily explore each other lost in our rapture. When he enters me, I moan uncontrollably. Such an amazing sensation. Oh, this feeling of rapture. My arousal is unleashed to new levels. Our coupling is primal. Magical. Unlocking my inhibitions, I suck in my breath in speechless ecstasy then scream with pleasure. We rock together more and more rapidly until our bodies explode in a simultaneous glorious pulsing majesty of complete fulfillment. Catching my breath and enjoying the afterglow for several minutes, I reach out to touch him. *What the…?* Patting around the area next to me, I can't feel him. I finally open my eyes.

No one's there.

I'm alone?

Huh?

Extremely confused and feeling foolish, I roll over and stare at the wall and finally go back to sleep. In the morning, I'm still aroused and then loneliness creeps over me. Too many years spent on pursuits instead of living my life. Shoving away that aspect of myself in favor of my characters having relationships and sexual satisfaction. My life has to change, that's the obvious message because I've never had a dream like that, so real. I smell the pillow, just a hint of the scent that has permeated my apartment for weeks. Nothing strong or immediate. Oh well. My subconscious mind is telling me that I'm in need of some male companionship. Basically, I'm desperate for it. For Alex, in particular.

The phone rings. I look at the clock, 11:00 a.m. And the date? It's the next day. Lunch yesterday finished at about 2:00 p.m., I think. Lots of fuzzy stuff about yesterday. I've slept for nearly 20 hours. Very unusual for me. And I'm still kind of groggy. *What the hell happened yesterday?*

"Hello?"

"Alexa, this Alex. How are you? Feeling better today, I hope?"

Oh boy. I start to stutter, embarrassed. Hey stupid, he doesn't know anything about your dream. *So, stop!*

"I...I...I'm fine, thanks. Just feel a little disoriented, quite frankly."

"Look, how about I bring you...us some coffee. You're up, right? I'm sure you could use a cup right about now."

"Oh ummm. I don't know. I should thank you for bringing me home, don't know what got into me, but…"

"No buts. Let me do this, just coffee. I'll be there in 30 minutes." He hangs up.

I text Margaret. *Can't make it today. Can you save the edit meeting for Monday?* She responds immediately. *Perfect. I'm really not ready. I need the rest of the weekend. I'll call Monday.* Okay. I'd better get dressed. Suddenly, I get a shot of adrenaline that propels me out of bed. Rushing around like a crazy person, I'm suddenly not groggy anymore. Excited. Energized. I shower, blow dry my hair, put on minimal makeup. Don't want to look like I've fussed too much. Not too staged. I choose my favorite white scooped-neck tee and just as I'm zipping up my super-tight jeans the concierge buzzer rings. He's here! "Send him up," I say. Adrenaline is flowing but I try and focus my mind on being relaxed. Take deep breaths. Be cool. Don't look needy or interested. My pulse is hammering. My stomach is queasy. Be calm. Stay calm.

The doorbell buzzes and he's here, smiling. That broad grin. Even bright-white teeth. Cleft in his chin. Sun-tanned skin. Sexily unshaven. Piercing blue eyes. Strong jaw. Thick, shiny black hair falling softly around his face. Just like I described him in *Foregone*. Just my type, actually. I show him in and before he can put down the coffee containers, I grab his shirt and pull him toward me and kiss his gorgeous mouth hungrily. He manages to set the coffee down on my hall table before I start ripping off his shirt and pushing him to the bedroom. He's a willing participant. Oh, yeah! Stripping off my clothes in no time flat, I go for his pants but he's already working on them. We fall into bed and I relive my dream in every detail. It's perfect. I couldn't have written this scene any better. This time when I reach over to him after we're temporarily satiated, he's there!

"You're real," I say. He looks at me puzzled and then says, "Let me remind you, just how real."

And we spend the next 24 hours in a world of our own design where it's just the two of us. Just us and no one else. Just us and the rapture of sexual enthrall. A day and night of bliss, an insatiable physical connection, making love, making our intimate selves known. No secrets. Our private world of lust and desire. Under a spell of sexual arousal for hours on end. Finally spent, we give into fatigue and sleep.

When I wake up, I instinctually check to see if he is indeed lying next to me. Whew. I'm not crazy. I carefully ease myself out from under the blankets to go into the bathroom and turn on the shower. As the hot, calming water flows over me, my mind wanders to the events leading up to this copulation marathon. Yes, this lovemaking was certainly epic. We connected on all cylinders. *Do I want to continue this?* But before I can answer myself, the shower door opens and he joins me. We play and giggle getting soap and shampoo in our eyes and everywhere. Scrubbing each other's backs. Rinsing each other with the shower hose. A comfortable happy couple. Blissful.

"It looks beautiful outside," he says after toweling off and drying my back. "Let's take a drive to the Cloisters and then eat dinner somewhere around Rhinebeck. In fact, there's an inn there and perhaps we can stay the night or maybe two? How about it? Just grab a couple of things and let's go. Okay?"

"Sounds wonderful, but I've gotta eat something right now, or I'll faint. My favorite cafe is just a short walk."

As we scarf down bagels, bacon and eggs and lots of coffee, I ask him if he has adjusted to his move. "I love LA and the West in general. Great scenery, skiing, hiking. But this opportunity is well…a once in a lifetime thing. I'll settle for Broadway, world-class museums, and the energy and the vibe of this city."

"Did you hurt your leg? I notice you have a slight limp while we were walking here."

"Yup. Tore it up pretty bad skiing last winter. I slammed into the ground…crashed actually…after a trick I wasn't ready for. I've been going to physical therapy and it's vastly improved. Might even try skiing in Vermont this winter."

Okay. My stomach knots up making me queasy. Bad feelings. That's exactly what I wrote about Rick. My pulse begins to race. I can either obsess about this strangeness and flee…or ignore it. I don't want to flee. I'm really attracted to this guy. Well, of course I am. He's my fantasy come to life. I'll try and make sense of all this later. Right now, I'm enjoying myself. We walk hand in hand to the loft and I pack a few things.

"What about you?" I ask. "Don't you need stuff, if we stay the weekend?"

"Nah. I'll buy what I need somewhere. I'm easy."

Top down, engine revving, we get on the West Side Highway heading north to the Cloisters. This special day needs a title. Something to tidy up my thoughts, so I can reminisce when I'm alone. The wind whipping his hair, his stylish Ray-Bans enhancing his strong bone structure. Chopin preludes blasting from the Porsche's powerful sound system complement his cosmopolitan style and sophistication. He's the quintessential New Yorker, no remnant of the laid back, pool-partying LA persona that I had written as a way to first describe him. No, this Alex is not Rick. Yes, of course there are implausible similarities. But the differences outweigh them. I choose to believe the differences outweigh them. No history. No past. No storyline. This day is all that exists. This glorious day. Puffy white clouds, azure blue sky, the magnificent power of the car. Yes, the title for today will simply be "Chopin and Cotton Candy Clouds."

The Cloisters, a medieval abbey in northern Manhattan, sits atop a hill with vistas of the Hudson River. Reassembled from pieces of several European abbeys, it offers modern visitors a glimpse into the medieval style of cloistered herb gardens that were maintained by monks or priests. It's part of the Metropolitan Museum of Art, and as such, it houses an extensive collection of art and manuscripts of that era. My mother took me here once after we moved uptown when she was studying at Columbia. It was like stepping back in time and traveling to far-off Europe, experiencing a lifestyle for souls long gone but reimagined in New York City.

On my first visit back then, a string quartet was performing an open-air concert. Today, however, we would hear an a cappella concert of medieval music sung in one of the chapels. The acoustics are perfect; the ancient music sung by the choir is tranquil and spiritually uplifting. In this holy place, I try to make sense of what is going on now in my life. It began with King, but where will it lead? This weekend can sort out some things for me. Of this I am sure. King is at the center of it, but there's also Alex. I must not be blind-sided. Notice all the details. Not be fooled by the sexuality of him. The loveliness of him. Alex, who seemed to spring from words typed on my computer.

"Isn't this just beautiful," he whispers jolting me from my musings. I notice his eyes seem moist. He's moved to tears by this music. His emotional engagement touches me. Perhaps, *I'm* the one who's really the fraud. A writer who believes that her characters are real and in the flesh. That I have the power to create a beating heart. It's just nonsense.

I'm nonsensical.

Afterwards, we remain in our contemplative mood and spend some time enjoying the views of the Hudson River in reverent silence. Instinctively, we rise together from our bench and head toward the car anticipating our fun-filled weekend. The green hills of the Catskills create a dreamy landscape as we speed along to our destination in upstate New York. This time, he plays symphonies of the Romantic Period. I recognize Beethoven and Strauss. A small voice nags at me that my character Rick loved classical music. He was also a nice guy. Remember that you wrote that he was quite helpful to the protagonist, Luanne. He found her a lab so she could run experiments until she found the right formula for her non-allergic cleaning product. So, *settle down*, I tell myself. *Enjoy the drive and the music*. But I get slightly agitated again when I see we've passed our original destination and we're getting off the highway at a sign for the Hamlet of Misty Falls.

"Where are we going?" I ask. "I thought you said, Rhinebeck. We passed a sign for that quite a while back."

"Yes, I know. I wanted to take advantage of the daylight and show you something before we went there. This area is quite charming. Such beautiful old houses. A beautiful little hamlet."

So we drive along winding country roads and pass beautiful homes overlooking the Hudson River. Finally, we end up on a secluded dead-end street with woods on one side and the river on the other. Behind an imposing and ornate wrought-iron fence with stone posts is a charming Gingerbread Queen Anne Victorian. The lavender house has a front porch with carved wooden posts painted white and white ornate wooden trim on the turret and windows that add a whimsical juxtaposition to the lavender. In fact, all the Eastlake style decorations are painted white and make the house a cherished architectural wonder. Flowery gardens and a circular driveway complete the stunning display of a lovely bygone era. Or right out of a movie set. I look at Alex perplexed.

"Why are we stopping here? It's a lovely home. Quite lovely, but is there something you're trying to tell me?"

"I think you should buy it."

"Buy it? But…why? You're kidding right? I have no desire to move out of New York City. I love my loft and love the city."

"It would be a perfect place to write the script and get out of the summer heat there. My production company has studios nearby and we could easily collaborate."

"What are you talking about? I haven't agreed to anything. I haven't even signed anything. Aren't you being premature?"

"But you did."

"Did what?" Now I'm becoming very uncomfortable. Quite nervous, in fact.

"You signed the contract at the luncheon with King. We were all a little surprised at your outburst about never signing because you had signed the contracts before dessert was brought out. We actually had a little fanfare ceremony honoring this important event. King loves rituals. He played a drumroll on his music system. Brought the pen to you on a silver plate. You initiated it. Asked King, if he had a legal copy you could sign. You were extremely animated and excited about the whole thing."

"That's ridiculous! I would have remembered that. I never signed anything. That's preposterous. Aren't you tired of trying to pigeonhole me? Besides I was told it was just a meet and greet, not a signing, so why would I even presume to do that? I'm waiting to hear back from my attorney…why would I…oh what's the use." I'm getting really annoyed at this. "I don't understand why you're lying to me. Look, I have no need for a house up here in the sticks, and I don't even see a "For Sale" sign. You know, suddenly I'm not interested in continuing this weekend. I'm not feeling very well. I think I want to go home." I'm angry and more than confused at this turn of events. "I want to go home right NOW," I shout. "Please take me home."

"Alexa, why can't you just relax and enjoy your good fortune. We'll have fun working together *and* we'll make lots of money."

"Show me the signed contract. Can you do that? You can't because there is none."

"It's in your loft. Right on your coffee table. You were a little indisposed when I brought you home."

"Drugged, you mean."

"That's ridiculous. You were asking for drink after drink. It was you who over did it. Let's work together up here. Please consider this house. It would be perfect and the location couldn't be better. King has about a ten thousand acre retreat here that includes my soundstage and two post-production studios, and, of course, a small mountain," he laughs. "But just look at this house. Who wouldn't want this house? It's beautiful. A dream house. A getaway to be creative. And it's waiting for you."

"It's NOT…FOR…SALE," I say emphatically while raising my voice. "Why do you think it's for sale? This conversation is ridiculous. I don't want this house. I don't want any of this. I'm done. Please, I'd like to go home." He nods and smirks and revs the engine. Then he pushes a button and the top pops up and takes care of itself locking into place. The drive home is somber. No music. No chit-chat. I'm stewing. Agitated. I can't wait to see if the contract is indeed signed and on my coffee table. I need to talk to someone. My mother. Margaret. What a strange end to this day of such anticipation. Now, I can't wait to get away from this guy. But, *can* I get away from this guy, if I indeed signed the contract? I want my old life back. Before Alex, before King. Before that stupid offer.

At last, we're on my street and I tell him to just pull over in front of my building. He obliges. Grabbing my packed bag from the rear seat and jumping out of the car, I run like a frightened animal into the lobby. No goodbye. No light kiss after the marathon sextravaganza. Just escape. Abject fear propels me to the safety of my elevator and my home. Once inside my loft, I immediately look for something on the coffee table.

Oh no! There it is, the dreaded paperwork. Right on the table mocking me. Just as he said. I grab it and flip through the pages hoping it has not been signed. Bile bubbles up. Retching convulsions. My signature is all over the damned pages. All the company contracts bear my signature. The management company, publisher, all of them. Creating my prison. Signed, sealed, and delivered. *How? When?* I can't remember any details. Just that the food was amazing and the weird coincidence of Jewel, and that chef, Philippe looking like characters I created. Just like Alex.

Eugenie. I remember King called for Eugenie, she was someone who gave me water. Was it in the water? What did she look like? No clear memory of her. Apparently, she wasn't one of my characters or I would've remembered. That's good. Some normalcy. I climb into bed and pull the covers over me. I need sleep. I'm exhausted physically and emotionally. Perhaps, I'll be able to figure this all out in the morning. Rest. I need rest. My behavior has been abominable and rest is definitely needed. Yes, the whole thing with Rick, I mean Alex, begins to embarrass me. Why did I attack him like that? Ashamed of my behavior on so many fronts, I slip easily into a deep sleep.

The morning brings some clarity. My usual routine of staying up to all hours writing and rewriting has taken a toll on my sanity. Margaret has been my only diversion. Not good. My social life is nonexistent. Not good. My obsession with writing another blockbuster—definitely not good. A break is definitely needed. A well-rounded life is needed. After Margaret shows me her edits on Monday, planning a trip somewhere would be just the thing. A cruise maybe. The contract is just a license for me to make lots of money. Being number one again. My innermost desires made real. Think of the positive outcomes and *calm down.*

I put on a pot of coffee to have a cup after going for a run to Battery Park and then up toward the Seaport. The fresh air will do me good. Another glorious day. I barely make it to the park because I can't get my rhythm. My breathing is labored, so walking is better right now. I hope I'm not getting sick, but being out of breath is unusual for me. There are tons of people waiting for the ferry to take them to the Statue of Liberty. Sitting on a bench to muster more strength, I enjoy the kaleidoscope of people and commotion. And then I notice a confrontation and my antenna goes up. A couple arguing on a bench further down and across from me. Arguing really loudly with no thought to their surroundings. It's a scary business. He grabs her arm roughly. Bruises on her upper arm come into view when she pulls away from him. Before I realize what I'm doing, I run over to them and get involved in their fight.

"Jodie," I yell at her. "You've got you stop letting guys treat you like this."

"Hey," she shouts back at me. "This is not your concern. Get away. Get out of here!" Her boyfriend, who is now standing, gets in my face and pushes me. "You heard her. Get out of here." The force of his push is unexpected and I lose my balance, trip over my feet, and fall down.

The crowd waiting in the ferry line becomes silent and freezes watching this interaction and some people take a step forward. A small group of nearby onlookers form a circle around me, their faces scrunched in anger looking like they're about to start screaming at me. They start closing in when a cop walks over. "Is everything okay here?" he asks pointedly. The crowd immediately disperses. Quickly getting up and mollified, I mumble something about mistaking her for someone else and apologize. *Jodie's* boyfriend calls me a nut job under his breath and we all walk away. No harm done. No handcuffs and courtrooms.

Flushed with the fever of this shame and fear of arrest, I stumble back toward my loft. All I want to do is get home quickly. I'm becoming a danger to myself with my imagination now on steroids. The characters in my books are not coming to life. *Stop this nonsense!* These are everyday people just living their lives. Philippe, Jewel, Alex. Not created by me. I must keep telling myself that they were not created by me. Although, strangely, I must admit, this woman did *seem* to resemble my description of Jodie. Wait. Here's a thought. Maybe, I'm just creating believable characters, so much so, that they seem to really exist in the world around me. That thought doesn't calm me but just whips up my paranoia about being able to conjure up people. In this agitated state, the street seems to become a moving walkway. I'm home in no time.

Once home, I pour out the coffee, get a glass of wine, and sit in my Jacuzzi. Maybe I should see a shrink. I realize that I am becoming a first-class nutcase and that venturing out alone is too dangerous for me right now. I fill up the day with rented movies and ordering in Chinese. The day passes. After darkness falls, I wander around my loft bored out of my mind. I'm not in the mood to write. I'm not in the mood to be by myself.

Some devilish urge is telling me to get dressed and go out. My carnal thoughts of Alex won't cease and fire pulses in my veins. Dressing very provocatively, I randomly choose a nearby bar. It's dark and dangerous, smells of booze and sweat. I order Scotch—a double, something I never drink. Quick, one-two gulps. I have another. Someone grabs the next stool. He offers to buy my next round. I let him. He moves closer and starts kissing my neck. I let him. Then he grabs my arm and takes me outside to the side alley and right there, I let him. Dizzy and quite drunk, I turn away and tell him I'm going. No, he doesn't want me to go and holds my arm tightly. I pull away and knee him. He curses me and releases my arm as he doubles over in pain. Well, that was interesting. Suddenly, I'm quite sober and walk casually home, unafraid.

Chapter Five

That damned contract

I get up very rested on Monday morning and while brewing my morning coffee notice the message light blinking on my phone. It's my lawyer. "Hello, Lex, this is Jeff Roseman. I've been reading over your contracts for all the subsidiaries and there are a few jarring sentences that appear concerning your rights' holdings. I advise you not to sign these contracts until we clear up the language, so please come in at your earliest convenience." Uh-oh. *Hmm*. When did he call? On Saturday afternoon. Working on the weekend, that's why I pay him the big bucks. Saturday afternoon. *Where was I?* Oh, yes, with Alex, a lifetime ago. I should check my messages more often. I look at the time. It's 9:30. He's bound to be in so I start to call his office. Just then, I hear the elevator stop and my doorbell buzzes. It's Margaret. Right, it's our meeting day. I'll call him later.

"Come in." I yell out to her. "You're just in time for a fresh pot of coffee."

"That sounds great!" She's carrying a whole stack of my mail and puts it on the kitchen table. "I guess you haven't gotten your mail in a few days," she says. "How was your meeting? Was Alex there? Is that why you haven't picked up your mail?" She laughs and winks. "I wish I could have seen that Rolls. Sounds like a wealthy organization. No wonder they can offer so much money."

"Meeting went well. We'll talk about it in detail at some point. And yes, Alex was there." I look at her innocently so as not to give her any ideas. The last few days have been too bizarre to delve into, and I must first sort out the whole business for myself. I quickly add, "Right now, I've got some focus. So let's jump on it. Tell me, what did you think? Just some minor grammatical changes and not much else?"

"Well, yes…and no."

"What do you mean?" I asked startled. I certainly wasn't expecting *that* answer.

"Overall, I loved it, but please take this the right way. We both want the trilogy to be your comeback and a literary achievement. But *Darkside* feels a little rushed and some tension is missing. Also some scenes are just not plausible and…"

"Stop right there," I interrupt her. "That's absurd. I just signed a humongous deal. Alex can't wait for me to write the script. You can't be serious. Show me."

"You signed? I thought you were hesitant to sign. Well, that's great. Congratulations!"

"Thanks. So show me."

"Well...for starters...here in Chapter Two when Jodie goes to a random bar and some dude starts kissing her neck and then screws her in the alley."

"Oh," I say, as a nervous dread washes over me. Then softly, "....I don't remember, let me see." Anxiously, I read the words in disbelief. Not plausible, she says. *But, oh yes, it is.* Of course, I can't tell her. Have to act nonchalant in the face of this growing strangeness. I read and reread that passage and try and remain calm. Something is happening to me. Something unnatural is pushing its way into my reality. Of this I am certain. *But what?* My characters are becoming flesh and blood, and am I becoming...*Jodie?* Is there some point to these experiences?

"What is it?' she says, noticing my demeanor. "You've gone white. Is something wrong? I'm sorry if I upset you."

"No. Nothing. Nothing's wrong, but suddenly I'm no longer in the mood to go over this. Just leave your notes. I'll decide if your assessment of the narrative has merit. Right now, I'm inclined to leave things as they are and just use your skills as a copyeditor. I'm sorry, but we have to stop. I just realized that I have an appointment that I had completely forgotten about. I've got to get ready." An obvious lie because I just told her I wasn't in the mood. I'm not thinking straight.

"Lex, there's no need to take it so personally. I didn't mean to make you so upset. It won't be much to fix some of these issues. Really. The majority of the book is brilliant. I'm just afraid you might lose readers before they get into it."

"Okay, thanks. No problem. I'll call you." She has a pleading look on her face but I ignore it and leave her standing there while walking into my bedroom and then closing the door. When I hear her leave, I come out and pour myself another cup of coffee and sit looking out my window. I'm in a daze and sip slowly. I don't even remember that scene. Maybe I should reread the book to remind myself in case...*in case of what?* The book now has become something else altogether and reading it is the last thing I want to do.

Numb. Frozen. I sit there, hoping these weird occurrences are just flights of fancy. Hoping I can just shake myself back to my former reality. But the contract definitely is real and life changing. Life changing.

Is that the clue? I go into my powder room and stare in the mirror. Am I physically changing too? Am I starting to *resemble* Jodie? My reflection stares back. No, thank goodness. It's still me. Hallelujah, my face with all its imperfections. Then I remember that I was calling Roseman when Margaret burst in. I finish my coffee and dial him up.

"Hello. This is Alexa Wainwright returning Mr. Roseman's call."

"Oh, Ms. Wainwright. I'm so sorry that I haven't called you yet." She begins to cry softly. "A terrible thing happened. Just terrible. Mr. Roseman was killed last night by a hit and run driver." She sobs loudly and I wait for her to continue. "He was on the sidewalk just on the street corner of his townhouse. Apparently, a car just careened off the road and ran over him. I mean…," she manages to say in her distress, "the car, literally ran over him several times." What she says next is almost hard to make out because she's so distraught. "The police are considering it a homicide," and then she almost wails.

"Oh no! How awful, who would do that?" I say through my own flood of tears. "Oh my god. No…no, such a young man with a family. I'm so sorry," I say illogically feeling responsible, worried that this has something to do with the strange world of King Blakemore and my contract. After we hang up, remorse, sorrow, and fear overtake me and I cry loudly, hard, and uncontrollably. Gagging, I run into my bathroom and douse my face with cold water. This is too much. I've got to get out of this contract and take back my life. The rush of events is too overwhelming. I feel isolated and quite vulnerable. My anxiety level borders on hysteria.

In a somber mood, I grab the contracts and get another cup of coffee only mildly concerned that sometimes I act rashly from being pumped up on too much caffeine. I've got to get a handle on what I've signed. I've got to have the energy and focus to figure this all out. To make sense of Roseman's message. Sitting at my kitchen table, I read slowly and very carefully. So even though there's a lot of legalese, I wade through it and try to make sense of it. I see that the giant advances are spelled out as well as the percentage of the film. All right, that calms me a little.

The Jameson buyout is disturbing because, reading between the lines, it could be extortion. Margaret's words about their A-list authors being managed by Trinity of Sixes rings in my ears. Becoming a little leery, I continue. Being the designated scriptwriter for *Darkside* is also in there. Okay, that's good. Final script approval rests with the production team. *Hmm*, don't like that, but at least I have input to the process. There's a deadline for my next novel, but not until next year. That's doable. So far so good. Then I find the dreaded sentence. Rewriting it on my notepad to try and decipher its meaning after researching some legal terminology, the sentence basically says: *In the event that any or all signed contracts are not fulfilled by Ms. Alexa Wainwright, or that Ms. Wainwright seeks to terminate said contracts, Trinity of Sixes Communications and all its subsidiaries shall retain all the rights to all of her work (i.e., novels, scripts, works in progress of any nature) past, present, and future. The name, Alexa Wainwright, and all its forms such as, Lex, Alex, or Lexi Wainwright is the property of Trinity of Sixes Communications and can no longer be used by Ms. Wainwright for future creative work once the contract is terminated. Additionally, the contract termination penalty shall be for a sum of not less than $100 million of which the termination penalty amount is subject to change at the whim of Trinity of Sixes Communications, et al.*

I read these scary words over and over. This sentence is on all contracts, no loopholes. A sinking feeling starts at the pit of my stomach and an awful sense of dread washes over me...again. This feeling of impending doom is now becoming my normal mood in its consistent pervasiveness. Creeping dread. A cold, clammy sweat breaks out over my entire body. Nausea makes it hard to swallow. *All the rights to my work. Past rights. Future rights. My name! My friggin name! They own my name? Can they really do that! Ethical Christian values my ass!* Stunned by the absolute horror of my entrapment, I go get my phone. I need help. I need to send a text to my mother. I need her to call me. She said to be careful. But I wasn't careful. I don't remember signing that damned contract. I tried to be careful, really tried, by sending it to Roseman. But he's dead now.

What should I do? I've got to get out of this situation. Is there a way out? I feel like a person sinking in quicksand with no one to pull me out. Reaching for the phone, I knock off the stack of mail onto the floor. There, on top of the disarray of junk mail, bills, and my grocery store's weekly specials' flyer is a brochure of the Victorian house in Misty Falls. The very house Alex showed me on Saturday, a million years ago. Shocked by its presence in my apartment, I pick it up gingerly, worried that it's imbued with a magical spell. No strangeness happens. No shapeshifting or trance inducing...it's harmless. Just a brochure and an unbelievably freaky coincidence...maybe. I study it. The house is undeniably charming and...friendly looking. Inviting.

Price Drastically Reduced, screams giant red letters. *Hurry this deal won't wait!* Really? How odd. That beautiful house, that very house. I flip open the brochure. The price is not listed but the phone number of the realtor is listed. The interior photos show how lovely it is inside. *Interior Totally Renovated and Upgraded. Perfect for weekends or summer getaway* says the heading. A delightful looking, funky mid-century modern kitchen is accented with contemporary furnishings. The retro-appliances are turquoise with a refrigerator that is specifically listed as having been fitted with an ice maker, the Shaker cabinets are white with steel hardware, the backsplash is turquoise and white patterned glass squares, and the counter tops are concrete like mine. An adorable breakfast nook is also a throwback and matches the vintage kitchen having a chrome rimmed oblong table with a white speckled Formica top and four turquoise tufted Naugahyde vinyl chairs with chrome legs.

Views of the Hudson through the floor-to-ceiling windows surround the kitchen, the living room, and dining area that's large enough for a wooden farmhouse table that can seat eight people easily. French doors provide access to the patio. Photos from the patio reveal English-garden landscaping, giant evergreens, and a rolling green lawn. The Hudson River shimmers in the light. The room sizes seem large but not too large. Cozy. All furnishings are included. Move in condition, turnkey.

The phone rings and I pray it's my mom. I answer trying not to sound too desperate so as not to frighten her. But, I really, really need to talk her.

"Hello?" I ask hopefully.

"Hello, Ms. Wainwright, this is Amber Blakemore. I'd like to welcome you into the Trinity of Sixes family."

"Oh," disappointment pulses through me. "Uh...thank you, Miss..."

She interrupts, "Please call me Amber."

"So, you're related to Mr...er King?"

"Yes, he's my uncle. The reason I'm calling, Alexa, can I call you Alexa?"

"Sure."

"We need you to send us the trilogy manuscripts. We want to have a segmented release before the movie hits theaters. We're certain the books will work to make the movie a blockbuster and the movie will, in turn, send viewers to buy the books."

"I understand, but it's come to my attention that *Darkside* needs some minor reworking. I can have it..."

"Please, let me stop you right there. Just send it as is. Don't worry about it. We'll do the final edits, as stated in the contract. We have a great team. You'll be more than pleased with the result and your sales."

Whoa. They have the final edits, as stated in the contract? Must have missed that. "Just give me a day or two and..."

"Well, we actually need them as soon as we hang up. We're on a tight deadline. So, can we count on you to send them directly? In Word documents?

"Okay…I guess…sure. Just give me about an hour to reformat from Pages."

"Great. Thanks so much. I look forward to working with you… I'm a big fan," she says as an afterthought.

As soon as I hang up, I grab the publishing contract. Sure enough, it's there. They have final edits and final approval. Okay. Let them have what Margaret thinks is a crappy version. LET THEM HAVE THAT PIECE OF SHIT!!! Let them fuss over it and fix it…or not. Amber seems so sure it will make money anyway, no matter what. *And isn't that the point to all of this? Money?* I can just sit back relax and enjoy my…wait! Wait just a minute. I think I've just hatched a plan to circumvent this contact. I'll give them crap. Write a crap script, write crap books. They'll want to break the contract themselves. That's it! I've got them beat. Ha!

A thought pops into my head. What if they keep me under contract but never publish my work? They could do that. Basically, I would disappear from the scene. Would they do that? *Do I really care?* I'll be filthy rich just from the trilogy, richer than I ever could have imagined. Go out with a bang by being number one on the bestseller list, unless I've missed something. *Uh-oh.* I'm sure I missed something. It couldn't be that easy to fool them with all their lawyers. Never mind, it's worth a try. That'll be my plan until I'm shown otherwise. Take my chances. Take back some control…if I can.

Rethinking this strategy, it does really seem too easy. Something is fishy, a gnawing restlessness creeps over me and I get an urge to take another look at the contract. I find a sentence about timeframes for future books with no set duration, no end. Not just two books, but for the rest of my life, if they want. And what does *fulfilled* mean? Can I fulfill the contract with giving them crap? Those horrible sentences stick in my brain about fulfillment and termination penalties, loss of my name. *Hmm.* I read them again.

Yes, lack of fulfillment will be considered termination requiring stated astronomical fee. And then, perusing the contract further, the definition of fulfillment is described as "at the level of previous published work or better." *I know these sentences weren't there before!* This contract is responding to my thoughts and changing the language, like it's alive. I'm not crazy. *Am I?* Shivering at the thought of this horrendous situation, I see my future self withered, wrinkled, humpbacked, and encased in cobwebs sitting at my desk. A frozen death mask of misery on my face with my fingers on my keyboard as if typing. A tableau for eternity.

My mind races to think of something else to break free from this deal. Yes! Another idea takes shape that has nothing to do with language of the contract, so it might have legs. Even though I'm signed, sealed, and delivered, basically owned by Trinity of Sixes, maybe I can sue for signing under duress. I'm sure I was drugged. I'll get a blood test. That'll prove it. Now, I picture King and his entourage getting arrested, shackled, and shuffling in orange jumpsuits. Sitting in prison cells with ugly toilets in full view waiting to humiliate them. My nightmare over, their nightmare beginning.

Suddenly, an icy draft from nowhere knocks me out of my reverie like a bucket of cold water. My vision of King's incarceration evaporates when logic enters. It's been days since the drugging, so what's the point of a blood test now? Anyway, they…King…probably used a drug with no residual traces. Anyone listening to my accusation would also see that the first part of the contract details the vast sums of money in advances and percentages. Who would believe I was under duress?

This is all new ground for me. I'm completely over my head. They really have me. Completely. *Be careful.* Did my mother see this? If so, why didn't she give me more information? Warn me in detail. *I really need to talk to her. I need her advice.* I feel so lost and vulnerable. I text her and it bounces back. Not delivered. *C'mon Mom!* I try again. No luck. I call and it doesn't go through like it's been disconnected. Something's up with her phone. Strange and very frustrating.

My coffee's gone cold but I drink it anyway. Numb, immobile, and detached, I stare out the window at the skyline. Time passes. I pick up the brochure again. *Ah yes,* it's a delightful looking house, very tempting. Many New Yorkers have weekenders in the country to detox from the hustle bustle. I imagine myself having coffee on the tree-shaded patio watching the peaceful flow of the river. I picture working with Alex on the script…yeah, I picture Alex. Well…if I can't get out of that damned contract, *what else is there to do?*

Who would blame me?

And so, in sound mind and totally aware of being a fly caught in a spider web, a bird in a gilded cage, and every other cliché about being entrapped that doesn't come to mind right now, I make the call and embrace my altered existence.

Chapter Six

Kip

Smooth as glass, it felt like there were no potholes or bumps on the road as we headed up the West Side Highway. Gliding over the Tappan Zee Bridge and racing past the light traffic to the New York Thruway, this high performance vehicle was a joy to drive. We also had an amazing view of the mountains through its panoramic roof of glass. "Handles like a dream, doesn't it?" asked Kip, my spur of the moment instructor and sales manager of the Range Rover showroom. After my impulsive purchase, we just drove right out of the dealership and onto the street, as he talked me through all my nervousness being behind the wheel of a powerful SUV with my limited driving experience.

No worries, this Range Rover practically drove itself. It was the perfect choice, a beautiful color called Luxor Metallic, kind of a pale gold, with the windows and top trimmed in black. Very elegant. Very, very expensive. Nearly the price of my house. *And why not?* I'm to be filthy rich. Besides, I needed to have a really good car right now, for my trips back and forth, for snowy roads and such.

How this all came about was quite accidental, not even given any thought, until it instantly became apparent that I needed a car. Choosing what to pack led me to sorting through my closet and carving out a giant stack of clothes, shoes, and purses to give to Goodwill. Being immersed in a mundane project was therapeutic and relaxing. I had decided to consciously make an effort to shift my perception of reality, to focus on all the positive things going on in my life, even though there seems to be another version of the real world that I'm experiencing.

The purchase of the house in Misty Falls was super easy. The price was really low, unbelievably low for being on several acres of river property and the house itself being quite ample. Four bedrooms, three baths, first-floor powder room, great room, dining room, study, that funky kitchen, four fireplaces and more details such as crown molding throughout. Rounding out this astonishing find was a swimming pool with a guesthouse and fully equipped gym and media room in the loft/ attic above the attached garage that I didn't notice on first inspection of the offer brochure.

Discovering these extras was another weird occurrence, among all my weird occurrences of late. I'd been thinking it was too bad there was no pool or exercise room. I was also wishing there was a media room like here in my condo loft. And sure enough, the house had it all. Two pages of the brochure were apparently stuck together and so I missed those photos at first glance. Or perhaps there was another explanation, my desire for those extras created them. An irrational extension of my ability to conjure up people like Alex and Jewel. Now I can create anything just by wanting it. Very powerful. An intoxicating ability that must be managed, so I'm trying to keep my thoughts simple and task oriented.

Logic is tossed as I sink deeper.

All in all, after closing costs and fees, the total out of pocket came to $325,000. A crazy low number and probably engineered by King or Alex who really wanted me up there. I bought it for cash. Transferred money from some investments. No bank involvement, just the title company, insurance company for homeowner's, and the real-estate lawyer for the closing. Did it all over fax, phone, and the internet. Fast and simple. There were no other offers. Like it was waiting for me. I told the realtor that when I first saw the house there was no indication it was for sale. He said it had just come on the market. The owners got in a jam, needed to leave the area quickly, and hoped it would sell fast and priced it accordingly. Curious how that really small amount in today's world would be worth taking such a hit from the home's real value, which probably was closer to several million dollars. The owners had no mortgage. But still.

I'm being romanced with riches on all fronts of that I'm sure. In a final attempt at making some sense of the deal outside of its pretty obvious manipulation by others, I asked the realtor how he got my address. He told me he canvasses my whole building because city folks love a weekend retreat. That made sense, even though it was a giant coincidence. So I made a conscious decision. I'm just going to go where this leads me and not fight it. Enjoy my good fortune.

In the taxi, on the way to Goodwill, we passed a billboard for Land Rover and the dealership was on the next street, walking distance from Goodwill. It got me thinking of a car, something big enough for all my stuff and with four-wheel drive if I'm up there in winter. As soon as I walked into the rather empty dealership, a strikingly attractive guy sitting at the strategically placed desk facing the door, looked up and we locked eyes and nodded. He didn't rush over and start crowding me and hard selling but gave me time to browse around looking at the few models. Then, after a few minutes, he sauntered over and extended his manicured hand and gently but firmly shook mine.

His engaging, disarming, and aristocratic air of the grown-up rich-kid tickled my imagination and it was easy to picture him dressed as a member of the court of Louis XVI. But in this life, he was hip, urban, and fashionably monotone. Wearing black trousers, a black t-shirt stretched tightly across his well-toned frame, and a black buttery leather sport coat, his casual city sophistication was complemented by his eye-catching Western belt buckle of silver and turquoise. Although tall, he wore medium-heeled Western black boots that played a rhythmic beat on the floor tiles when he approached me.

But it was more than his clothes that fascinated me one second after I took a good look at his face while we shook hands. He was Michelangelo's David. A Greek god. Perfection and beauty. His disheveled mass of thick, black curls framed his large, bright blue eyes, giving him an angelic cherub-like innocence that at once charmed my sensibilities while bringing forth my heretofore unrecognized maternal instincts. I guessed him to be in his very early twenties and, alas, too young for my taste. "Hello," he said. "I'm Henry Bartholomew Knight, but everyone calls me Kip. How about I show you your dream car."

And there it was. Another spontaneous purchase followed by an impromptu lesson in the joys of driving a Range Rover given by my new friend, Kip, who would become from that very first meeting, a beloved acquaintance. Kip offered to drive up to Misty Falls with me the following day to continue his lessons, so I wouldn't bruise or dent this beauty of a car. Although, one could think this offer quite odd, as well as my acceptance, it seemed perfectly appropriate. A train enthusiast, he looked forward to the Amtrak ride on the trip back, and so it was a win-win. I welcomed the company and not sleeping alone in the big house for the first night.

When we got back to town after my driving lesson, he nurtured me through the city traffic and stayed with me until I got to the garage in my building. We hugged goodbye agreeing to meet in mid-morning for our drive upstate. I immediately bought a parking space for the exorbitant price of $1500 per month. Can't leave this classy car parked on the street. Anyways, I'm filthy rich now. Filthy rich. My new mantra to justify my behavior.

My daft, impulsive, and manic attitude had a slight setback after listening to a message when I got home. A whispery voice, disguising the caller's gender, left a sinister sounding message, "Don't move to Misty Falls." That was it. It was an eerie warning because of that strange sounding voice. For a second, I wondered if it might be my lawyer, Roseman, since he called to warn me before about the contract. But then I remembered, *he's dead*. The caller ID said number unknown. I deleted his previous message, so I couldn't compare the voices. I shrugged my shoulders and tossed away the warning. Probably a vengeful person from my agency or publishing house. But…*hmm*…no one knows I bought the house because it really just happened. Perplexing. Oh well. I'm not going to let it creep me out. There's enough about my life right now to creep me out, if I stop, take a beat, and mull over things. Whatever…I'm going. Taking this new world order to its conclusion because there's really no other choice.

Yes, I'm a bird in gilded cage, but no matter, *gilded* is good. Every book a blockbuster. A triumph. Final edit pressure lifted. No matter what I write, as long as I write something decent, will sell…and sell well, stratosphere well. The dream of every writer. What's there to complain about? And I love writing. There are a million ideas living inside me waiting to become a story. And there will be millions upon millions of readers. Suddenly, the image of the old crone typing for eternity surfaces from deep within my consciousness. "Stay away old crone," I shout to my empty room. And again for emphasis, "Stay away. Success and wealth beyond my wildest dreams trumps you and your ominous message." *Please let that be true.*

The weird phone message wasn't the only uncomfortable and mood-deflating attack on my new found enthusiasm for Trinity, et.al. My agent Gloria called as soon as she got her formal letter this morning severing my relationship with her. I had given her no warning about all that was going on and, true to my chicken shit way of dealing with confrontations, didn't take the call and let the machine pick up. Her voice sounded high-pitched indicating her distress. She, along with my publisher, have become collateral damage, an unfortunate turn of events dictated by the terms of my ironclad contract.

But there's nothing I can do, so why put myself through that awkwardness? Why deal with all the drama? There are some residual royalties she's owed, along with the generous contract buyout that will more than compensate for terminating our relationship. I'll write a nice thank you for all she's done for me. If it weren't for her, there would be no me as a writer. I owe her a big thank you for that. However, when you consider how much money she's earned from my books, well, I'm thinking we're even. But still…there's some guilt…in fact, a lot of guilty feelings concerning dumping her.

It will also be extremely tough to tell Margaret that I no longer need her services what with Trinity's final edits clause. I'm not going to drive myself nuts with giving them perfection. Anyway, she had no idea what she started by bringing Alex over and now she's paying a big price for it. Besides, she's always been too subservient and that trait is the one thing about her I find really tiresome. This will ultimately be good for her. Get her to find the husband she longs for and move to Waspy Connecticut where she will bear 2.3 children who will become part of a future freshmen class attending Harvard or Yale. She'll thank me for it… later. She's another one I'll reach out to in my cowardly way by sending an email. It's been written but is still in my outbox. I'll hit send after I'm settled in Misty Falls, so that when she rushes over here, I'll be gone.

The keys to the house arrived yesterday. Now it's time to finish packing and eat at my favorite kosher deli on Second Ave. One last dinner of corned beef on club bread, Dr. Brown's cream soda, and a potato knish. Like I'm going away to prison, or a university in Oklahoma. I know the move won't be very far, just a few hours north, but it will be a tremendous change. I grew up in the city. Country life is foreign to me. Roosters crowing, farmers chomping on a sprig of hay, the smell of horse manure everywhere. That's my mental image, as soon as I think about living in Duchess County. Granted, it didn't look like that when Alex took me there. But still. I'm really glad that Kip is going with me. My driving needs oversight on the winding country roads and steep inclines when going through mountains and such. It wasn't just for the driving that I was glad. Striking out alone is daunting. Having my mother come with me for a few days would have been quite comforting.

Where the hell is she when I need her so much?

I spend a very sleepless night. The corned beef didn't help, turning my stomach into a war zone. I'm a jumble of nerves. Today is the day. No more walks on Wall Street on a Sunday. No more South Street Seaport, no more…SHUT UP! I yell out loud to myself and then the concierge calls. "Send him up," I say. And so my adventure to the hinterland begins.

"What's wrong?" he asks as soon as he walks through the doorway sensing my distress.

"Nothing, nothing." He raises his eyebrows in disbelief. "Well, I'm overwhelmed with the move…and all the other changes…and my mother hasn't called…and I'm lonely…and…"

"Shh," he says gently and gives me a bear hug. We stand like that for several minutes. It calms me…a calming energy, my heart rate slows down, my breathing relaxes. Anxiety is hugged right out of me, like I just took a hit of a joint. "Hey," he says lightening the mood, "this penthouse has some great views. I knew when they started building these, the lofts would be spectacular."

"Oh, were you thinking of buying one?"

"No, my dad is…was the developer that built these. He's built half of downtown and owns several high-priced apartment buildings. I don't have an appetite for turning New York City into a place just for the ultra wealthy, so he couldn't entice me into joining his firm. He thought that buying me an elitist car dealership would give me something to do. But it bores me, when it doesn't annoy me." He throws up his hands and squeezes my shoulder. "Enough about me. Are you ready? Let's hit the road. We could run into traffic, if we don't leave soon. People head to their country houses by midday on a Friday, so we're good if we leave now."

His words about elitism knock me back. The antithesis of what I'd been telling myself these past few days, that being fabulously rich is good, not just good, but good times a zillion. My words to live by. His somewhat socialist point of view now makes me uncomfortable. Don't dwell on it, after all he's the *owner* of the Land Rover dealership. Why didn't he become a grade school teacher or charity worker if he's so against the spoils of inherited wealth? I'll ask him...later.

"I'd offer you coffee but I'm bringing my cherished coffee maker until I buy another one. It's so hot and dry out, do you need hydrating? Would you like some bottled water?"

"Sure. Love one. Is that the pile of stuff to be loaded into the car?"

Loading up the car means about five trips up and down the elevator to the garage. Finally, we close the cargo area on the last load. It was more of a challenge than I had originally thought. One thing led to another and I brought books, photos, and emptied my refrigerator. Meeting Kip and his offer to help move was like a gift from the gods.

And we were off.

Life changing off.

This drought had its positives. Another sunny day with no clouds made for a spectacular drive. I find myself grabbing sideways glances at him when I should be looking at the road. Occasionally he has to yell, "Look out!" when the car in front slows down. I'm not experienced enough to take my eyes off the road, but he's so damn cute in profile. Plastic-surgery perfect straight nose that gentiles have, dimples, cleft. Curls bouncing when he laughs. Today, he's dressed for a weekend in the country, very casual. Shorts, slip on canvas shoes, tee. All black. The guy loves black. His muscular and well-shaped legs make him look a lot stronger than his clothes from yesterday. His arms are built as well. Clearly, an avid gym goer, strong but not muscle bound. I want to cuddle him, not ravish him. And that's good. A calm, friendly, long weekend. Happiness.

We talk about the weather and the danger of our diminishing

water supply, but in a small talk kind of way. Not a too serious and worrisome kind of way. Then he turns on the radio and immediately our joyful mood is sobered by an alarmed reporter. We hear dire warnings about the drought and wild fires. This newscaster is reminding everyone that although there appears to be no weather events, lightning can still strike causing dry brush to ignite.

"That's where the expression *like a bolt out of the blue* comes from," the newscaster says. I tell Kip that's exactly what happened the other day as I looked out the window. He tells me he's never seen that. And so we talk about the scary results of the drought again. Future water rationing, fire danger in Misty Falls. The problems of flooding and drought that are becoming common all over the planet. We become silent pondering the climate change implications.

"Why do people call you Kip?" I ask suddenly.

"Oh," he says, "I was wondering when you'd get around to asking me. Not a very interesting story. It started at boarding school. Everyone had nicknames there, either given to them by their families or by the students. Heather was Honey, John was Jack, Horace was horse face." He laughs.

"That wasn't very nice."

"Well, he did look like one. As for me, I was a knight in process because I always held the door open for girls and it also was a play on my last name. So, Kip, and it stuck. How about you? How'd you come by your name? It doesn't feel real. Classy, but somehow not belonging to you."

"How perceptive of you, but I'm not sure I liked that you picked up on that. How?"

"Just a gift, I guess. So what is it? Your real name?"

"Gladys Lipschitz." And we both laugh. "Well," he says, "that doesn't suit you either. You're more worthy of an exotic name, like…Riva, I think."

"*Riva?* Wow. What made you think of that name of all things? That's my mother's name. How weird that you would think of it."

"That name just popped into my head when I was looking at you just now. Probably read it in a book or something." That explanation makes no sense to me because Riva is an unusual name and not very common in this country. Never seen it in a book or film. Strange.

"So *Gladys*," he says with a smirk, "I've got a present for you," and he takes out an iPod and plugs it into my console. "I loaded it up with music. There's everything from Bach to Mumford and Sons."

"That's so sweet. Thanks so much." I have my own loaded iPod, who doesn't? But I pretend to be very excited anyway. At a rest stop, I get worried because I lose him for a few minutes but then I find him stretching and jogging outside. A real health nut. The remainder of the trip, we spend listening to music, laughing, and enjoying the day. Before we know it, I'm turning into the driveway of my new house and can turn off the nice but authoritative lady living in my GPS.

Chapter Seven

The house

There it is in all its splendor. We sit in the driveway for a moment marveling at the architectural wonder of this fantasy house. The white trim wooden ornaments against the soft lavender exterior, the turrets, porch, and etched-glass inserts of the cherry wood double front door. No rockers on the front porch like in the picture and I was curious about that but still charming and inviting.

"What a place," says Kip. "You weren't kidding when you said it's right on the river. The house suits you, quirky and classy. A great retreat. And even a pool. Hey, we, or rather you, could turn it into a B&B, if you want to get out of the writing business." His enthusiasm rubs off. Excitement gushes through me. My decision was so right, so perfect, so spot on to come up here. Great days ahead. A fun-filled summer. Since I'd never been inside the house (and if Kip thought that strange, he never said so), we decide to investigate before unloading the car.

As we step into the foyer, we're aghast at what we see. *What the…?* Broken glass is everywhere. The missing rocking chairs were in pieces as if smashed against the walls that now have deep holes. The sofas look as if a knife were used to slice their fabric. The TV is knocked off the wall, cracked, and lying on the wooden floor along with smashed unrecognizable whatnots. Lamps are crashed and broken on the once beautiful floor now marred with giant deep gashes. Plastic bags full of smelly garbage are thrown all over everything, so the room stank. The kitchen can be seen from the living room and it's destroyed. The cabinets are thrown open and dishes are smashed on the counter and probably on the floor.

"Oh my god! What a freakin' mess! Why would anybody do this?" But I knew. Adding to my upset of facing this unsettling scene, I had a sinking feeling that I knew something more unsettling. *Jodie.* Jodie did this to her trailer before she ran away. Was this another materialization of a character I had written, like the crazy scene at the ferry? No! That's nuts! But I started to shake with fear. Kip noted my extreme distress and pulled me close. "It's okay. It'll be okay. I'll help you fix this place back up." Then he lets go and faces me, "Are you sure these people weren't in foreclosure or a short sale? Sometimes the anger of their raw deal takes control and they lash out. I've seen this kind of mess left behind after my father has foreclosed on people."

"I don't know. I wasn't told that. Only that the owners needed cash and fast. As far as my purchase, I hardly paid anything for this place and now I know why. The deal seemed so easy. *Too* easy, I guess. *Move in condition. Turnkey.* That's what the brochure said. Ha! It's not just this mess that needs to be cleaned up, but now I have to buy all new furniture, dishes, probably beds. Everything! It was very stupid of me not to do a walk-through before the closing. I never imagined anything like this and coming up here earlier wasn't really convenient. So stupid of me." I shake my head in disgust.

Slowly, we walk around. Each room looks the same. Destruction and chaos as if a wild animal got trapped in here. Upstairs is no better. Sure enough, the beds are destroyed. Just like Jodie. Mattresses sliced. And the lights don't turn on. No electricity. No air conditioning. Why hadn't the account been switched over? I had talked to the company myself. With trepidation, we walk over to the guesthouse by the pool. An oasis of calm. Clean, neat, and welcoming. Left for me to live in while I fix everything else. We sit for a moment stunned and then look around. At least there's a well-supplied kitchen, full bath, one bedroom, and the small living room. A little cottage. It'll do for now.

Looking more closely at the pool through the sliding glass doors, I jump up and shout, "Oh no! Look!" Floating around the pool are several dead squirrels and perhaps even a rabbit. This is too much. I'm beaten. This was a big mistake. I see that now. *What was I thinking?* The phone message from that mystery person was right, I shouldn't move here. It probably was the disgruntled former owner angry over lost money, not my strange and far-fetched notion that it was Jodie. I don't care, I'll just walk away. Leave the mess. Lose the money. I can't deal with this.

"I'm going back to the city, Kip, *now.* I don't want to stay here, even one more second."

"Wait. Let me make a few phone calls. I know people because of my father's business. Don't be too hasty. This is still a lovely place. It's a challenge to be sure, but it could turn out fine. I can take the week off and help. Call the electric company and then call your realtor."

"No, I'm beaten, Kip. It's too much. I want to go home."

"Please, let me help. This will all work out, I promise. Please, don't be hasty. Trust me. Make those calls."

"I just dealt with the selling agent, so I don't have a realtor," I say giving in but still unsure. "I'll call him, but I have a bad feeling that somehow I've been suckered."

The first call is to the electric company, the house and guesthouse are stifling. *Oh ma'am,* some jerk says, *we're so sorry. We'll turn it on right now. Give us about an hour.* I hate being called ma'am. Then, I call the cable company, internet access is my life line. They can come out tomorrow. Finally, I call the realtor. The number's been disconnected. I try his cell...nothing, doesn't even connect. I call information trying to find the main number for the agency in Misty Falls, but the agency apparently doesn't exist. Yeah, sure. Figures. I try to locate the former owners but no luck there either. Kip says we can look up the tax records and get some info about them, but I'm too depressed to do that right now. And then suddenly, the air conditioner unit clicks on. We spontaneously shout, "Yea!" And begin to laugh.

Kip was more successful with *his* calls. He tells me the plan. Cleaners will get here first thing tomorrow as will drywall contractors who will match the wall paint. We should get some lunch, but first we must put my food in the refrigerator in the cottage. We check out the refrigerator. It's clean. Thank goodness. My food is in coolers packed with ice, so it's still good. We put the other stuff in cabinets. I hook up my coffee maker. Kip checks his phone for nearby furniture stores. There's a big furniture store chain about an hour from here. Hooray. Then he suggests I should just order the same mattress I have in the city, if I like it. Good idea, but I'm skeptical because it takes a while to get a bespoke Savoir bed. As luck would have it, there's an available mattress with all my exact requirements because it was not delivered to a client whose check bounced. I get it for a deep discount but pay extra for express delivery and the distance. It will be here overnight. Amazing. Things are looking up. We go to lunch.

Misty Falls is a quaint hamlet with one main shopping street and a handful of side streets ending in a sprinkling of houses with roads leading up to the mountains and thruway. Street lights are fake gas lamps with hanging flower pots, and store-front window boxes are full of spring flowers. The flowers are all real and give off a sweet perfume. Green mountain vistas wrap around blooming ornamental cherry-tree lined streets adding their scent to the luscious aroma. A little piece of heaven. Welcoming and picturesque. No sign yet of the creeping drought. Jane's Joint grabbed our attention with her sign that read, *Home cooking, but I ain't yo' momma.* Seated at a booth by the window, we studied our menus that offered a giant array of selections from Italian food to Greek, like a Jersey diner.

"You're like my guardian angel, Kip," I say with my eyes glued to the menu.

"Yes, I know," he says and I look up to see that he's serious. Just then the waitress appears and almost makes me gag. She's wearing a pink uniform, hairnet, and looks just like my imagined failed self, Gladys, the waitress. *Can this be?* Is this a reminder of what might happen to me, if I do not fulfill the contract? She takes her pencil from behind her ear and pulls the order pad from her pocket. Her nameplate is pinned to her shirt. Gladys! Unbelievable.

She's my sad-faced, life-sucks-for-me twin, looking at us with bored dark eyes waiting for our order. Yes, she's a ringer for me having the same build, similar coloring, and similar facial features. My legs start shaking and my heart begins to race. I look at Kip to see if he recognizes her resemblance to me, as he orders a Greek salad and some water. He seems to take no notice of it. I can barely spit out that I want the same order. "Sure, two Greeks, two waters," the could-be-my mouth says to us, as she walks away.

How come Kip didn't notice the startling likeness? Or is it just me? Have I been hallucinating all this time? With Alex, Jewel? Some kind of brain damage? I'm relieved and unnerved at the same time. Maybe, there's something seriously wrong with me. Maybe, I should see a doctor. But, now I'm up here for the summer and all my doctors are in the city. I need to verify my hallucination, so I nudge Kip.

"Did you notice her name? The waitress?" I ask Kip.

"No, why?" Just then she brings the waters. "Thanks, Phyllis," he says looking at me strangely.

"Oh, I made a mistake, never mind. I thought her nameplate said...forget it."

When she comes back her uniform isn't even pink and she's blonde. Okay, I'm going nuts. Really having a mental problem. Delirious. Nuts is better than the power to conjure up people...maybe. Thinking this through, I suddenly realize that Kip is someone I'd never thought of before, never wrote about...so, that's good. That's a path to being sane again. Perhaps Alex isn't really Rick. If I can get Kip to meet Alex, get Kip and Alex in the same room, I might see who he really is, realize my mistake. A simple plan to bust through my mental illness, opening the floodgates of truth. A strategy to move into normalcy. These thoughts begin to calm me, lighten me up.

Also, I must change my warped thinking about the house. Kip said that disgruntled owners in short sales sometimes tear up their houses. Only, I don't think there was a bank involved on their end, but whatever. Most likely, it was the angry former owners and not Jodie who destroyed my house, and, also, it wasn't a conjured up version of my sorry self waiting on us. It was someone named Phyllis. I have to shift my perspective and think of the positive. Meeting Kip for one. Living up here with its beautiful setting. Focus on immediate tasks. There's a lot to do. When the salads come, we laugh at how enormous they are and dig right in. We eat hungrily and in silence finishing in no time. Yummy. I'm feeling happy…a little.

Shopping commands our attention after lunch. As soon as we get into the car, we come up with our strategy during the one hour drive to the furniture store. There's a lot to purchase. An entire house of furniture. Sofas and such are first, then linens, and finally kitchen and dining items. We run through the furniture showroom picking out floor models available for immediate delivery. I have a color scheme in mind to match the area rugs that luckily weren't ruined. There are numerous selections that fit my criteria. It's all so easy. Boom. Boom. Boom. That one, that one, that one.

Then it's off to an electronics store for two flat-screen TVs. One giant one for the den area and a slightly smaller one for my bedroom. The media room has a screen that comes down from the ceiling and it was in good shape. At least, I wouldn't have to figure out how to replace that. Next we buy sheets for all the beds. Luckily, in the guest bedrooms, the knife slices never made it to the mattress. Next are dishes, flatware, glasses and such. All these purchases are put on my credit card. I had to call my bank at the electronics store because the fraud department thought someone was making bogus charges and declined the card.

The cargo area and back seat are stuffed with linens, dishes, drinking glasses, and TVs. The rest will be delivered. We're exhausted and satisfied that all will be normal in about two days, at the latest. The furniture will be delivered by tomorrow afternoon after the damaged furniture is removed, the cleaners are finished, and the floors polished. Amazing. Kip is like a magician. Presto! Everything is fixed. On Monday morning, we marvel at what we've accomplished. It's all perfect. Everything's installed. My bed is fabulous and I bought a padded leather headboard to accent it. Heaven, just like at my loft.

On a whim, I bought a fancy espresso machine, a worthy contender to my cherished coffee maker. We sit on the patio sipping our frothy lattes while enjoying the light breeze from the river and the beautiful early-summer flower garden. The sprinklers come on, reminding me that there were no April showers this spring and we could really use some rain. The drought is so worrisome, and I feel guilty watering, but so far there's no rationing up here. At least I think so, because I've seen lawns being watered. Can't let this beautiful and expensive garden just dry up and blow away.

"Will you really stay for the week, Kip? Enjoy this place with me after all our work?"

"I'd like to, now that we've got this place looking like a page out of Martha Stewart's magazine. I haven't yet given my sales manager a heads up, we were so busy. A few days off to relax we'll do me good before I set out for Nairobi and Buenos Aires." He sees my puzzled expression and tells me that every year he makes a trip to disadvantaged locales to help feed and clothe the poor unfortunates that populate our world. An overwhelming number of the world's population wallow in abject poverty. Both he and his father's way of giving back. His father realizes that the family's wealth is more than anyone could spend in ten lifetimes and so totally supports Kip's work with numerous charities, here and abroad. It's not just throwing money at these organizations, Kip rolls up his sleeves and helps out with the day-to-day. He has spent time on poor Native American reservations that get no casino money because they are too remote, and in the inner city in Detroit, South Central LA, the Southside of Chicago.

When he tells me of meeting the garbage people of New Delhi who pick through the giant trash mountain known as the Ghazipur landfill to find items to sell and who even live in that awful environment, his face takes on a glow and his eyes sparkle. It amazes him, how people so disadvantaged can still have optimism and grace. His obvious care for all humanity and his sweetness becomes tangible, a window to what makes him tick. I feel such a kindred connection with him, the brother I never had. After our coffees, he excuses himself to make his calls and I stroll around the redone interior. Each room takes on its own welcoming aura and I marvel at the transformation from trash heap to idyllic retreat. The Hudson River becomes part of the decor being visible from all rooms. The river becomes narrower up this way and the other shoreline is visible. A changing kaleidoscope of colors and shadow, depending on the time of day. Kip, my voice of reason, counseled me not to run away. It was wise of me to listen.

I set up my computer and finally send the email to Margaret. On cue, my cell phone rings 10 seconds later. I'll check the message later and respond to her in due course, when I have the time to soothe her ruffled feathers. Margaret is the least of my concerns right now. I need to find out the backstory on this house. Who were these people? The name I wrote on the check can be found in South Dakota and Portland, Oregon. So who were they? Now I wish I took out a mortgage so the bank could identify the previous owners. I'm trying to find the right website to look up tax records when the buzzer by the gate sounds off. *What the…?* I speak into the intercom. It's a delivery from the Lodge. Very curious, I buzz them through and meet them as they drive up.

It's a gorgeous floral bouquet that could have been picked right out of my garden. The flowers are in a beautiful porcelain vase not of flower shop quality but possibly from an ancient Chinese dynasty. There's a card. *Welcome home. Looking forward to working with you up here. Come to Trinity Lodge around 8:00 pm to celebrate the beginning of the best adventure of your life. Alex. P.S. King says to enjoy the Qing Dynasty vase from his private collection. The Lodge is not far from you. Just follow the easy directions on the back of this card.*

Kip comes back into the room and sniffs the bouquet. "Nice flowers," he says nonchalantly but looks aggravated. "Well, originally I thought it would no big deal to stay a week but I'm sorry to say, Lex, I've got to go back tonight and take care of a few things. How about I come up here on Thursday? Looks like my trip will be delayed a bit, for a few months actually, and perhaps I can stay on for a while. Be your permanent house guest," he laughs. "But don't worry, I'll stay in the cottage," he adds.

"That sound's good…great in fact. I'd love the company. We can explore the area, swim. You can invite friends up. Maybe for July fourth. I'll be writing here most days."

"Oh," he says alarmed, "I was just kidding about being permanent."

"Whatever you want to do. I would love it though. It would be great to have you here for the entire summer." And it really would. I didn't realize how lonely I was until Kip entered my life.

"We'll see. It's a possibility. The dealership has a buyer. So I'll be happily rid of it soon."

I drive him to the train and have just enough time to take a luxurious bath in my jetted tub and get ready for the soiree. But a gnawing question keeps churning in my mind.

How did Alex and King know I had moved up here and into this house?

Chapter Eight

The soiree

There are flowers everywhere. Daffodils, roses, tulips. So soft. A bed of flowers all around me. Deep, perhaps a foot deep. The fragrance fills my nostrils with a sweet aroma that becomes a flavorful taste on my tongue. Immersion among the petals brings forth an epiphany. I understand now, we are connected to all things. We are all one. A spiritual joy emerges from deep within me. Love. Love is in the flowers. And then, suddenly, a shift. I can sense that something is amiss. A discomfort. I awake in a rush of anxiety. *What? Where am I?* Strange room. Suddenly I'm aware that a doorbell is ringing nonstop, urgently. I have fallen asleep and I look at the clock. *Oh my god!* It's 9:00. *The party!* The incessant ringing propels me out of the bed. *Who? What?* I'm disoriented.

"Who's there?" I shout through the closed door while peering through the glass. Two giant men in dark suits. Uh-oh. How'd they get there? *Damn!* I forgot to close the gate after I got back from driving Kip to the train. Not used to such things.

"We've been sent here by Mr. King Blakemore to take you to his gathering. Are you alright, Ms. Wainwright? He was worried when you didn't show up."

"Yes, I'm fine. You can go now and tell him I will drive myself there, as soon as I get dressed."

"Our orders are to bring you. We'll wait in the car."

What the…hell? Our orders? How creepy. I've been summoned by the king. Can't blow it off *now*. I'm stuck with the goon squad and, suddenly, in a rush. There's no time to figure out what to wear. Half of my things are still in boxes. I spy my summer-weight sweats on the floor next to my running shoes. Quickly putting my unruly hair in ponytail, I look in the mirror and put on some lipstick. There. At least I'm clean. *What if I refused to go?* Would those scary guys break-in and kidnap me? One last look in the full-length mirror. I know I'm probably not dressed right but… too bad. This is what you get when you force me to hurry. It's the country anyway. Casual should rule. Probably not this casual…but still.

I open the door and almost pee in my pants. A Hummer? Who has Hummers anymore? The car maker is long gone, but apparently not for King's grass roots militia. The men in black wear ear pieces like bodyguards. Even sitting they look huge. The driver gets out and opens the door and towers over me. Their size and obvious strength make me uneasy. Very uneasy. What's in store for me tonight? *I wish Kip hadn't left.*

The drive in the dark to Trinity Lodge keeps me disoriented because I am so new to this area and totally unfamiliar with the winding roads…also, I'm a city girl used to the grid of streets and avenues. The headlights eventually shine on a metal plaque on a stone wall bearing its name. Automatic gates open, so we can drive right through. Now, I pay close attention trying to make out landmarks in the dark. Firstly, the drive is about a half hour from the front gate to the house. That in itself is impressive. Along the way there's nothing. Well not really nothing, but acres and acres of forest and pasture. Probably beautiful in the daylight.

When we finally reach the house there's a tumult of noise from a mélange of peculiar looking people of uncertain gender milling around the front door and entrance steps. *What the…?* I had no idea that this party was going to be such an event. I thought it was just going to be Alex, Jewel, and perhaps a few more. Bright outdoor lighting and landscape lights make everyone as visible as if it were an afternoon gathering. Chopin's Nocturne in E-Flat Major, a personal favorite of mine when relaxing with a glass of wine, plays loudly from speakers creating an elegant vibe that would be extinguished once I got inside. There are valets to park cars, although at the moment there aren't any. Food trucks are just pulling around the circular drive for later in the evening when departing guests can have one final go at sweets, liqueurs, coffee, and novelty foods while they wait for their cars, parked who knows where, to be brought around.

Jameson threw a Christmas party last year at his North Shore estate and had gourmet food trucks as well. Must be the latest rage. Ah, I see trucks showcasing designer doughnuts with cappuccinos and lattes in all flavors, and others with Asian and Indian fare. My stomach rumbles because I'd forgotten to eat dinner. My thoughts swiftly change to being mortified at being so underdressed, as I alight from the car and pass the group by the steps. Couture and high-end off-the rack from Saks or Barney's drape tiny waists of these, at minimum, six-feet tall unisex oddities.

Cigarette holders sparkle through pursed lips, but no one is smoking. And then I notice that they're not actually human, but mannequins in pose. Quite strange this department store display-window vignette. Adding to the strangeness is hearing this crowd of dummies engaged in conversation and realize it's emanating from speakers inside them. Even stranger. I walk up the steps with my head down wishing I could just turn around and go home. At least my ridiculous attire is lost on them. Maybe, I could just grab something to eat and hide in a corner until this is over.

No luck.

"There you are," says King loudly walking up to me as soon as I enter a large entranceway leading to an enormous room full of guests. Looking me up and down, his puzzled glance becomes a frown. He's clearly not pleased with my choice of clothing. Then he leads me into the center of the room and claps his hands together to get everyone's attention. All stop and turn to look at him. And...me. Oi vey. Awkward. Embarrassed, my face becomes flushed and hot at this unexpected attention.

"I'd like us all to welcome our newest protégé to the Trinity of Sixes family. Most of you probably are familiar with her work and her international appeal. Let's all give a warm welcome to the talented writer and bestselling author, Alexa Wainwright." I stand there fake smiling and notice celebrities in this crowd. Familiar faces from TV, film, and other well-known writers and this makes me even more uncomfortable wearing this ridiculous outfit and stupid ponytail.

However, as I take a more in-depth look around the room, an assortment of bizarre-looking party-goers makes me suck in my breath. Scattered among the famous faces are weird-looking creatures right out of Star Wars or children's books' myths and legends and the like. Alice in Wonderland comes to mind. A collection of freaks and monsters. *What the...? Is this for real?* They're completely accepted among the celebrities and smiling at each other. Somehow, I've slipped into a parallel universe. The oddballs of this other-world co-exist with my intimates, normal people. Margaret, Gloria and even poor Roseman. And Mom, she also exists in this awful new reality. I want to go back to my old reality, where only humans dwell. This strangeness is more than unsettling. Please, let me wake up from this nightmare of horrors. *Please, please, please.*

Scared out of my wits, I spy Alex and Jewel in the mix. They have their arms around each other's waist. I focus my gaze on them, rather than the specter of these other-worldly oddities. Jewel looks me right in the eye and then moves closer to Alex. Definitely a message. But at least it's somewhat comforting to see normal humans. King asks everyone to toast me with a glass of Champagne. Uh-oh. I don't really want to drink anything. My paranoia over what happened to me at King's luncheon meeting is still fresh, but I'm stuck. Champagne is quickly poured by an army of red-faced and pointy-eared denizens that could easily be carrying pitchforks instead of the bubbly. Everyone raises their glasses and toasts my success. I take a tiny, teensy-weensy sip. All stand still in place and look at me for an uncomfortable eternity. Then I get it. I'm obliged to say something.

Trying to gain some decorum and control my shaky voice, I say, "Thank you all for honoring me like this." Then I come up with a fiction that I've been thinking about for a short story, taking a page from my mother's playbook. "King," I say in a forced lighthearted manner, "I realize you must think I came underdressed for this occasion, but you're mistaken. This light-weight track suit is an experimental prototype from NASA and will be worn by astronauts for our first trip to Mars. It can keep a person comfortable at 160 degrees below zero or 160 degrees above zero. It was given to me as a thank you for a short story on Mars that I wrote for their newsletter." Sounds of delight and approval travel through the room, and then another round of applause.

A strange looking individual, with a gravity-defying bright green toupee, heavy eyeliner surrounding wild green and orange eyes, steps out of the crowd. This gender-bending creature is wearing a red and white sparkly striped jump suit accented with red sparkly, chunky heels that have an unsettling but oversized resemblance to Dorothy's heel-clicking footwear in the Land of Oz. *It* moves forward while reaching out to touch my garment. I immediately step back to get away. Giant buck-teeth pop out when it starts giggling at my response. Another guest with creepy bugged-out eyes, bluish skin, and dressed as strangely as a Dr. Seuss character, moves forward. And then a furry one. And then another. The freaks start to crowd around. All want to feel this magical cloth.

Totally aghast at what I started, I say loudly over the murmuring ghouls, "Actually, what I just told you is a promo for my next novel about space travel. This track suit is exactly what it looks like. It's an off-the-rack selection from Sports World. My apologies to all. I fell asleep and didn't have time to get ready." I look at King with concern at this blatant manipulation. He laughs. And then everyone laughs and thankfully moves away from me but stays nearby not dismissed yet by King. Still laughing, he puts his arm around my shoulders and speaks to this tricked-out assembly. As soon as he starts to speak, a respectful hush falls over the crowd.

"I'd like to take this opportunity to tell everyone some wonderful news. Our foray into publishing has produced its first casualty among our competitors. Our strategy to become the only publisher of consequence is on track. The acquisition of Alexa Wainwright and all of her past, present, and future work, and the last remaining best-selling author in their roster, has resulted in Jameson Publishing closing its doors after seventy years in the business." A murmur of shocked sounds ricochets around the room. "Here's to shutting them all down one by one." Everyone applauds loudly, whistles, and starts swaying with arms linked, and singing a weird anthem to Trinity of Sixes with King's voice the loudest and strongest.

> *Trinity of Sixes now and forever.*
> *Trinity of Sixes will change the world.*
> *Trinity of Sixes will work hard and endeavor,*
> *to be the one and only pearl.*

When it's finished everyone hugs and kisses the person next to them. I hang close to King not wanting to get involved in the icky love fest. A sick feeling comes over me when I think of King's announcement. *Jameson closed!* And I'm responsible. King said that my leaving clinched it. Bob Jameson, a descendant of the founder, is a nice guy. Granted, he's made a fortune and probably won't be hurting for money. But all the others, the staff, from the mailroom guy to the acquisitions editors. Looking for other Jameson authors, I spy the master of the thrillers genre, and there's the number one author in mysteries. I must talk to them. Both of them seem dazed, zoned out. Better wait. My thoughts are interrupted by another loud hand clap and announcement by King.

"Let the fun begin," he shouts. Everyone takes their seats at their large round banquet tables as a group of latex dressed diminutive acrobats run into the center of the room. I slink over to the buffet and throw sideways glances at these adroit child-sized gymnasts as they tumble, make human pyramids, and jump through circles of fire. They're quite skilled and mesmerizing. But the amazing spread on the far wall takes precedence. I'm starved. Choosing sparkling bottled water that I hope hasn't been tampered with, I say "no thank you" to the wine pourer who wears an odd, shirtless costume of black tie, cummerbund, and tights, but who is otherwise normal looking. The Champagne-pouring devil doppelgängers are nowhere to be seen.

Munching on the delectables of sushi, prime rib, filet mignon, fresh salmon, Caesar salad, I make my way to an unobtrusive corner, having no desire to make chitchat with this peculiar assortment of notables and kooks. It's a challenge to balance my plate on the tiny table, but it's away from everyone. I have to crouch over while sitting on the adjacent armchair to keep my bottle of water from falling off my lap.

Finally, I have a chance to look around and take note of my surroundings. It's like a carbon copy of Teddy Roosevelt's Sagamore Hill. First of all, and most unsettling, is that I didn't notice at first that the entrance to this room is flanked by two giant ivory tusks. Ivory! Killing elephants for their ivory. Disgusting and barbaric. The tables have Zebra-striped coverings that probably are real skin and the chairs are covered in blood-red cloth. Gruesome. But that's not all. Lining the walls are trophies of Bambi and his mother along with moose and elk. Lions and bears are upright in savage pose with their mouths wide open and teeth bared.

Far worse than the customary targets are several unusual specimens. Clustered together in one corner of the room, and near where I'm sitting, is an exhibit entitled, Endangered Species. Framed photos show King, the savage hunter, posing with these poor dead animals who are about to go extinct. There are trophies of a white rhino, a black rhino, a Bengal tiger, an African elephant, an upright, giant polar bear, and several species of primates. Sadly, there are empty spots waiting to be filled after King destroys them, just to hang their taxidermic remnants in this room.

I see a spot for the Asian elephant before it sickens me too much to read further. It surely must be illegal for him to hunt them, but I'm sure his money can buy silence. This blatant disregard for decimating the diversity of life on this planet is beyond sickening. Speculating from this gaggle of aliens, he must be doing the same thing on other planets. *Is that possible? But where else could this strange group be from?* A highly disturbing thought.

The room's other eye-grabber, apart from the poor former wildlife, is a giant walk-in fireplace made of stone boulders. Whole trees look like they could burn in there. The mantle is thick mahogany with dental-style carvings and shines with a high polish. Its high reach does not make for easy adornment so right smack-dab in the center of the wall above it is a giant buffalo head. Disgusting. Everywhere you look, if you don't see stuffed wild life, you see wood. A luxurious wooden extravaganza. Ceilings are wide-wood beams that strikingly form a hexagon shape, or rather, the top half of a hexagon. Floors are polished dark wood and walls are paneled with rustic rough-hewn logs. Area rugs are an array of animal skins. The whole place is a sick and twisted version of the Museum of Natural History.

This enormous room is similar in size to King's uptown mansion. There must be 20 round banquet tables large enough for seating eight people each. Even with all these tables there's still room for a grand piano placed in a corner alcove and floor space in the center of the surrounding tables for the acrobat show. Except for the familiar celebrity faces, and in addition to my first assessment of mythological leviathans, all others could have stepped out of a circus ring or Marvel comic. Applauding politely or ignoring the entertainment are persons with neon pink or purple hair, clown-face makeup, and dressed in bizarre and colorful clothing that stands out like a beacon of light against the African jungle decor.

Sprinkled though the crowd of Bozos and Homer Simpson characters are old film star impersonators. I know them because my mother had a collection of vintage movies she grabbed from a video store going out of business. Gloria Swanson slinks around with Greta Garbo, Rock Hudson chats with Cary Grant and Rudolph Valentino. OMG! There's Elvis dancing with Marilyn Monroe. What a sight! So authentic looking. And skinny Elvis, when he was hot. Like the pictures in the article I read about him. And Marilyn, young like in the movie *Some Like It Hot*. At least, I hope they're impersonators. A sick feeling overtakes me. *Could they be resurrected from the dead?* My flight into fear is abruptly diverted.

"Well, hello!" says Alex as he pulls a chair over and sits down at my makeshift space. Having just put a whole sushi roll in my mouth, I can only nod back.

"Listen," he continues, "I'd like to start sending you my ideas, my treatment for the script. I realize you're still settling in but we have imposed deadlines to start filming in the fall. We thought filming against the fall foliage would add some interesting texture to the setting." I look puzzled. "Oh, we're filming it here. All the outdoor scenes. And setting it in Misty Falls for the town scenes." I haven't yet spoken, partially because just sitting next to him makes me tingle. *What is it with this guy? I want to grab and kiss him. I want him to envelop me with kisses and more. Why? Why am I so drawn to him? Because he's my male fantasy come to life, remember?*

Finally, I force myself to stop these titillating thoughts and tell him he can send over the treatment. Then, we're startled by King clapping his hands again and introducing Merlin the Magician. The lights in the room darken and there are spotlights focused on the figure of a man dressed in a silk maroon Moroccan hat with a tassel and matching flowing caftan. First I am blown away that this room is rigged with spotlights. Then I am blown away by the mannequins from the front steps walking behind him. *What the...?*

Merlin does typical magician tricks, sawing in two a now alive mannequin, rabbits pulled from hats, doves flying free to who knows where when a cloak thrown over a cage on a small table is dramatically swept off. Then he's ready for his final trick. He'll make someone from the audience disappear. Two mannequins walk over to an unsuspecting woman and grab her arms. "No!" She screams. Over and over. "No...no...no!" Then "Please don't! Please!" Why is she so frightened? She's practically carried up to the center of the room and then put in a chair, while wiggling and squirming and screaming. Strong mannequins hold her, as her arms and then her feet are bound to the chair by Merlin.

This is no longer amusing. Merlin wheels over a square cage made of curtains on all sides and envelops her with it. Snap! The curtains are shut. She lets out a blood-curdling scream and then there's abrupt silence. "Presto!" he says as he waves the wand. The lights come on. Merlin opens the curtains. She's gone. Everyone applauds. I turn to Alex. He's gone too. I spy him sitting next to Jewel clapping and laughing and then he nuzzles her neck. She's stunning in a white silk safari shirt and tan jodhpurs, hair pulled back with sexy strands hanging down. A perfect outfit for this jungle room. I become nauseated with jealousy. Time to go.

As I get ready to leave, I keep searching for the woman to come out from somewhere. Her purse is still on the table where she was sitting. No woman. A bad feeling takes hold concerning what I just witnessed. In fact, this entire event has been stomach turning, except for the food. I get up and feel someone grab my arm. It's King. I look at him clearly annoyed at his arrogance to grab my arm. He ignores my displeasure.

"Alexa, there's someone I would like you to meet."

"What happened to that woman? Where is she?" My anger and concern bleed through every word.

"I wouldn't worry about that right now. She's probably laughing at the theatrics and enjoying a martini in her favorite locale." He nudges his companion forward. "Alexa, this is Hyacinth Malachite our director of editorial. You and she will be working closely, as I've assigned her personally to oversee your endeavors. She's quite excited to work with you on *Darkside*, and will also go over the first two books in the trilogy to see if Jameson missed anything."

I am face-to-face with the green-faced (like her surname, Malachite) fierce evil witch from the *Wizard of Oz*. Another bizarre *Oz* connection, a place that was also an altered reality. Her repulsive and shockingly big, hook nose, minus the wart, is only scarily outdone by her crocodile grin revealing mismatched teeth and fangs that could easily devour a small mammal. Her coarse, long hair gives the illusion of being made of cardboard scraps and has a hint of green with gray highlights. She reaches out with bony fingers to shake my hand and when we touch I become mesmerized by her threatening gaze. I get the message, *don't mess with this editor.* King is satisfied and leads her away to...whatever...

cast a spell on someone else. I'm stunned and just stand there wondering what to do next, when Alex and Jewel come over and lock arms with me.

"Come," says Jewel. "Join us." And before I realize it, I'm walking with them into another room, a library lined floor-to-ceiling with books and an imposing desk in the center with a high-backed throne chair behind it. As soon as the door closes behind us, my attention to the detail of the room shifts to my bodily invasion. I'm being molested. Sexually attacked. Jewel grabs me and starts kissing me pushing her tongue into my mouth while Alex kisses my neck and massages my breasts. He reaches into my sweat pants and starts to tenderly explore my most intimate places. My emerging arousal at Alex's touch overtakes any hesitancy. Thick with lust, they lead me to a sofa and lay me down. Jewel starts to undress me, while Alex removes his pants and underwear and enters my mouth.

Wait! No! This isn't me! I break free, pull on my clothes and run. Out of the room, out of the wall-lined haven for dead-eyed beasts while knocking into the food buffet and crashing plates to the floor. Out the front door. Run! Run! Escape! I see the Hummer parked in the circle across from the food trucks, now with a small group of guests mingling around them. I leap down the steps, race over, and jump in the Hummer. The keys are in the ignition. My heart is pounding, I'm exploding with fear and disgust as I turn the key. The engine wines and whirs. I turn the key again. *C'mon. Let's go. Gotta get outta here!* It roars to a start. I see the men in black running to the car in the rear view mirror. Luckily, I can adjust the seat electronically while I step on the gas. I'm off. One minor thought crosses my mind as I speed away.

How the hell can I find my way home?

Chapter Nine

Jewel

I awaken with a start. Ominously, I hear something ringing…again like last night. Déjà vu. *Was it just last night?* But this time it's my cell phone. The display says Trinity Lodge. I stare in disbelief and nausea waiting for the call to go to voicemail. The ringing stops, and I realize I have been holding my breath. Last night was a living nightmare. I desperately want to go back to my old life. Turn back the clock. Before Alex. Since he came into my life, my world has become more than strange. It's so bizarre, like I'm in some preternatural existence and I hate it. I've gone down the rabbit hole where nothing is familiar. All is twisted and the people are nightmare characters. I need my mother and Margaret. People I can trust. Normal people. And Kip. I need him to come back here or go see him in the city. I need to move back into my loft and fast. Today, in fact.

Going downstairs, I'm feeling hopelessly out-of-sorts as I go into the kitchen to make coffee. Another sunny day. The river shimmers in the sunlight. Daylight and a normal scene. I sip the coffee and plan my escape. It's amazing, I'm not dead. The Hummer was too big for me to handle. Luckily, the road was straight and not winding at all as I raced toward the gate. The only near mishap happened when I became absorbed by the sight of a truck near the line of trees unloading a large herd of deer onto the property. Deer that would become hunters' trophies, I suspect. Taking my eyes off the road for that split second nearly caused me to crash right into the entrance gate. Or so I thought. Sigh of relief as the gate opened right up as soon as I approached. It must have some kind of bar code/ embedded signal.

When I got on the main road, I gunned it and almost crashed into a tree on a turn, so I pulled over to calm down. No one was following me. Seeing the navigation system on the dashboard, I typed in my address. Then I drove at a very slow speed until I saw my driveway. I ditched the car outside the gate and used the remote on my keychain to open it. This time I would close it behind me. I ran into the house, ran into my bedroom, stripped and hid under the covers. I was fucking scared. I'm still scared. But I'm also at a loss of what to do. I hate this place. Hate everyone.

Finally, I decide to listen to the message. It's Jewel. She's worried about me. Hah! A load of shit. But more importantly, she's coming over. We need to talk. I don't want to talk to her. She tells me that if I don't listen to what she has to say, it could have dire consequences. Ugh! Another threat. All these messed up people do is threaten me, or trap me, or coerce me. I have to get out of here before she comes. And then I hear someone buzzing at the gate and her voice on the intercom. She must have called on the way. I ignore her. Maybe she'll go away if I don't respond. A few seconds pass. Silence. I'm safe.

Crap! She's at the front door. A key is opening the lock. *What the...?* She just walks right into my house! My body begins to shake from fright, "Get out!" I scream. "Get out of my house right now or I'll call the police!" She looks me right in the eyes and tells me coldly and sternly to calm down and to get her a cup of coffee. Her scary demeanor and evil gaze subdues me. I'm so flummoxed that I do as she says. She follows me into the kitchen and sits at the table.

"I've always loved this house. I love how you decorated it." I slam the hot cup on the table and some splashes on her face. She jumps up and wipes her face with her sleeve and grabs my arms.

"You need to stop this attitude right now. You wanted this. You wanted all that we can give you. There's nothing wrong with being wealthy beyond your wildest dreams and becoming one of the most popular authors in the world. Now sit down and listen to me." Woodenly, I sit down and stare at the face I created with my thoughts and words. My anger surges again.

"How were you able to get in here?" I ask heatedly. "The gate was locked. You are invading my privacy. This is my home. My sanctuary. I only signed a book deal. Just a book deal. How dare you try and take over my life."

"Settle down," she says. "You don't understand, realize, that now you're under the protection of King and what that means. He looks out for his people. You're part of his family now. He makes things happen. This house. How do you think you got it so easily? King owns Misty Falls. Everyone here benefits. It was a hardscrabble town before he sank a fortune in it, his own money, to make it the haven you see today."

"Well, I don't think the people who lived *here*, in this house, were too happy. They trashed this place. It was a total mess. A lot of anger created the destruction I witnessed. I had to redecorate every room."

"Yes. And aren't you happier having your own signature in the look and feel of these rooms?"

"Are you saying King did this? To spur me to redo everything? I was going to just walk away. It was very depressing to see. If it weren't for Kip, I would have."

"Yes, we know."

I reel back at that comment. Really…physically reel back. Kip a ploy? A King disciple? It's all too much to take in. But then I remember something.

"I met Kip by accident."

"There are no accidents in King's world. King has amazing powers of perception. He knows how things work. How everything is connected. How time and space interact. He truly is a master of the universe. With King on your side, anything and everything is possible. He loves all his chosen ones and keeps us close."

"Not all of us. What happened to that woman at the party? She just disappeared. Where is she? Her scream was a blood-curdling scream of abject fear. And, as for me, I don't feel *chosen*, I feel I've been duped and manipulated into a cult that keeps me prisoner. And also, while I'm asking, why do you resemble, almost exactly I might add, one of the characters in an earlier work of mine? Explain that!"

"First of all, there are those who question, keep questioning what King has provided. Isadora was, is, one of those people. King put her where she belongs with her doubts. She's now shunned and can never come back. We don't want the same thing to happen to you. Just enjoy the spoils that come with your connection and devotion to King." She pauses to take a sip of her coffee and to see if I have grasped what she's telling me. Yeah. I get it. And it unnerves me. I understand that, basically, I've been warned. Ignore the warning at my own peril, the risks and ramifications as yet unknown but, of which, can only be guessed. Worried, but also infuriated, by this obvious threat, I convey my disgust by staring at her through narrowed eyes and furrowed brows. My arms are folded in an adversarial manner. I'm impatient for her to leave.

She continues, "I also should remind you to look over the contract you signed. You are free to leave but there are consequences. Trinity of Sixes Publishing owns your brand, your name, if you will. So if you default on your contract, you can never publish under that name. Trinity, however, can publish whatever it wants under your name, and whatever advances were paid must be returned with interest plus a substantial termination fee."

That fucking contract. Yes, I knew about the termination fee but not about returning the advances with interest. I read about them owning my name, but I didn't realize it meant that Trinity can produce *new* work using my name. *What bastards!* I knew it. That damned contract changes based on my behavior to keep me locked in. It swallows me whole like the whale swallowed Jonah in the Bible. I'm trapped.

"Look, I understand your confusion," she says seeing the shocked look on my face. "I know you can question our ethics, but this is business. I know King mentioned Christian values, but we're in the business of staying viable. Our morality is staying true to what benefits Trinity."

I unfold my arms. I'm beaten. What's the use of acting out? Jewel notices my changed body language acknowledging my defeat and pats my shoulder gently while nodding, as if to say, *It's okay, it'll be okay.* She takes one last gulp of her coffee before she resumes speaking.

"Now I'll answer your last question, as to why I look like a character in one of your books. *The Lucky Ones*, right? Jessica Warren was not only classy but a nurturing woman as your creation. Someone to put you at ease. All of us see the world around us uniquely. Our own interpretations of reality. It's a rather simple concept, really, and one King finds quite useful. How I look to you, is not how I look to someone else or myself. King knows that and understands for some authors their characters become real, direct their own narratives.

"We have come to realize, especially for you, the epitome of your writing experience is creating characters who become so real they jump off the page and lead their own lives. We all make our own reality. We all interpret the world around us from our own particular perspective. King gives you the gift of a world populated by creations of your unique imagination. Those you have loved while writing their thoughts and dreams, been intimately connected with when writing their personal journeys, and those that will become future storylines. Just know, you are surrounded by love. I'm advising you, for your own good, don't question so much. Just enjoy. King holds you in high regard. You are very special to King. To all of us."

"What about those odd creatures that were at the party last night? Some looked like they could be aliens from another planet. It was beyond creepy."

"Oh, that's just King's sense of humor. He enjoys a good laugh creating an adoring crowd out of figments of *his* imagination. You, me, Alex, and King were the only real people there."

"What about the other Jameson authors I saw?"

"Just to make you feel comfortable."

"So everything I saw last night was just a mind game? Well, what about that poor woman Isadora? You just told me that she brought it on herself to be made to disappear. So are you changing your story now?"

"All experiences are lessons for you. So learn."

"You must think I'm a complete idiot to tell me this ridiculous pile of horse shit. The only lesson learned is that I'm sorry I got involved with any of you."

I stand up to signify the end of this conversation, but she's not finished and doesn't get up. She wants to apologize for the encounter in the study. Monogamy doesn't exist among the inner circle to which now I belong. It was too soon, she realizes, but eventually I will come to enjoy the playfulness they all share. "Hardly," I tell her and she just nods.

Then, she tells me something really strange, as if anything can get any stranger. This house has been among King's possessions for a long time, even before the town came to be. Of course, it's been updated several times. Perhaps, the house will give up some of its secrets, if I look for them. This knowledge will help sort out my ambiguousness about accepting King's love and protection. Next, she tells me that later today the new authors, Trinity's editorial, and a few others will be taking Trinity's private jet to go to King's private island in the Caribbean to celebrate and relax for a few days. A car will come around for me at 1:30. No need to pack. Everything will be provided.

She gets up to leave and I take notice of what she is wearing. The exact outfit I described in her final scene in *The Lucky Ones*. A white cardigan tied across a white turtleneck, white jeans, and white slip on-canvas loafers. I almost gag but manage to blurt out, "I need you to give me back my key and my gate remote you've acquired without my permission."

She hands them back to me and says, "We will honor your privacy but be rest assured gates, doors, locks are not deterrents."

Huh?

"See you later," she says.

"Wait. I haven't said I'd go."

"You're to come. No discussion." She finally leaves.

I'm so agitated by her visit and its implications. Nurturing! Bull shit! That was far from nurturing. She's as evil as any of them. An evil character that I certainly didn't create. I run into my study and tear through my desk drawers until I find the contract. SON OF A BITCH! There's the paragraph mentioning the use of my name by Trinity for new work if I should terminate and also a paragraph about returning any advances received with interest. Right before my goddamn signature. I start to primal scream and I scream until my voice gets hoarse.

Ping!

A text message from Mom. Oh thank goodness. I really need to talk to her and get her advice. I read the message.

Hi Hon. I will be away for at least ten days in an area with no mobile service. In case of an emergency you will have to call the university and they will be able to get a message to me through our encrypted server. Miss you. I'm shutting my phone off. I'll call when I can.

Oh no! "Wait!" I scream out loud and go to my favorites and press her name. Hurry, hurry! It's ringing! Yes! Nope...right to voicemail. *Shit!* But I don't have time to be too depressed because the phone instantly plays my ringtone. Hope against hope. It's not Mom, but it's Margaret. That'll do.

"Margaret! Hi, sorry I haven't called you but I've been so busy."

"Where are you? The concierge at your loft said you moved for the summer. I'd like to have a face-to-face conversation with you, Lex. I've been so upset. I thought we were more than business associates. I thought we were friends."

"We were...I mean...are friends. I miss you and would love to see you too. I'm going away for a few days. How about I call as soon as I come back? I moved to a town called Misty Falls. I own a beautiful Victorian right on the Hudson. I'm working here with Alex. I signed a contract not only with Alex's production company but with Trinity of Sixes Communications, as well. Just like you explained at the loft, it *is* a multifaceted company in the entertainment and book publishing industry, of which Alex's company is a part. I'll tell you all about the deal when I see you. When I get back, we'll plan a weekend."

"I'm so relieved. I miss you. Okay, that would be great. I look forward to it. Talk to you soon."

"Talk soon. Bye."

That felt good talking to Margaret. I do miss her...desperately. Maybe she and I can figure a way out of this inexorable contract. Or maybe I can entice her to join me in my new strange world. I certainly have enough money to pay her to be my friend plus editor, like before. Or just a companion with the ploy that she's an editor because of Trinity editorial's final say. My old life seems a million years ago, and how I miss it. Sitting on the patio drinking another cup of coffee, I review my conversation with Jewel.

She was sent to warn me not to try any funny business. I'm sure of it. She said not to pack a bag, but there's no way I'm not going to bring something. Not into a nudist colony kind of experience in case that's their idea of, what did she call it? Being *playful*? Sitting here with the scent of my beautiful flowers, lavender being the most prominent, induces a calm over me. They are a delightful rainbow of colors with strong fresh blooms. This is such a fabulous spot.

My inner turmoil is assuaged by the peaceful scene before me. Sparkling river, cloudless sky, trees still green but becoming slightly parched. My grass is a lush green from watering, a soft carpet of nature's gifts. My sprinkler waters everyday even though the town now only allows every third day because of the drought. So far, no one has stopped me and the timer was already set and a bit confusing to change. I don't really want to go anywhere. I haven't enjoyed this house yet. And what did she say about the house? Reveal its secrets? That was peculiar.

A light breeze ruffles my hair and kisses my cheeks. Maybe I'll just stay here and the hell with the trip. There's nothing they can do about it. Right? I'm not breaking any contract by just staying here. Suddenly the breeze picks up and a few rose buds fly into my face. Then a rush of them. Then daffodils and tulips. The breeze, a howling wind now, knocks the chairs around and a small branch blows off a tree and hits me smack on the head. I run into the house and have trouble shutting the French doors against the blowing force. Reluctantly, I pack a few things and put them in my large purse to hide. Don't want Jewel to know that I've ignored her *no need to pack* instructions. If my thoughts about not going caused a windstorm, what would a suitcase cause? A firestorm?

Grabbing a light sandwich of turkey and cheese, I wander around looking for secrets. Secrets. How silly. "House, can you let me in on your secrets? Tell me your hidden stories to enlighten me? Oooh…puh..lease house," I shout. Laughing at myself for these antics, I abruptly stop as I almost crash into a wall. A partial wall separates the kitchen from the great room. *What the…?* A wall? And then I notice a door.

Hmm. I cautiously open it to find a staircase leading down to a dark basement. *Huh!* How weird. This house has no basement. My stomach tightens. Luckily there is a light switch above the stairwell. I begin to make my way down the stairs with unsteady legs. I can see there's a lot of space down there. A large room with dark, eerie corners. I'm frightened and really don't want to do this alone. Just then my intercom buzzer sounds. My ride is here. I run back upstairs, shut the light, and slam the door. The appearing-out-of-nowhere basement will have to wait.

Thank goodness.

Chapter Ten

The island

The car pulls up and it's not the military style Hummer with the two gorillas. That's a good start. Stepping out of his black Porsche with the top down is Alex. Another good start. He's alone. Better.

"Are you ready for some fun in the sun?" he asks cheerily while he walks over and takes my large purse. Like nothing happened last night, he kisses me on the cheek. Electricity. I wish I wasn't so physically responsive to him because he spells danger. Yeah Jewel, I get it. My reality is my creation, figuratively and now literally and just like her, he's not to be trusted. But dangerous can also be sexy. I lock up the house and get in the car. Off we go to paradise. At least I hope it's paradise.

All in all, King's world is not your average world of dreams and although logic says my life has spun out of control, and there's a sinister underbelly, going to a private island on a private jet is not too shabby. I'm bracing myself for anything but hoping for the best. Alex reaches over and squeezes my shoulder and winks at me. Yeah, this could be good if Jewel doesn't show. But do I want to pretend there's nothing between them? That he's a free agent? I look at his handsome profile. His seductive charm. His causal sophistication that brings out my primal lust. Hell, yeah.

We get to a private air strip at the outer perimeter of the Lodge. There's a runway large enough for the Gulfstream to land and take off. It's a beauty of a plane and more extravagant inside then anything I've seen in movies. The cabin has seating for all 20 of us. There are large leather seats, singles or doubles that face each other. There are two private staterooms and a full kitchen. Alex and I choose seats facing each other with a table between. A hostess makes sure we're all comfortable and enjoying drinks before takeoff. We have a choice of steak or lobster and a fine selections of wines. It's all surreal.

When my cocktail is poured, I decide to throw caution to the wind and take small sips to test its potency. The drink appears harmless. Fun in the sun is just what I need. I sit back and relax and take it all in and dash off a text to Kip that I will be away for a few days and will call him when I get back. I look around the plane. Still no Jewel but I see some authors I know casually and Hyacinth Malachite, the editorial director.

We exchange pleasantries. I look puzzled and Alex explains that King believes that working vacations are very productive. Now, I remember Jewel mentioned something about editorial. Must have pushed it right out of mind. Okay, so right away this trip is not as it seems.

We take off smoothly and the view is spectacular as we gain altitude. The only blight on the landscape are the areas where the drought is becoming obvious. Trees should be lush with new leaves this time of year. Instead, some are already turning brown, while places where people water are sumptuously green. Areas of brown grow in density as we fly over state parks and national forests. Alex distracts me by toasting my good fortune. Our drink hostess serves our lunch and is helped by the chef who prepared our feast in the fully decked-out kitchen. After we eat and while the other guests are settling in for a nap, Alex whispers in my ear to join him in one of the vacant staterooms. We still have a few hours until we get to our destination situated way down the Bahama islands chain. He grabs a bottle of wine and two glasses and I follow him. Shutting the door, he draws down the shade for privacy, sets down the drink items, and grabs me and kisses me deeply.

The double seating pulls out to make a small bed and in a mad frenzy, we soar to our own heights of passion and pleasure. In the back of my mind, I wonder if he's brought Jewel to a stateroom on this jet, but then he touches me so erotically that I tingle, melt, and focus on the sensations. All of him explores all of me. Gently and then urgently. We are both aroused and insatiable. On fire with lust, there are no taboos. Over and over we explode in ecstasy together. But quietly and secretively, which only adds fuel to our ardor. Finally, we rest and the island is sleepily in view as we make our final approach for landing.

The Caribbean looks just like the photos. Turquoise water surrounds white sandy beaches. Trinity Island is quite small and bordered by a reef on one side keeping the surf there calm as a bay. Naturally, the accommodations are world-class. We each have a well-appointed bungalow with private pool and hot tub. Alex nuzzles my neck and tells me he has some work to do and will see me soon. He takes off to some building in the thicket of trees. I can barely walk after our intensely passionate hour or more and admire his supernatural energy. I'm assigned to bungalow three. Right on the beach, the bedroom looks out to the calm water and the gentle waves hitting the edge of the reef.

The well-stocked kitchen has fruit, snacks, and drinks and opens to the welcoming living room. Flat screen, satellite radio, overstuffed sofas invite the guest to kick your shoes off and relax. On the small breakfast table is a menu and itinerary of things to do. Four days, of which the first three are without a schedule. On the last day, two hours are set aside for work right before we leave. My work assignment is a focus group with the editorial staff to discuss *Darkside*. *Hmm*. Not going to worry about it now. I see that dinner is in the main house in two hours. The sun is setting, so I decide to take a bath and get ready. I'll explore the beaches tomorrow. There's a soft knock on the door. I think it's Alex, so I open without thinking.

"Hello, Miss Alexa, I'm Carla. I've come to give you your daily massage," she says in a lush Caribbean accent. An island beauty with coffee-colored skin and light green eyes, she walks into the bungalow with purpose and a massage board. She tells me to undress while she sets up the table on the lanai and draws together the silky-looking white curtains for privacy. Wearing a light-weight, ultra-soft cotton bathrobe from the closet, I hop on the table. The table is cushiony and comforting, both physically and emotionally. I indulge in the sweetness of it and enjoy the sound of the ocean while feeling the gentle breeze. Although, I am quite satiated sexually after being with Alex, Carla immediately arouses me with her expert touch.

Light and then strong, deep and then shallow. She kneads my skin and moves to private, intimate places without pause. Completely relaxed, I enjoy it. When she's done, she tells me to close my eyes for a moment while she starts my bath. I doze while listening to the glory of the pulsating sea. Gently waking me, I follow her into the bathroom. Candles burn around a tub filled with rose petals and sweet smelling lavender body wash to cleanse my skin. Carla bathes me and shampoos my hair with the same love and care as my massage. When the bath is done, she blow dries and styles my hair and puts on my makeup. A shimmering strapless dark purple thigh-high dress appears from the closet with matching strapped sandals with medium heels. My favorite color. *How did they know?* Carla kisses me on the cheek and tells me she'll be back tomorrow. Okay to that.

I'm now ready for dinner.

The main house is a stunner in a plantation style design with a wide veranda. Inside, floor to ceiling windows capture the sea at every turn. The bamboo floors and vaulted teak ceiling stand out against the all-white furnishings to subdue the senses, making the interior light and airy, enhancing the island vibe. Surprisingly, the room is awash with people. Perhaps King entertains in shifts and these folks will be leaving tomorrow. They certainly didn't fly in with us. I suppose he could also own more than one jet. Or possibly they're not real? More figments?

The guests mill about with champagne flutes continuously

replenished with Dom Pérignon. I see Ray Russell, a best-selling sci-fi author, Jennifer Darling, the romance queen, Henry Avondale of literary fiction fame, who won the Pulitzer for *A Town Revisited*. All Jameson authors, or I should say former Jameson authors. We nod politely. There are some celebrity authors that were with other houses, like Pike Barker, a singer/songwriter from the UK whose break out song *Slut Girls* went through the roof. I had heard she wrote a memoir about her abused and neglected childhood. All these people left their publishers to go with Trinity. Interesting. I'm in good company. Looking around for Alex, who's not here, I realize that King and Jewel are absent as well. Good.

We have assigned seats for dinner like at a wedding or a cruise ship. A tasty meal of fresh fish, conch fritters, and yellow rice is topped off with fresh coconut slices. Renaldo Rivera sings and plays Spanish love songs on a beat up guitar through dinner and continues for those who decide to hang out afterwards. I look forward to falling into bed. Alex still hasn't shown, so I walk to my bungalow. There's no moon and it's spookily dark. I hear a rustle in the trees.

"Who's there?" I hear the rustle again.

And then a man's tortured voice in a loud whisper speaks, "This island is not what it seems, miss. Be careful. Watch out for yourself, if you learn its secrets."

Then I hear a thwack, fists hitting something. A muffled scream. Thump! A large heavy something hits the ground hard and then is being dragged. Silence. *What the...?* I race back to my bungalow. Someone's in there. I see a shadowy figure walk by a window. The front door is not closed fully. Uh-oh. Should I go in? I hesitate not knowing what do to. The front door flies open and momentarily frightens me, so I actually jump and let out a low scream. Oh, thank goodness. It's Alex.

"Hey sweetie!" And then he looks closer at me, "Aren't you glad to see me?"

I rush into his arms and tell him what I thought just happened. He seems concerned and calms me saying he'll look into it. The island natives are superstitious and come up with all kinds of scenarios to frighten the guests. A game of sorts. It's happened before. They've been warned. Not to worry.

He adds, "It probably won't happen again because it sounds like that guy, at least, learned his lesson."

"Do they usually get beaten up? These islanders?"

"I wouldn't think so. That would be an overreaction, I would think. But I'll check. Don't let it ruin your time here. We're here to have fun. King's orders."

I'm so relieved he's here. His clothes are thrown over a chair in the bedroom and he's in sleeping shorts. Right. Good. He's spending the night. "You look stunning in that dress," he says before unzipping it. Afterwards, we cuddle and sleep intertwined for the rest of the night. In the morning, he nuzzles my neck, something he apparently likes doing, and gets up. I hear kitchen cabinets opening and closing, pans slamming on the cooktop. The sound and fury of breakfast preparation. I love this domesticity. *Why have I lived alone for so long?* My writing has consumed me, so only when I finish a project, like now, do I realize how lonely I am. Gotta change that...and soon. Maybe, I'll quickly write another book where I kill off Jewel. It's not murder if she's not real, right? *Hmm.* Maybe all I need to do is to think it.

As an experiment, I picture Jewel nonchalantly walking down... say, Fifth Ave. Browsing the Bergdorf Goodman window and about to go in. A disheveled homeless man stealthily approaches, snatches her purse and runs across the street. She runs after him not realizing that a city bus is rambling down at the exact spot trying to make the light. She's hit so hard that she flies through the air and crashes onto the sidewalk. The scene switches to a hospital room. King is there. Somberly, he holds her hand. She opens her eyes for a brief moment and then she's gone. The flat-lined heart monitor sends out the sound of death. Doctors and nurses rush in and try to revive her, but alas, she's gone. Whoa. *What am I doing?* This is sick. I blink my thoughts away and picture Jewel alive and well playing tennis.

Lumbering into the kitchen, the smell of breakfast gets my stomach rumbling. A busy Alex is flipping pancakes, perking coffee, and frying bacon. Tropical fresh fruit and muffins are placed on the small table. Yum. Grabbing a muffin and some mango, I walk out onto the Lanai. The fresh ocean breeze, clear sky, and turquoise water promise a day truly in paradise and extinguish all of my apprehensions. This new world order designed by King is not too shabby. Breakfast is ready and I eat heartily.

"Let's make the most out of today," he says. "Some of my staff is arriving later. There's a complete post-production studio here. We have some final cleanup for a film scheduled for a July fourth opening, hopefully, a summer blockbuster. Lots of CGI, car crashes, explosions. The usual pap for teenagers and guys of all ages. So what we do in post can make a big difference."

"Why would you want to work anywhere else? If I were you, I'd just stay here. It's glorious. By far, a much better setting than Misty Falls."

"True, but a little too remote for my taste. And I have many different crews with different specialties. To bring them all here would not be practical. In fact, Misty Falls also has drawbacks with its location. I prefer New York City. Much more convenient. But anyway, I say we beach it this morning. Have a fabulous local lobster lunch at the house and...afterwards...," he winks.

And so we lazily finish our breakfast, put on the swim suits provided, and head toward the beach. Our bare feet sink into the warm powdery sand and the calm water beckons with its gemstone color and clarity. There are no other bathers, so we laughingly decide to swim au naturale and frolic as sea creatures. Splashing and floating, laughing with childish horseplay. Breast stroke, back stroke, dog paddle and diving down to the sea floor wearing masks and snorkels just lying at the shore for us to use. There are hordes of shimmering schools of tiny fish that instantaneously make a perfect zig-zag in exact unison to avoid my pokey finger. Colorful coral form a protective wall around us. The water, a warm velvety cocoon, nourishes our playfulness. A perfect morning.

"I've never swum in this cove before," says Alex, as he plants a wet kiss on my lips. I must say it's quite delightful being so calm. The last time I was here, my bungalow was on the other side of the island. The surf is a bit rougher on that side because the reef is much further out. You should feel flattered. Only the important guests get the bungalows on this side."

"Why am I considered important?"

Before he can answer, I hear faint sounds of distress coming from way down at the other end of the cove. Someone is screaming. I vaguely make out some figures. Someone is being dragged into the water.

"Alex! What's happening? We need to do something! Now!" And I race out of the water and put on my swimsuit and head toward the commotion. Alex grabs my arm.

"Wait! Stop! It's just some islanders fooling around. Some of the locals think that this cove is evil because the fish population has been decimated. But just in this shallow cove and not all year. The water temperature increases in the summer season and that's probably the reason for the dying off. Some locals believe there's a curse here and that swimming in the water changes you or kills you. Those that know better think it's funny to throw someone in. It's just a game."

"So it's not true? Why do they play so many scary games?"

"Doesn't it sound silly?" he laughs. "These islanders are so superstitious. Some islanders also believe the water for this complex is the scourge of Satan and when you drink it, he steals your soul. But King wants the purist tap water and ships it in. Stores it in giant water towers.

Island lore retells the trials the natives suffered when they were brought here as slaves on ships and they equate any ships with evil. Won't set foot on one or help unload the cargo. King has to bring his own personnel." He sees my worried frown. "It's just superstitious hyperbole. Now, forget it and let's get lunch."

"So the important guests get the cove of death? But, we saw giant schools of fish in the water. Tons of fish."

"Right, so there you are. Utter nonsense."

As we walk to my lodgings to change, I try and figure out how much water I might have consumed since yesterday. This business of King providing the tap water is something that totally blind-sided me. Even though the rest of the day is magical, I keep worrying about the incident this morning and the hauled in water. I drink only bottled water or wine at lunch. No ice cubes for the water. The lobster was broiled, not boiled, I made sure to ask. I felt that my being careful about the tap water, although a day late, made me a little safer, not a victim, until Alex told me that the label on the bottled water is made-up because it's bottled at the complex. People like to carry bottles on hikes and such and King provides.

I almost gag and try and stop my fretting. Just like the contract, I'm stuck and there's nothing I can do. After lunch, he tells me that he will be busy for the next few days and on top of that he's staying longer. He won't be coming back with me on the jet. Later, after a nap and a room service dinner, his mastery at arousing me to new heights is consistent and so blissful sleep cocoons me until morning. After we enjoy the sunrise from our comfy bed, we kiss goodbye and set up our meeting for the following week in Misty Falls to begin our collaboration. Okay, whatever. I'll explore the island, have my massage with Carla that I canceled yesterday because I was with Alex, and enjoy the food. Anyways, I have that focus group thingy tomorrow.

After coffee, fruit, and muffins, which apparently are bought around daily, I throw on shorts and head out. It's a blustery day and the soft sand swirls up in the air and gets in my eyes. A storm is coming. Heavy dark clouds are forming on the horizon and are moving quickly. I see white caps hitting the reef and realize that the cove gets an infusion of cooler water and probably carries all varieties of fish during storms, so maybe that's why there were schools of fish yesterday.

But come to think of it, there were no larger fish poking around the reef as you would expect. It saddened me to think of this natural wonder becoming devoid of sea life. Giving in to my curiosity and in an exploratory mood, I follow a well-trodden path that leads away from the beach and toward the center of the island. It takes me to a small power plant that probably is the culprit for the warmer water. I'm sure there's a pipe that discharges hot water into the cove.

Obviously built with no thought of the consequences to the ecosystem, I see a pipe extending from the building and then disappearing underground. What does it matter if fish are killed off each summer? Some come back when the water is cooler. And so what if they don't come back? King has no need of them in the placid cove. And what of the reef itself? Surely, it must be compromised by the water temperature. At least on one side. Then I think of the deer. The thought just pops into my head. That truck full of deer just for the sport of killing. In King's world, it's all about consumption. All about devouring anything in his sphere for his own amusement.

I'm like the deer in that truck. I'm like the fish trapped in the over-heated cove. I am King's sport, his captive. To have my creative integrity be exploited and consumed, to have him own my essence, my spirit…my soul even. And in some twisted way, it was my greed that was preyed on and brought these people into my life where they spun their web and took away my freedom. Stop! I have to stop this constant internal diatribe of woe. These thoughts must be silenced, if I'm to have any sort of a fulfilling life. And life is good right now. Great sex. Private jet. Private island. Fortune and fame for the taking.

Continuing down the path, I see a little village appear ahead. Ramshackle concrete dwellings grouped together. Their bright colors are marred by large swaths of chipped paint exposing the bare cement. Emerald green, pink, orange, turquoise and yellow form a child's coloring book of tiny houses with small gardens, broken shutters, and battered roofs. In this little cluster of cottages, people of all ages mill about, sit on porches, or scurry in servant's uniforms to and from what must be the path leading to King's main house.

A strong aroma of vanilla mixed with licorice fills my nostrils, like a giant potpourri pot or perhaps scented candles. The pleasant odor masks the smells of outdoor kitchens with chickens roasting and soups boiling and also of pig droppings, horse manure, and cow patties from casually roaming farm animals. Children are giggling and playing tag. Dogs are running around and barking at colorful parrots who sit on well-placed perches flapping their wings in protest. Hearty laughter bellows out from a cadre of women wearing brightly colored print dresses with matching head wraps and carrying infants on their hips. A happy free-spirited vibe emanates from this friendly group…until they spot me.

Suddenly, everything stops and a few men wearing different versions of a torn t-shirt, cutoffs, and dreadlocks walk toward me in a threatening manner. Then a few more. They're joined by the brilliantly dressed women carrying their babies. Everyone is sweating profusely and their strong scent of licorice overwhelms me. I try and retreat but misstep and trip on a rock. Another stupid fall when crowds threaten me. My sandal straps break apart and I land square on my behind, as the group moves closer. The children who were romping and playing push through to get a better view. The townspeople surround me. I can sense their growing anger reflected in their cold, mean, and squinty-eyed gazes. An adult male, a member of this angry mob, picks up a small stone and fear flashes through me. They start to chant a word that sounds like evil or devil or both. "Evil." "Devil." Over and over. The babies begin to wail.

"No wait! Stop. Please. I'm not…HELP! Someone HELP!" I scream, "HELP!" My entire body is shaking, but I manage to stand up. I want to run, but I'll have to break through the group to do so. *What should I do?*

"I'm not evil." I say in a pleading voice. "I'm a writer, just a writer…of books." I say stupidly. Someone spits. *Oh God.* Suddenly a woman shouts, "Stop it!" And breaks through the circle of angry islanders. It's Carla! She grabs my arm and pulls me toward the path to the main house.

"What are you doing here?" she whispers angrily through clenched teeth. "Didn't anyone warn you not to come to the village?"

"No, no one. What happened back there? Everyone seemed relaxed and joyful until I showed up." I begin to sob with relief. "I didn't realize…"

"Just never do that again. Go back to your cottage and stay on the grounds of the resort." She pushes me in that direction and turns toward the group who are slowly dispersing but still keeping an eye on me, as I make my bare-footed way up the path. Once back in the cottage, I find a bottle of rum and a coke and make myself a stiff drink. I order food from the main house and stay put. Tomorrow, I have to get through that damn focus group, and then I can get back home. If I can just make it until then. Carla doesn't show up for my massage and that's good. I didn't enjoy her attitude, and I want to be alone. How would I know that the islanders had so much hate…no, not hate, fear. They were afraid. Afraid of me as if I were evil, or the Devil or both. Why? Perhaps I know why.

At dusk, I sit on the porch and watch the stars begin to peek out of the dark sky. There's no haze just a pure, clear vista of the awesome number of stars in our Milky Way. I can even make out Orion's Belt and the Big Dipper. As I sit there, a low rumbling drumbeat vibrates the wood floor. *Ba bum. Ba bum.* Over and over. Like a dirge. It seems to be coming from an area not too far from this cottage.

My curiosity gets the better of me and I get up and walk toward the sound. It's coming from a small hut nestled among the tree line, at edge of the swamp. How come I didn't notice it before? Something is weird about it. It seems to glow with a red light like it's on fire. I move closer to get a better look. *What the…hell?* There are flames, shooting flames licking at the windows. I'm about to yell, "Fire!" when someone puts his hands over my mouth and shuts me up. It's Alex.

"Shh. Don't make a sound," he whispers. "Don't disturb the ritual. Go back to your cottage! Didn't you see on your itinerary that tonight was a night of rest for you? Now go back and rest."

"Are you kidding? There's an out of control fire in there, Alex. People could get hurt. We have to do something."

"It's just an illusion. It's not real," he says starting to get annoyed while grabbing my arm. "Let me walk you back." Someone screams.

"Alex, someone's hurt! We have to do something!" I pull away and start to run toward the fire. Just then the entire hut bursts into flames. "Oh my god, Alex! We've got to get help!"

Then a whirlwind spins around the hut and drills down into the ground. A giant hole forms and swallows the structure whole. In a flash, the hole seals up and the night stars sparkle peacefully.

"What the hell was that?" I scream at him. "That was no illusion. The hut is gone! Vanished. Just like that!" I snap my fingers and then run over to the now normal looking spot where the hut was on fire and where it fell into the gaping hole. I stomp my feet. Solid earth. "Answer me, Alex. What the hell is going on here?" I begin to get hysterical. "This is crazy, Alex. Tell me, WHAT'S GOING ON?" I scream at him.

He grabs me and hugs me tight, trying to settle me down. "Look," he says, "there's magic going on here. King has amazing powers but what you saw was just a trick like the magician at the Lodge."

"That's bullshit, Alex! The magician at the Lodge? You've got to be kidding. The woman who disappeared was petrified. If it's all pretend, where is she, Alex? Jewel's explanation was that she is shunned, sent away as a nonbeliever, you tell me it was just a trick. Which is it because her blood-curdling scream still haunts me and is very troubling."

"Look Jewel has her own agenda. She gets a kick out of keeping people on the edge and off-kilter. She senses King's strong interest in you.

It worries her. Worries her about maintaining her status. But what you witnessed was all part of the magician's act, a trick. Just like sawing a woman in half or having someone levitate. So, don't listen to Jewel. In fact, I think the woman is the same one they made disappear last year. Part of the troupe. And I saw her here, yesterday, snorkeling on the other side of the island. Listen, the first time I came, there were different tricks. Different magic. Five cottages that overnight became the ten that are here now. Sinkholes swallowing trees and then filling up by themselves. A swarm of spiders that just evaporated. A blood red moon for two nights. And of course the fires, like the one tonight.

"I was concerned too, like you are, but then King explained that he wants all of us not to take our reality for granted. To be open to sudden changes. To embrace the wonder of existence while preparing for eternal life. He's all about lessons. All about enlightenment. C'mon Lex, don't get yourself all worked up over nothing. Let me walk you back to your cottage, you have a big day tomorrow."

The islanders chanting "evil" and "devil" rings in my ears as he walks me back. What do they *know*? What was really going on in that hut? Later that night, I'm awakened by again hearing a far off drumbeat. Another ritual somewhere? Was that a scream? There's no sleeping for me after that, and I pace the living room like a caged and crazy animal in a zoo. In the morning, I'm clearly not ready for the focus group that awaits me in the main house conference room. Bleary eyed, I manage to get there. I am introduced by Hyacinth Malachite's assistant Bijoux Lovely, who will conduct the session. *What's with the jewelry names?* Everyone is polite.

Hyacinth sits with a dour expression in the corner of the room. She keeps her scary mouth tightly closed. There's a panel of five discussants sitting behind a table. All women. All middle-aged, unkempt, and homely. There are two chairs placed in front of the table. Bijoux and I each take a seat. Bijoux is dressed as if a schoolmarm in a period piece with her hair pulled back in a tight bun, glasses, and sensible shoes. Her silk blouse has a bow at the neck and her softly pleated skirt reveals no curves. Once the discussion starts, I get the joke. She's the schoolmarm in a porn flick.

She starts the Q&A with, "Panel, do you think the title *Darkside, based on a true story of bondage and submission,* captures the essence of the book? Would you buy it based on the title?"

I immediately stand up and jump in. "Wait! Are you kidding?" I ask, my fists clenched threateningly at my sides. "What the hell are you talking about? This is not a true story. There's no bondage. Are we talking about *my* book? Did any of you actually read it? What are we talking about here?" But my nightmare is just beginning.

"Please sit down, Alexa. We're discussing the edited version. The new version that had reached consensus by our staff, didn't you get our draft?"

I remain standing. "No. I never received anything. And I'm not sure what's going on here. *Darkside* is resoundingly fiction and is a psychological riff on a tormented and fractured woman with inner demons. A relatable character. Although there's violence, there is no kinky erotica and..."

Hyacinth interrupts from the corner of the room, "Now there is. And this focus group agrees that it works well."

"I thought the purpose of this focus group was to try and find out what *they* think. But you say they already have let you know?"

"Yes, they filled out a survey. We're just testing the title and some cover art."

"And these five women in, I'm guessing, their 50s and 60s represent...what?"

Bijoux takes over, "Your base, your readership. Women in this demographic will buy your book in droves."

"This age group of women want to read BDSM crap?"

"Precisely," interjects Hyacinth. "These are the books that sell. If you want to see where well-written literature is read, take a university English Lit class where it's required. The real world wants erotica and actually in all age groups of women. We had two women in their twenties and two under twenty for the panel but they had to cancel. In fact, young women are the fastest growing demographic. Contemporary, historical, paranormal erotica are in such high demand that books from known authors in that genre are selling in advance of publication. End-of-the world dystopias are also selling fiercely, so we are trying to somehow create a spin off for Jodie to grab that demographic as well. In any event, we expect a movie deal that will be quite lucrative for you."

"I already have a movie deal for *Darkside* with Trinity of Sixes Productions. Don't you people talk to each other?"

"Yes, but not for this new version and not for the trilogy. We are in discussions with Alex."

"So what's the point of this? Of my being here?"

"To inform *you* of what readers want."

"I see. So they want Jodie to be sexually brutalized in that trailer?"

"Oh no. That doesn't work at all," says Bijoux and nods to the grandmas who all laugh in agreement. "Our focus group wants something else entirely. Jodie's unnamed mister has to be filthy rich. Live on an estate in the English countryside, away from public scrutiny. He has chauffeurs, a private jet, and a loyal staff who looks away at his perversions. He must shower her with fabulous jewelry and furs. There's a giant demand for that kind of story. We predict this book will sell millions of copies. Trailer trash settings have no market. The current demand is for billionaire erotica."

"In the stratosphere, just like you wanted. Isn't that so?" adds Hyacinth and guffaws and runs her tongue over her jagged teeth before she snaps her mouth shut with a thudding sound. Just like her crocodile doppelgänger would do. There's an audible sucking in of all our breaths as we watch this display in horror. *What the…?*

Then changing the mood, one of the panel members starts to speak. She has frizzy hair and giant pores on her flat, wide face. Her shirt is stretched tight across her big round stomach and her fat underarms flap when she runs her fingers through her hair.

"I think I know who the unnamed billionaire in this story is based on. I read a lot of gossip magazines and I think it's that rock star, Jasper Ripley. Right? Only I don't think he's such a con man in real life. You have him swindling his record label and I don't believe he's done that. I haven't read that in the tabloids or anywhere."

"Well, it's only *based* on a true story. We have license to change things. It's not non-fiction," says Bijoux.

"None of it is based on any fucking real-life thing," I say angrily. "It's fiction. Fiction. FICTION!" I yell disgusted. "Fiction means all made up, pretending, like when you think some good-looking man is having sex with you when you're working your vibrators. You daft idiots, you subhuman mentally challenged assholes."

Hyacinth jumps up and moves forward from her corner, "Now, wait just a minute!"

Bijoux throws daggers at me with her eyes and says, "I don't think that was called for, Alexa."

"You ask for decorum from *me?* That's a laugh when you people are porn pushers preying on sex-starved matrons." The panel rises in anger and begins to shout obscenities and threatening to never buy any of my books. Ignoring them, I grab the mockup of the cover placed on the table in front of one of the angry panelists. It shows a nude woman whose face is in ecstasy and a tuxedo-dressed gentleman doing who knows what to her. I scream at the top of my lungs, waving it in all of their faces. "THIS IS SHIT! JUST PLAIN GARBAGE. IT ISN'T EVEN MY WORK, ANYMORE. HOW CAN YOU PUT MY NAME ON IT?"

"Not too many authors write their own books these days. Once they're established anything sells," Bijoux says quietly treating me like a child having a tantrum.

"Oh my god, what bullshit!" I answer through clenched teeth.

"You should know something else," Hyacinth says slyly and wickedly. I brace myself. "We decided the current trilogy doesn't work but a trilogy out of *Darkside* would multiply sales. Something like *Darkside: The Surrender, Darkside: The Master, and Darkside: The Bonds of Love.* And, of course, adding based on a true story in all the titles. We'll write them. And the movie scripts from the future deals. We can see it's not your thing."

Suddenly, I'm overwhelmed with nausea, a gripping overwhelming spasm. Turning my work into trash, well, I literally can't stomach it. I walk over to Hyacinth to tell her that I'm done with this stupid focus group, but instead, the contents of my stomach and rising bile eject and I throw up in her face. I run out while she gags trying to wipe her shirt clean. My purse packed with my few items is with me, my ride to the airstrip is waiting, and now, I can finally get off this fucking island.

Chapter Eleven

Margaret

Throwing my keys on the kitchen counter, I kick off my shoes and collapse on the sofa. As soon as I got home from the trip, I had to run to the store because there was no food, laundry detergent, or paper products. I spent like 200 bucks. When I got back, I realized that I forgot to buy toilet paper, so I ran out this morning. What a pain. I always had my groceries delivered in the city, a convenience I didn't realize was rare. Living out here is like the Dark Ages. When I called the local chain, the manager said, "We don't do that unless you are without transportation and housebound. We would need a doctor's note to that effect. And the charge for that is quite high, with the starting price at one hundred dollars just for delivery of one or two bags." I cursed and hung up the phone.

Before I went out yesterday, I called Margaret. After several attempts, I just left a message telling her I really needed to see her and that I was back. "Come up as soon as you can, I'll be here waiting," I said in a desperate voice. Maybe between the two of us, we can figure out how I can get out of this strangle-hold on me. I don't want the vast sums of money that I thought I wanted. I don't want to be number one on the best-sellers' list. I just want my old life back. My old life blissfully innocent of all the weirdness that can be accessed by associating with the wrong people. All I have are regrets. Every day and every waking minute. Firing Margaret could be at the top of the list of regrets. Why I did it is beyond my comprehension. Dazzled by the glitter of wealth and seduced by promises of the superficial. Chasing rainbows that turned into storm clouds and my ruin. A life lesson learned the hard way.

It's weird that she hasn't called me back, even when I tell her she doesn't have to call, she always calls. Margaret. I picture her cute face and wide smile with gleaming white, straight teeth. A poster child for the expensive braces she wore as a child to achieve that perfection. I was so comfortable with her right from the start. She was so relaxed and mellow taking all my shit with no complaints. She idolized me and was my first fan. Totally psyched at the mega success of my debut and thrilled to be a part of it. She was always there for me. She helped me with writer's block, with thorny plot problems. Pulled all-nighters to make my deadlines. Cooked me breakfast. Cooked me dinner.

Margaret Hathaway. A card-carrying member of the one percent. Her real name, not a made-up name like mine. She abhorred shortening her name to Marge or heaven forbid, Peggy. Never call her anything but Margaret. Never. So this fragile-looking petite young women, always laid back, would become brazen, bold, and threatening if someone tried to call her Peggy. I was tempted to call her Peggy because Margaret seemed too imposing for her sprite-like appearance, but she would always give me the stare when she heard the letter, "p," about to come out of my mouth. So I would finesse and change it. "Margaret, Margaret. Okay, okay, I know. I'm sorry." That was her only area of contention. Otherwise she was a bubble, a sparkling dancing light. My sweet and lovely Margaret. Why she said nothing when Alex called her, Peggy, is probably the spell these people hold on everyone.

Being the recluse that I am, she was also a social buddy. We looked so funny going to bars on the prowl together, especially when I put on my stiletto heels and towered over her. Me, from the mythical island of Amazon women, she, tiny, slender, Peter Pan. Flat soft shoes, leggings and a tunic are her staples. It made me self-conscious to be so big in comparison, but I felt sexy in heels and only wore my comfy flats for daily errands and such. Most of the time, I walked ahead of her and sat down at the bar first. One time I made her put on my Louboutins for fun, to entice her to think about adding some height when we went clubbing. First of all, they were giant on her small feet, so that was a big mistake. Luckily, we were in my carpeted bedroom because she fell so hard she almost broke her ankle. She hopped around for nearly a week having sprained it so badly it turned blue. I was mortified that I was responsible, but she brushed it off, as always.

Then, there was the time I bought her a tennis racket and took her to Chelsea Piers. She said that she played as a kid and in college but she stunk at it. I got tired of playing easy and served a hardball right into her face. I could have killed her. For a minute, I had forgotten that she was so short. My fast and low killer serve, perfected with the aid of my instructor, was just at the right height to hit her in her face when she ran for it bending down. She had a black eye for a month. Poor Margaret, she sure has suffered bodily harm knowing me.

I thought about Margaret's privileged childhood, so different from mine. Equestrian training, private boarding school, country-club golfing and summers yachting on Martha's Vineyard. She brought me home one weekend to see firsthand her family's Southport Connecticut estate overlooking the Long Island Sound. Both her parents came from inherited wealth. Her mother from the blue-blood Davenports who dated back to the first settlers in the 1700s and made their fortune in shipping and mining. The company had long since been bought out by an international conglomerate.

The family has more money than they can count. Margaret's mother will inherit additional vast sums when her confirmed bachelor brother, who's suffering from terminal cancer, passes. Margaret's father is from new money, being the heir of a large hotel chain that was absorbed by an even larger hotel chain. He holds an honorary seat on their Board and is a majority stock holder. There is no office grind culture model from which Margaret has somehow developed her work ethic.

Although Margaret had a childhood of luxury, she's the classic case of the neglected rich kid. Her parents do a lot of charity work and have their own foundation so, as usual, they were away in China attending a global conference when she took me to Overlook Cliffs. In that respect, my humble upbringing trumps all of her material advantages. I was the apple of my mother's eye and felt loved and cared for. Perhaps Margaret was attracted to a life of earning her own way, as a form of rebellion. We were both only children and so naturally our friendship evolved into becoming more like family. The sister we both longed for. And like sisters, we fought and sometimes she got on my nerves. I was annoyed at her when I fired her. Caught in Trinity's web because she brought Alex to my doorstep.

Margaret. Margaret who didn't need that stupid job working for me, but wanted to try being self-sufficient. Except for her living arrangements, which were quite grand, she took nothing else from her parents. Her parents' pied-à-terre used for evenings at the opera, museum galas, and charity balls was an entire floor at the Dakota. Margaret always said that living there was just temporary until she could find something she could afford on her own. But the perks were too enticing.

There was a full staff at the ready for whenever Mr. and Mrs. Hathaway chose to spend an evening, so Margaret did not have to concern herself with keeping it clean or cooking for that matter. We spent Thanksgiving there last year and the meal was absolutely first rate. Her parents were at an Ashram in India, so I gladly accepted her invitation. She also included my mother who was duly impressed. I had thought Margaret's apartment in the city was grand until she took me to their estate in Southport. Maybe that's why I thought I didn't have enough money, seeing the world from Margaret's perspective. Shouldn't really blame Margaret, though. It was *my* greed. Just plain greed that propelled me.

For all the fancy living that we both enjoyed, our favorite evenings were staying in at my place, streaming movies, and ordering take-out Chinese. She'd talk about my most recent project as if the people were real, as we watched some asinine blockbuster. She'd say the book I was working on was so much more interesting than the stupid rom-com we were watching. Or that my characters were so much more believable than the hit family drama starring all A-list actors, and so on. Yup. She's my biggest fan. Most people never have a one good friend like Margaret and on top of that she was a great collaborator. Lying on the sofa, I'm so nostalgic for my old life that I begin to weep. *Okay stop this.* She and I will figure a way out. There has to be a way out. *Now enjoy this beautiful house with its beautiful view,* I tell myself.

So, I get up and go out on the patio. How beautiful the river looks today. The ever-changing river. Sometimes it's peacefully still and calm, a river of glass. Sometimes there's the slow boil of anger and unrest like the light chop today. The perfect pairing to my mood. The balmy breeze is pleasant and I sit with the warm sun on my face for about a half hour trying to relax my anxious mood and enjoy the outdoors.

The drought is showing its effect on the distant vista. A brown blight is snaking its way along the hills devouring the green leaves and grass in its path. My water-soaked garden with its colorful array of early summer flowers and emerald lawn is a beacon to the world shouting my self-indulgence and disrespect for the current scarcity. The alternative is to have my landscaping dry up and blow away. Having this outdoor space is such an enjoyable change from condo living that I'm loath to part with it and stop watering. I know that soon enough, I will be forced to curtail my automatic sprinklers. But there's always hope for a heavy downpour.

I've become uneasy at seeing the advance of the scary drought and my selfish watering but mostly I'm concerned about Margaret blowing me off. It's not like her. *Why hasn't she called me back?* So, I go into the house to call her again. As I walk toward the phone, I start to recall there was a strange event here before I left for the island. An unsettling feeling pushes its way into my consciousness. Something unusual. *What?* And then I remember. The magically appearing wall with the door! And the basement! I walk over and touch the air where the wall was. Nothing. No invisible wall. *Hmm.* What did I do?

Oh yeah.

Chapter Twelve

The mysterious basement

I take a step back. "House can you tell me your secrets?" I ask out loud. All of a sudden, the room starts to vibrate and I hear a high-pitched squeaking noise, then grating and scraping like rubbing sandpaper, followed by a loud rumbling. After that, there's a sharp tearing sound like the ripping of the fabric of reality. I hold my ears as an ear-drum breaking boom explodes in the room. And then again. BOOM! Then nothing. Peacefulness. Birds are chirping outside. A far away dog is barking. But there's utter silence now in this room. I'm stunned. Stupefied. Because there it is. The wall. Right where there was…nothing before. This noise lollapalooza is quite contrary to the first time the wall appeared in complete silence. If throwing me off kilter is the motivation for this blast of sound to mark its appearance, it worked.

I feel the wall…cautiously. I open the door…hesitantly. I flip on the inside light switch…tentatively. The staircase is there leading to a basement that looks cavernous, ominous, and creepy. Just like before. I pause just inside the door on the top step. *Maybe this isn't such a good idea.* Then, a draft out of nowhere shuts the door behind me pushing me half-way down the stairs. There's stuff down there. Something's there. A large trunk is near the bottom step and I walk down to investigate. Suddenly, I feel strange. More unsettled than I was a second ago because I recognize this trunk. It's my dress-up trunk. My trunk full of play clothes. When I was a kid, it was filled with my mother's throw-aways. Old high-heeled shoes and out-of-style skirts that became dresses on me. Gaudy necklaces and scarves. I open it. *What the…?* All the play clothes are there. I touch them. They're real. *How can this be?*

Then I turn and look into the basement room. *Oh my.* It's not a basement. It's my bedroom in Brooklyn when I was growing up. There, on the bed, is my cherished stuffed turtle that played *It's a Small World*. Smallwee. My four-year-old self called it Smallwee, and the name stuck. It got all matted down from a million hugs and scrunches as I slept with it by my side. Bought with love by my mom on our one and only trip to Disney World. I carried it everywhere until it looked foolish for my age. Then I kept it on my bed like it is here in this altered reality room until we moved to New York City. I still have it in a box at my loft. All the familiar objects in this room flash into my view boggling my mind.

There are my pink sneakers with Velcro fasteners in a heap on the floor. My green converse low tops are tossed in the corner. My white desk with junk all over it. Books, pads, pencils, empty drink cartons thrown willy-nilly, so there's no room to work at it. The room is also a mess. Yeah, the same old mess. Like I always kept it. I walk in gingerly and sit on the bed. It's real. It's my white iron daybed with brass accents that I loved so much. We sold it before we moved to the city to get some extra money. My pink comforter. I loved pink. My white dresser that matched my desk. My Disney princess lamp. And there's my old TV. I turn it on. One of my favorite shows comes on. What was the name? *Full House.* I change the channel. Oh! My! *SeaQuest.*

I spy the hallway that leads to the kitchen and living room. Suddenly, I really miss my mom. Miss my childhood. Miss having her close. *Maybe she's here somehow.* I walk over to the hallway and stop cold. A good thing. There's a chasm, a black hole of nothingness. A sheer drop to a teeny, tiny red glow way, way down…far down. Miles down maybe. I jump back into the room. The TV has mysteriously turned off. I walk over to the pair of windows where sunlight is shining through. I look out and think I see my old neighborhood. I try and open one window but it won't open. Then the outside goes dark.

This eerie, weird version of my childhood bedroom is frightening and yet not. It's *my* bedroom after all. So many happy memories. Sitting on the bed, I hug and sniff Smallwee and become nostalgic for things past. We lived here with Miriam, who was my mother's only relative and her sponsor to come to the United States. A first cousin on my grandmother's side, Miriam's widowed mother had left the Soviet Union with her years before. Already an adult at that point, but treated as a child and dominated by her mother, Miriam's ability to think for herself never took hold. A thickset, rather plain woman, Miriam was blessed with a sweetness, however, that endeared her to all who interacted with her when she shopped in their stores.

After Aunt Clara died, she immediately married a recent refugee from a shtetl, a small Jewish village in the Ukraine, after being introduced to him by one of the shopkeepers she frequented. But alas, Miriam was widowed soon after she and Morris moved to Brighton Beach, a growing Russian community. His untimely death was the result of careless thinking and small village mentality. A man not used to all the traffic coming and going, Morris stepped in front of a city bus and was snuffed out in an instant.

Even after living in Brooklyn for many years, Miriam never

adjusted to life in America, never learning fluent English. She only shopped in Russian speaking stores, read Russian and Yiddish newspapers, and never watched American television. So it was with great joy that lonely Miriam took my mother in during her confinement. It also was no hardship to enjoy the extra money to which my mother was entitled under the refugee program. As a young child, I was naturally curious about my father but sadly he was killed in a freak accident before they were to be married, or so I was told. The story of his death was horrific. Walking in the city near a construction site, a hammer fell out of the hands of a worker on the tenth floor hitting him on the head and killing him instantly. A most unfortunate instance of literally being at the wrong place at the wrong time. Of course, it made no difference that my parents had planned to wed, my mother's condition was totally unacceptable to her family. Another freak accident stealing two men in my family.

Our time living with Miriam was full of happiness. There was never any discussion of us leaving that apartment after I was born, and we stayed until my mother finished her undergraduate degree at Brooklyn College. It took her far longer than four years because she worked at various jobs to support me and help Miriam. After she graduated, and I was ready to start high school, she was accepted to Columbia University to earn a doctorate in Theoretical Astrophysics and Cosmology with a concentration in Elementary Particle Physics. Given full tuition and housing, we moved from Brighton Beach and Miriam's apartment into graduate student housing in NYC next to campus.

Finally, my mother had a bedroom. At Miriam's, she gave me the one free bedroom while she slept on a pullout sofa in the living room. By the time we moved to Columbia, Miriam was also ready to leave her apartment and move to an assisted living building right near the boardwalk. We visited her as often as we could but she died within a year. Sad, lonely, and still missing Morris. It broke our hearts.

In an unusual turn of events and not a normal path for doctoral students, Columbia University offered my mother an assistant professorship after her dissertation and defense blew away the faculty. I had been prepared for her to join the faculty at Stanford, or some other far off place upon completion of her doctorate, not realizing how disturbed it made me until she told me she didn't have to leave the area. My load was substantially lightened. Mom and I would remain near each other, as it always was and should be. Smith had been a relatively short train ride from Columbia and I came home often. Once I graduated, I would move back to NYC to find a way to support myself while writing my first novel.

Now, my mom would be there as well.

I always felt in awe of my mother's genius. Science courses left me cold and confused. Compatible with her inner strength and superior intellect, and already having a child, she never thought of marriage as a necessary or desirable option. Preferring relationships to remain in the courtship phase, like the romances of bygone eras, she enjoyed being handled with utmost care while being impervious to entreaties for commitment. This aloofness makes most men wild with desire and foolishly obsessive, at which point she becomes bored and moves on. Choosing a male dominated field in which to work guarantees the abundance of suitors.

Although my love and admiration for her is beyond measure, she also had her quirks, as we all do. Why, for example, did she decide to name me Gladys, a name I despised? She also was insistent that I would never speak Russian. Emphatic about it. Paradoxically, she both hated and pined for all things Russian. Her conflicted feelings remain to this day. Sometimes I would catch her humming a Russian folk tune and when she noticed my immediate interest, she would abruptly stop and mutter under her breath, "Never mind." Or when strangers on a train would start speaking Russian, a nostalgic look would come over her face.

These contradictions were especially obvious concerning her parents of whom she never spoke. She was devastated by Miriam's news of her mother's death and sobbed quietly for days. She never discussed my dead father, whose untimely exit from this world put her life in such turmoil and whose memory seemed erased. Yet, she carried around a worn photo of a fountain with statues of horses, an obvious treasure of which there has never been any explanation. I guessed its significance had something to do with him.

For Riva Lipschitz from Moscow, I was to be American through and through. No stain of the foreigner, and so, I cannot converse in my mother's native tongue and had never spoken directly to Miriam her entire life. Unbeknownst to my mother, however, I did develop an understanding of the version of Russian mixed with Yiddish that was spoken at home, as children are wont to do. Naturally, because of my mother's feeble attempts to deny her heritage, I was drawn to Russian culture and its literary scene by the lure of forbidden fruit and a consuming curiosity. I developed a passion for the great Russian writers and have read all the works of Tolstoy, Chekov, Pasternak, and Dostoevsky. Devouring Russian literature from the unique vantage point of the Russian Jewish peasant mentality that I acquired naturally from my upbringing.

I'm still on the bed in that out-of-nowhere basement holding

Smallwee, but now finished with my musings of things past. The cherished memory of living in this room will not let me go. My childhood of bliss will not be overshadowed by this strangeness. I loved this room. And yet, it's not really *this* room with the hole to hell right outside the door. Although my instincts tell me to flee, something else is at work keeping me here. I call out, "What is this? What is the secret?" And then, tentatively, "Mom?" And…there she is.

"Mom! I'm so glad to see you! I've missed you so much." I hop off the bed and run to hug her but when I reach out there's nothing. She disappears. "Mom?" She pops into view again a little farther away, but this time I just wait. She looks different. Her hair is different and worn in a style from a different time period. Piled on top with curls. Like in black and white movies. And her clothes. From the '40s? She's talking to someone who's in shadow. Then she crouches down and is talking to a little girl. Who? I walk over and get a sideways glance at the girl in the scene. Oh my. She looks like me. *What the…?* The scene fades. "Mom? Mom?" She appears in another spot. Now she's wearing an elaborate silk gown with a big hoop skirt. Like Scarlet O'Hara. She's dancing with someone. I walk over to get a better look and she fades again. When she reappears, she's dressed like Marie Antoinette or someone from the 1700s. Her powder blue silk dress has a tight waist, low-cut top, big full, skirt with layers of fabric and a bustle, and frilly lace cuffs on three-quarter sleeves. A white elaborate wig having thick, long curls covers her hair.

She's talking to someone. Who? Then he walks into the scene. He takes her arm. They're walking in a park. Horse-drawn carriages wait patiently. They're holding the hand of a little girl. Their backs are turned as they walk away. I can't see their faces. The little girl turns and looks at me. Oh my god! It's me. My mom and the man turn and look at me. Oh my god! It's King! I run upstairs on a sprint. Run upstairs to get away. Run upstairs to answer the phone before it stops ringing.

"Hello," I say in a breathless voice. "Margaret, is it you? I've been waiting all day for you to call back."

"No, this isn't Margaret. It's her mother Elizabeth Hathaway. Something awful has happened. Terrible, terrible." She starts to sob. "Margaret was in a really bad car accident. Her car was crushed between two semi-trucks on the highway. She was stopped behind a semi because of traffic but another semi came barreling down the hill losing control of its breaks and slammed into her which…caused her car to…crash into the truck in front. There's nothing left. Nothing left of…her car…or of…her…just…the stain of her blood on the road," she wails uncontrollably for a few minutes. Finally, she manages to say in a nasty and angry tone,

"She was on her way to see you. She called me just before she left. Said you were back and that she had something important to show you about your new publisher and it couldn't be delayed. So, she couldn't attend our garden party this weekend. If only you hadn't called…If only you had stayed away longer." She's sobbing and hiccupping and I can't make out what else she's saying. The funeral. Something about the funeral. She hangs up before I can speak.

I'm too shocked to move. Tears well up and flood my face. My sweet Margaret. *Why?* I stare at the wall. Sinister is the only word to describe that basement. Sinister. The room, Margaret's death. Something sinister is at play. "Go from whence you came you evil wall," I yell. Nothing happens. I need to get rid of it. Suddenly, the scent of licorice and vanilla fills my sense memory from that hardscrabble island village. I look it up on the internet. Yes, sure enough both are used to ward off evil. I rummage around in my spice rack and find vanilla and then a small box of black licorice pops into view. *How did I get that?* I must have packed it by mistake from the island. Carla! She always had licorice bits. Hurriedly and with shaky hands, I put some pieces in a small pot over a low flame and pour some vanilla over them. After a few short minutes, I can smell the combination and just as I am about to yell something at the wall again, it dissolves. Just like that. Gone. I walk over and touch the air where the wall stood. It's just air. I walk around the area and jump up and down. The floor is solid. No basement. No stairs.

My hysterical flurry of activity over, I sit on the sofa and have a good cry. Devastated beyond any sorrow that has come before. Even Miriam's death. I picture my little sprite. Her smile. Her good nature. My only friend in this harsh world and I banished her in a fiendish manner. In an email. What a despicable coward. After how close we had been. I was trying to make up for it but, instead, summoned her to her death. Her mother was right. I'm responsible. I'm the cause. She may have started my miserable journey into this new life but it was I who signed the contract. I brought this sinister, evil world to my door. Tears and more tears flow freely. Misery. I have the urge to total this place. Crash everything to the floor like Jodie. Oh my, like the last inhabitants. I've got to get out of here and quickly. I have to go to the city. I must go and right now. I need to talk to someone. Kip. I need… must…talk to Kip.

First, I have to find him.

Then, I need to get the funeral information, so that I can attend.

And finally, I need to talk to Mom. I need to find out if King is my fucking father and how that's possible.

I need. I need. I need this nightmare to end.

Chapter Thirteen

Imprisoned

After I throw a black dress in a bag and a few other necessities, I jump in my car and tear away. Bearing down on the gas, the speedometer hits 95. I want to get back to my loft in the city and away from this house as fast as I can. But I'm a new driver and swerve all over the road at this speed. The world flies by and matches my racing heart. Nothing can stop me from my purpose. Even the knowledge that Margaret died in a car accident doesn't make me cautious. I'm frantic to get away from that house, that poisonous place. *What the...?* What the hell is that? Red flashing lights in my rear-view mirror. FUCK!!! I'm being pulled over. I don't need this. I don't have time for *this*.

A car bearing a sheriff's decal parks behind me after I ease my car onto the shoulder. An officer wearing an ugly brown uniform with matching ranger-style felt hat and stereotypical Ray-Ban sunglasses gets out of the car and saunters over. After I roll down the window, he asks me if I realize how fast I'd been going. Stupidly, this is what I say, "Of course I do. I have a very important matter to attend to. I don't even have time to talk to *you* right now, so give me the goddamn ticket and get it over with. I'm in a hurry."

He touches the brim of his hat and grins while chewing gum, "I understand you're in a hurry. Must be something *really* important. Well, just let me think about that for a minute." He rocks back and forth on his heels for a brief moment and then he says, "Yes, I've thought it over and I think that you're a safety risk right now, and if I let you leave, you'll just continue to ignore the speed limit. Please step out of your car and turn around and put your hands behind your back."

"Wait a minute. Please...I didn't mean to say..."

"Step out of the car, NOW!"

The bastard handcuffs me, shoves me into the back seat of his vehicle, and his partner gets into my car and follows us to the local jail at the Misty Falls police department. My humiliation is sobering and humbling. I'm also quite frightened. This is America, can you be locked up for having a smart mouth? Well, for starters, telling him I was in a hurry when I was caught speeding was just plain dumb. But I'm not myself. I'm traumatized and must get back to the city for my sanity. Part of me wants to tell him of my terrible predicament, but who would believe me? Certainly not this guy.

The door to the cell locks behind me. There are just two empty cells side-by side and they are down a corridor and around a corner from the front desk. As soon as the cop walks away, I feel isolated, alone, and quite vulnerable. Must not be a lot of crime around here. Or maybe these are just a detention cells for minor stuff. Just for a few hours, I hope. I don't think they can keep me here for more than a few hours. I'll look that up on my phone. *Where's my purse?* No purse. Oh yeah, they took it.

I sit down on the narrow wooden bench to think. The good thing about this cell being empty is I don't have to deal with making small talk with a real criminal. But maybe a real criminal could help me figure out what I'm supposed to do. *What should I do?* As I sit there, the scent of disinfecting fluid fills my nostrils and is quite distasteful. I look around. Not much to see. The cell is sparse with wooden benches against the bars and concrete back wall. Sterile and unfriendly, this horrible cell throws me into a panic. *I've got get out of here! Call Jeff Roseman, call your lawyer.* Why didn't I think of that right away? I'm shaking because I don't know his number and they took away my phone. And then I remember, I can't call my lawyer because he's DEAD. Oh my god, my lawyer's dead!

Something else gnaws at me. What? Oh no, I remember. He left a message about not signing the contract until we talked. Margaret! She wanted to tell me something about Trinity. My stomach does flips. Are they connected? His death and Margaret's? I start to gag. But I can't throw up here and stink up this cell even more with the smell of my vomit on top of this awful chemical smell. Oh, *Margaret, Margaret, Margaret,* I scream in my head. I *knew* Trinity was evil. I should have told you I knew that and kept you safe. How could this have gotten so twisted? This started out as a goddamn contract. Just a *book* contract. What is the danger to which I have exposed the people around me? To Kip? To my mother? I'm so agitated, I get up and start to pace in circles and moan.

"Keep it down over there," a harsh voice yells and I stop moaning and just breathe heavily. After about an hour that seems like two weeks, a cop comes over and tells me I need to get finger printed. I can't tell how many police are here. They all look the same, like clones of each other. All serious, unfriendly, with downright mean faces. He has me stand in front of a mugshot camera and takes my photo. I know I look mortified and petrified. Horrible. Then I get fingerprinted. *Oh dear.* He asks me if I'd like to call someone to make bail.

"Yes, yes, please, but their numbers are in my contacts on my phone. May I have it back for just a moment?" I should have thought to write down Kip's phone number before they confiscated my purse where I keep my phone in an outside pouch, but I was too nervous to think straight. Can't call information collect, right?

"Sorry," says one of the cop clones, "we're checking it out."

"What for?"

"Standard procedure."

"Can someone call information for me?" I get a cold and annoyed stare. Once back in my cell, I start to pace again. After several hours another clone brings in a disheveled and smelly, homeless drunk and puts him in the cell next to mine. That really brings up my bile and I manage to make it to the far corner of the cell before I throw up. The cop says, "Sleep it off, Rusty." And then, "I'll bring a mop so you can clean up your mess, Miss *Lipschitz*." I look at him perplexed and feel invaded. "That's your real name, right? Before you changed it?" And then he adds, "We'll call your wife, Rusty, and let her know you're here again."

Reeling from the venomous way this cop pronounced my birth name, I check out Rusty as he tries make himself comfortable on the narrow and too-short bench. His stink keeps me gagging. So he's not homeless. *But who would live with such a bum?* Not my problem. My problem is bigger than that. Much bigger. The guy's feet hang over and it's hard for him to turn on his side, but with eyes closed and before he starts snoring, he says, "Call Alex."

"What? What did you say?" No response. He's out cold. "Did you say call Alex? How do you know Alex?" Now he's snoring. I'm not going to call Alex, that's the last person I'd call. I bang on the cell's bars and yell, "I really need my phone." I hear a rustling sound coming from Rusty's cell and then behind me but when I turn to look, the guy is still dead asleep. Pacing again, I step on a crumpled piece of paper. *What the...?* There's a number written in pencil and with an obvious shaky hand. But readable. Ah, I recognize it. Damn! It's Alex's cell phone number. *Hmm...oh well...*

What else can I do? And so...

Chapter Fourteen

My unexpected stay at the Lodge

A bright beam of sunlight shines in my eyes and awakens me from deep slumber. Heavenly plush linens, a sumptuous bed, and soft cushiony pillows cocoon me in a most pleasant and delightful sensuousness. *Where am I?* Oh yeah. I'm a "guest" at the Lodge. This beautifully appointed room is what one might find at a luxury 5-star hotel. Everything is white. The bedding, the sofas, the desk, chairs, and lamps, plantation shutters with one slat open causing the sun to wake me up… white. The wing where this room is located is called, by an amazingly poetic choice, the White Wing. All rooms are…white. To keep the rustic lodge feeling going, the walls and ceiling are wood paneled, albeit painted white. The furniture has been created out of white birch trees. There's a blue wing and a green wing, according to the map. I'm sure King's wing must be black, all things evil must be black.

Of course, I called Alex. Weighing my options of being stuck in that detention cell until they could find a court appointed attorney with getting out of there immediately was a no brainer. In no time at all, Alex swooped in, paid my bail, and took me to the Lodge instead of my house. Since I won't able to drive because my driver's license was confiscated, all my needs would be looked after quite well at the Lodge. My date in traffic court was not for six weeks. Six weeks!

My mind started to race trying to figure out how to call a cab and take a train to my loft. But, once at the Lodge, the staff took my purse for safe keeping and then they took my clothes for "washing." So now, I'm imprisoned *here* wearing the Lodge requisitioned attire of comfy pajama-type clothing that's not appropriate for taking public transportation into the city but is acceptable to wear to dinner when there are no other guests. This was told to me by the woman who took my clothes. Stuck here and at their mercy. But I've got to admit, there are worse places, like the police station for example. Last night's dinner was a scrumptious leg of lamb, roasted potatoes, fresh asparagus, accompanied with a lush Malbec, and followed by a baked Alaska to die for. It was served in the more intimate breakfast room, rather than the dining room that was adjacent. Soft music played. Classical symphony type music. So elegant and very snooty and totally strange given the masculine, savage hunter decor run rampant here.

Peeking into the massive dining room out of curiosity was not a pleasant sight because it complemented the trophy ballroom with its blatant disregard for god's creatures. There was an enormous wooden dining table of dark red, highly polished to almost black, that looked like an entire tree trunk with all the grains. Probably an endangered sequoia. The table comfortably seated about 20 people in roomy armchairs by quick count. The room had another enormous rough-stone fireplace but not as large as in the trophy/ballroom, whose mantel was adorned with bric-a-brac wooden pieces of primitive art. The dark wide-plank wood floors, throughout this part of the house, had numerous animal skin throw-rugs of all species and the zebra-striped wallpaper kept the slaughter-of-animals theme going.

Wood beamed ceilings and rough-hewn wood logs were just like the trophy room but in here the wall logs were thinner and placed in sections creating spacial demarcations. This gave the effect of showcasing the realistic artwork probably created by masters in the field, depicting with almost photographic quality an array of African landscapes in oil on canvas and placed in thick, ornate gold-leaf frames.

There were scenes of the Great Plains and snow-capped mountains, grazing elephants, and lion stalking prey. Strewn among the collection were mesmerizing portraits of natives in full costume or going about their business in their villages. But one painting stood out as paramount among them all. The eye was riveted toward a mural-sized piece of what appeared to be thousands of migrating wildebeest with all the dust, commotion, and feeding frenzies by predators that accompany that annual event. The perfect vulgarity for Neanderthals devouring their quarry, the Serengeti slaughter as a dining-room theme.

After dinner, I was given a reflexology treatment when I finished soaking in my personal hot tub room connected to my private bath. The bath is all marble with gold taps. Matching the bedroom decor, there's white wood paneling on the ceiling, rustic white birch towel racks, and a birch chair with a white cushioned seat for the vanity area. The giant walk-in steam shower is amazing and there's a large whirlpool tub with numerous jets for bathing, the hot tub being just for soaking. I have used all the bathing options in turns and my skin has been exfoliated by pressured swirls of hot water and my pummeled muscles are relaxed and stretched. It's been marvelous.

I'm the only guest so everyone makes a fuss over me, offering me water nonstop, bringing snacks to my room. I'm aware that my euphoria seems to be escalating with each passing minute. Perhaps my dinner was laced with anti-depressants. *But really, who cares?* I like feeling good. Feeling good is…good. My room also has live streaming just-released movies as well as oldies shown on a giant flat screen. No need to use the media room in the main area and besides it's too spooky to be there by myself. It's really kind of fun to watch movies still in theaters in the comfort of my room and for *free*. I got caught up on several movies that were of interest and I watched until I got too sleepy. There's a whole bunch more on my list. It's all so relaxing. All of it, and I slept like a baby.

Peaceful sleep with no dreams. Glorious sleep all through the night until morning, haven't done that in years, when there's a soft knock after the sun awakens me. "Breakfast, Miss," says one of the staff in a soft lilting voice. Everything is so soothing here, when you stay away from the stuffed wildlife. The staff, the bed, the clothes, the food. Breakfast has all my favorites when I'm not dieting. Crispy bacon, over-easy eggs, grits, blueberry pancakes cooked to perfection and a perfect latte. After breakfast, I'm scheduled for a facial in the spa area and then the rest of the day, I will be sunning by the outdoor resort-sized pool.

I really needed this break because I sort of remember being very unglued. I was desperate to get to my loft for some reason. *When was that? Yesterday? Last week?* Anyway, it seems a while ago. There was the police station incident but not sure why I was there. Every once in a while, an embryo of a thought tries to nudge its way into my consciousness but then evaporates. I'm told King will be here tonight and spend a quiet few days. That should prove interesting. Oh, there's an engraved invitation on my tray. I'm expected at dinner tonight. Okay.

Clouds roll in and the wind picks up in while I'm eating breakfast so that takes care of sunning by the pool. This persistent drought allows clouds to form but never brings any rain. Like the terrible drought in Ethiopia that left the entire country to starve. It's beyond odd. Prices for produce are already starting to rise. The lack of rain is apparently everywhere. Oh, well, I'm sick of salads anyway. Guess I'll go for a swim in the indoor pool. My 90-minute facial awaits and the world-class spa is just what one would expect at a luxury resort. New Age music, pervasive cascading waterfalls, dim lighting, and an attentive and soft-spoken staff. One wonders what goes on when King isn't here and the Lodge has no guests?

After my facial, I set out from my first-floor room with the map of this hotel-sized home to find the indoor pool wearing my Lodge supplied swimsuit. I'm surprised that the pool is not near the spa and workout room, but in some sort of underground level accessed by its own passageway. Of course, I get lost so decide to use this ploy to poke around and really see this place. The staff is off doing whatever, so no one notices when I dawdle checking out the whatnots in the trophy room, the heart of the house, and where the party was held.

Last night when I was escorted to dinner, we used the hallway from my bedroom wing that passes through the main entrance lobby to get to the dining rooms. The trophy room is a straight shot from the front door and all of the two-story wings where the bedrooms are located in this H-shaped house flank this wild-game cemetery, as shown on the map. It would be easy to mistake this private residence for a hotel. It must be more than 100,000 square feet. Like the manor houses of British royalty or palaces of German kings. Or almost any European royalty, for that matter.

As I stand at its entrance, the room is imposing in both size and grandeur. The two-story glass-domed ceiling, adds to the majestic ambiance. It also feels twice as large without people. All the carefully placed doodads, ashtrays, and throw pillows, add to the casual elegance. Passing the door to the library, I get a funny feeling, but can't remember why, and then find a hallway leading to another wing. The door to the hallway is wide open, I guess in readiness for King. His room must be near here. I grow excited to see it. As I follow the hall, it ends at an intersection. The left corridor leads to a rather large conference-type room and peeks my curiosity.

Several white boards have writing on them. I guess the staff hasn't gotten around to erasing them yet. Curious, I try reading the clipped sentences. I see the words "drought," "climate," "and "rain forests." Then, "Possible Future Strategies: Mass Extinction." *What the...?* There are brochures and pamphlets in the center of the huge conference table. I pick one up. Under a logo of three sixes intertwined with the numbers 666 clearly written below it, is the title, "Bringing farming to the Amazon Rain Forest." It has pictures of clear cut acreage and seeds. Another one says, "How to get Logging Permits in the Pacific Northwest Rain Forests," and "The Idiots Guide to Overturning Anti-Fracking Legislation." Finally, there's one that's more horrifying than the others, "Maintaining and Escalating Global Water Pollution Strategies." So this is a planned attack on our climate? Cutting down our rain forests? Throwing our planet into chaos by poisoning our water supply? And 666, the sign of the Devil, is the real company name. I knew it!

Then I remember that the trophy room is a showcase for species going extinct populated by poachers and hunters with blood lust like King. I suck in my breath feeling horrified. My euphoria is waning. I'm waking up from my mania. The feel-good meds must be wearing off. What didn't

I eat at breakfast? I didn't touch the juice or the Good Health Water, flavored water with all essential vitamins according to the label. But I did drink the coffee. *Hmm.* I'm about to continue my investigation of the rest of the rooms down the hallway when a cleanup crew enters.

"What are you doing here?" asks an older woman with vampire teeth obviously in charge.

"I…uh…got turned around trying to find the indoor pool."

"Really? Well, it's nowhere near here. Go back the way you came and follow the hallway outside of your room that leads to the spa. There's a sign in front of the staircase. And now I'd thank you to leave."

I scurry out of there disappointed that my investigation of all the evil crap that goes on here is cut short. I did find out plenty, though, and now a wave of desire to leave has returned in a flash of recovered memories. A wave of despair overwhelms me and I cave against the wall sobbing. Margaret…the funeral. Oh my god, Margaret. *How could I forget?* My world has gone haywire in such a short time. Sadness and depression take over. But I'm angry as well. That bastard can't keep doing all this. Hurting those I love. Fucking up the planet. As I turn to leave, I realize the door to the conference room has closed and the crew inside won't know that I've decided to continue down the right corridor to the double doors at the end.

I jiggle the knob and the door is locked. *Damn!* Quickly looking down the hallway to see if I'm still alone, I do something I saw on a TV show. I kick the door hard by the lock. Voila! It works. Amazing. Crime shows can actually be educational. Once inside I'm startled by the size of the room and begin to snoop around. First of all, it's not a bedroom but a living room and the huntsman decor is totally absent. The furnishings are more luxury second-home than Africa. Velvet fabrics in burgundy and gold adorn the furnishings giving the room a Medieval regal feel.

Plush wall-to-wall carpeting soften the footsteps and feel almost therapeutic. A hideaway fit for a king. There's a beautiful, shiny wood bar stocked with everything from beer on tap to brandies. A mid-sized refrigerator next to the bar holds snacks and drinks. There's a collection of candies and dry nibbles like pretzels in and chips in giant bowls on top of the bar. On the far end of the room is a bedroom with a canopy bed that I can see through the open door. Outside the sliding doors, there's a single-lane lap pool protected by a privacy fence. King never has to leave these quarters.

Aside from the enormous size, nothing seems weird or kinky. Then I spot it. A walled off area jutting out into the living room in the far right corner and not noticeable on entering. At first glance, it looks like it could be another room or a closet. Investigating what's behind the wall, I see there's a vestibule leading to a floor-to-ceiling door with a giant stone in front of it. The stone is too heavy to remove, so I press my ear against the door. I jump back in fear and then cautiously listen again. Sounds of screaming and moaning. Evil screeching, the licking of flames, the whirling of wind carrying these noises from below. *Below where?* The hole outside my mysteriously appearing basement bedroom pops into my mind. The bottomless hole. *Oh my god!*

I run out of the room and all the way back to mine. Panicked, I turn on the shower and primal scream. I scream until I can scream no more. This is all too much. All signs point to the supernatural, to pure evil. And to me. Can this stuff really exist? I want out of this nightmare. I must get out. I finally calm down and try to integrate all I have seen and all that I think I know. *What will save me from this?* I'm trapped. Imprisoned here. I still have no clothes, so I can't leave just yet. *What to do?* I decide go for that swim. Exercising, especially swimming, has always made me think more clearly, and so I find the pool.

The comfortably warm room with the lap pool is in sharp contrast to the quite chilly air-conditioned hallways and rooms set to temperatures accommodating King's personal taste to vanquish the oppressive and relentless summer heat. Even though the Olympic-sized pool is down a level, this side of the house is on a hill so the room is actually above ground with tall arched windows on three sides. The almost sky-high ceilings and large windows afford plenty of daylight and a sense of being outdoors. The pool itself also is heated to a comfortable temperature for easy entry. The relaxing warmth, however, does not assuage my distress.

Somehow, I must get out of here. I must get back to the city. I start to swim...and think. I must confront King tonight. The time is right. Just he and I alone at dinner. At least I hope so. I hope nobody else shows up. Like Jewel and Alex. Oh why did I think of that? I shake that thought out of my mind and dive down to make my flip turn at the end of the lane. Breathing and swimming. Clearing my head. Breathing and swimming. Breathing...and...my mind starts to riff on random thoughts. Those scenes. Those home movies through time. Holograms of another life shown to me in my recreated childhood bedroom *on the border of hell* are at a minimum horrifying. Stomach turning. I can't be related to King. I'm nothing like him. And my mother...my mother is in no way involved. She's just a hard working scientist. This is a trick. An evil trick and there must be some way to figure it out. Yes, tonight at dinner is my best chance.

First, I'll throw him off guard by confronting him right away.

Something he won't be expecting because he thinks I've been drinking his mind-numbing potion. Right, he probably thinks I'm still drugged and docile. I'll hit him below the belt. Tell him he thinks he has some power over me but he doesn't. And certainly not my mother, a Jewish immigrant who sought religious asylum. Jews don't even believe in the *Devil*. So this magician's trick is just that...a trick. I don't know how he has been able to pull all this off but it's bullshit. Just bullshit. This thought calms me...somewhat.

After the confrontation, I'll demand to go back to the city. If he's *god forbid* family...not family, my *father*, he won't hurt me. I can't believe I'm even thinking these bizarre thoughts. One thing rings true and bums me out even further, if that's possible. It's that I'm so alone in all this. So isolated. Yes, nobody but my mom to care whether I live or die. Whether I'm missing or safe. And she's never around! Realizing how solitary my life has become again crystallizes how much I must make changes. Expand my circle. My circle has always been quite small even before Trinity. But at least I had a few people, Margaret, my agent, my publisher.

Now, there's no one. It's hard to believe in so short a time. No one to talk to. Kip was a possible friend but for some unknown reason, he just disappeared. At least, he would be someone I could talk to about all this weirdness before he took me to Bellevue Hospital's nuthouse. As soon as I get back to the city, I've got to find him somehow. I'll go the dealership. That's what I'll do. But why has he gone missing? Is he in danger? He said he'd call. Or has something already gone wrong, like Margaret and Roseman? Oh no! But wait, Jewel implied he was one of King's disciples. I'm so confused.

When I get back to my room after more than an hour of doing laps, there's a lovely casual slacks outfit laid out on my bed. Tonight one must dress up for King, no pajamas. Still no sign of my own clothes but the fine fabric of this stylish ensemble is more posh than anything I have and probably cost thousands. No hardship to wear this. There's also shoes with sensible wedge heels. I look inside for the name of the designer. Stuart Weitzman. Not bad. A note is slipped under my door, a reminder. Dinner is at 6:00 sharp. Then later, a soft knock.

"Yes?" I open the door. A maid in a neat uniform.

"You didn't drink your Good Health Water at the pool. You must be thirsty. I've brought you some. It's important to stay hydrated," she says like a New Age guru.

"Thanks." She comes in and places the tray on the coffee table.

"I can wait for you to drink it, so I can remove the empty bottle from the room."

"That's okay. I'll place it outside when I'm done." *So that's where the meds are hiding.*

I pour it out with relish when she leaves.

Another knock. How annoying, what now?

"We've come for your relaxing massage, hair, and make-up."

"Oh."

And so I give myself up to being pampered. At the very least, it will maintain the calm my swim achieved and perhaps help me have the focus and strength I need for hurling my shocking accusations. But also, there will be begging for mercy, pleading for pity, and imploring for my freedom.

From the man who might be my father.

Chapter Fifteen

Dinner with King

At exactly 6:00 sharp and as I'm about to leave the room, there's another knock on my door. *What is this Grand Central Station?* Being the only guest has advantages and disadvantages. When I open the door, there's a young, delectable guy with movie-star quality good looks wearing the Lodge t-shirt and jeans. He's to escort me to the dining room. Message loud and clear, nobody wants me snooping around again. But it's no bother to check this guy out as we walk to dinner. A nice diversion from my jittery thoughts. Unexpectedly, we don't go to the dining room but to a cozy salon. So many rooms in this place. Or do they just materialize spontaneously like my basement or the contract that adds sentences at will?

This room is also devoid of the Lodge vibe and has more of a sophisticated country manor feeling. More in keeping with King's personal quarters and probably attached to his private retreat. Antique furniture, soft colors, and flowery motifs of silk linen cover the sofas. A charming oasis from taxidermy world. King has his back toward me standing in front of a large bay window and sipping a drink. He's looking out at a fabulous view of a colorful manicured English flower garden surrounding the outdoor patio, the emerald green lawn, and the thick, lush forest in the distance. No signs of brown and dying anything. The sun has now come out and throws spotlights on this scene in its end-of-day ritual.

He turns when he hears me enter and puts his drink down. Walking over to me, he takes my hand and kisses it like knights of old. "My dear, don't you look lovely tonight." Our eyes meet. Glowing, yellow mesmerizing eyes peer into mine. His eyes inhabit me and my brain begins to feel numb, invaded, and peculiar. Dressed in a country gentleman's green tweed jacket, moss-green shirt and matching silk pocket square, his demure and elegant clothing mismatches his seething dark energy. "Can I offer you a drink before dinner?" he asks. I nod in the affirmative, not yet trusting my speaking voice after being unnerved by this initial strangeness.

He motions at a server hidden in the shadows and a drink cart is wheeled over. The cart has a complete array of choices. Keeping up my charade of normal social behavior for now, I choose a glass of Malbec, my current favorite. As I take the seat that's offered me, another shadowy server immediately presents a tray full of hors-d'oeuvres, but I wave it away. Except for the brain-eating greeting, the atmosphere feels low key. The waiters are dressed in black silk shirts and black jeans. A far cry from the half-naked staff at the grand soiree. After taking a sip of the wine, I get afraid it might be spiked with the anti-depressants I have avoided all day. Carefully, I spit it back in the glass while making it seem like I'm taking another sip.

"I hope you are enjoying yourself and taking advantage of all the Lodge has to offer," he says in a very friendly tone but doesn't sit next to me and remains standing.

"I...well...you see," I say clumsily trying to figure out how to lead into the dreaded but necessary conversation. Surprisingly, he's no longer engaged, looks at the entrance to the room, and walks right by me.

"Ah, Sofia, Harry how good of you to come."

SHIT!!!

An older couple with Palm Springs golf tans and wreaking of wealth enter the room walking briskly. The woman is a warning label for plastic surgery gone awry. Her eyes are stretched and pulled back tightly toward her ears. Puffed-out cheeks and fat lips add to her freak-show face, like the frightening reflection that stares back at you from a fun-house mirror. It's not a good look. Her husband is no better with an ill-fitting toupee and Botox everything. They're inappropriately overdressed. He in a tux and she in a chiffon ball gown, as if this were a Manhattan socialite's dinner party. I'm introduced as the world-renowned author that just signed with Trinity of Sixes Publishing and they are, aptly, the Tanners. They feign interest but immediately turn their attention to drinks and gobble up the hors-d'oeuvres as if they hadn't eaten in days.

People start flowing in dressed in various attire. There's a couple wearing sandals, shorts, and tees. A woman wearing a red bandanna and a long, flowing red and green tie-dyed poncho over red tights spins in circles as she advances into the room. A guy all in blue velvet, even his shoes, tiptoes over to the crowd. An elderly man in white tie and white tails struts arm and arm with a young girl in a wedding dress. The room fills up with other assorted characters that are part of this strange brew and, who I discover, are guests at the Lodge for King's annual Summer Fling. There's a welcome sign in the corner of the room that I hadn't noticed before, being so bent on my plan of attack. There will be hunting, fishing, dining, and entertainment. Designer trunk shows for the wives. The place will be packed for the next few days with King's entourage of weird wackos.

King works the crowd. He's laughing. They're gulping drinks and gorging. He's charming and making conversation while they continue to gulp drinks and gorge. Finally, we're ushered into the Serengeti dining room and find seats with our names on place cards. I'm seated between a tall model with a regal neck and long, flowing blonde hair and a short, be-speckled, pot-bellied gentleman wearing a sports fisherman's vest with pockets full of lures and hooks dangling out. The first course is served. Everyone wolfs down the foie gras as if it were peanut butter. Next is French onion soup. I watch as the soup bowls are raised and the cheese topping hungrily pulled off with their teeth. All of them eat this way, as if animals let out of their cages. Everyone concentrates on the food. There's no small talk. King doesn't seem to notice and chats with his quests sitting nearby who ignore him and eat like lions in the wild eating a gazelle. Or like the Neanderthals I envisioned when I first investigated this room.

As I observe this bizarre scene, one by one the dinner guests take on the appearance of animals. The model becomes a giraffe; the chubby man becomes a toad. It goes like that around the table. I've been careful not to drink too much. Is this what the guests really look like, or has the food been laced and I'm hallucinating? King has not changed his demeanor but his yellow eyes glow evilly again, as if unmasked as well. His skin is red and horns appear on his forehead. I excuse myself and run back to my room and immediately look in the mirror. Am I changing? Is there a red tint now to my skin? I see a hint of horns and feel nubs on my head. OMG!

I run back to the dining room and scream at King, "I need to get out of this evil place, I'm changing physically. I'm not like you and I don't want to be!"

King stands up and says calmly, "Let's continue this conversation in the salon, shall we?"

The motley zoo continues attacking the third course of roast beef and never looks up. King follows me into the salon. We sit in the armchairs facing one another.

"I can see you're agitated. But you've just arrived and I was looking forward to spending some time with you. Certainly, you'll stay until your court date. Without a car, it's impossible up here, unfortunately. We can provide all your *creature* comforts." My head jerks back at this reference and his smug expression when emphasizing that word. He continues, "And Alex will be able to work with you on your project right here. He's anxious to get started. Alexa, it's very important to me that you stay. I'll hear no more talk of leaving."

"You're absurd. I would never stay here for six weeks. This place is too strange for me. And what's with the circus animals that came to dinner? I didn't see any cars drive up. Where did those *creatures* come from anyway?" I ask mocking his tone. "From that portal in your private quarters?"

"Ah, you went snooping around? I was hoping you would. Your curiosity and aggressive personality is what I admire in you. So you think there's some sort of portal in my private living room? Very astute. I can give you a personal tour," he says with a wide grin.

"I really have no interest in anything you want to show me, King. This place makes me very uncomfortable. *You* make me uncomfortable. I don't know what magic you performed on my own house but now that *house* makes me uncomfortable. In fact, it creeps me out. First thing in the morning, please have a car take me to the train. I have to leave tomorrow. I have urgent business in the city." I stand up to indicate this conversation is over.

"You mean Margaret Hathaway's funeral? That will be held at the weekend and besides, as I understand it, you wouldn't be welcome there," he says pointedly. He continues snidely, "Her parents blame you for the accident, n'est-ce pas? She was rushing up here to show you something because you finally reached out to her. Rushing to her death on that highway because you needed to see her after you hadn't spoken to her for weeks. Her loyalty knew no bounds. The moment you called her, she hastened to your aid. Nonetheless, such a horrible way to die. By its very definition, an accident cannot be your fault, my love. Although her parents most probably do not see it that way. My guess is that you would be made to feel quite uncomfortable at the funeral. Do you really want to put yourself through that, dearest?"

"Don't ever call me that. I'm not your dearest. I'd like to know how you came by that information about Margaret? I haven't spoken to anyone about it. I certainly don't want to discuss Margaret's funeral with you because you are the reason she's dead. She had some damning information about *you* she was frantic to show me. Her death was certainly not my fault and it was no accident. It was you who killed her. *It was you, you bastard!* Just like you killed Roseman!"

"Now wait a minute, Alexa. Let's not get carried away with accusations. Let's not make things unpleasant between us. If you want to leave tomorrow morning, of course you can. There's no need to take the train. I'll have my driver take you to your loft."

This shocks me. I didn't expect him to be agreeable. Then, he does something that makes me cringe. He walks over to me and pulls me up gently. Towering over me, he puts his arms around me and hugs me while kissing my forehead gently.

"Come. The chef has planned a wonderful dinner for us tonight. Take my arm and experience a meal you'll never forget."

"But what about all those *things* attending your Summer Fling? I really would rather not have dinner with them."

He snaps his fingers. "They're gone. I thought they would amuse you, as they do me. Oh, well. Shall we go back to the dining room?"

It's empty. Indeed, they're gone. As if they had never come. Just like Jewel explained. That in itself is unnerving. Were they really creations of King's imagination, or worse, undead slaves from the portal responding to his whims? The dining room is now set for two. Clean plates, as if we had not started dinner before. We sit together at one end of the enormous table and consume the meal in silence except for King making sounds of pleasure with every bite, interspersed with the words *delicious* and *quite tasty*, as he nods towards me for validation. I know he's trying to get me to lighten up, but I remain stony and stiff even though the meal is quite flavorful.

As our dinner progresses, my courage increases to hit him with a barrage of questions. For starters, how does he know my mother and what has he to do with this endless drought? The ever-gnawing question of his relationship to me is way too scary to broach right off the bat…the elephant in the room, so to speak, and smirk to myself looking at the herd of elephants in the painting behind him. But I plan to do it. Yes, I will ask. At some point before dessert. The servers come in and add two more places, in preparation for dessert. I look at King puzzled.

"Alex and Jewel will join us."

That's it. Now or never. Looking right into his eyes, I ask, "What is your relationship to my mother? How do you know her?"

"Oh…well…your mother… *hmm*. Why do you ask that?"

"I saw you together. In a dream of sorts. You and she through time. How is that possible?"

"Do you believe in the concept that we make our own reality? That sometimes what we think happens? Or in your case, write. We have the power to bring forth a world of our own making. A world populated by our thoughts. By people we have created with our imagination. You are very advanced, Alexa. More advanced than I had originally envisaged. There are many ways thoughts can become actual events. A dream can be a vehicle for these sorts of things."

"It wasn't really a dream but more like an experience. It occurred in a room that appeared out of nowhere down a flight of stairs to a basement in my house. But there's no staircase leading down from the ground floor because there's no basement. In that suddenly appearing basement was an exact replica of my childhood bedroom. There, I witnessed events, or scenes through time of you with my mother. And a child. Like a silent film."

"Yes, you definitely have a gift. I..." At that moment Alex and Jewel enter the room. "Yes, speaking of people that were formed from your conscious thought."

Alex and Jewel are holding hands and sit down staying close. Jewel is whispering in his ear. They both laugh. Seeing them cuddling each other and whispering at the table makes me so jealous I become nauseous. I certainly didn't create these people. Jewel wasn't an insatiable cougar or Alex a happy boy toy. Well, for starters, they weren't even in the same book. Disgusted, with them, disgusted with everything, I angrily push my chair back, stand up, and make ready to leave the room.

"Please stop getting so aggravated tonight, Alexa. It's becoming tiresome," says King. "We still have much to discuss. We'll have after dinner cordials back in the salon and have a nice chat. Please sit back down and enjoy your dessert." As an afterthought he adds, "Alex, Alexa needs to go to the city tomorrow morning. Would you mind driving her back to her loft?"

"You're leaving already?" he asks after he manages to extract himself from Jewel's embrace. "Oh that's a shame. I thought you would be staying a while and we could work on the script here. It's so convenient, you being such a short distance from my studio. We're already behind in our deadline goals. We shouldn't really delay any longer."

"What's the point? Trinity of Sixes Publishing has changed everything, so I don't even know what the book is about anymore."

"We'll figure it out together," he says.

Moving behind my chair and pushing it in for emphasis, I take a deep breath and say in the most offensive manner I can muster. "No, we won't figure anything out *together*. I want you all to listen very carefully. I'm done with everything here. D. O. N. E. Done! I'm not interested in pursuing anything. I don't want to work on any FUCKING script. In fact, let me make this perfectly clear. I don't care about the FUCKING contract. I. WANT. OUT! I want my life back. The life I had before, except now my best friend is dead! *DEAD!* DEAD! I can't even fucking believe it. So...final. I'll never see her again. Never hear her laugh again. So...all of you can just... FUCK OFF!"

King stands up and becomes taller than before, as tall as a tree dwarfing me. His increased stature makes me quiver in fear, tiny nothing that I am. "There's no need for such profanity, Alexa," he says in a very loud deep voice like the giant he's become. "We understand the anguish you feel over your loss. But you can't just walk away from your obligations. You think you can turn your back on arrangements that have already been made? And there's one important point that you have not addressed, my dear." Now he becomes normal sized and looks me right in the eye. A look of pure maliciousness connects to my core, as he says in an acid-toned voice, "You summoned me into your life."

"*What?*" I ask in an urgent whisper.

"That's right. You wanted me in your life and I have obliged. I have answered your desire for great wealth and fame. And quite frankly, I have been waiting a long time for this and am overjoyed that you have finally come around. I say again. It was you who summoned me, and as such, I remain. There's too much at stake now and too much invested. A lot of planning went into our covenant. Accept and enjoy the spoils. Now, please sit back down, Alexa, and let's partake in this fabulous *devil's* food confection," he says in a light-hearted manner and he winks at me as he sits back down.

Mollified and horrified about what he just said, I'm frozen. Summoned him? *How? When?* Suddenly, King looks up and mesmerizes me with his glowing eyes' stare. Thoughts flood my brain and I remember thinking that I'd give anything, do anything, to once again experience my initial success. Yes, those were my thoughts, just before Alex came into my life. His eyes hold me in their gaze. I succumb and submit. And sit back down. When dessert is finished, we make our way to the salon. King is very animated and asks Alex and Jewel to give us some time alone. They willingly oblige. Alex winks and looks knowingly at me when he says he looks forward to our drive to the city. What a cad he is, but I'm just too wooden and depressed to care. Can't I just *undo* this summoning? There must be a way. I know there's a riddle here that I must uncover. And what does my mother have to do with this?

I'm still so confused.

Chapter Sixteen

The big reveal

Even though my aggressiveness has waned, has been assuaged probably by King's metaphysical power over me when his eyes bored into mine, I remain curious.

"Tell me, King, what is my mother's involvement in all of this? How do you know her?" I ask him, as he pours me a brandy and motions for me to sit down again in one of two comfy armchairs in the salon that face each other.

"Your mother and I have known each other a very long time."

"Centuries?"

"One could say that."

"How's that possible?"

"The bending or warping of space-time is how it's referred to now, which as you know, is your mother's field of study at the moment. She was enthralled that science finally caught up to our reality, hers and mine."

"So tell me then, is she one of your...demons or whatever you call them? A ridiculous notion because she doesn't have a mean bone in her body. She's sweet and her only flaw might be she's too focused on her work. But certainly, she's nothing like a disciple of yours."

"Alexa, eternal life is seductive. I mean real life on this plane. Not in some religious sense. I offer that to some people along with all the comforts to enjoy life to the fullest because we all learn too quickly that life is short, *tempus fugit*, as the Romans said. Others repay me in the traditional way and dwell in the regions described in Dante's Inferno," he laughs heartily with a glint of humor in his eyes. He continues, "Your mother was just a child when we first met and quite poor. In that period in history, if you weren't nobility, landed gentry, your life was worthless with no hope for change. Income inequality was much more rigid than now, no fluidity. If you were born poor that's how you stayed, no dot com child billionaires. All wealth was inherited. Before that, wealth came through conquest. I did very well back then as I am expecting to do so now with the social unrest brought on by the same inequalities.

"When the poor see what they're missing, they'll do just about anything to change that situation for themselves. Crime, drugs to numb their emotions, or make a pact with *me*. Well, not all, of course. But enough for my amusement. Throughout history, the unfortunates have caused social upheaval, civil war, and the like. The new leaders become what they once reviled and the cycle continues. Even a large number of the monied class live in fear of losing their wealth or are always hungering for more, never satiated. In fact, they are easier to turn than the unfortunates. Some of my Summer Fling attendees belong in that category, as you might have guessed. You might recognize those traits in yourself, I might add." He winks at me and then claps his hands together, "What fun I've had through the centuries and my stable of followers is quite impressive both in number and the status of those who have willingly become my votary."

"Please, stop, don't lump me in with your Fling degenerates. It's extremely disturbing to me to think my insecurities brought me here, to the situation I now find myself. But, also, I don't want to hear your philosophy on the human race. You're *subhuman*. A scourge on humanity. The lowest of the low."

"Thank you, dear, for the compliment. But the greediness of humans created me and not the other way around."

Greed created *him? Preposterous!* I continue, "If my mother belongs to your live-forever acolytes, why is she off contemplating the origins of the universe and not living in that hole in your private quarters?" I'm extremely reluctant to ask this, but I must. "How do I fit in? Why were we all together as a *family?* Are...we a...family? If that was me I saw in those scenes in my creepy basement, why don't I remember my previous lives?" Before he can answer, I add, "And I have feelings of empathy. I care about people and would never consider enslaving anyone for my own enhancement and amusement. You disgust me at the very fiber of my being."

"Okay, let's not be so harsh, my dear. I will answer your questions. Firstly, your mother. She is special to me and as such has been allowed to follow her own path. This recent life, she asked to be totally autonomous. Created an identity for herself that guaranteed some government support at first, so she could start her career on her own merits after she graduated. Although, I've kept an eye on her and tweaked things a bit to make her academic hurdles easier, but don't tell her. As long as she's willing to be my companion, keep me in her life, or I should say, *lives,* I let her fly, from time to *time,*" he chuckles. "Contrary to all conventional wisdom, I do have a heart and for some unexplained reason, your mother fulfills my needs. Call it love, maybe." I'm shocked and filled with revulsion to hear him say that.

"Please, King, I'm not a complete idiot."

"Haven't you heard the myth, that I'm a fallen angel? Well, there's some truth to that and probably the reason you have been estranged from me until now. You have some of that spark of goodness and decency. On the insistence of your mother, I gave you the ability to choose your destiny all these centuries when you came of age. You always chose a different path from working with me, a path, most distastefully, of helping others. You've been a nurse in two world wars, an anthropologist, a teacher, among other socially conscious endeavors. In truth, I thought you were a lost cause until you chose to be writer in this life. And you haven't disappointed, having all the traits that put you in my crosshairs, so to speak.

"Anxiety, competitiveness, jealousy, depression, neurotic self-doubt with its cousin delusions of grandeur, and, of course, avarice, all made you an easy target. Had you chosen to be, to coin a phrase, a celebrity whore on a reality show or sought public office, it would have been even easier, but I digress. In short, ego and greed form the personalities of most players in these pursuits, and, so finally, you came back into the fold. I couldn't be happier. Your life will be big, Alexa, huge beyond your wildest dreams. Everything you've ever wanted will be there for the taking. All I want from you in return is to stand beside me, acknowledge me, be a part of my life, all of them for eternity. Not at all what others had to pledge."

"But I don't want the big life anymore. I want my old life back before you existed for me. I want to erase the memory of you, like it was before you say I summoned you. Please let me go. One life is enough for me. Let me go...forever, I beg you."

"Oh no, no, no. Never, my darling. You're family. It's too late. I should have done this long ago, brought you into my life. I see now what I have missed all this time. So just stop this nonsense."

"Isn't Jewel your daughter? Won't she do?"

He sighs, "Jewel. She's nothing. A fabrication to make a point. The manifestation of one of your characters. Now you know how powerful thought can be. The notion of creating your own reality is very exhilarating for a writer."

"But except for her appearance, she's nothing like the character I created. And I didn't call her Jewel."

King shrugs his shoulders, "People change, and, yes, sometimes our creations are stubborn in exploring their own identity. Haven't you ever had a character change their name in your writing? You know, when you sit down to continue where you left off and another name for your character pops into your head?"

That just happened with my Trilogy. Jodie was originally Donna.

Strangeness just gets stranger. King's world is too unsettling. I have to stop this weirdness *but how can I?* My mind races to try and devise a way out of this entrapment. I need to know everything, so I can figure out my escape. "You said greed created you. How and why is that?"

"All life on this planet is greedy. Even plant life will succumb to invasive species. Survival of the fittest is all about greed. You see it everywhere in nature. Invasive species takeover the habitats of native species. Swallow them up, so to speak, and so they die off. Kudzu in the Southern states has choked off natural vegetation. Brown tree snakes introduced accidentally in Guam have caused the extinction of native birds. And so on and so forth. For humans greed is an art form.

"They have created proxies for their greed and called them corporations. Destroying this planet is a sideshow to their lust for wealth. In this lifetime, I can just sit back and relax and be entertained. Greed feeds me. I get stronger. The proliferation of greed increases my ability to enforce my will. My existence is the embodiment, the realization of that greed. The intrinsic force of humanity is its greed, rapacity, and avarice. I'm here to ensure it hums along, is not quashed, and fulfills its manifest destiny."

"Not all humans are like that. There are many selfless humans. Religious and secular. Activists who fight unselfishly for human rights. Sacrifice their lives if needs be."

"Ah, religion. How perfect. Even in this century, religious zealots do my work for me. Throughout history, the massacres in the name of religion have been genius. I realize that there is no universal statement one can make concerning religion. Unfortunately for me, there is the odd outlier, saintly personality. But mostly it's about slaughter, stealing property, and power. Power as a vehicle to feed the avarice of those who rule. I have enjoyed the spectacle. Of course, humans have devised all sorts of reasons for combat of which religion is just one. But conquest is all about greed, the underlying uniformity of greed, making what I do exceedingly simple."

"And what is it you do?"

"I collect evil doers. Perpetrators. Perps, in the current vernacular. Boardroom members who sanction products created by corporations that are purposely addictive. Members of organizations that foster race hatred through propaganda and violence. Neglectful parents who basically put loaded guns in the hands of children. Blackmailers, pedophiles, pimps, rapists, murderers. I could go on and on. And when I've gathered them, their souls become part of my vast network of laborers who do my bidding." And with a twinkle in his beastly yellow eyes, he adds laughing, "Mine forever, no union, no minimum wage."

Once he stops laughing, he says very pointedly, "You've seen them in the city, on the island, and here. They are the staff that has made you so very comfortable. But my reach is not just for providing domestic servants, you also see them in government. Take a good look next time the U.S. Congress is in session and see if you can pick them out. It's quite an achievement how much I've infiltrated the legislative process and something of which I am most proud. And not just in this country but here is where I have the most fun. Anything else you'd like to know?"

"What about all those pamphlets in the conference room? Are you trying to make this planet uninhabitable for humans? Won't that defeat your mission, if there are no longer people? Mass extinction of our species, how can that benefit you?"

"Ah yes, I was expecting that question. Well, you see, Alexa, climate change with its droughts, floods, and rising sea levels creates chaos. And chaos is good for business, one could say. Also, the seas are being overfished and becoming polluted with mercury and detritus, especially plastic, and no government is willing to even slow it down. But, if programs spring up like the ridiculous climate change summit that happened recently to thwart the impending mass extinction of marine life, among other irreversible events, well, we need to develop a strategy to stop it. You see, when humans with their incessant need to acquire money and power actually destroy their habitat, and they eventually will, I'll just take my business elsewhere. Find another place in the cosmos to set up shop. I've done it before.

"Mars, for example, used to be teeming with life. You saw some of my collection of life-forms from around the universe at the soirée. And as some archaeologists believe, the Earth had a massive extinction of humans when the northern and southern magnetic poles switched positions millions of years ago, as they are in the process of doing now. However, humanity is very tenacious and managed to thrive again, as I can attest to, having been there. So you see, I'm always seeking opportunities to wreak havoc, either making things happen for my benefit or adding a tweak here and there as they unfold in my favor. What? You've gone white."

"So those things at your soiree were not figments of your imagination, like Jewel told me? And you really did kill Margaret and Roseman too, didn't you?"

"Dearest. There's no difference between real or imaginary when I'm in charge. As far as accusing me of murder, Alexa, accidents happen. Random events just happen. You yourself met a stranger in a bar, didn't you? And then put yourself in some danger? It turned out fine, no harm done, but it could have turned out differently. The world is a scary place and I thrive on that. But having said that, I'm sorry for your loss, really I am. However, both of them would have held you back from your destiny. So things really do happen for the best."

"Certainly not for *them*," I say emphatically while feeling awkward that he knew about my random sexual encounter. Or was my evil self engineered somehow by King bleeding through that night? Is that why I became so strange then?

"Anything else? I can tell you're not finished."

"Why don't I know you? Why don't I know this?"

"Your mother's idea. As I said, this time she wanted to make it on her own. Didn't want to *ride on my coattails* is how she put it. She's become quite the modern Western woman."

"Was anyone going to tell me the truth about who I am?"

"Didn't need to. Today's conversation was waiting to happen. But I tweaked that a little as well by revealing truths to you with scenes from your past lives in the basement I conjured up for you. It was getting tiresome to have you be so hostile to me."

I become quiet taking in all this information and sit stone-faced for several minutes thinking. This is an identity crisis of epic proportions. The devil is in the details, as they say, and the Devil is my...*father*. His lifestyle is lavish, the luxury with which he surrounds himself is like a venture capitalist billionaire. His mansions, private island, and probably prime real estate in all the major cities of the world. He probably owns a sports team and a casino in Vegas. Can I really turn my back on that? I'm royalty of the underworld. As repulsive as that is, it's also seductive. My success as a writer would be unmatched. Would last long after I left this life for the next one. Forever. King breaks my reverie.

"I see you are lost in thought. What is it?"

"Well, I do have one last question. Aren't there good people? People who can't be turned? Like my friend, Kip for example? Unless he's one of yours, as Jewel implied."

"Oh, yes. I have my enemies, the angelic rabble. I always must be on my guard to outsmart them. The eternal battle between good and evil. So far, I've been quite successful."

"How?"

"That information will have to wait for another time. We'll continue this heart-to-heart later. Come, Alexa, let's have a toast to celebrate your new life of fame and fortune."

"Have a drink? Well, I've noticed your drinks seem to be laced with something. Drugs to elicit feelings of euphoria. Why do you need to do that if everything is so great?"

"Why not? Why focus on the negative when your focus can be on the things that make you happy. Be happy. Enjoy your life and stay blissful. You can reach that state through meditation and denial of the physical or...you can just have a drink with me."

I look directly at King, as he motions to me to have that toast, and raises his glass. Our eyes lock and his ability to mesmerize me takes hold. I realize, he never answered my question about Kip. I take a sip. And then another. The familiar feeling of euphoria immediately starts flowing through my blood stream. King gets up and walks over to me with a look of tenderness on his face.

"We had such fun, you and I. At that park with the carriages. It was such a great memory that I showed you. Let's hug and be family again."

I stand up and when he hugs me there's such a feeling of elation and a sense of belonging. He said family. This is who I am, according to him. I don't have the guts or desire, at the moment, to embrace that fully. To interpret the implications of what this means at a cellular level. I desperately need to talk to my mother...and soon. When we part and I'm about to walk back to my room, he says, "I'll have your mother come see you in New York."

How the hell can he do that? I laugh to myself at the pun.

And then I know, I've really lost my mind.

Chapter Seventeen

Back in NYC

Pressing the dimmer switch that darkens or lightens my windows by degrees to either block out the daylight sun or city nighttime lights, I squint at the brightness. The neighboring windows bounce beams of sunlight into my sleep-gorged eyes. Rooftops and clear-blue sky are just as pleasing to me as leafy trees and flowers. It's good to be back in the city. The total blackout option for the windows gave Alex and me just the right sense of isolation we craved when we first got here. Sipping on the latte that Alex brought me before he left this morning, I survey the view as I contemplate the last two days. King saw us off and made sure I had a case of Good Health Water to get me through the funeral and any other tough issues. Alex had a good laugh, as he put the case in the trunk of his Porsche.

Racing down the highway, absent patrol cars, was just what I needed after all the confusion roiling around in my brain. The wind whipping my hair into a tornadic mess while the warm sun bathed my face put me a numbed state that was cathartic. When, at last, we pulled up to my loft building, William gave me a warm "hello" and told me I'd been missed. He tipped his hat at Alex and told him he'd put the car in my garage spot and bring up my luggage and such. Initially, I was afraid that I had grown horns and a tail, but to William I was just the same Ms. Wainwright.

My loft was also just the same. How I missed this place. It felt like years instead of a few weeks. I walked around throwing loving eyes on all my stuff. I looked at the view from my living room and remembered the day of the weird lightning bolt and Margaret bringing Alex. Margaret. Uncontrollable tears. Deep sorrow. I grabbed a tissue and sat down. Sobbing because it really was my fault. Alex held me, letting me sob on his shoulder. He comforted me like that for several minutes and I was grateful for his sensitivity. I needed that. Needed him.

"Come," he said as he lifted me up, and we retreated to my bedroom where we stayed until this morning. I was hoping he would go with me to the funeral, but no, Jewel called. He took the call, which in itself aggravated me, and she told him she was back in the city and for him to meet her. He looked at me embarrassed but told me he had to go and then he jumped in the shower.

"I was hoping you'd come with me to the funeral," I say playing the guilt card, while he's toweling off. He's an Adonis in the bright light of the bathroom. "It's going to be tough for me. Tell her you're busy. Tell her you're with me."

"I can't explain my situation with Jewel very well except to say that I feel very protective of her. We have a strong kinship and I never want to upset her. It's not logical, but nevertheless, ever since I first met her something took hold of me. Of course, I'd prefer to be with you, Alexa. But I have no choice. Sometimes I feel very trapped, but I can't change things. She knows it and uses it."

"That's just stupid. The only thing you have in common with her is that I created you both."

He stops toweling off and stares at me in disbelief. "That's a very bizarre comment. Why would you say something so odd? How could you have created us?"

"I don't want to get into that right now. Can you pick me up a latte from next door before you leave?" I roll over and fall back asleep and awaken when he kisses my forehead and sets down the coffee on my nightstand. As he tiptoes out of the room to rush over to Jewel, I say in my groggy voice, "Thanks for the coffee and drop dead." And suddenly I hear a crash in the living room. Oh no! I don't want that! King said... "Alex!" I scream and I'm about to jump out of bed when he pokes his head in the doorway.

"Sorry, I tripped on the hassock that was sticking out. Did you say something?"

"Thanks for the coffee," I say feeling stupid.

"Happy to do it. I'll call later." And he's gone.

That was very odd. The coincidence of Alex falling down at the moment I told him to drop dead. King said that my thoughts can make things happen. He also said that Jewel and Alex had been formed from my consciousness. But Jewel said the way my characters appear to me is my unique interpretation. I remember my weird experience in Battery Park, Jodie springing to life. So did my made-up character Alex almost really drop dead when I said that? *Hmm.* I sit back on the pillows and sip my latte. But they certainly don't act like the characters I wrote. This conundrum really disturbs me. *Do I have the power to create reality or not?*

If I could create reality, I would write Margaret back into it. I would write that by a miracle she weaved away from the truck in front. So I find a pencil and paper and write that down. And I wait. Then I run to front door and grab my daily newspaper left on my lobby table. Furiously flipping the pages until I come to the announcements, I scan the list and then see it. Margaret Hathaway funeral service today, 1:00 pm the Cathedral of St. John the Divine. Damn it. My heart is racing. I had so hoped I could fix it. *What to do about all this?* My mood is full of so much dread and fear. But it's clear that I'm adjusting to my new life. Accepting my changed circumstances. Even without the euphemistic Good Health Water. Perhaps, though, I need a sip or two before I go to the funeral. I need to prepare myself emotionally.

As I luxuriate in my bath after downing an entire bottle of "water" in practically one gulp, I feel so much better. My thoughts move to my wild and crazy sexcapade with Alex these last two days. Constantly on the verge of exploding in ecstasy, it was beyond anything I've ever experienced. He just keeps getting better at what turns me on. Does he do that for Jewel? That sours my high somewhat and a kernel of a thought flashes through my mind. If I really created Jewel, maybe I can uncreate her. She's annoying, not really King's daughter, and has definitely outworn her welcome.

She shouldn't have that much control over Alex. She certainly won't be missed. My powers might only extend to those characters I created. Okay. It's worth a shot. I try and remember the scene where I killed her before but it's vague. I check the time, and set the scene as happening right now. Alex had told me she was shopping at her favorite stores and would meet him at King's. I towel off and sit down at my computer and this time I write:

Rushing to meet her lover, Jewel pauses at the corner of Fifth Avenue and 57th street to wait for the light to change and wipes her brow. The noonday heat is piercing and the crushing crowds on Fifth Avenue are just as one would expect at lunchtime. Bedecked in her signature white attire, her silky platinum hair is as white as her blouse and makes her appear cool and fresh to the idle passerby. But she is agitated and quite overheated with the mob at the sale and the crowds in the street. As she enters the crosswalk, one of her Bergdorf Goodman bags is knocked out of her hands by the onslaught of the teeming hordes and tumbles under the rear fender of a car stopped for the light. Quickly, it's snatched up by a disheveled street person who then races down the block knocking people aside as he hurries to get away.

Frozen in the crosswalk watching her $1000 silk shirt being ripped off by the opportunistic immoral stranger, she doesn't realize the light has changed and the cars have begun to move. Furiously honking horns cause her to become disoriented, so she doesn't notice an oncoming taxi driven by a harried and tired cabbie anxious to get home from a long double shift jockeying around the traffic to make the light. Only after her smashed, limp body gets caught under the chassis and is dragged across the intersection, *does he realize what he's done. She's pronounced dead at the scene.*

Done. I have to hurry to make the funeral on time. So I put on my black dress and have William hail me a cab to take me way up town to 115th Street and Amsterdam Ave. We sail up the West Side Highway arriving with time to spare, as a large crowd of people slowly and solemnly enter the church. There's quite a large group of the Hathaway's social set and quite a large turnout of young men and women who probably were Margaret's school chums and friends. Quite surprising to me, because I always thought she was a loner being at my beck and call.

People are milling about in the hallway offering each other condolences before entering the sanctuary. Special hugs and kisses are extended to a forlorn young man who swallows hard and blinks away tears. *She had a boyfriend?* How awful for him. Suddenly someone taps me on the arm and whispers, "Aren't you Alexa Wainwright?" Thinking that this person knew that Margaret worked for me, I answer, "Yes...and I'm so sorry for..." before I realize what's happening the group of twenty somethings crowds around me asking for my autograph and in hushed tones inform me they are fans of my latest sensuous *Darkside* trilogy. "What? What are you saying? Sensuous?"

Before I can find out anything, we are ushered into the service. Margaret's parents are sitting in the first pew and Mrs. Hathaway is sobbing. She stands up to speak to the priest and turns to look at the people filing into the sanctuary. At that moment our eyes meet and she loses it, screaming at me. "You killed her! You killed her! It's because of you that she's dead. I told you not to come to the funeral. Why are you here? Get out. Get out!"

I wanted to scream back at her that I loved Margaret. That I had no idea...what would happen...an unforeseen accident, but instead I push through the crowd behind me and run out. Before I hit the hallway, I think I spy Kip sitting in a pew. *Was that really Kip?* But I can't turn back because of all the commotion I've caused. I hope he'll follow me out. As I reach the outside steps, there's a crowd on the street. They surround me begging for an autograph or take a picture.

Someone holds a book for me to sign. *What the...? The Darkside Trilogy: Blood, Sweat, and Tears* with a provocative cover. I grab the book. The cover art shows the back of long, slender, naked legs in an upside down V-stance with feet shod in stiletto heels. The legs frame a bare-chested male wearing jodhpurs and boots seated crossed-legged in an armchair placed at a slight distance in front of the unknown woman. Smiling lustily, he holds a riding crop in one hand. The subtitle is *Tears*.

No amount of happy juice can overcome the shock of this travesty. I throw the book into the crowd and someone yells, "Hey, don't do that!"

As I run down the street, I try to make sense of this. That scary editor, Malachite, and her evil mouth said they had already edited the trilogy and made it erotic, perverted. *A fait accompli!* Seeing the printed book brings up my bile. The truth of that is just too much to take. *Son of a bitch!* I don't want to be known as a porn writer. A city bus drives by and there's my photo and the book cover on the side of the bus. *International Sensation!* I hail a cab and head home feeling disgusted and thinking about that scene at the funeral. What *was* that? Did her mother really think I wouldn't come to Margaret's funeral? I loved her. Oh god, Margaret. My stomach clenches at the thought. I need to drink the case of Good Health Water right now.

I ponder the magnitude of being an *international sensation.* That's what I wanted. Groupies following me and wanting photos and autographs. That's what I wanted. Maybe. Maybe I can deal. After all, I really didn't write it. Trinity's crew did. I probably should read it. See what they did. No…no. I'll just collect the checks. But everyone sees my picture. Knows my name. Thinks I wrote it. I need a trip back to the island or at least go to Misty Falls. Get out of this city. I hate it here, now! And I have to find Kip. He'll give me good advice. And Mom. The Mom I knew all my life, before King ruined it with the crap he told me.

When we get to my building, there's a throng of women of various ages milling about. "Go around to the back entrance," I yell at the driver. Once there, I crouch down and hurriedly put the numbers in the keypad to unlock the door. Before I can open it, a group of teenage girls encircles me asking me to sign my book, shoving it into my face. *What the…?* It's a different book. The cover art displays a vampire with mouth wide open about to bite the neck of a sexy looking woman. She's wearing a dress from the 1800's showing cleavage and they are in front of a grand estate under a full moon. The title reads *Darkside Trilogy: Blood, Sweat, and Tears* with the subtitle, *Blood.* Oh my god! As I try to open the door another book is shoved in my face. "Please sign this, I love your work," says a girl of around fifteen. A different cover.

This time the artwork shows a crumbling university campus surrounded by a dried-out landscape with blaring hot sun. A clan of zombies in the background is shuffling toward the ruined buildings, while in the forefront, a normal looking woman in torn clothing, her breasts partially exposed, and with an expression of abject fear looks on from a safe distance. The subtitle is *Sweat.* Okay. I get it. Erotica, or rather, porn, monsters, and dystopia.

Malachite and her devil crew gave me the impression that was for future projects, but I guess not. All the crap that beats out literature of high quality is now my new brand. This is how low I've sunk. They certainly know how to work fast; I'll give them that. I sign the book and enter the building. So all my heroines are victims now like Jodie in *Darkside*, instead of being empowered and strong? That disgusts me to my core. The *final edits* clause has been the price paid, the retribution, for lusting after fame and fortune. I certainly got what I wished for, noting the swarming crowd of fans. At least the books are not all S&M porn, like I originally thought.

But who knows, unless I read them.

Chapter Eighteen

Mom, Alex, and Kip in that order

Once in my loft, I grab a large envelope lying on my lobby table and breathe a sigh of relief. I really don't enjoy the attention of mobs. Who would? Is that the shower running? "Alex?" I call out. But it can't be him. He doesn't have a key. So then I get nervous. A crazy stalker? Carefully, I walk into the guest bathroom and peek inside.

"Mom! When…how…did?"

"Hey, hon, wait a sec," she stops me, "I'll be right out."

Boy, have I missed her. I call down to the concierge and order a giant quantity of her favorite Chinese dishes. Humming, I set the table. My mom finally being here overshadows my awful afternoon. Then, I open the envelope sent by a delivery service. This is it. Money has been transferred into my new Trinity bank account that I can access with the ATM card enclosed. The money is guaranteed and insured by the bank for the multiple millions that's in there. It will earn ten percent if I choose to put some in savings. The checking account will earn five percent. *Really?* No bank offers that much interest today.

Ten percent of millions is a lot of money. So it's like as fast as I spend it, it will grow back through interest to the original amount. I like that. I look at the zeros. My trilogy has already earned back the advance and there are additional royalties. My head is spinning. Here's the reward. Rich. Rich beyond my wildest dreams. I look at the ATM card that looks like all other ones out there. No one would know the vast amount of money this accesses. I'm given a pin number that I can change at a machine or online. The bank has arrangements with all other banks, so there is no extra charge to draw money out. As if that matters at this level of cash. King thinks of everything. So now he owns the banking industry?

As I'm daydreaming of how to spend this windfall, Mom enters the room looking fabulous. "Oh that hot shower was divine. It's been so long since I had one." With perfect timing the food is delivered. "Oh, you ordered Chinese? How wonderful. The food there is awful. It's been ages since I had anything good to eat," she says, "and these are some of my favorite dishes. You are such a sweet child to remember." We catch up while stuffing mouthfuls of dim sum, fried rice, and egg foo young into our mouths. Mom makes sounds of pleasure with each bite.

"How's the universe?" I ask facetiously.

"So many exciting discoveries. We're seeing things on Mars that perhaps give clues life once thrived there."

Wow, just like King told me. "And you, Mom. How are you?"

"Never better. How's the book deal coming?"

"You don't know? I thought you spoke to King."

"Who? Oh, by the way, why didn't you answer your phone this morning? I called to let you know I was coming."

I grab my phone and turn the sound back on. "I had to go to a funeral, so I turned the ringer off."

"A funeral? I'm so sorry. Anyone I know?"

"Yes." And my voices catches when I say, "Margaret, my assistant. A tragic car accident." My phone displays two missed calls and one voicemail from Alex. "Excuse me, Mom. I have to listen to this."

"My god Alexa," says a hysterical sounding Alex. "Why don't you answer your phone or your texts? Something awful has happened." *A bad feeling swamps me.* "It's Jewel. She was killed in a horrific accident on Fifth Avenue. Run over by a taxi. Terrible. Terrible. King is coming to the city to help me make all the arrangements. I don't know when I'll be able to get back to you." End of message. Oh…my…god. It worked. My experiment worked. Now, I'm a murderer.

"Is everything okay? You've turned pale and look quite frightened."

"Have we lived for centuries? Is Satan my father?" I blurt out in a panic.

"Sweetheart, whatever are you talking about? What nonsense is filling your head? What's that paper you were looking at when I came in here?"

So I show her my millions. "Oh my," she says. "Let's do something fun. I'm only here for a couple of days and then I must get back. Call the Red Door and set up spa treatments for today and then let's go shopping tomorrow."

"Mom, can you please answer my question?"

"Stop it, Gladys. Don't be absurd."

She hasn't called me Gladys since I changed my name. That was strange. But I drop it. I want her to be my old mom. Not the weird, century hopping, devil-loving, mom. We change into comfortable clothes for our spa treatments. There's one on Fifth Avenue and one at Union Square. For obvious reasons, I steer clear of Fifth Avenue. We order ultimate facials, massages, and spa manicures and pedicures. Since it closes at 9:00 pm, there's enough time for us going so late in the day. I put away the left-over Chinese and we leave. As soon as we enter the spa, the soft music and dim lighting puts us at ease. We are both whisked away separately for our services. Not the mother and daughter experience for which I had hoped. But being by myself did give me time to think about all that had happened on this most unusual day.

Basically, I can kill people. People that spring from the pages of my books. I could kill Alex, if I wanted, or King's chef in his NYC mansion. If I can kill them, can I also make them come back to life? I mean Jewel was annoying, but still what I did to her was beyond awful. In the waiting area after my facial and drinking water before my massage, I decide to try another experiment. I grab some note paper and a pen that's available for customers to write reviews.

This time I write a different scene. Jewel still is being robbed, but this time, there's a decent young guy witnessing the perpetrator going for the bag. He grabs it from the guy before it can be whisked away and gallantly hands it back to Jewel while the would-be thief flees down the street. A thankful Jewel and her shirt make it across the street before the light changes. And then I wait. After my massage, I check my phone. Alex's message is still there. Not good. My stomach does flips. I really killed her. Staring at my phone, and for no particular reason, I decide to listen to his morbid message again. "Hi Sweetie. Sorry I had to run out on you this morning. I hope you got through the funeral okay. I'll call soon."

The message changed. Jewel is not dead. I undid it. I brought her back to life. The incident erased. I sigh in relief. I'm omnipotent. I'm powerful, but within limits. Only for those I created with my words. How I wish, I could bring back Margaret. The rest of my spa experience flies by on champagne bubbles of joyful relaxation. I didn't like being a murderer. Satan's spawn is a decent human being. I have free will. This puts me more at ease.

"Wasn't that great, Mom? I'm feeling so relaxed now. I have a grand idea. Instead of going shopping for clothes tomorrow, let me buy you a Park Avenue apartment. I certainly can afford it, and it would be a great investment for me. Why don't you call Jerry and have him join us?"

"Jerry? Oh right, Jerry. No, let's just be the two of us for this short visit." She doesn't want to see Jerry? Maybe it's over. None of her beaus lasts very long, but I wonder why she never mentioned it. We go to bed early exhausted from being so relaxed and have breakfast at my favorite deli. I tell her about the great success of the trilogy but not all of it. Why ruin the day by hashing out all the stuff that makes me uncomfortable? I do admit I have a new publisher and that editorial made some changes to the narrative. Substantial changes that are appealing to a readership I hadn't reached before. That was true. I ask, tentatively, "So about that little outburst I had yesterday...do you know King Blakemore?"

"Can't say that I do. Why?"

"He owns the publishing house, Trinity of Sixes."

"Odd name." And then she quickly changes the subject. "I'm so enjoying this breakfast. This bacon is yummy. Haven't had a breakfast like this in ages."

"Are your accommodations there adequate? You seem to have been deprived of many normal things. Like a good hot shower and basic breakfast food."

"We are like astronauts in training, hon."

"Is that what you're doing?"

"It's all hush-hush. Can't say anymore. So what's on the agenda for today?"

"Don't you remember? We're going house hunting. We're meeting the realtor at our first stop in an hour. Park avenue and fifty-seventh street is a brand new luxury building with great amenities. Then we'll look at some pre-war co-ops. I told her my budget was 17 million for at least three beds and three baths and updated kitchen."

"Gladys, that's ridiculous. I don't belong in such a fancy building. I'm too middle class and I like it that way. Spend your money on yourself. You deserve it. I'm perfectly happy where I am and it's near campus."

"Humor me. It'll be fun. And why are you calling me Gladys all of a sudden. I changed my name years ago."

"Oh, did I? Sorry, I didn't realize. Okay, let's go and pretend we're part of the wealthy elite."

The first building is near Saks and I impulsively decide to stop and buy her a pair of comfortable, and kind of sexy, ballet flats. Traipsing around all day in her signature heels would be painful, I tell her. She protests at first then finally agrees. An unexpected surprise. A giant shoe sale. Frantically grabbing shoes off the rack, we're tickled at the marked down prices. $200 reduced to $25. *Practically free,* we both shout simultaneously. Laughing and having fun, like the good old days. Just a mom and her daughter spending time together shopping. How I've missed that lately. I hate her secretive government assignment. I want her just to be a professor, not an astronaut, so I can see her more often. But I'm super proud of her and it would be amazing, if she actually went into space.

We load up on shoes. At first, she protests because there's not enough room in her government-issued housing. When I tell her there's plenty of room to store them in my apartment, she goes nuts. Lots of shoes for her tiny feet are available. My size not so much, enough though for me to have fun. We do a lot of damage in a short period, but still have to race to make the appointment with the realtor. I arrange to have the shoes delivered to my loft. Sweet.

We spend the rest of the day looking at real estate and it's a huge eye opener. It seems in NYC, $45 million, my entire nest egg at the moment, is still not enough for some of the fabulous properties on the market. The first stop is a brand new condo building. Way over my budget, available units on the high floors start at $22 million with property taxes and fees of about $10,000 a month. One can see the entire landscape of the city from the numerous picture windows. All of Central Park is the view while taking a bath, the expanse of Manhattan bordered by the East River when relaxing in bed, and the Hudson River and most of the West Side while reading a newspaper in the living room. It was like being in your own personal castle in the sky. Its steel and marble kitchen made my head spin. My loft felt dated in comparison.

Next we go to an art deco gem on Central Park West where a duplex lists for $60 million. Lots of square footage and beautiful outdoor spaces that overlook Central Park. These older places have loads of character and enormous rooms. Plaster ornaments abound on the walls and ceilings. Smaller units in my price range just didn't do it for me. Bottom line, I needed more money. Caroline, my eager real estate agent, was very dejected that we didn't make any offers. I tell her that as soon as my royalties begin to flow, I'll call her. But she knows loyalty in her business is a scarce commodity. My mother liked her though. She was also petite and so they were eye level to each other, both having to tilt their heads back to talk to me. Quite funny.

Afterwards, Mom and I go to The Russian Tea Room for an early dinner. We had gone there once several years ago to celebrate her successful defense of her doctoral dissertation. It had been exhilarating to have her finally acknowledge the heritage she had mostly eschewed. We had to be frugal back then, so we only ate borscht. Since we don't have to be frugal anymore, and remembering that wonderful evening coupled with my new found curiosity about her background, I suggest we go there.

She loved the idea and was exuberant. The Tea Room's main dining area hadn't changed at all. It still had red leather booths with gold wood trim and gold trim on the decorative wall treatments. Memories of being there bring a wisp of sadness. My normal, innocent life, before King. Surprisingly, my mother speaks some Russian to the waiters after she winks at me. Only words, no sentences. Flirting with them in her native tongue, she laughs when they start rambling away and she can't answer. I'm so glad to feel connected to something real, to be there with her, to watch her have fun.

"Order anything you want," I tell her. Surprisingly, she seems confused about what to get and brushes it off by saying she's not really familiar with these fancy dishes. "Besides," she says, "after so many years of looking at the stars, I haven't thought much about food." I order for us. Blinis, pancakes that you fill with caviar, and, of course, borscht. As an afterthought, I add a bottle of Champagne. She's leaving in the morning, so tonight's a goodbye celebration.

"Let's toast to your new digs as soon as I get my next big royalty check," I tell her and we clink our champagne glasses. After we eat, the owner, who overheard my mother speaking a few Russian words, gives us a tour of the restaurant's ballrooms for private parties. Reminiscent of over-the-top elaborate Russian palaces from photos I'd seen in my quest to connect to my heritage while in college, they're decorated with golden candelabra chandeliers, chairs painted gold, enormous banquet tables, mirrored walls, and red ceilings. Bright red and gold, a combination that cheers the soul.

An idea had been forming as we ate. I would sell my loft and buy myself a new place in that pre-war Art Deco gem and a townhouse for my mother near her campus. It motivated me to start my next book. Since Trinity changes my work to suit its own needs, all I have to do is create a rough draft. Let them do what they want. My inner calling to be a writer has been hijacked, so now all I want is a privileged lifestyle and to collect the checks. Even if it becomes known as shiterature, as some bestselling pap is currently described. Money heals all embarrassments.

In the morning, we have a traditional cup of Russian tea, a quick kiss and then she's gone. I sit here musing about our visit. Something was off. Why did she keep calling me Gladys? I worried about her faculties but she was doing heavy-lifting brain work in her science career, so that couldn't be it. It was rather odd she didn't seem to know what to order in the restaurant. She didn't want to see Jerry, never called him. She said she would be back at the end of the summer in time to teach the fall semester. I'll reassess the situation when she comes back.

Because of what happened after the funeral, staying here in the city, with my new notoriety, is out of the question. I made sure I looked nothing like my book-cover headshot when I went out with my mother. A few teeny boppers were hanging around in front of my building, but we immediately grabbed a cab and left. Before I call Alex to drive me back to Misty Falls, there's one more thing I've got to get done. I must find Kip. I remember, I thought I saw him at the funeral. I try to relive those moments of rushing out of there. Yes. It *was* Kip seated there in the church. *But why?* How did he know about Margaret? Why didn't he follow me out? Yes, that was definitely him sitting there looking very judgmental.

My first stop is the Range Rover car dealership. There's a sale going on, so the place is busy. The nameplate on Kip's desk now says Ralph Axelrod. Oh right, I guess he actually did sell the dealership. Oh, boy. Now, I'm left in a quandary of how to find him. It feels wrong to have a different nameplate on this desk. These silly thoughts race through my head out of impatience and nervousness. Finally, someone notices me snooping around at this desk and saunters over giving off a snooty vibe.

"Can I help you? I'm Ralph Axelrod," he says with a British accent. He's tall, slender with blonde hair neatly combed straight back, a button-down light-blue shirt, thin tie, khaki chinos, and penny loafers. Straight out of Abercrombie and Fitch, stylish but casual. He's the ivy-league poster boy for this car dealership.

"I'm looking for Kip, the former owner of this dealership. Perhaps someone wouldn't mind giving me his personal address? We're friends but his cell phone is no longer working and I have no other contact information, unfortunately."

"There's no former owner. This dealership has been owned since it opened in nineteen seventy by the Headly Corporation, a private company based in Toronto that also owns the Bentley and Rolls Royce dealerships here in New York, Los Angeles, and Buenos Aries."

I'm stunned. Why is nothing as it seems anymore? And why do corporations own everything now?

"Well, did someone by the name of Kip work here then? Henry Bartholomew Knight is his real name. I met him right here. He was sitting at this desk and sold me a car."

"No, I'm sorry. No."

I turn to leave. "Wait a minute," he says. "Bartholomew. Yes. This building used to be called the Bartholomew Building and the dealership rented this space. About forty years ago this location sold Roll Royce automobiles and there was a terrible fire. Everything burned to the ground. The upper floors were a single, private residence. I believe people perished, at least a member of the Bartholomew family who lived in the residence did, if I remember correctly. The Headly Corporation seized the opportunity to buy what was left. It was gutted and rehabilitated. Now it's the Headly Building and they have sold the upper floors as condo businesses. There's a computer graphics company and various other businesses, a non-profit for clean water and so on."

"What year did you say the fire happened?"

"About five years after the dealership opened. Nineteen seventy-five, I think."

I thank him and leave in a rush, anxious to get home and search online. In the grip of a dark foreboding, my stomach tightens, my skin crawls, and my pulse throbs. If indeed, it was Kip who died in that fire then how was it that I met him? How was it that we spent so much time together? Was he a hallucination? I must find out, but I'm also afraid of the answer. Once in my study, I try to come up with a search strategy. The fire happened before the internet, so finding newspaper coverage might not be possible. I decide that maybe census data might list his name and the year he died. I decide to just type in his full name and see what comes up. *What the...?* He's listed in Wikipedia? And so I read in horror.

Henry Bartholomew Knight, also known as Kip, was an accomplished minimalist composer, performer, and visual artist known for his whimsical installations featuring everyday objects from backyards in suburbia. A Renaissance man of many accomplishments, Mr. Knight raced cars for a hobby and held doctorates in archeology, anthropology, and music. He sat on the boards of several foundations and charities, to which he started giving his family's vast fortune. Bartholomew Henry Knight, Kip's grandfather, who died before he was born, started the dynasty in his thirties when he went from being a West Texas dirt farmer to a man of considerable wealth practically overnight.

The never confirmed story is that Mr. Knight, the grandfather, was bequeathed the mineral rights to his neighbor's land within the Permian Basin. Unbeknownst to the neighbor who left the rights on his deathbed to cover an unpaid debt, but perhaps known to Knight, the land was exceedingly rich in oil reserves. The family fortune grew quickly and remained stable from wells that have pumped more than 100,000 barrels per day since the mid-1920s.

Tragically, in 1975 at the age of 35, Henry Bartholomew Knight perished in a fire that broke out in his residence, a large, multi-level single unit that combined the upper floors above a Rolls Royce dealership, which was spared. It was concluded that the fire was the result of arson but the perpetrator was never found. Considered a murder investigation, it remains one of many unsolved crimes. Richard Bartholomew Knight, the father of Henry Bartholomew Knight, owned the building and subsequently sold the burned-out property for pennies on the dollar to the Headly Corporation, owner of the dealership renting the street-level space.

Headly Corporation, a wholly-owned subsidiary of King Blakemore LLC, which recently changed its name to Trinity of Sixes Communications, had been feuding with the Knights concerning the dealership's rents and fees. This contentious relationship put King Blakemore directly at the center of the investigation and under suspicion for the arson. However, his connection to causing the fire was never proved, thus clearing Blakemore of any wrongdoing. Lavinia Knight, Kip's mother, died many years prior to the fire from complications during childbirth. Subsequently, Henry Bartholomew Knight was Mr. Knight's only son and heir. Richard B. Knight continued as a board member of the charities his son started until his death in 1985 at the relatively young age of 65, never having gotten over the loss of his son and wife. The Knight Foundation, supporting the numerous charities created by Henry Bartholomew Knight, continues today funded by a trust set up solely for that purpose.

Chapter Nineteen

The ceremony

The city has become stifling for me in quite a short period of time. There's always a small crowd hanging outside my building, obstructing my comings and goings, wanting autographs and photos with me. My mother thought it was cute when she was here and a validation of my great success. I actually hated it because it continuously mortified me that my trilogy's narrative, and with it my dignity, had been completely destroyed by Trinity of Sixes Publishing. Even without reading it, I knew that. Teeny-bopper groupies had never been my target demographic, proving Malachite right in her assessment of the growing interest of young adults in these genres.

The covers of all three books in the trilogy said it all. Give the public what it wants and it wants smut, horror, and an eighth-grade reading level. This formula apparently sells millions of books and fast, so it's quite appealing to publishing houses where a sure thing always trumps niche market esoterica or literature written for discerning adults. At least, that's the business model for Trinity of Sixes Publishing, a junkyard that appeals to those who watch reality TV. Jameson, always a classy outfit, applauded and heralded thought-provoking, well-written fiction in any genre, appealing to the type of audience that enjoys the intelligent programming of public television.

Jumping on the Trinity bandwagon, an ideology that I had been adamantly against, might be justified only in the context of making tons of money to enable freedom for important but less commercial pursuits. But no one realizes that writers like actors get typecast. Once you write work that panders to the lowest common denominator, it defines your future promise or lack thereof. So basically, my debut and previous works aside, I was now finished as a respected literary voice. So what. Great wealth, my heretofore heart's desire, is the coveted door prize and is all that's left for me now. At least I had a body of work that made me proud, that I could hearken back to, as my brand gets swept into the gutter. Trumped by Trinity will be my slogan going forward. I'll cry all the way to the bank, as they say. I guess that was the plan all along. The contract's main demand, I initially thought, was that I keep writing. Having control over my finished product was my natural assumption since my previous work had attracted them. But that "final edits" clause was the killer. That clause changed my life's focus. There are worse things than just managing one's investments and traveling the world.

I had wanted to confide all this heartache and confusion to my mother. Tell her about my connection to King through his company but every time I tried to broach the subject, she cleverly maneuvered away from it. At one point, I just wanted to grab her and make her tell me everything about her relationship with King. Make her listen to how I sold my soul. But I just couldn't do it. I'm a chicken when it comes to conflict and, besides, I still held on to some hope that this was all a charade. That I am not the Devil's daughter. That my mother isn't a demon woman. She went back to her world of black holes and such without resolving my dilemma and in a strange way I was relieved. Better not to know.

Ironically, the thought of being royalty, even of the evil and ugly underworld, had held some fascination for a brief second. But when I stay away from the happy juice and can think clearly, my revulsion to all things associated with King is steadfast and true. He, and everything he stands for, disgusts me. When all who have made similar pacts have their markers come due, no one wants to spend eternity like that. The spoils and the riches are all well and good when living, but quite different when the portal to hell awaits.

This morning, when Alex picked me up to drive me back to Misty Falls, there was something odd going on with me. A shift in my thinking. He wanted a quickie before we left, but I just wasn't interested. The whole thing with Alex is just too fake. After my experiment killing off Jewel, and telling Alex to drop dead and his crashing on the floor, I suddenly realized that I also created Alex's lust for me when I had that very intense copulation dream. Knowing that I can control him with my pen, with my words, and even with my thoughts is annoying beyond belief.

He's suddenly become dull and boring. My robot sex toy. A big surprise because he always turned me on. And his relationship with Jewel is also a turn off. She's old enough to be his mother and yet he worships her. I might kill them both off just for fun. For a few days at least before I write them back to life. Power corrupts... seriously. But it's also a bore. Killing King with just my computer and my thoughts, however, would be pure bliss. But he's not really alive. He's an eternal, depraved, and malignant force.

Besides my urgent desire to get away from the city and all the adoring crowds, I also need my car. I need to be flexible, to be able to run away and start over somewhere, squirrel away enough funds to start over.

Change my name. I know that's delusional. King has powers. But maybe I do as well. Something will come to me…I hope. Jewel's another reason to go up to Misty Falls. She mentioned something about Kip. I must find out what she knows. A disturbing possibility about Kip has been percolating in my thoughts and making me very uncomfortable.

I'm afraid that Kip made a deal with King and the deal somehow went south—really south as in that dark and burning awfulness. If he were an accomplished minimalist composer, why hasn't his work been listed somewhere? Recorded by an orchestra, string quartet, or pianist? On an initial superficial search, no sites listing his music came up. So that's the first task in my research. Find the backstory on Kip and figure out why he showed up in my life. He seems to have an agenda of some sort, a raison d'être. Thoughts of him further aggravate my already dark mood as we drive upstate. When we get to my house, Alex wants to come in and I nastily brush him off. He's like a trained dog.

Surprise. My car is there. A note on the windshield says the charges have been dropped. Okay, it's true, this entire town is under King's rule. Creepy, but good for me right now. The house is welcoming and feels unexpectedly safe. There's no magical wall with a door to a nonexistent basement. I stock up on groceries. I actually enjoy the drive, until I think of how patient Kip was in showing me how to handle this car. My plan is to hole up here and do some extensive searching online and then to invite Jewel over for lunch and quiz her. As far as the screenplay, there is no way I'll write it. Because I'll never read how that witch editor turned *Darkside* into crap. Uh-uh. No. I'll write some garbage based on my original work and let Alex create the travesty. My main focus is Kip. Gotta figure out how to bring him back from wherever he's gone.

When I come back from shopping, I decide to take a swim. Maybe having a swim will help me sort out this impossible situation. Relax me and crystallize my thoughts. It's hot as blazes. There's no let up from this drought. Just in these past few weeks, the reservoirs are becoming depleted and watering lawns is forbidden on certain days. My flowers are drying up. My grass has brown patches. Now that I know how much this pleases King, it makes me doubly upset. I keep hoping all this is a bad dream and I'll wake up. I'm a broken record, annoying, even to myself. I constantly teeter between giving in and not giving up. The money, the money, the money. But this is not winning the lottery. This is not a game. The reality of my situation is dire. How can I conquer the beast? What's the key to saving myself? It's just little ole me and the personification of all that's wrong with humanity. The bright sun is squint worthy. Glaring sun with no let up. Burning up the earth. Making it hell. This metaphor only adds to my distress.

All the swim does is make me resigned to my fate. There's no hope. No way out. All I can do is collect my vast sums of money, buy spectacular residences for me and my mom, and just before I die, throw myself at the feet of a priest. I can't throw myself at the feet of a rabbi because Jews don't believe in Satan. Hello? Wait! There's the plan! After great wealth has been transferred into my bank account, I will denounce King because he doesn't exist for me as a Jew. I'll take all the riches and then repent in a church as extra insurance. The lengths to which I'll go to enjoy a wealthy lifestyle even disgust *me*. Then I remember, there's no death for me and my mom. We just bounce along century to century enjoying being profoundly maleficent.

If this is who I really am, why don't I know these things? Why don't I understand the rules? So maybe…it's really not true. Maybe if I close my eyes and click my heels together like Dorothy in the Wizard of Oz, I can really go back to my other life. As I dry off in my lounge chair catching some rays, I feel a presence. Opening my eyes, I think I see a shadow move across the sliding glass doors of the guesthouse. *What the…?* I get up and walk over.

Sliding the door open very carefully, I poke my head inside. "Who's there?" I ask tentatively. The house appears to be empty. Nothing is out of place. Dark and ominous, it's unwelcoming but apparently vacant. As I step into the living room to get a better look, a force knocks me forward, takes hold of me, and whisks me up into the air. Up through the roof, above the house, tossing me about topsy-turvy in a swirling wind then stopping abruptly and setting me upright in a gentle caress.

All around me is a white cloud of nothingness. A place with no up or down. Just white smoky air and isolation. My balance is thrown off and I reach out to grab something and gain purchase. Nothing. There's nothing. No floor. No walls. But I don't fall. My legs are like rubber swaying from side-to-side as if floating. Yes, I'm floating in this dense white fog. It's disorienting and makes me quite nauseous.

"Help!" I scream, but no sound comes out. I try again. Nothing. *Oh my god! What is this place? Where am I?* Suddenly, a tiny figure slowly emerges from far away in the nothingness and floats over growing ever larger. My fear is whipped up into such a frenzy that my whole body begins to convulse. I try to run away but can only float in the same spot. I start to silently whimper and it becomes a mournful wail in my head. I close my eyes to shut out this terrifying experience and try and think of something peaceful. A beautiful beach, turquoise water. But my noiseless wailing continues.

"Hush," says a voice in my head. "Don't be frightened!" *What? How?* My eyes pop open and I'm staring at...Kip. I abruptly stop wailing. "Kip! Oh Kip. Is it you?" *Is it Kip? He looks somewhat older. The age he was when he...died?* Nothing comes out of my mouth but I can tell we're communicating. He understands my question. He doesn't answer but looks at me with deep meaning. His long hair is not really hair but a mess of curled tubes, like fluorescent bulbs, framing his face and flowing behind him creating a ribbon of visible sparkling energy. His robe is a pulsating cluster of tiny stars. His glowing eyes throw off such brilliance that I must look away. No! Don't look away, he says telepathically. And so I look into his eyes and then he raises his hand and points it at me. A bolt of electricity hits me and vibrates through my body making my senses tingle and my skin throw off tiny bright flashes of electrons. *For your protection.*

This positive energy washes over me like a warm cocoon, calming me. *Who are you?* I communicate with my thoughts. *Are you Kip? Will you help me? Please? Help me get my old life back! I'm so miserable. Please, Kip. Help.* Agonizing moments of silence. Just a transfer of his energy into my deepest core. I float in limbo pleading with all my being. *I haven't yet passed the test* his eyes tell me. "What test?" I ask out loud with no sound. And he fades. "Come back! What test?" I'm shouting so loud that I wake myself up from my nap on the lounge chair. I lie there dazed not knowing if I'm awake or asleep. A few minutes pass before I'm aware of my surroundings. The sun is gone and a fog has rolled in. Unusual for this time of year. An eerie fog that puts me back in my dream and unsettles me. I look around for Kip. *What was the message?* He said something to me. *What was it?* I'm more confused than ever. The dampness and my befuddled state-of-mind propel me indoors.

The phone is ringing. It's the Lodge. "Please be ready in an hour to be picked up for the ceremony," an unfamiliar voice says. "What ceremony?" Click.

Thoughts flash though my mind as I become panicky. I don't want to go there right now. And I certainly want to drive myself. I'll hurry up and drive myself back to the city. That's it. I'll go back to the city right now. I start running around the house, grabbing my things and changing out of my bathing suit while I stuff my overnighter. Fifteen minutes. Good. *Now let me get out of here.* I pull open the front door and scream in surprise as I run into two giant bodyguards standing in the doorway. They throw my bag back into the house and escort me to the Hummer.

"Darling, so glad you could come," King says, as I'm ushered into the trophy room. The ridiculousness of this statement throws me off and I stare at him in disbelief. Putting his arm around my shoulders, he escorts me over to a small group of some sort of beings. "Come," he says, "let me introduce you to the other neophytes." It's an amazingly odd array of living things. There are definitely human-types probably from other planets, with normal looking parts but their skin is reptilian in texture. Some have turquoise-colored hair, some have horns and tails, some have webbed feet and all the above-mentioned features. But there also are homo-sapiens. Celebrities I've seen on TV. One is a very well-known loud-mouthed boor and boozer. Another is a short-squat politician from NYC.

"Oh, wow there's..." King stops me and says there are no names used here. At least the humanoid types have limbs, eyes, and heads resembling people. But there are other things that are amorphous red blobs that ooze around the floor. They make gurgling noises and smell awful. The distorted-looking humanoids with their non-human hair and skin color are actually less off-putting than these shapeless creatures from who knows where. Our subconscious night horrors? When I was grabbed from my house, it was a very stress-inducing trip in the car. Being summoned for an unknown ceremony struck fear in my heart, as they say. Being among this monster mix of alien entities validates that fear. Are these just creations from the mind of King? I surely hope so.

"What are these things and why exactly am I here?" I ask King as he maneuvers me around the room.

"Oh, you'll see very soon, my sweet." And then he starts introducing me as a newly discovered member of his family, keeping it thankfully vague. Each bow in reverence. *Run! Flee!* My instincts take hold, but King has got me in a tight grip. Suddenly, a glass of orange liquid is shoved into my hand and King makes a toast. He welcomes everyone, first speaking in English and then he starts making squeaking noises and strange grunting sounds of which the monsters seem to understand. We all drink the sweet tasting liquid. "Bottoms up," King says and makes me finish it all. As soon as it enters my blood stream everything becomes altered, strange, and possibly dangerous. Just like the effects of Good Health Water, reality is blurred and bubbles of giddiness take hold of me.

We are all told to gather in the center of the room and the floor becomes an elevator going down and down. Oh my, like an amusement park ride. I giggle. We end up in a cave-like room lit up only by candles. Dark and ominous shadows hop wildly about the room. I suck in my breath feeling anxious. My crazed, light-hearted mood slowly begins spiraling downward. For some unknown reason, the drink has lost its power or maybe it was a false reaction on my part. After we all walk off the elevator, we are told by King to take a robe from the ones hanging on hooks on the cave walls. Wearing a nasty robe that has been worn by someone else or some *thing* else is not a pleasant thought but there's no alternative.

The robes are beyond awful. They are scratchy and sticky with goo and reek of offal or other scents that make me retch. Once I put on my robe, even though my instincts of fear and dread remain charged, I become numb and placid like cornered prey. The putrid stench of things long dead burns my nostrils and I gag convulsively. The stink is worse than the oozing sour smelling blobs now hidden under the large hooded robes thrown over them. A herd mentality pervades and we move in unison toward the center of the room. We're all connected and communicate without speaking. I hear King talking to me in my head, as he sits in a king type throne chair on a pedestal at one end of this hollowed-out cave room. The chair overlooks a giant pentagram painted on or chiseled into the center of the stone floor. His eyes have once again become beastly, yellow fires with weird oval slits for pupils. *Welcome, my dear*, to your initiation, he tells me in my head.

There's chanting by the others of which I join in. A screaming sound of a human or animal can be heard off in the deep recesses of the cave. There's to be a sacrifice. A palpable excitement races through the neophytes. Blood lust. Monotonous ritual humming further seduces my consciousness. And then the louder hum of the elevator as it goes back up. At this, my conscious awareness snaps back and overtakes my drug-induced numbed state. Immediately claustrophobia sets in. The robe, the walls, feel too close, the depth of the cave feels too far underground. My breathing becomes labored. No way out. Stuck down here in this dungeon. Down, way down in this hole. I hyperventilate and can't catch my breath breaking out in a cold sweat. The room starts to spin. Coughing and choking, I feel myself losing consciousness and then I totally black out.

I wake up in my former room in the White Wing of the Lodge far away from the cave of darkness and treachery. Pleasant soft music calms my nerves. The cloud-like softness of the bedding, makes me feel safe. All is clean, soothing, and the sweet scent of roses envelops the room. Surrounded by luxury, I shake the memory away of that horrifying place.

And then I realize, I'm not alone.

Chapter Twenty

Alex in wonderland

My eyes flutter open and a blurry figure sits facing me in the corner of the room. "Kip? Is that you? Kip?" I say in a soft, raspy whisper. "I thought you were... dead." He gets up and walks over. "Shh, now... rest."

"Oh...Alex. Sorry. I thought you were…" I slowly reach up and feel bandages wrapped around my forehead. I look at him quizzically.

"You took a really bad fall from a standing position," he says gently. "Cracked your head on the hard stone. Got quite a deep gash." Answering my unvoiced question, he says, "King's personal physician in Misty Falls rushed over here right after you were brought upstairs. You've been out for three days."

"Three days?"

"Jewel and I have been taking turns watching for any signs of swelling, a concussion can prove deadly. How are you feeling now?"

"Really bad headache. Sore." Alex nods sympathetically.

"Doc is coming in a few days to check your wound. But here's something for the pain."

As soon as I swallow the pills, my eyes close, and I'm out. Powerful drugs. For the next few days, I float in and out between waking and sleeping. I dream of Kip every time I fall asleep. He's my guardian angel looking out for me. He takes me to magical places of rainbows and puffy pink clouds. A chorus of sweet heavenly voices hums in my ears. Soft as velvet, the greenest grass cushions our feet and fragrant blossoms glow in the brilliant sunshine.

"This place is yours when you're ready. But you haven't passed the test," he tells me.

"What's the test? Why do you keep saying that? What do you mean?" I ask.

He disappears and my mother's there sitting under a lush, leafy tree. I rush over and try to hug her. I hug the air. She's not really there, like the holograms in my mysterious basement. "Mom," I call out and she materializes in a different spot. We're in a boat floating down a gentle river with thick vegetation along the banks. Birds, scores of them, of various species, sing in unison with the sweet angelic chorus. They follow us, dancing in the sky. A handful alight gently on the bow of the boat. "Mom," I say urgently and reach out to her. She morphs into Jewel who tells me, "I know what you are looking for. I know about Kip." She fades and Kip reappears, but no, it's Alex not Kip and then I wake up. I feel sad when I awaken preferring to be in that heavenly place. I gladly take the pain meds and return to my dream world.

The doctor comes but my confused state keeps me suspended between reality and never-never land all through my check-up. He asks me simple questions to see if I'm deranged or brain damaged. I know my name. I know I'm at the Lodge. I know the name of our President. I'm aware that King is standing by the bed looking very concerned. *Really?* If I died wouldn't I just come back to life? That's what he told me. Or go to that hot house for eternity? Isn't that what he wants? There's a lot I don't understand. And really don't want to understand. One thing I know is that being in bed so long has given me a really bad backache.

The doctor leaves giving instructions for more rest. I start to wean myself from the pain pills to get out of bed. Slowly, I come back to myself and finally can get up and take a shower. I shuffle over on stiff legs from a tight dull ache in my lower back. When the doc came he removed the large bandage replacing it with a Band-Aid type thing. The gash on my forehead, which had to be glued, is healing well and protected. I can immerse myself in a hot shower, and it feels wonderful. In the shower the Band-Aid on my head gets wet and while I'm replacing it, I can see there's a small scar forming. It will be inconsequential when it finally heals. Time to get out of here and go home.

But there are other plans for me.

"Now that you're up and about, King wants me to take you to the island to continue your recovery," Alex says, as I emerge from the bathroom luckily wearing fresh pajamas.

"Don't you knock before entering a room?"

"Well, all this time, you were in bed sleeping and I didn't want to disturb you. Sorry, I didn't realize. Just got used to..."

"No worries," I interrupt. "I'm not going anywhere but home. Now if you'll excuse me, I need to get dressed, if I can find my clothes."

"Here are some clothes and here is a packed suitcase. The jet is ready to go and we have to leave soon."

"Get out of here. No one is telling me what to do ANYMORE! I'm done. I'm out of here." Shouting makes my head throb.

"Please Alexa, be reasonable. We'll have fun. We'll be staying at the main house. Just us. Great food. Beautiful beach. C'mon. I've been looking forward to getting away with you." He walks over and puts his arms around me. There are faint stirrings of desire. But no. Gotta go. *Why does he have to look so damn good?*

"I had some food brought here. You must be starving. Have a bite and let's have fun. Just you and me."

Suddenly, I'm ravenous, so I dig into the best kosher corned beef sandwich I have ever eaten. The corned beef just melts in my mouth and the flavor and texture is perfect. Corned beef on club bread, one of my favorite delights. French fries crisp on the outside and chewy on the inside. I devour it all and drink the can of Dr. Brown's diet cream soda. Boy was that good. So hungry before but now totally satiated. Yum. Yet, I could eat another one.

"What were we talking about?" I ask feeling a pleasant rush of elation.

"Going to the island for a few days. To help you relax and recover."

"But I don't have any clothes," I protest weakly, as the island now is sounding like a great idea.

"You said that already, and I just gave them to you. They're on the bed. Here," he says handing me underwear, shorts, a top, and sandals. As I change, I begin to hum uncontrollably, my mood becoming more and more upbeat. We leave for the private airport with a toast of Champagne in the limo. Fun in the sun.

I sleep soundly on the plane still exhausted from my ordeal. While I sleep, a message from Kip takes hold of my dream state. He's shaking his head in disapproval, but I'm not sure why. Then, he's standing in front of the grease board in the conference room at the Lodge and writes the word GREED in all caps. With a pointer he repeatedly taps on the word and hits it harder and harder until the board breaks. Thwack! I jump in my sleep but don't wake up. I'm in the salon with King. We're having that conversation about greed. How greed fuels him, is his life force throughout time. He builds his armies on greed. He snags humanity with their greed as he snagged me. Yes, my greed had defined me. Greed. Greed. Flashing in my head, the word greed starts a thought process, a growing realization of what I must do. Yes! Now I know. It's clear and within reach. Hallelujah!

When I awake, the crux of the dream, the vital knowledge brought forth in the dream is lost, totally forgotten. An *important message* is the only thought that remains. Dreams are like that sometimes. Alex is curled against my back. His arms and legs are wrapped around me and he's softly stroking my cheek while tickling my bare feet with his toes. I turn and see love in his eyes. *Love? Really?* How strange, but sweet. We're lying in bed in one of the private cabins on the aircraft. With my guard down and relaxed, no matter where my head had been recently, he stirs me to the core. He acknowledges my acceptance of his closeness by beginning to snuggle and nibble my ear. He knows I love that, how it drives me crazy.

He then moves down and begins massaging my feet with oil from a small bottle on the table. It smells like lavender, my favorite scent and is most soothing to my emotional well-being. The sensation of him rubbing my feet is also incredibly sensual and enjoyable. My arousal begins to take hold. There was some reason I shouldn't be doing this, but it's gone from my mind. *What the hell?* And so, I give in and give myself up to an insatiable desire that leaves us both spent by the time we land. Ecstasy is a lot more satisfying than movies on demand or music channels.

We arrive at the main house and are shown to King's private guest quarters, which are, of course, expansive like the Lodge. A house within a house. There's a living room with a kitchenette having a full-sized refrigerator full of drinks, cheeses, caviar and more, a pantry full of dry snacks, and a fully stocked wet bar. Off the living room behind French doors is a study complete with a new state-of-the art iMac and other office equipment. The center piece of the master bedroom is an oversized bed, larger than a king, facing a wall of glass overlooking the ocean. In fact, all rooms in this private apartment have ocean views because the house sits atop a small hill right on the beach. The marble bathroom is a spectacle to behold. A saltwater tropical aquarium is embedded in the floor, so that while one bathes, showers, or uses the toilet the colorful fish swim across the room providing enchanting entertainment.

Alex and I race to the giant bed and jump on it to feel its feathery texture. Then we grab two splits of Dom Pérignon out of the fridge and drink right out of the bottle. We are like two kids having fun and being wowed with the extravagance of this place when I realize my healthy self has returned. Yay!

"Let's go for a swim before it gets dark," I say enjoying my newfound energy.

"Sure. I'll put on my suit."

"No, let's just go nude. The beach looks very secluded."

"What a great idea," he says laughing.

Running into the water completely naked is exhilarating. The water temperature is perfect like a mild bath. This beach is protected by a reef like the swimming area near the cottages. The water is as calm as a lake not hampered by currents or waves and we luxuriate in the joy it brings. No sign of compromised sea life, thank goodness. We are joyful and erupt in laughter. We tease each other playfully and then kiss under water. We are like dolphins frolicking, jumping, and diving.

The softness of the water against our nakedness is like a caress. The sun's warm heat, a protective womb. Afterwards, we decide to take our dinner in the private guest quarters and feast on succulent lobster, fresh local tropical fruits, and finish with confections worthy of a French pastry chef. Bottomless glasses of champagne. This is our private oasis and we vow not to leave these quarters and our private beach for our entire stay.

The second day of our stay, I decide to venture out of our cove for a walk along the water's edge on the beautiful white sand beach while Alex is napping in a lounge chair. We're still naked, never putting clothes on after our first swim. The staff takes no notice and we take no notice of the staff. This is pure freedom. I'm enjoying getting an all-over tan that being nude affords. Happy fish jump out of the water teasing the birds who hunt for them. The sky is cloudless, the wind is calm, and the scent of blooming florals intoxicating. My joyful mood transcends all doubts, fear, and anger. I'm blissful in the rapture of love, and the contentment of a fulfilled life. I could stay here forever. And then I crash right into Kip who has appeared out of nowhere. *What the...?*

"Kip! I've been looking for you? What happened to you? Why did you disappear?" He doesn't answer but looks at me with deep meaning. Again with the deep meaning gaze. He's dressed in the cool clothes of our first encounter, and so I realize something's amiss. "Kip?" He answers in a tone that brings me up short. "Do you realize what you're doing? Do you realize how dangerous are the choices you are making? What consequences you will suffer?"

My bubble bursts and I realize what he's saying. I'm transported back to witnessing my encounters with King, his beastly eyes. My loss of Margaret. My eternal damnation. I'm reliving these scenes as they fly by and leave me dizzy. The evil of King Blakemore. The willing disciples drawn in by their lust for wealth. Now I am one of them. Their greed, now my greed. The dungeon ceremony comes back in full force. That awful pit. The weirdness. I'm pulled out of my selfish haze. Pulled into sharp focus. "No!" I shout. "I don't want to be like that." And all the anger and fear return. Whoosh!

"You know what you must do," says Kip.

And, suddenly, I do.

Chapter Twenty-one

I know what to do

After the image of Kip dissolves and I am standing there in my nakedness, real and spiritual, I am spurred to take immediate action. My mind is no longer in a fog of bullshit bliss; my eyes have been opened. Yes, I remember all of it now. Yes, I realize my circumstances are dire and I need to be done with this diabolical scourge on humanity. Yes, in a rush, I remember the urgency with which I tried to escape. The fainting spell and subsequent blow to my head saved me from that awful ritual that would have inducted me into Satan's army. I run back to the house leaving Alex sunbathing in his chair at the other end of the beach. I need his help and there's a sure way to get it. Once in the house, I throw on a robe and boot up the computer. I write as fast as my lousy typing allows:

Alex closes his eyes as he rests on the chaise lounge enjoying the soft sounds of the surf lapping at the shoreline while the balmy breeze cools his skin from the hot sun. The past several days convince him that Alexa is his one true love. Whatever it takes to win her, whatever she asks, he would do. He would never let her down no matter who tried to come between them. He needs to tell her this and right now. To let her know what she means to him. And so when he doesn't see her walking down the beach, he decides to see if she has returned to the house.

I wait a minute and hear Alex coming through the sliding glass door. This ability to manipulate my characters through my writing is heady stuff. I know it will disappear once I am free, but I will have no regrets.

"Alexa, I…," he says.

"Alex," I interrupt. "I need your help and quickly." He nods. "Please find an SUV and drive it over to the door of these quarters. OK?"

"Of course, but why?"

"No time to explain, just do it. Also call the pilots and tell them we need to leave the island in a couple of hours."

"Wait…why? We're enjoying ourselves."

"I must get back to Misty Falls tonight. Please. It's important."

"Okay, my love." And he throws on some shorts and leaves.

After I jump in the shower and say goodbye to the beautiful angel fish swimming at my feet, I grab the landline, because my cell phone has no service, and call my financial advisor. I call his office. No answer. Then on his private number at home. He's there.

"Hi John, it's Alexa Wainwright. Sorry to bother you on a Saturday. I think it's Saturday anyway," I laugh awkwardly, "I've lost track of time lately."

"Hi Alexa, nice to hear from you. Actually it's Sunday," he laughs. "How can I help you?"

"I'd like you to close all my accounts that receive direct deposits from Trinity of Sixes Publishing. Before you do that, please exhaust those accounts by giving equal donations to several non-profit charities for which I will send you a list directly. I want nothing left. Zero."

"Alexa, are you sure? That's a lot of money. Several million. At least save some for yourself. I assume you're more than satisfied with the earnings from the investments we set up previously and I can do the same with this new influx of cash. This is legacy money."

"Yes, I realize all the implications of what I'm doing. I have more than enough money. I'm quite comfortable, actually, thanks to you. You've appreciated my principal quite nicely. That's all I need. But all the recent publishing money that I thought I would use to buy NYC real estate, I don't want anymore. I want nothing more to do with Trinity of Sixes and that money. So please remember to close out those accounts after you make the donations. And do this immediately. Whatever it takes, get this money to these charities today, immediately. And whatever the transfer costs are, I authorize you do it. I'm also going to send you a copy of a manifesto of sorts about Trinity of Sixes Publishing. If anything happens to me, please make sure it's published in the newspapers. I'm counting on you to get it out there. Widespread exposure." He agrees half-heartedly expressing concern about my using the words "if anything happens to me" and also cautioning me about liable lawsuits and the like.

After we hang up, I make a quick search on the internet and email him the names of twenty non-profit organizations that feed the hungry, protect wildlife, provide healthcare to the poor and disadvantaged masses worldwide, and those whose mission is to clean up the world's water supply. Then, I dash into the kitchen and start emptying the drinks and food from the refrigerator, and finally, the bar. I put everything in a heap by the door. Next are the closets, drawers, linens, and pillows in the bedroom. I add this to the already giant heap. We'll have to make two trips. When Alex comes back, he almost trips over the pile of stuff.

"Load all this in the car," I tell a shocked Alex. "Don't ask. Just do it…please. We'll probably have to make two trips. Hurry." I tell him to drive quickly to the center of the little village, where we start unloading the car. A small group of curious bystanders watches us but none move forward. After we're totally unloaded, we drive back and finish the job. It goes faster because the pile is much smaller. We race back to the village and see a massive crowd grabbing stuff and running to their cottages. We add our final load and race to the airport. Once on the plane, I breathe a sigh of relief. Nobody at the main house has shown up demanding the return of the goods. Success!

As we take off, I see the security cars racing toward the airport too late to stop us. We are free, that is until we land. I'm sure that I'll have to answer to King or one of his henchmen for this, but I'm prepared. Nothing can stop me. I see a smiling Kip in my mind's eye. He'll protect me, I'm sure. But King holds the trump card and my cockiness will probably dissolve and turn into fear and dread as soon as we land. Despite my uneasiness, the plane ride is pleasant with an attentive Alex and a delicious sandwich. I fall into a blissful sleep unaware of the shocking danger that awaits.

I dream of simple times. I am back in my loft before everything that's happened or is it after I have successfully executed my plan? I'm enjoying my morning cup of coffee as I sit on my balcony looking at the familiar cityscape. My trilogy in its original form is stacked next to me. Completed. I pick up the first in the series. It's published by Jameson. Pretty covers. I smile. Then I'm running in the neighborhood. Taking my usual route. A pleasant runner's high. The day is glorious. Scene switch. I'm at Battery Park. Happy families waiting for the ferry. All is good.

At least in the dream.

Chapter Twenty-two

Mom!

I t's a smooth landing. So smooth that Alex has to wake me. Still lost in my pleasant dream, it's hard to shake myself awake. But then, wham! A swirling wind grabs me and carries me out of the plane and into the air. Spinning around and around, I get exceedingly dizzy and almost pass out. I'm abruptly dropped down hard causing a shudder to wave through my body from my heels to my head. My teeth bite down hard on my tongue. As I recover from the stupor brought on by being caught in the grip of this powerful unwanted summons, I realize where I am. It's King's dungeon. That awful place where, thankfully, I had been spared the initiation ritual. *What the…?*

I try to move, but my legs turn to rubber, as I see King rise up from his throne and grow as tall as a tree. His deep bellowing voice shakes me to my core, as he calls out my name, while his yellow beast eyes are ablaze in anger. Quaking in fear, I watch his skin turn the darkest red, nearly black, enhancing his evil aspect. He bends down and puts his face close to mine, as he grabs my arms and shakes me hard. His putrid breath fills my nostrils.

"What do you think you are doing?" he snarls. "Do you think you can outsmart me, little feeble one? No one is as powerful as I. Even your precious Kip does my bidding. He imagines himself a saint, but in the end he's mine. Has always been mine. These tricks of his are meaningless. So stop this nonsense or you will be sorry. Sorrier than you have ever been."

My whole being becomes infused with the enlightened ideas given to me from another plane where Kip resides and fills me with positive energy and strength. Armed with this knowledge and pretending to have the courage that I do not feel, I shout back, "I'm done with you! You will never own me. I have free will. You are powerless in the face of goodness. I spit on you." And then I really spit at him. With great anger, his eyes narrow and their gaze weakens my resolve and impertinence. My courage crumbles as I feel myself shrink to the size of a small dog, as I'm tossed down a hole that appears in the floor. Down, down, down I go into the darkness. A furnace of heat surrounds me. I hit hard and my eyes slowly adjust as I shake in abject fear.

Figures in chains and wrapped in rags are moaning, as they are whipped by an army of King clones. Skeletal arms and legs in constant motion shrinking from the painful lashes belong to dead-eyed miserable once-human creatures wearing dazed and confused expressions of overwhelming suffering. This scene, the heat, and the stench make me start to choke and bring up my bile, triggering a return to my normal size. Immediately, the walls close in making me claustrophobic. Hot stone walls press in on me from all sides. I begin to scream but no sound is emitted as hysteria overtakes me. Buried alive. Buried alive is the panic that swirls through my brain. Being buried alive has always been my biting fear. My agonizing and hysterical fear. Then, suddenly, I am whisked upward. King's hot breath is in my ears, as I rise from the world of the damned to stand in front of him once more.

"Know that your fate will be worse than those wretched souls who dared to refuse my commands," his voice hisses. "You have crossed the line and you will be punished for this insubordination. It will not be pleasant. Go to your home and see what awaits you. Be gone!" Before he turns away he growls like an attacking bear and then sears my skin with fiery tendrils that flash from his fingers.

Before the pain of this assault registers, I'm thrown back into the whirlwind that carried me to this dungeon. Tossed about like a weak fly and jostled mercilessly, I'm dropped with no fanfare at the front door to my house. I can hear my cell phone ringing from deep within the house. My cell phone? How did it get there? I had taken nothing with me from the island in my rush to leave. My front door is thankfully unlocked. I scurry into the house and race to grab the call from my cell, which is just lying on the kitchen counter. Too late. The call went to voicemail. Mom. It was Mom. I quickly call her back and it goes straight to her voicemail. She's left me a message. I hurriedly play it back.

"Hi sweetheart. I have some exciting news. I have a month break before classes start and I'm rushing home. Maybe we can go somewhere together. It's been so long since I've seen you. These past months have been very exciting but also lonely. I've missed you so much. And I've been dreaming of going to the Russian Tea Room for some good food. It's been ages since we've gone there and my taste buds have been in hiatus. The food here has been beyond atrocious. *I'll get there sometime later tonight. It's a long drive. Love you."*

Doesn't she remember that we were just there? That we spent a few days together? Then I feel like I just got punched in the stomach. It wasn't my mom! That woman wasn't my mom. She was an imposter. King did that...*why?* Immediately, a shocking thought frightens me and nearly brings me to my knees. I know what he's up to. I grab my phone and dial with shaky fingers. I misdial. *Shit!* I try again. I'm screaming out loud. "Mom! Mom! Please answer your phone." It goes straight to voicemail. "Mom, get off the road right now. GET OFF THE ROAD, MOM! PLEASE LISTEN TO ME. GET OFF THE ROAD NOW! Call me right back. Please call me right back."

"Oh my god," I whisper to myself. "What can I do?" I call Jerry. Ring. Ring. The phone picks up. "Jerry, have you…" "Hi, this is Jerry. I'm not available…" I hang up and squelch the urge to throw my phone against the wall. *What? What?* Something. She rented the car. She rented the car. If I can just find out where she rented the car, I can get a license plate number and call the police. *How?* Wait, there's something I can do. I call the astrophysics department at Columbia using my landline. A secretary answers.

"Hello, this is the Department of Physics and Astrophysics. Jennifer Bailey speaking.

"I have an urgent request. My mother is a professor there and has been on assignment all summer for NASA. I need to find out just where she's been, the location. Can I speak to the department head? Right now. It's a matter of life and death."

"I'm sorry, but Dr. Fisher is away on vacation until next week."

"Do you know anyone who was also on this project that I can call?"

"I'm sorry, but the professors handle these kinds of assignments by themselves, so we have no way of knowing."

"Can you send me the faculty roster with their home phone numbers?"

"I'm sorry, we can't give out that information. But you can go to the department website and get their office numbers."

"GODDAMN IT! This is serious. A LIFE and DEATH situation. Can't you help me? Please. Please."

"I'm sorry…" I slam down the receiver. "SON OF A BITCH!"

With trepidation, I turn on the news. And there it is. A terrible car accident at the northern New Hampshire border with Maine. Two semi-tractor trailers and a passenger car. Just like Margaret! The announcer is saying:

Sometimes it's even upsetting to me to report a car crash that is such a horrific accident. The driver of a passenger car was squashed beyond recognition between two semis. The semi in front was slowly going up an incline and the semi behind was barreling down from the downhill behind and lost its brakes. It plowed at high speed into the car, which was then pushed into the truck in front. Police are still trying to remove any identifying information from the wreckage. They believe that because the car was a rental, the unfortunate driver's identity can be determined. If the license plate number isn't too crumpled to read, they will contact the rental car company to find out who rented the car. Wait. Wait. This just in. (And he presses his head mic closer to his ear.) The police have just acknowledged that they know the identity of the driver. All we can say is that she was a female in her late forties or early fifties. We are not releasing her identity until the next of kin are notified.

As soon as he finishes that statement, my phone rings.

Chapter Twenty-three

The beginning of the end

It's hard to see through my tears, so the drive to the hardware store was rough. As I run helter-skelter around the aisles in my grave distress trying to find what I'm looking for, I absently knock items off the shelves. Leaving a trail of crashed cleaning fluids, nails, hammers and the like, the manager easily discovers my whereabouts and offers to help me. I yell at him to leave me alone. He acknowledges my distraught state and backs away slowly while repeating his desire to help me. I realize I have to find what I need quickly before he calls the cops, and I brush by him.

Luckily down the next aisle are the gas cans and matches. And in the next one are bags of rags. I throw $200 dollars on the check-out counter knowing this will more than compensate for the commotion I've caused and race out. Next stop is the gas station. I have four large cans and it takes much longer than my patience allows to fill them up. I place them in the back of my SUV. Stupidly, I didn't change to perform this task. Running out of the house like a crazy person in flip flops and shorts, I now must return home and put on long pants and hiking boots.

I'm crazed and screaming. Frenzied and crying. Devastated and filled with extreme fury, hatred, and blood lust for vengeance. Slamming the front door behind me, I'm initially shocked to witness the destruction I left in my wake. After that horrible phone call telling me about my mother's death, I went nuts. I grabbed everything within reach and threw it against the wall. Lamps, figurines, and candlesticks gouged big craters in the walls. Screaming at the top of my lungs, I had grabbed a long, sharp knife from the kitchen and tore open the sofas. I dumped out all my dishes and glasses onto the floor and watched them crash into pieces. I knocked the artwork off the walls and stomped on them. Then I ran upstairs and did the same to my bedroom and all the guest rooms. I slit the mattresses and tore the linens. I threw all my perfume and cosmetics onto the marble floor. Every time something crashed, I screamed louder. Screamed so loud, I became hoarse. Screamed until I could scream no longer. And yet, I still screamed.

Agitated at the front door and looking at this mess, it dawns on me that I should wait for darkness. In the hardware store and then at the gas station all I could think about was racing over to the Lodge. But I really need the cover of night. Sunset is approaching and so after I change, I force myself to wait. Since my house is destroyed and I've nowhere to sit, I go over to the guesthouse. *Mom, Mom.* I scream in my head. *I'm so sorry. I did this. This is my fault. King, that bastard warned me. Why did I think I could win? But maybe...maybe now I can.*

Once inside the guesthouse, I throw myself on the bed and fall asleep from exhaustion brought on by my crazed screaming and weeping. In my sleep, I feel a soft feather stroking my cheek and my eyes pop open. It's Kip. I hop out of bed.

"How dare you come here. Get out. You're one of King's followers, his slave. You convinced me to stay here. You made it possible. You drove me up here," I bark at him in a raspy voice. "My mother is dead because of you. Oh my god, she's *dead*." That word horrifies me again. "Get out! Get out now! I hate you. I can't believe I listened to you. I thought you gave me a way out. I never thought my mother was at risk. King made me think they had a history. But you must have known the charade. You tricked me and now the most important person in my life is dead." I become hysterical crying again and start hitting Kip with my hands and fists. He lets me wear myself out and then he hugs me and we are instantly gone from this room and this moment in time.

We are in a sunny and spacious room dominated by a highly polished grand piano. The windows of the room frame an outdoor scene of luscious trees and flowery bushes. Thoroughbreds graze in the distance, a bucolic country setting. The room itself offers the comfort of walls lined with books. Wingback chairs and plush leather sofas, with tufted backs and antique brass nailhead trim, provide elegant seating. The scent of leather permeates. Sumptuous Turkish carpets cover the dark oak floor. Tiffany lamps are placed atop antique tables. A room that one might find at a private men's club. A substantial room. Probably the music room plus library of an estate-sized home in Connecticut or the horse country of western New Jersey.

Slowly becoming audible in this scene is the sound of the piano. At first, the music is distant and weak and then the melody gloriously fills the room with rich chords and strong strokes. A young boy slowly takes form as he plays the piece with the love and grace of a more seasoned performer. The word *prodigy* pops into my mind. I know at once that this is Kip. When he finishes with a flourish, an older man stands up from the sofa applauding loudly. Yes, of course, this is his father. There is so much pride and love in his eyes for this child. The father is dressed casually but elegantly in a sweater of fine wool and perfectly tailored slacks. A moneyed gentleman, all manicured and tidy except for his unruly shock of white hair. The physical resemblance of this child to his father, as well as the grown-up Kip to his father, is remarkable.

I turn to look at Kip who has vanished. Suddenly, the scene changes and a man is kneeling beside a bed in a dark bedroom. It's a modest room, so I interpret this to be an earlier time and different place. A pale, stone-faced woman is lying prone with her head on the pillow and not moving. She is dead. Recently dead from the looks of her. The man is sobbing. There's a bassinet in the room where an eerily quiet, and very pale, almost blue child, lies sleeping or in a coma. A door opens. The man turns and looks up. Wild, unruly hair but handsome features. Another clone of Kip and Kip's father. I look at the man coming into the room. It's King! *What the...?*

"Bart, I have the best doctor who can look after your son. I know you're still grieving for your wife, but we have to act quickly. The poisons she transferred to him are taking hold. He needs a transfusion. My people will make him well, the fact that he's a mix-race will not be a problem. Sign this contract, and I assure you there will never be any more money problems for you and your infant son. But hurry!"

At this point, I realize that the woman who is lying on the bed is black. The man called Bart takes the pen from King and signs the contract hurriedly. Bartholomew Henry Knight. Kip's grandfather! I don't have to read the contract to know what it says. At that point, the scene fades again and I'm in a large living room, which feels like it's in a very large house. Bright sun shines through the picture window revealing a prairie of sparse grassland and tumbleweed. A youngish blonde woman with dazzling blue eyes like Kip's is having a heated conversation. She's arguing with a young man who has a light-brown complexion and piercing dark eyes. Was he the baby in the bassinet?

"You're not my mother! Don't tell me what to do!" he says shouting as he slams the front door and exits. I float after him and squint in the bright sunlight as I watch him get on a motorcycle and speed away. An overwhelming odor of sulfur, tar, or creosote fills my nostrils as I notice the pumping oil wells around us. Turning to look back at the house, I see that it's a massive structure made of stone like a palace in Europe. Now, I'm on the bike feeling the wind in my hair. Faster and faster, we're flying on the desolate road when suddenly out of nowhere a car crosses our path and we swerve away. The bike goes off the road and flies into a ditch then flips over. Standing in front of this young man, I see that his head is lying in a funny position and realize his neck has been broken. Suddenly a chasm opens up and pulls his soul from his body. It is dragged down and down into the deep opening. *Oh! That was beyond strange and quite unnerving.*

The scene changes again and now I seem to be in an apartment. Outside the window are other buildings. A city. New York? Slowly appearing are two people. Kip and...King! King is in full fury with his beast eyes, flaring nostrils, and red-toned skin. Kip is calm and angelic with a beatific smile.

"Get rid of your ridiculous charities at once," King says and snarls. "I won't have you mock me. Mock what I stand for. You belong to me. I own you and you must obey."

"That's absurd. My father and I are free agents. You may have made a deal with grandfather, but not us. Now get out and never approach me, or my father, again. We denounce you."

"Your grandfather gave me *his* soul, the soul of your father, and the soul of his half-brother, and the souls of all future generations. That was the deal to acquire and keep the oil wells pumping. Your vast fortune has been generated by those oil wells. I can stop the flow at any time. Are you ready to become impoverished?"

"Stop those damned wells. Damned by you. My father and I cleverly invested the money from those wells, which has grown exponentially. If we never get one more cent from those wells it wouldn't matter. I'm not greedy and have more than enough to fund my charities and live a simple life. Now begone, you foul beast." And with that Kip raises his arms and I think I see angel's wings attached to them for one split second. King growls and shrinks back cursing and rushes out the door. At least I've got validation that my instincts to give away my money to charities was the perfect antidote to King's evil powers.

And then a terrible thing happens. The room fills up with smoke. I can't breathe. I see Kip lying lifeless on the floor, as the apartment goes up in flames. Awful. Slipping out of his body his soul takes flight and then is brought down by a demon entity. They wrestle and finally Kip's soul pulls away with the aid of a glorious shining light emanating from a woman. A beauty of the ages with the fairest complexion and nearly white long curly hair. A divine goddess of purity and love. And then Kip, wrapped in the aura of this bright light, rises upward and upward and the sound of angels singing fills the room as the roof falls in and I see puffy soft clouds wrap around his ascending soul.

Dumfounded by this scene, I'm more amazed by something else. I have met that woman before. I *know* her. *How? Where?* Seeing her face instantly unlocks childhood memories held deep within my subconscious mind. A recurring dream as a young child. A message whispered in my ear, *Rejoice, you are one of us.* A mysterious message of which the meaning is just now starting to take shape. And then visits by this woman come forth, secret visits when I was alone playing in the park or by myself in my room sleeping. Along with those visits was the calming scent of lavender, long thought by me to be associated with my mother. Lavender surrounded me when I stumbled in life and stumbled as a writer. My guardian angel, Evangelina is her name…yes, Evangelina, it comes to me now. She protected me and instilled in me a sense of what is good and right. *But then how can King, the Devil, be my father?*

As I try to get a better look at her, I suddenly realize my travel through time and place has ended. I'm back in my guesthouse and I'm alone. Normal reality takes hold as those visions evaporate. "It doesn't matter about you being a force for good, Kip, or the angel lady," I shout out to nobody. "You encouraged me to stay here to work with King, to see firsthand his evil ways. Now my mother is dead. I hate you! Hate you!" And I start wailing as the horror of losing my mother returns. Immediately, thoughts flash in my mind. Thoughts about enjoying the spoils of the deal. Yes, I had thought that. Embraced the idea that the enormous sums of money would give my mother and me a good life.

I was going to buy her an apartment and got caught up in the greediness, until I snapped out of it. Until I realized that I really wanted out. To make a break from all that King represented. And suddenly, like a bolt of electricity, I realize all this was the test Kip kept talking about. To prove myself worthy, rise above my inclinations, my pursuit of false gods in my longing for fame. Perhaps it was the reason Kip helped me to stay. So that I could finally see the evil wrapped in cold cash. Reject all that King offered. But that doesn't change this devastating outcome. The revenge laid at my mother's feet. Her death was the price I paid, and it was too much. My rage returns and I grab my keys and jump into my car.

I know there's a road of sorts to the Lodge from the landing strip and that's where I head. My four-wheel drive will get me over the dirt paths leading to the back of the house. I bump and sway over the rough terrain noticing how the never-ending drought has even turned King's forest into dead and dying trees. The wide trunks of old oak trees hide my parked car from the surveillance of the security guards. I alight with my fire starters realizing this may be the end for me. I may perish, that my own life is at risk when the flames start. But I don't care. Twigs snap under my feet and miraculously no one is alerted. After several trips back and forth to the car, I'm ready.

I soak several rags in gasoline and take the box of matches and put it in my pants' pocket. As an afterthought, I grab only one gas can because that's all I can manage. Jiggling the doorknob of the small back door, I realize to my dismay that it's locked. Undaunted, I kick the lock, like I did when I busted into King's private area. Miraculously, the door gives way. I pause for just a moment to look around and get my bearings. I'm right outside the entrance to the salon.

Thankfully, it's deserted. I can barely make out the furniture and the main hallway's location in the dimness, which is slightly illuminated by the outdoor lighting that bleeds through the windows. My destination, the trophy room, is quite close and that knowledge recharges my energy for this dangerous mission. The entry point door was a lucky guess in the dark. A very lucky guess.

Tiptoeing gently toward the hallway and crossing through the salon, as if a ballerina, I breathe softly, and bump into the chair that I sat in when I had my meeting with King. Our conversation flashes through my mind and shivers of disgust make me twinge. Then a calming feeling overtakes me. *What's that?* The scent of lavender? The overpowering aroma of lavender overwhelms the strong smell of the gasoline soaked rags. A scent, that until my experience with Kip, I have always connected to my darling mother, and I'm reminded once again of my loss and need of her. *Mom.* I miss you so. A silent sob catches in my throat and brings solid determination to complete my task. *This is for you, Mom.*

Carefully and slowly, I traverse the hallway to the trophy room sliding my free hand along the wall for guidance. Once inside, the massiveness of the room, even in the low lighting from scattered small lamps, brings me up short. *How did I forget that?* There's no way these few rags and only one can of gasoline are enough to engulf this room in flames. My haste to seek revenge made me stupid and naive. Shit. Now, I must go back and get at least two gasoline cans to pour all over the wooden floor, walls, and furniture to soak the room as best I can. As I turn to make my way back down the hall, I hear talking. Shit. I grab the can and rush over to hide behind a giant, stuffed grizzly bear standing on its hindquarters as if to attack. Within seconds of doing that someone turns on the giant chandelier. *Whew!*

"Ah yes, Penelope, you can set the tea down here. Now leave us."

It's King! What bad luck. Miserable luck in fact. I was counting on him being in the city. With him here, his security team must be on high alert. It's amazing my opening the back door didn't set off alarms. Whatever the obstacles, I will do what I came here to do. I know that burning down this house can't physically hurt him, the fires of hell being his habitat, but I know he loves this prized collection of animals slaughtered for his amusement. And this Lodge with its doorway to Hades. Stuck here with my fire starters, these heavily soaked rags nearly make *me* gag, so I'm praying the stench won't permeate the room. I've got to tone down the smell. I put the rags under my shirt in a desperate attempt to confine the odor. The conversation over tea is not interrupted by King or whoever he's with becoming aware of the smell of gasoline. Relaxing somewhat, I hear the click of fine china and low laughter after a lewd remark about Penelope. *Assholes.* However, what I hear next makes my knees start to shake.

"We have to do something about Alexa and quickly. She's too unpredictable and capable of exposing all my schemes when we are so close to achieving havoc on an epic scale. Fracking for oil, for example, is already causing earthquakes in Oklahoma, heretofore not common in that state and also compromising the ground water. Of course, the oil companies are denying the connection. The promise of great wealth and dismissing the potential disturbance to the continental plates and fault lines are already enticing additional states to join the fray. The release of these previously unreachable oil reserves will accelerate this planet's demise from climate change much sooner than scientist's have predicted.

"Also, Antarctica is heating up faster than anyone had thought now that carbon dioxide has reached dangerous levels in the atmosphere. In addition to all this acceleration in climate change, global unrest is taking hold. Scarce resources brought on by droughts and floods and the incessant need for oil by the developed countries has opened Pandora's box causing a tidal wave of intolerance by religious zealots. A backlash, a denouncing of modernism, by the disenfranchised and refugees of the oil-rich countries is sweeping the world.

"Mass murders, executions, destruction of antiquities are becoming commonplace. The tribal warfare in the Middle East, land grabs in the name of religion that have gone on for centuries, has moved beyond its borders and now puts the human race at the precipice of extinction. A world war today between the major powers make the stakes extremely high because of the proliferation of nuclear weapons. It would be most amusing to watch.

"All could be lost if Alexa creates a sea change by exposing me in order to motivate my enemies, those selfless fools lacking the normal traits of lust, greed, and denial of reality when it's inconvenient to their cash flow. Disgusting do-gooder trash. It's a tragedy that we weren't able to get her through the initiation ritual. We would have owned her soul immediately and not had to wait for the terms of the contract to be fulfilled.

This torments me." At that, he makes a frightening noise, a low rumbling growl coupled with a high-pitched ear-piercing scream like a trapped feral animal. The sound makes my entire body vibrate uncontrollably. I grab on to the back of the Grizzly and almost topple it over.

"What's that?" King asks recovering his normal voice.

"Probably some rodent getting caught in one of the traps we've set. There's a colony living here that keeps setting off the alarms, so we had to shut them off for a few days while the extermination is being taken care of," says the other man speaking audibly for the first time. "Shutting off the alarms is not really risky because we never have intruders anyway. Most of your guests fight to get *out* once they're shown the dungeon." They both laugh.

"I know it's presumptuous of me to ask," he continues, "but why are you so concerned about Alexa Wainwright? She's just a lone wolf among your new crop of souls. You have many adversaries, of which she is just one. But your fixation on her is apparent. What is so special about her? Why is she so important? You strategized for months on what to do to get her interested in becoming a *devotee*, so to speak. Why is that?"

"Well…yes, Damien, unfortunately, there are people whom I cannot reach. Failures that I cannot lure to my side, to my way of thinking. An epic battle that has gone on for millennia. My interest is born from an unfortunate mistake on my part that happened long before our association. Alexa has been touched, or perhaps I should say, infused with the light of someone who came into my life several centuries ago. Evangelina was, is, her name. Perchance, she reminds me of her because of that connection. As soon as I gazed upon Evangelina, as she administered to the wretched poor in her village in what is now Belarus, I was lost, under her spell, captivated. To be sure, the attraction was the purity of her spirit, her delicate nature in sharp juxtaposition to my own. I showered her with gifts, but she would have none of it. I offered her my heart but she steadfastly refused me. A maiden beyond my reach. I have never before, or since, felt the emotions she stirred in me. A butterfly of grace choosing selflessness over greed. To be a force for good.

"An ethereal creature, she was so pale she was almost transparent. Hair so blonde, it was nearly white in color, extremely light blue eyes that shone with a celestial gaze as if touched by angels. I became obsessed. Desperate to subjugate her to my will. Turn her. But I could not break through the protection around her. The barriers to my gaining access to her inner core. To woo her. With me, she could have had anything she wanted but instead she chose austerity, poverty, and celibacy. We would have been a formidable team. We could have ruled the underworld together. We could have lured untold numbers to our side with her charm and innocent appeal and my cleverness. A waste, a sheer waste. The ignorance and vacuousness of the self-righteous always amaze me.

"Her rejection of me, and all that I stood for, was extreme in its intensity. A knife slicing through me. Painful. I usually get what I want and so my obsession heightened. I tried to break through the barriers put up against me. Eventually, after many years, perhaps centuries, as she dwelled among her kindred spirits, I gave up. I vowed to never put myself through that again. Never. I had refused to even think about Evangelina for decades but, alas, something would stir up my memories and I succumbed again to my longing for her. I was lost in my fervor, my fixation on her increasing. I followed her or had others follow her. I had to know what she was doing.

"But, I would lose her for years at a time. She was quite good at hiding from me, disappearing for long stretches. It drove me to distraction when I discovered she was creating an army of sorts to fight me. I had to show her how fruitless that was. To make her realize that I reign supreme. Will always reign over her weak-willed fools. I would demonstrate my power by becoming King Blakemore, a media mogul controlling the minds of the populace, bending the trends in popular culture to be subordinate to me. The drug culture, the loss of the family unit, indiscriminate sexual encounters, rampant internet porn, all instigated by me. All whole-heartedly embraced and interwoven into the fabric of modern society, such as it is. Then, Alexa Wainwright was brought to my attention after my decision to enter the world of publishing.

"When I saw her photo on the jacket of one of her books, the likeness was uncanny. Not her coloring because it's almost like she's the antithesis of Evangelina, a photo negative if you will, with her black eyes and hair, but the smile, the features, the light in her eyes. My inexplicable sense of loss came flooding back. Why did this young author arouse these feelings? What had she to do with Evangelina? Then, I remembered a relatively recent incident in Moscow, when Evangelina emerged again in my awareness after years of her remaining out of sight and removed from the world.

"I discovered through taunts by her that she was still continuing to build her army to conquer me and had imbued a child with her positive energy, a piece of her light. A child related to Evangelina through her father. A child I tried to kill in the womb but failed. Alexa was that child and, as such, protected until she came of age. Eventually, I lost interest, my attention turned elsewhere with so many souls easily coming to my side and my army growing in strength and numbers. But seeing Alexa's photo brought it all back. The synchronicity of her being an author and my foray into publishing was probably designed by Evangelina to see what Alexa would do.

"And to see how strong my power has become. The war between us with Alexa the spoils. And now was the time. Alexa was no longer a child. Free to choose. Here was my second chance to find a replacement for a partner and in doing so reduce Evangelina to a mere annoyance. I made Alexa my focal point. Studied her. She had a vulnerability. A weakness in her character. Evangelina's influence fading, brought on by the harsh realities of survival. Alexa, now exercising her free will might become my good fortune, or so I thought. Ah, the sweetness of revenge, to hurt the one that had the power to hurt *me*.

"I was under the misconception that I could control Alexa because of that weakness of her character. A chance perhaps to redeem myself. Once and for all to rid myself of the sense of defeat and compulsive behavior that made me feel weak. I would present myself in a fatherly role and fabricate a relationship with her mother. Give her vague suggestions that implied I might be her biological father. A man she had never met, hoping that would make her more accepting of me. Get her unflinchingly over to my side. But she never really embraced the idea. Even when I created scenes with her mother through time, she refused to accept it. I also gave her doubts about Kip and she was thrown for a while, but he's gotten to her now.

"Unhappily, it turns out she despises me even more than Evangelina does, if that's even possible. I didn't think that kind of enmity was in her, she seemed malleable. Starved for a father figure. Our most recent confrontation, where I showed her the pit of hell, and my extreme anger toward her, could not dissuade her, or make her submit out of fear. More's the pity. I was so sure it would be easy to form an alliance with her. She is a modern woman. Loose morals, edgy. And more importantly, she's greedy having an insatiable need for fame and riches. What a joy it would have been to replace that unenlightened sycophant, Jewel, the character she created, with the author herself. It amuses me how her characters evolve in unexpected ways. Who would have thought that Alex and Jewel would form such a bond?

"His devotion to her adds some tension between him and Alexa and that keeps her interested. Like all women wanting what they can't control. It was a good interference on my part. But that loose cannon, Jodie, became the manifestation of Alexa's anger and mistrust of us.

Destroying that house was totally out of control and not what I wanted to happen. Although her appearance at the ferry was amusing, it would have taken too much time and energy to change her. She had to disappear."

I am seething with anger. Taking in all this information has given me clarity of thought. Of course, it was Jodie who made that ominous phone call warning me not to move up here. My first instincts were correct when I came upon the mess in the house and had thought, in some strange way, it was the work of Jodie. But at that point in time, it hadn't fully integrated into my consciousness the notion that my written words had power. That all my fictional characters had become real and acted on their own accord or played out scenes of my own creation, like with Jewel. I now know that the rage inciting that avalanche of tumult wasn't about the former owners losing money from the sale, like I had rationally surmised. But that Jodie and I had merged. In fact, I *felt* like Jodie, *was* Jodie while I was destroying the same house just before I came to burn down this place. It stemmed from the con, the game, the evil, the contract. Her unleashed anger about having been deceived, the murder of my mother, was *my* anger and anguish written into her. Finding that mess really was a foreshadowing of my own final scene. My scene of destruction.

"Alas," King continues, "when I think of the loss of Alexa, it saddens me. An alliance with her would have been a twofold win because I would finally conquer Evangelina by conquering Alexa, her chosen one. The final showdown between us, when I would prevail. But, regrettably, this has been denied me."

His voice becomes hoarse and he seems to sob. Wow. I can't believe what I've just heard. This entire conversation is very disturbing. I wish I could get a peek at this Damian person. I was really lucky I fainted in that dungeon. More than lucky. I know now that some positive force has been watching out for me. That force is Evangelina, my protector, who became lost in my subconscious. Forgotten. Yes, now I understand. So that I could choose freely. Choose to come to her of my own free will. And Kip, who also enveloped me with his protective energy, to protect me from the evil dungeon by helping me collapse as well. And the knowledge that King has been in love, or whatever he can feel, with Evangelina, is astounding. But most importantly King's not my father. *Not my father!* I knew it! A wave of relief flows over me. I'm more determined now than ever to proceed.

Suddenly, King says, "What's that odor?"

I suck in my breath silently. Oh no! Can he smell the gas? *What should I to do?*

"Yes, I detect a strong scent as well. Quite strong. *Mmm...* Lavender I think. Yes, quite pleasant. Do you have lavender sprayed into this room?" asks Damian.

I almost choke with relief but I must be quiet. *Thank you, Evangelina.*

"How strange that the scent of lavender, Evangelina's scent, is permeating this room while we are discussing her. It's as if she's scoffing at me. Because of her ceaseless quest to reduce my power, I have come to realize she watches my every movement. Perhaps she is the very reason that difficulties arise for me from time to time, although my power is growing while hers is weakening. All too soon, she will be of no consequence."

"So," Damian asks, "how can we keep Alexa from being protected by Evangelina? What shall we do to stop her? If she had gone through the initiation ritual, she would be yours at this moment. She could have been sitting by your side right now enjoying the spoils that accepting you and partnering with you offers. How unfortunate she fainted, so the contract has yet to be executed. She escaped eternal damnation. And now, she has some chance of being rescued by your enemies. Even more unfortunate, I know how much fun you would have had if she rejected you. Watching her agony in the fire and brimstone of the underworld, if she had at first refused to become your chosen one. I'm sure that after dwelling in that horrible place, she would have pleaded with you to give her a second chance and change her status to be your partner. But, you, King, relish the torment of others. You would have enjoyed her begging you to free her from the inferno."

"Yes, you are quite right," King says haughtily and I can imagine his sneer. *The bastard.*

Damian continues, "And I'm sure you will take great joy informing Alexa that her friend, Margaret, and her mother will not have an afterlife. No eternity for them because they will just become dust...nothing." And he laughs wickedly.

"Yes, those who make no pact with me can neither enter hell nor heaven when it is I who takes their lives. They just disappear into nothingness, as you well know."

Oh no, Mom! She's lost for eternity.

"But there is no joy in that for me," King continues. "I wish I had some way for last rites, as do some religions. Then, I could capture their souls forever. But, alas, rules cannot be broken and those are the rules. Now, Alexa might possibly be saved by the angels, just like Kip was saved. Saved by Evangelina, who watches over her, unless we get rid of Alexa before she can intervene. I know she will try to save her. Because the history of Evangelina's interest in Alexa started with her mother, Riva Lipschitz, and her relationship with the biological father, whom I mentioned earlier. Especially, because of the father. Evangelina's bloodline was the connection with the father, a distant relative. A branch of her family tree. Part of her grand plan, I suppose. Building her army against me with her own family through time. Kip being another distant relative on his mother's side.

"Of course, I had to interject some disruption in her plans. I got rid of the father, hoping by doing so Riva Lipschitz would be coerced into ending the pregnancy. Destroying him, thus, would have a twofold effect. The bloodline connection would end with him as well as with the child when the pregnancy was terminated. But Riva Lipschitz thwarted my plans. When Alexa turned up, I was reminded that this chapter had not closed. My obsession had not subsided but lay dormant. I realize now that my pain from Evangelina's betrayal is unceasing, endless. However, Riva Lipschitz finally earned retribution for her insistence on keeping the child. It gave me much pleasure on many levels.

"Anyway, it distresses me to give up on Alexa. I wanted to show Evangelina that infusing the child with the light of goodness and purity can be overturned by greed and corruption. I had such hope. Unusual for me, I have some regret that the history I manufactured was just that, a pretense. Her mother returning unexpectedly was inconvenient. Destroying her gave me pleasure because I knew the impact it would have on Alexa. A just retaliation for her rejection of me. The price that had to be paid. But I would have preferred a different ending to this story. I was sure Alexa's greed would bring her to my side. It seemed such a certainty…seemed it would be so easy to woo her and her lust for success with a just a little help from pharmaceuticals. Not nearly as much as I've used on others. And it was quite easy to excite her wanton sexuality. It still puzzles and offends me why she refused me and the life I offered. But this is not over. I have other cards I can play. I see you are curious. But let's just deal with the situation at hand for now, shall we?"

I clench my teeth at this and will myself to stay put. The stench of my rags, the sourness in my nostrils from the bear's fur, and the sweet lavender make me woozy. Lavender. Not my mom's but Evangelina's scent of lavender. Mom sent into nothingness. No chance of ever connecting again. My heart breaks for the thousandth time. *But Evangelina related to my biological father!* This thought eases my struggle to remain silent and still. Yes, I'm definitely getting help with the odor of lavender overshadowing the stench of gasoline.

Damian asks, "How should we get rid of her then? I could lure her by becoming Kip, again. Perhaps take her on a hike and then toss her off the side of a mountain? An accident that befalls inexperienced hikers and does not attract suspicions? Something like that?" *What?* My legs start to shake again, as I listen to them plan my demise.

"I don't think impersonating Kip would work anymore because we've made an error in insinuating he was one of us," says King quite irritated. "Because she has turned from us and now finds us repugnant, she is leery of him, questions his motives. He's been visiting her since his spirit has escaped our clutches, but my sources tell me she's not totally convinced of his intentions. And with his new availability, it would be easy for him to interfere and convince her of his true identity. It was perfect, however, for you to become Kip when she first drove up here. A stroke of luck that we grabbed him when he was jogging at the rest stop. She probably would have turned right around and gone back to the city. I thought having her spend time here with me would bring us closer. More's the pity, it didn't work."

"Yes, she thought Kip was a saint. Her guardian angel," he laughs.

Huh? Yes, now it all makes sense. It wasn't really Kip who made it so easy to clean up that house. It was a mistake to mistrust him. I believed King when he told me Kip was one of them. Now I know why he disappeared and didn't return my calls. He was held captive. *Yes, you bastards*, he's come back. He's come back to show me the light and steer me away from my tendency for avarice, my greediness for fame. *My wonderful Kip, guiding me to make the right choice. Leading me to Evangelina. Working together with her. My guardian angels. If only he could have protected my mother.*

The two evil beasts continue their planning and casually walk through scenarios on how to kill me. It's difficult to remain immobile behind this damn Grizzly and listen to them. I want to scream. I want to burn this place down right now. They discuss using a hired killer. Someone to slit my throat in my apartment. Replace the concierge on duty with one of their own. Or perhaps, I'm raped and choked to death as I walk in my neighborhood at night. They can be patient for just the right moment. However long it takes. Lull me into a false sense of safety. Of being able to resume my old life. Keeping Alex away.

Damien says, "We could stir up her lustiness. Make her become reckless like we did that night at the bar. Only this time, I would finish her off instead of her hurting me, the bitch! But the sex was pretty good, I must say." I'm so overwhelmed with nausea hearing that, I nearly gag. He continues, "We also could stage another incident like the one at the ferry, only this time, it gets out of hand and the crowd could…"

King interrupts, "Much too messy. We'll think of something that is appropriate payback for her betrayal. But a car accident is always a good choice. Easy. Clean. No police looking for a perpetrator."

Bastards. Damien, a shapeshifter. Now I realize he must have turned into that weird version of my mother when she came unexpectedly to visit me and we shopped for real estate. Her mission, Damien's mission, was to placate me and encourage my avarice by purchasing an expensive apartment for her. Her hesitancy for me to do that played into my trying to please her. Always seeking her approval had propelled me into thinking about making a really grand purchase when more royalties rolled in. *Mom. Mom. Mom.* I sob silently. Anger reaches down to my core and throws off irrational thoughts. I picture myself leaping out and setting Damien on fire and then grabbing King by the throat and squeezing the life out of him. Taking pleasure as he turns blue and rolls his eyes back in his head while his tongue hangs out. *Except how can you kill demons that never die?*

It also now becomes clear that my Kip was sent to me by Evangelina. *You are one of us,* she had told me. But, I had to prove it. Prove that I would not be a disciple of King and lust for material riches, be lured by greed. And I almost succumbed. Yet, thankfully, I remain intact. I have learned my lesson well, although, tragically paying a very dear price. Now I know what I must do. Now I know to which side I belong. I can't save my mother but I can save others.

Perhaps I can even save myself.

Chapter Twenty-four

The final showdown

King finally decides to kill me by a drug overdose. Still behind the Grizzly, I listen while these fiends plan the strategy for my apparent suicide. Damien will pour lethal doses of drugs in all my drinks and then stage open medicine bottles all over my apartment. At first, King chose his preferred method for eliminating someone, a car accident, like Margaret and Mom. Smashed beyond recognition between two semis. It would happen when I drove back to NYC or whenever on a highway. They would monitor my behavior and then—smoosh. The end of me. But then, Damian pointed out that it might arouse suspicion, might cause an investigation, if I died exactly as my mother had. Too coincidental. So in the end, it would be drugs. *Less painful at least*, pops into my head as I grow nauseous picturing my demise.

This cause of death had worked before on many celebrities who had tried to break their contracts with King. They get what they want, all the fame and fortune, but don't want to meet King's terms. He laughs when he reminisces about some famous people toiling in the fiery pit. As for my suicide, it would naturally be concluded that I was depressed over my mother's death. Perfect. Overdose it is, and they laugh conspiratorially. "The sooner the better," he tells Damien who will handle it. I let out a soft groan unable to contain my distress any longer.

"What's that?" asks Damian.

"Yes, what *was* that? It sounded like a person. A moan or groaning sound, I think. Do you think there's someone hiding in here? That would be very unfortunate. No one needs to know what we've been discussing. Go and take a look around this room, Damian."

I freeze in fear. I'm to be found out. I hear this Damian creature get up and start to poke around. Moving sofas, tables. Opening closet doors.

"Nothing here," he says.

"How strange," says King. "I'm sure there's someone hiding. It was definitely a moan of some sort. Check behind those large animals. The lions and that Grizzly. The sound seemed to come from that side of the room."

Suddenly, I'm startled silly by a most unexpected occurrence.

Dozens of tiny mice, babies, scurry near my feet and race out into the room. And then bigger ones. Not a one touches me. My natural instinct to scream is assuaged by not feeling any sensation of mice running around me. I watch this event as if having an out-of-body experience, stunned, silent, and frozen. From the corner of my eye, I see the rodents running out from all corners of the room in my line of sight. Hordes of them. This giant room must be full of them. And they keep coming. More and more. In droves. A deluge of mice. Some instantly blow up like a balloon and become giant rats. And the sound. The squeaking sound reaches a crescendo. I force myself not to react but to remain still because I sense this is an otherworldly deflection engineered by my lavender-loving protector. King starts shouting.

"These disgusting things. GET AWAY!!! Look how many there are. Do something Damian. Do something!" He lets out an angry bellow. "Call the exterminators at once! NOW! These filthy beasts. Ouch!" And then I hear him get up and rush out of the room knocking things over. He's actually running and moaning. I would enjoy seeing his distress, if I weren't so distressed myself and needing to remain hidden. Damian picks up the phone and calls for help.

"Come to the trophy room right now and rid us of these nasty mice! And filthy rats! It's a massive attack. There are so many you can't even see the floor. Come at once! It's DISGUSTING!" he shouts angrily into the phone. "Ow!" he screams and I hear him fall over hard and then there are no more sounds from him. I peek out and the mice and rats are all over him on the floor. The sight is from a horror movie. I'm hoping he'll be completely devoured but the bastard gets up and brushes off the rodents. He races out just as an army of people come running in while spraying the room. They're wearing gas masks and hazmat suits. Uh-oh. Now what? Gotta do something and right now.

A strong chemical smell fills my nostrils. The squealing mice quiet down somewhat as they start to die. Will I be poisoned before they get to me? I've got to do something and fast. Just as I'm about to reveal myself and light a soaked rag to throw into the room, a heavy fog cocoons me. The fog is infused with the calming and lovely aroma of lavender. The overwhelming scent is thick and pure and I feel arms wrap around me in a loving embrace. For a moment, the fog lightens and I gaze at the visage before me. She's Botticelli's Venus, a glowing, rapturous beauty beyond description, the manifestation of Evangelina, my protector. Before I can make sense of what's happening, I'm whisked away to another place and time.

My feet gently touch the ground and when the fog dissipates, I see that I'm in a city. On a street in a city. *New York?* It certainly looks like it could be New York, one of those tree-lined quiet side streets uptown off Fifth Avenue. Then I notice an abundance of beautiful structures in the neoclassical style, as far down this street as I can see and probably beyond. Like an architectural outdoor museum, a collection salvaged from centuries before.

Although this type of architecture can be found in New York City, it's the colors they're painted that make them seem foreign and from centuries past. Pastel colors of pale yellow, light blue, salmon-pink create the magic. Each building has its own unique decorative white trim to complement the appealing exteriors. Graceful confections in stone. So no, not New York, *but where?* I am lighter than air as I study my surroundings, bobbing up above and then back down. What fun. I float down the street and notice that apparently among these architectural delights are churches because those buildings are adorned with crosses. The churches feel whimsical in their presentation with their onion-shaped domes. One is all white and the onion-shaped domes atop the spires are gold. They are very oriental looking. Moorish. These designs seem familiar, like I've seen this type of architecture before in photos or somewhere. *Hmm...just where is this?*

My educational seminar floating among this bounty of beautiful buildings is abruptly cut short by the sudden appearance of people. I nearly bump into two young women who appear out of nowhere walking in front of me. There's something familiar about one of them. She has curly red hair pinned back on each side with barrettes and she immediately captures my attention. I hover in front of them to get a really good look. Amazingly, I take my ability to bob about in stride finding it rather enjoyable.

I am transfixed. Staring at her. The red head. Just staring...hard. Then my heart starts to pound and I'm about to be overwhelmed with sorrow. I quickly take control of myself. This moment is too important to waste on tears. This moment can hardly be fathomed. In a sudden rush of recognition, I realize that the woman I'm staring at is my...*mother.* Seeing my mother as a young woman of perhaps eighteen or nineteen years old is very disconcerting but also leaves me awestruck. Oh my god, it's Mom. Mom! *It's Mom!* Resisting an urge to grab and hug her, I hover in wonder trying to grasp this reality. Of course, I'm in Moscow. Yes, that's where I've seen photos of those onion-domed churches, the most famous being in Red Square. I can see that my mother is enjoying an early spring day in the city where she was born. New leaves are emerging from the many trees planted evenly on the sidewalk. Reawakening from their winter's sleep. A rebirth from death. Just like this experience of my mother being reborn for me.

It's mesmerizing to watch her walking nonchalantly with a friend. Every detail of my young mother, my mother *alive*, is a cherished sight and will forever be seared in my memory. I have always thought my mother to be a beauty, fantastic to behold, but this youngster had not yet been sullied by the many disappointments that would come later. She just beams. Her very essence reflects this innocence. And so I study this miracle of seeing my mother in her youth.

Her creamy complexion is so fair it appears translucent, like the faces of beautiful angels in church paintings. Her dazzling, enormous bright blue eyes in her young face reveal her sharp intelligence and independent spirit, as they always have to me. As she walks, her thick red hair, a wild mass of curls, bounces on her shoulders. It shocks me to see her with long hair that is surprisingly curly instead of her signature spiky short cut that she has worn as far back as I can remember. It dawns on me, in that instant, that I have never seen any photos of my mother when she was young and living in Moscow. She had left all that behind her and had never contacted her parents nor did they contact her after she emigrated. At least not to my knowledge. I have always been curious about her life in Moscow, and now, perhaps, some of her history will be revealed to me.

Gliding around her from every angle, I can see that she is much shorter and much more slender than her female companion who is rather stout with plain features. Yes, she is tiny. Just like her tiny firebrand future self that I know…knew…and I stifle a sob. They both are dressed similarly wearing light gray wool sweaters and dark gray wool knee-length skirts. Perhaps they are school uniforms. My mother wears black dress flats with white ankle socks. Her friend wears loafers and knee socks. They are giggling and speaking to each other in Russian and Yiddish. …*Mom*… *Mom*. My heart breaks again. I can't help myself and try to hug her. To feel her. My arms just grab the air, but my being merges with hers. I become privy to her thoughts and can understand what she's saying. She loves this street, *Bolshaya Ordynka*. Ah yes, she loves these walks around the historic district with its fabulous collection of beautiful buildings and then to cross the Moscow River over the Moskvoretsky Bridge leading to Red Square.

Her family's apartment is near Red Square by the Choral Synagogue, a Jewish treasure. She loved to go inside whenever it was open and look at the splendor of it. When she thinks about the synagogue, I can see it. A spectacular structure that's quite impressive. The façade is neoclassical in pale yellow but the interior is in the Moorish style dominated by gold accents in the moldings and murals. Most certainly, there are no synagogues in the United States so glorious.

My connection to her thoughts is suddenly severed and I'm thrown out to just float around her. I try to hug her again, so we can merge, but I'm kept out. So, in my floating state, I accompany her and her friend Ida as they walk over the bridge, stopping for a moment to gaze upon the narrow and winding Moscow River. Listening to their banter, which luckily I can still understand, I realize they are two silly girls. Boys and shoes. Strict parents. Stuff like that. As they approach Red Square, they walk toward the whimsical St. Basil's Cathedral.

The orange brick facade is adorned with decorative shapes using the colors of green, blue, or red and trimmed in gold or white. This one-of-a-kind structure, with its numerous spires created to look like the flames of a bonfire, immediately captures your eye and your imagination. The spires all have multicolored onion-shaped domes displaying stripes or geometric overlays painted for maximum effect of the designs. The tallest spire in the center has a smooth gold dome. This truly remarkable architectural wonder keeps my attention, so I don't notice a young man in uniform approaching us.

"*Privet, krasavitsa,*" he says to my mother while getting quite close to her. Hello beautiful, a universal pick-up line. My mother and her friend start giggling like the school girls they are. My mother acting like that makes me uncomfortable. Giggling. She doesn't giggle. Never have seen her giggle. But, hey, she was just a kid really, and a girl giggling at a boy saying hello is timeless, I guess. It doesn't suit her, though. She's not a girly girl, my mother, but a strong and independent woman. They walk away quickly with hurried steps and put their heads down, so as not to look at him. He pursues. He won't be dissuaded. They whisper to each other.

"*Sheyna dreykop,*" says Ida speaking Yiddish, so he won't understand. My mother agrees.

"*Meshuga,*" she says. So they think he's cute but nuts. He starts to speak again and my mother stops short and turns toward him with an annoyed look. Now we're talking. This bold action is more like it. Ida turns also following her lead.

"Stop following us. We aren't interested in you soldier boys," says Ida.

"Well, sorry miss, but I'm really not interested in you. Just interested in your friend and her unique beauty," he says looking pointedly at my mother. "I am Alexai Glazkov," he says while taking off his officer's visor hat trimmed with red and gold braiding. He bows slightly in a formal manner to make her acquaintance. "And you are probably the prettiest girl I've ever seen. Your scarlet hair…and your eyes…so blue…like the sky. You will haunt me forever, even if I never see you again. Can we please meet tomorrow? In Alexander Gardens. By the fountain with the horses. Three o'clock. I'll be waiting. I have to go now." His eyes beg her. His dark, soulful eyes. He puts his hat back on and his soft and shiny thick black hair is once again hidden.

This handsome young man cuts quite the figure in his khaki green army uniform with its short belted jacket revealing his slim waist. The braiding on his broad shoulders matches that of his hat. As he turns his head toward a group of soldiers standing in front of St. Basil's who have started shouting to him, he says again, "Three o'clock. The fountain with the horses. Meet me then." When he's slightly further away while walking backwards and staring at my mother, he smiles, "Please," he says softly, "tomorrow, three o'clock." He turns to rejoin his comrades, strutting over in his black leather boots worn over his army jodhpur breeches. Sophisticated and so debonair, he's captivating, even to me.

My mother looks spellbound watching him. She nodded when he told her his name but didn't offer her own. In fact, she never uttered a word. Only after he falls in with his group does she begin to turn away. She starts to make her way across the square with Ida and then turns back to get another look at him, but he's gone.

In a flash of awareness, I'm starting to register the importance of this soldier. I don't know why I hadn't realized it at once. Now I understand why I'm being shown this encounter. Shown this day in my mother's life. Pretty stupid of me not to get this before. It's plain to see, and now I realize, that this soldier is my…father! And his name is Alexai. Oh my. My mother never blinked when I changed my name. And the significance also of the name for their meeting place, Alexander Gardens. All these connected names. This is more than a coincidence. I always thought it odd that every time I asked my mother what was my father's name, she would say, "Why does it matter?" But it did matter. I'm flabbergasted by the unseen hand, the guardian angels that guided me. All I ever knew was that he was a soldier.

Any filial connections to King are totally erased with this knowledge. Hallelujah! So, this casual and random event is the beginning of my existence. My father. The soldier. Amazing and awesome. A gift to be able to see him. To know what he looked like. Words of gratitude could never be expressed adequately. Evangelina, my miracle protector, thank you, most humbly.

I turn my attention back to my mother.

"So, will you meet him?" asks Ida.

"Of course not," my mother says. "Did you think he was cute?"

"Of course! Very good looking."

"I did too. Such clear olive skin and beautiful brown eyes."

"Don't even think about it, Riva. Your father would never allow you to date a goy. Only Jews for us. Anyway, he's probably an atheist being in the military."

"Yeah, you're right about my father. But why would I have to tell him?"

"Riva!"

"Just kidding. He's handsome though. A gorgeous specimen, very tempting." And they both laugh heartily like adults. Not giggling like school girls, thank goodness. Now the two of them dissolve and fade away. Suddenly, I'm alone. Red Square also disappears and the lavender-scented fog surrounds me once again. Now what? I'm in some sort of botanical gardens with lovely tulips planted in neat rectangles of yellows and reds. There's a large iron gate. I see my mother running through it while furiously glancing at her watch. Her thoughts are once again revealed to me.

Conflicted but excited, she made up her mind at the very last minute. When she reaches the fountain with the horses, it's ten minutes after three o'clock. Searching frantically through the crowd of people, she cannot find him. She's dejected like she was made the fool. As she turns back around, she spies him. There. Strolling slowly toward the Tomb of the Unknown Soldier where the changing of the guards has begun. A broad smile replaces her frown but she doesn't want to appear too excited as she approaches, so she comports herself appropriately. Standing on tiptoe next to him she says his name in an urgent whisper. He turns and she can see his tears. She's shocked by this display and he quickly brushes them away. She thinks, *is he crying for me because he thought I wasn't coming?*

"I'm so glad you came," he says. "I was afraid you forgot all about me. I know it's not manly to cry. But ever since I was a small boy, I get emotional here, especially when there is such a respectful changing of the guard. It makes me so proud to be Russian and a lieutenant in the army. Come, *milaya moyna*, let's watch until the end and then have some tea."

She's not convinced that his crying wasn't because he thought she wouldn't show, but she can't know for sure. He called her *my sweet*, milaya moyna, an affectionate term he would use toward her on a regular basis and it touched her to the core. Never again, for the rest of her life, would she allow anyone to call her my sweet. Now I know why. After the ceremony, they strolled to a cafe near the Kremlin while chatting away discovering their common interests. Music, literature, and astronomy. Astronomy, imagine that! He was fascinated by the universe and its mysteries, just like she was. She told him her name finally and he repeated it with awe and respect. It was perfect for her. Her blue eyes like the blue rivers that flow through Moscow. Riva for river. She told him, it was also a Hebrew name, from Rebecca in the Old Testament. Testing him. "Really?" he said inquisitively and quite unperturbed. He wasn't at all familiar with the Bible.

They sat in a dark corner of the cafe holding hands under the table. The centerpiece of each table had a colorful samovar trimmed in bronze and painted blue with artwork portraying flowers in a lighter blue and white. There was a matching teapot and both were placed on a matching metal tray. Tea leaves were brought and they steeped the tea and poured it into cut crystal glasses with metal handles. The charming cafe had embossed bronze metal ceiling tiles and plasterwork decorations on the columns and walls. The seating and tables with red and gold accents brought a cozy ambiance. A romantic place for a romantic assignation.

I float over and sit in the vacant chair opposite. I needed...no wanted to get a better look at this earnest young man who seduced my mother so easily. What a wondrous gift to see my father alive and in his prime wooing my mother. I could see myself in him. I had his eyes, his dark hair, and his height. Yes, now it makes sense why I look nothing like my mother. His DNA, his gene pool dominated my mother's and made me almost a carbon copy of him except for gender.

And so I sat and studied his every movement. How his eyes twinkled when he laughed, which he did frequently. His straight and even pearly white small teeth enhanced his handsomeness when he smiled or displayed his impish grin. His strong hands served the tea with delicate motion. How he took charge when he decided to get some food. Caviar and blinis sparing no expense. His obvious enthusiasm for life. How he was so totally besotted with my mother. When they kiss goodbye, it's a long and hungry kiss. Naturally, a bit uncomfortable for me to watch but I am too fascinated to turn away. This is how it started. The passion that led to me.

Another realization pops into my head. Now, I finally get why my mother chose Gladys as my name. Gladys...Glazkov. Close enough to honor him. Though Alexandra would have been a superior choice and a name I would never have changed. But then it dawns on me that speaking that name out loud would be too close to speaking *his* name. The pain. The hurt. The loss. She could never heal. But then *I* did it, changing my name to be like his, unknowingly, but so many years later. Maybe at that point, the memories were soothing to her. *Who knows?* Did I just think that or did Evangelina impart that to me? With that thought, Evangelina appears. She acknowledges my shock to all that I've been witnessing and folds her ethereal arms around me.

When she disappears, the fog rolls in again. This time when it thins out the scenes are quick vignettes depicting the events shaping my mother's destiny. In the first scene, she and Ida are in a park sitting on the grass in the shade of a large tree. My mother is weeping and telling Ida that she's afraid she's pregnant. Ida is horrified but consoling. She tells her about some homemade remedies to cause an abortion and writes them down on a slip of paper. She also tells her where she can go for a state-sponsored abortion.

My mother reads the paper sobbing while she pockets it. She looks dreadful with puffy eyes like she's been crying for days. Her greasy unwashed hair is pulled back in a ponytail and her skirt and blouse are all wrinkled. They sit sadly together never noticing the beautiful sunny day. Never smelling the few wild flowers. My mother stares blankly mumbling about the mess she's in and how she could be so stupid. Ida keeps telling her there's a simple solution, an abortion, and no one needs to know. Finally, they get up and hug goodbye. When my mother is by herself on the path back to her home, she rips up the paper and throws it away. I know how this ends and it's not an abortion. Thank goodness.

Next scene, she's with Alexai in an apartment. This time, she looks put-together. Fresh face, clean hair, pressed clothing. They're in a sparsely furnished living room sitting together on a worn, black leather-looking tufted sofa. In front of the sofa is a simple metal coffee table and a lone ashtray with a smoldering cigarette. No artwork on the walls save for a poster of Mikhail Gorbachev. A beat-up linoleum floor in gray and white faded geometric design rounds out the shabbiness of the place. Alexai tries to kiss her but she pushes him away.

He cajoles her. He pleads, "*Moya lyubov*, my love, I have very little time before being sent to Afghanistan." He's agitated, his cousin Vlad only gave them the apartment for two hours. My mother sulks. Over and over, he asks what's wrong. Suddenly, she runs into the bathroom and throws up. When she comes out, he's sitting on the sofa smoking a fresh cigarette looking distraught.

"I thought you were using the birth control pills I gave you. They were very difficult to get," he says stunned.

"I did, but I was stupid. I didn't realize they don't work right away.

I needed to be on them for a full month. I'm such an idiot. My father. How can I tell my father? I'll be disgraced in his eyes. A disgrace for the family. I can get an abortion. No one would ever know. But…I don't want to Alexai. This is our child…a child conceived by our love for each other."

"Shh, don't worry, *angelo'chick moi'*(my angel.) *Ya tebya lyublyu*, I love you. Yes, this is a shock but it just speeds things up. I want to marry you. I wanted to wait until I came back from my tour of duty, but we'll just get married right away. I leave in two days, so we have to do it tomorrow. I'll arrange everything."

"Alexai, are you sure? First I have to get my father's permission. I'm sure he'll accept you given the circumstances. Can we tell him we'll bring this child up as a Jew? In secret, of course, until things change."

"I don't care about religion. So, of course, you can do whatever you want, *milaya moyna*."

"Come to my apartment tomorrow afternoon. I will speak to him in the morning, when he's rested and in a good mood."

This scene dissolves and now I'm in my mother's apartment looking at my grandparents. My grandfather is livid. He's snarling and making such an ugly face that his pleasant features are camouflaged. When he stops to catch his breath, I see he has bright blue eyes that are filled with rage. His sparse hair is pure white and so is his mustache. My mother resembles him with her soft features and pert nose except for her flaming red hair. My matronly grandmother is quite stout and thick waisted.

She looks to be in her fifties but is most likely in her forties, given the age of my mother. Her wavy hair is loosely pinned back in a bun at her neck. It is a shockingly red color. Hard to describe. Neon red? Really bright. An awful dye job from probably an off the shelf product or maybe a home brew. She probably was at one time a natural red head like my mother. She's wearing a plain grey dress with a full, white apron tied over it. She's holding a dish towel as if she was interrupted drying dishes in the kitchen.

They're in a living room with dark wood traditional furniture. Part of the room is a dining area with a highly polished mahogany table. The four chairs have scrolled backs and fluted legs. The sofas have ill-fitting slipcovers in floral prints to protect them, I assume, from the two cats that are wandering around on the wood floors. Numerous paintings and photos adorn the walls. Through the glass panel doors of the bookcase, I can see knickknacks placed here and there in front of stacks of books. An apartment revealing much more prosperous people than Alexai's cousin.

"You have disgraced us," screams my grandfather. "You're a

whore. A *shanda fur die goy*. You have brought a shame on all Jews for the world to see allowing this to happen with a *sheygets*."

"*Oy gevalt*, Samuel! Oh my goodness, that's a horrible thing to say. This is your daughter. Think before you speak. So he's a *sheygets*, a non-Jew. Would her situation be any better if the boy were a Jew?"

"He wants to marry me, Papa. We're in love," says my mother. "He's coming to talk to you. He said twelve o'clock. That's when he can leave his post. Please Papa, listen to him. We can get married today."

"Samuel, you must give him a chance," says my grandmother. "It's better for her to marry. Much better. The rest we can work out. He can convert. Would he convert, Riva?"

"Perhaps. He has no loyalty to any religion. So maybe."

"Why would he want to?" says my grandfather. "Jews have a hard time here. There is so much anti-Semitism. Even parts of our beautiful synagogue are used by the government."

"Things are starting to change, Samuel. But our grandchild would be a Jew. That's what's most important. So let's meet him. Let's talk to him at twelve o'clock."

My grandfather is silent but shakes his head in agreement. I can see that he's not convinced but is beaten by circumstances. And they all sit down at the table to wait. My mother looks anxiously at the clock on the wall. Time passes but no one comes at 12:00 pm. There's no knock on the door at 1:00 pm or 2:00 pm or...ever. My mother's mood shifts to desperation and extreme sorrow. Her parents accept the fact that she's damaged goods with no salvation except for one. It's decided, she must have an abortion and then my mother flees the apartment.

Now, I'm taken to another scene. Alexai is making his way down to Red Square. He's whistling and practically dancing down the street. As he turns on a side street towards my mother's apartment, he notices a sweet little girl holding a doll in one hand and her mother's hand in the other. They're walking toward him. Strolling under some scaffolding from a five-story building under renovation, the girl drops the doll and continues walking unawares. Alexai watches her lose the doll and walks over to where it has dropped. He stops and bends down to pick it up just as a hammer falls from the top level of the scaffolding, hitting him directly on his head and killing him instantly. Bad timing. Really bad timing. My poor father. And ultimately, poor Mom. The situation has now become quite dire for my mother, but she doesn't know it yet.

Abruptly, I'm whisked away to see my mother running to the building that was their meeting place, cousin Vlad's apartment. She's furiously dashing up the stairs and banging on the door, "Alexai, Alexai," she yells and the door opens. My mother believes that the person opening the door is Alexai because the resemblance is striking. She throws herself into his arms hysterically crying. Vlad is obviously confused but holds her as they shuffle into the apartment. At that point, my mother realizes her mistake. Vlad is not wearing a uniform and he's crying. He's not Alexai. "What is it? Where is Alexai?" She senses something is terribly wrong and starts to panic breathing rapidly. "Tell me," she shouts through her tears and sees the sorrow on Vlad's face as he tells her. Then in a whisper, "Oh...my...god."

As she begins to collapse, he grabs her before she hits the floor. I watch her body language as she learns Alexai's fate and thus her own. He comforts her in a gentle voice through his own sobs. It's hard to watch this intense scene. Like a mantra, she says his name repeatedly. Over and over, "Alexai, Alexai..." As if speaking it out loud would somehow bring him back. But she knows, all is lost. There's no future, no hope, no chance for happiness. She would never speak his name again. Darkness descends upon her wrapped in wails of grief and a broken heart. I start to cry myself. This is too much to witness. Too hard.

Suddenly, Evangelina appears and I am given confirmation of what I heard King tell Damien. Evangelina had chosen my parents to be under her protection. My father, a distant relative of her family, and his pure love for my mother gave forth a positive charge of goodness needed in this world. To propel this good energy forward, Evangelina gave me her spark by touching my mother's stomach where it passed through her womb and into me. This angered King when he found out her plan to build her army of positive energy to fight his influence. His twisted evil mind knew no bounds. It was he who dropped the hammer changing the trajectory of my mother's life and, of course, mine. He's a trickster, she warns me. Don't believe anything he tells you.

The scene changes again. Because of losing Alexai, my mother is sitting in a reception room of a clinic with dozens of women waiting for an abortion. King, that bastard King. But Evangelina intercepts again and appears as one of these women who tells my mother of a Jewish charity that provides passage and papers to leave the Soviet Union and go to the United States. With this information, my mother immediately gets up and walks out. She walks out, follows her instincts, and winds up at Miriam's apartment in Brooklyn.

King has been thwarted. But in the end he did away with my mother, which I will never get over, and nearly got my soul. My hatred of him is visceral. And with that thought, I'm immediately brought back to his trophy room and my mission has become supercharged. I realize now that it was King's influence over me that pushed me in directions for which I have regrets. But no more, save for this one last hurrah.

How ironic that my dark side empowers me to do my task. I know King is an eternal malevolent force that can never be killed. But I can hurt him. I can show him how much I despise him by destroying what he treasures. A gesture, but a big one. And so I peek out from behind the bear. The room is empty and dead rats are everywhere. Disgusting. The room is rank with the odor of rat poison or whatever was used and dead rotting rodents. No one will enter this room for a while, I think, so there's time for me to go back to my car and get more gas and more rags.

Big mistake.

Chapter Twenty-five

This is really the final showdown

I slip out the door from the salon where I came in without so much as glance around and start to walk quickly over to my car…only it's not there! Instead, I find a bunch of security guards with their guns drawn pointed at me. Shit! Quickly, I drop down in a crouch like I've seen in TV detective shows and scurry back inside the house. Who knew watching those shows would wind up being so informative? A gun is fired and bullets whizz by my ear just as I close the door. *Now what?* I lock the door in a feeble attempt to keep them out and go back to Plan A. This time, I'm running back to the dead rats' mortuary as fast as I can. I still might be able to pull this off. Maybe the stuff that killed the rats is highly flammable and I have enough gas and rags to get things going. I make it to my hiding place behind the bear but, unfortunately, my luck has run out.

Just as I get there, dozens of people enter from the opposite hallway and the guards have gotten in the back door behind me. Think! Grabbing as many dead rats as I can, I start flinging them willy-nilly as King's men close in on both sides. This gives me a brief respite as they all make a minor retreat. Nobody wants a dead rat in their face. I grab the rags and dose them again heavily with gas. They're dripping wet. Perfect. I grab a match from my pocket and just as I am about to light one, I'm grabbed from behind. With my arms held down at my sides, I'm unceremoniously dragged and pushed into the salon where King sits patiently waiting in his favorite chair, smoking a thin cigar. *He wasn't there a moment ago. How did he get there so fast?*

Wearing a smoking jacket and a silk scarf loosely tied around his neck, he's the picture of elegance and not at all like the frightened man I heard fleeing from a room full of rats a short while ago. It's a startling transition. He waves his men out of the room.

"Well, hello my sweet," says King in his smarmy, slimy voice. "You've caused quite a stir. How nice of you to join me. Please have a seat," he says pleasantly. He's sitting in that same chair where we had the heart-to-heart talk a million years ago, at least it feels like that right now. There's some irony that we're going to have our final conversation in this very room. Final…for me. Fear flashes through me at that thought.

With a shaky voice and mustering the courage I do not feel, I say, "I'm not your sweet. How dare you. You plotted to kill me. I heard you.

Drug overdose. And I'm not your daughter. We are not family. I know everything. Everything. My mother was never your paramour." And then my disgust and hatred become stronger than my fear. "Lies all lies, you... you...filthy cockroach," I say, venom dripping with every word.

"There's no need to be so vicious. We had a little fun at your expense, I daresay. We knew you were hiding behind the Grizzly, one of my favorite trophies, so ferocious looking posed in his attack mode. We knew you were there because there was a mirror on the wall behind you." He laughs that awful laugh and then sips his tea and continues, "We had fun creating that scenario for you to hear, Damian and I. Please sit, Alexa. Have some tea with me. We can be civilized. Your fate has already been decided. Why not make these last few moments more enjoyable. Sit." And he points to the chair opposite his. Like that long ago night when he spewed his fabrications, his wild notions at me, that he and my mother... Now I know the truth but there's no real comfort, after all. Poor Mom. Poor me.

"What do you mean my fate has been decided? Are you really going to kill me? I don't think so," I say with conviction that I don't really feel.

"I don't have to do away with you, my darling Alexa. We have a contract. I own you and you will do my bidding."

"I never completed the deal because I never went through the initiation. You said so yourself."

"Alexa, dear Alexa. Do you think there really are such rules? I decide what is or isn't. It was all theater. All for your benefit. Shock and awe, so to speak," he says with a smirk. "Anything you heard was just to toy with you. Have a little fun at your expense."

"Well, I think you're bluffing. And besides, I know all about Evangelina," I say vehemently. "She's my protector and a force for good. She despises you and would do anything to stop you. She showed me who I really am. She took me back in time and I saw him, my biological father. My real father."

"Yes. I know that you think that. How appealing for you. Such a sweet romance to see your young mother in love with a dashing soldier. He, a virtual stranger, she, so trusting and naive. And then there's the tragedy of his untimely death. A romance for the ages, waxing poetic. Perfect for a tear-jerker movie or bestselling novel," he says pointedly.

"Wait...what are you saying? What are you implying? That *you* made this up? My family history is fiction? That's utter nonsense. I heard you tell Damian about Evangelina. The scent of lavender. The rejection.

You're just trying to poison her influence on me. Destroy the clarity she's given me. She showed me my truth, my father, my heritage."

"Yes," he says laughing heartily. An awful low-decibel noise interspersed with screeching animal sounds that pierces to my core causing me to break out in a light sweat and my hands to shake uncontrollably. Ignoring my distress, he says nastily, "You think you're the only one capable of creating a good story? Think about what I'm about to say... seriously. Knowing your mother as you do, does it seem plausible she would have been led astray for love? Would she have allowed her future to be decided in such a precarious manner? Be subject to the whim of others?"

I think about what he just said for a moment. He's hit a nerve. "Okay...you may have a point. My mother is…was…a very strong woman. But we're all different than who we were as teenagers. And let's not forget that we are formed by our circumstances, the sum total of our experiences. She was unwed and pregnant at a time and place where it was totally unacceptable. Forced into making a life-altering decision. We can get stronger when faced with adversity. We can change based on how we respond to what life throws at us. So okay, seeing my mother as a crying, simpering weakling or as a giggly schoolgirl may not have resonated with my image of her. But she did leave her family and come here totally on her own. Defied the pressure to have an abortion.

"The strength that would later define her was beginning to form, to take hold of her personality, surely. And she certainly came from Russia. I know that. That part is definitely true. And what about Miriam? I knew her. This was my childhood; I grew up in her apartment. She and my mother spoke Russian, shopped in Russian stores." Suddenly, I remember Evangelina's words in describing, King, a *trickster*, she said, *don't believe him*. With this vivid memory, I become stronger.

"I don't even know why I'm bothering to have any kind of conversation with you. You are a scourge on humanity, certainly not trustworthy. A trickster without a conscience who will say anything to confuse me, lie about anything. Why would you kill my mother if she was so important to you? You told me how important she was to you the night we had that conversation right here in this room. But you orchestrated her death. It was no accident. It was murder. MURDER! There's no family connection going on here King. No relationship through time. So...bottom line is, I don't believe you. You think I'll accept that my encounter with Evangelina was orchestrated by you? Like your fake Kip and the fake mother that you foisted on me? Alexai was not a made-up story, Evangelina's positive light exists, and my being disgusted by you is also REAL!"

"Please Alexa, try and calm yourself. Stop shouting, it's not becoming. Sit and have tea with me. There is so much to discuss, Alexa. Please." I remain standing with my fists clenched. *Oh, how I would love to punch him in the face.* He continues, "My dearest Alexa, you more than anyone should know this fact. You, as a writer, a weaver of tales, know that circumstances, events, or story lines can easily change and very often do. Quite simple, really. Hit delete and entire conversations vanish. In rewrites, characters who were killed off come back to life when the author decides to go in a different direction. Lovers become enemies and enemies become lovers. It is part of the writing process. It happens every day, perhaps every second in your world. Rather commonplace, I believe."

"What are you implying? That my life is being written as if it were a novel? That I'm the lead character in a work of fiction? That's absurd. I'm real. I am not the whim of some mythical writer somewhere. I know who I am."

"If you say so."

I'm thrown by the weirdness of this conversation's change in direction. "All right then. Let's say this ridiculous notion of yours is viable. So, my entire life is someone's...or perhaps it's the product of your imagination. If that's true, then rewrite the death of my mother. Delete her death. Do that if you are so smug about what's real and what's fiction. In fact, rewrite everything. Margaret's death, Roseman's. Rewrite it now. Bring my mother back, my real mother, not some evil doppelgänger, if what you say is not some twisted joke."

"Yes, a complete rewrite, a do over, if you will. Quite an intriguing thought and part of a plan I've been working on for you, my sweet. To see whether you would make the same choices. Become my partner or try and stop me. Join with my opposing forces knowing the risks, the losses you would suffer, or enjoy the spoils I can provide with no perilous outcome for those close to you. Hmm. Ah, yes. What fun it would be. Or maybe I'll just erase your memory of these events concerning your loved ones but leave some vestiges deeply embedded in your subconscious mind. See if your instincts push you toward me or away. An experiment for your immortal soul.

A challenge I put forth to Evangelina, I daresay, who you were right to believe existed. She resisted the idea because she says you've already proven which side you're on. That annoys me and isn't satisfying. I hate to lose. So we will do a reboot. No coercion this time. No drugs. I do hope you would choose me with your free will, Alexa. I know there's a part of you that would. That's why I'm giving you a second chance. To see if I prevail over Evangelina and the age old battle between good and evil. You're important to me. What you overheard me tell Damian about how I feel about you is true. We both need second chances."

King pauses for a moment as he sips his tea, lost in thought. He stares through the windows at the flower garden that's finally starting to whither in this endless drought. This gives me the opportunity for which I've been waiting. We've been alone in this room since he dismissed his men when I was first brought to him. Also, I never sat down, so I was poised to run. I had a bit of oil-soaked rag in my pants pocket and a matchbook stuffed in the other. Quick as a frightened bunny, I seize the opportunity and bolt out of the room. Catching King off-guard while he's ruminating over the rewrite of my life. I fly out of the room before he realizes what I'm doing.

Running with all the speed I can summon, I sail straight down the hallway to the trophy room. Once there, I light the rag and toss it into the room. The gas can is still where I left it behind the Grizzly and I pour gas everywhere before it runs out, especially dousing the Grizzly because King singled it out as a cherished possession. I light another match and throw it and ...whoosh...the entire room ignites. The chemical covered rats go up in flames and explode. Yuck. And then, I watch the destruction of the room as if happening in slow motion.

First, the Grizzly starts to attack me, moving forward with its mouth wide open, its giant claws extended. I scream before I realize that it's really just falling over as the flames disintegrate it. The wall trophies crack and break off the wooden walls that are separating and disintegrating as they are set ablaze. A fiery wind whirls around the heavy drapes that cover the windows and they become burning flame-throwers igniting the sofas.

I hear the crackling clamor of the giant fireplace logs as they catch the heat and flame up. Electric wires start to buzz and spark. The room itself begins to sway and the wood-beamed ceiling catches fire and begins crashing down into the room. I see King's men start to enter the room but back out thwarted by the superheated air. The hot air burns my lungs. I can't breathe. I look for an exit and realize that I will die before I can reach it. I will die here in this inferno. And I accept my fate. *Mom!* That's all I can think of as I lose consciousness and begin to fall onto the wooden floor that's now ignited.

As my body goes limp, I feel someone lift me in their arms and carry me upward. Up and up through the flames as the ceiling breaks into pieces around us. Up. Up. Into the open sky. Clear fresh air fills my wounded lungs and I start to revive. We're above the fiery mess that once was the trophy room. Booming vibrations of walls collapsing pound my ears, as the entire roof over the room caves in. High pitched sounds of hot metal hitting glass make me wince. Tingling sounds of exploding glass punctuate the air. It is the end of the trophy room. A symphony of destruction.

I turn my head and look at Kip. There's another symphony playing. The sound of sweet violins. The music of Henry Bartholomew Knight, the music of love and goodness. He smiles down at me and with one swoop of his free arm he gathers the power of the universe and throws a lightning bolt at the forest surrounding the Lodge. The entire water-starved forest explodes in a fiery storm. The second bolt hits the Lodge square at its center and it explodes in flames. A third bolt puts me in dizzying whirl. Whirling, whirling, and then…

I'm standing at my window looking at my city view. I feel disoriented, as if I just arrived from somewhere else. I attribute this to the slight dizziness that sometimes comes on when I'm peering down from this height, so I step back into the room. I look at my watch. 1:40. Forty minutes exactly is the thought that passes through my mind when the door buzzes and I let Margaret in.

Epilogue

Tiptoeing into the kitchen, so as not to wake my sleeping dog, I pour myself a coke and then add a good dose of Macallan Scotch whiskey. Of course, Trinity has already followed me into the kitchen from my bedroom. I know that's an odd name, but when I chose him at the breeder's, he told me the puppy was so attached to two others from the litter that he called them the Trinity. So the puppy basically named himself. He's a Russian sled dog, a Samoyed. White and fluffy like a giant stuffed toy and he's a good watch dog but also quite cuddly. Because he hasn't yet grown out of the puppy stage, he always wants to play when he first wakes up. So I try to avoid waking him in the middle of the night. But on the nights I have trouble sleeping, well…uh-oh he's looking at me with those playful eyes.

Sleep has become a problem of late. I'm having strange dreams that disappear as soon as I open my eyes. In fact, sometimes I'm so frightened by these dreams that I find myself sitting bolt upright in bed with my heart pounding and totally confused as to why this is so. I placed a lined yellow pad on my night stand to capture the dreams as soon as my eyes open. The pad remains blank. I meditate on these words; *I will remember my dreams* before I close my eyes. The pad remains blank.

Losing a good night's sleep keeps me edgy and irritated all day. It's affecting my work. My final rewrite and edits of the *Darkside* trilogy are not going well. Of course, Margaret has been a blessing for grammar, style, and usage edits but when she comes around all I want to do is hug her. It's such a strong urge that I think she's become uncomfortable. She has stopped taking my calls. Today, she texted me that she's involved in a relationship and needs some time off, a respite she calls it. Well, I'll have to accept that for now. Unasked for, she gave me the phone number of her mother's therapist in her message. I delete the text. Just because I hug her? In fact, the last time she came over, I didn't hug her at all. I was satisfied to just hold her hand. I know it got a little awkward when I wouldn't let go to type some of her changes. Whatever. Since when is being affectionate a sign of having emotional problems? I try not to take offense, but it's difficult. I'm thinking of firing her, but then what?

I don't like being alone so much and that's why I got Trinity. But he needs walking and I don't feel like leaving my loft. The concierge found a dog walker and I put a bowl of water and a dog bed in my private lobby area and leave Trinity out there to wait for the walker three times a day. I've never met the person, so I don't even know whether it's a male or a female. I hear the elevator and know that Trinity's been picked up and he scratches on the door when he's brought back. It's a good set up.

I realize my personality is beginning to change because I'm loathe to leave my loft and my childhood fears have returned. In fact, paranoia seems to be my singular state of mind. When my eyes first open after a restless night until I go to bed, a kernel of fear dwells in the pit of my stomach waiting to become full-blown panic. A terrific thunderstorm with repeated flashes of lightning passed through the other day and I raced into bed, pulled the covers over my head, and whimpered uncontrollably. Since then, I keep my windows in their darkened mode in case an unexpected storm catches me by surprise.

Perhaps being here alone days on end is having a negative impact. I want to be alone but I also need my sanity. Trinity has been a real help. I talk to him and he looks at me and cocks his head as if he knows what I'm saying. Sometimes, he even makes whimpering sounds as if to tell me not to worry. I hope my mother calls again. She called two days ago and I just sobbed and sobbed and couldn't get any words out. She tried to soothe me, but I was unable to control myself. The thing was, I didn't know why I was crying. I think she said she's coming to see me as soon as possible. At least, I think she said that because I couldn't hear too well through my hysteria.

I'm also becoming obsessed with my sales numbers and rankings. Every hour on the hour, I check the sites where my books are listed and those figures are posted. Even when I wake up in the middle of night because of all the global time zones. All have fallen in rank. My debut that was on the bestseller list for a year is not even in the top anything. My sales nosediving agitates me beyond belief. Well, not really nosediving, but still. My trilogy must do well or I might have to sell things. Like this loft. Well, I paid cash for it and I have money invested and also plenty of cash but the HOA fees here are astronomical. I also check my bank balance every day. I have direct deposits and direct debits. So far it's stable with deposits equaling withdrawals but if that changes…*what will I do?*

Also, the publishing industry is changing and not in a good way. This trend of giving books away for free is absurd. I told my publisher, I would never participate in a site that promotes giveaways. So far my books are still selling online as well as in stores but again not like before. If they ever become remainders, well then give them away. I won't care then because they've become garbage. But I'm not at that stage yet, thank goodness. It seems though that there is an ever increasing number of sites that push free ebooks. And on top of it, make the publisher pay to advertise their free books. I wouldn't do that even if I self-published. Writing a book takes hours and hours, months even, perhaps years. If you go to a craft fair, no artist is giving away a beaded necklace, or a watercolor landscape. Now the public expects free ebooks and this makes me so angry. But it also frightens me. How can I live on giveaways when ebooks have become the desired format? Are advances and sales of paperbacks going to become the sum total of royalties?

All this negative thinking has me wishing I had a cigarette, and I don't even smoke. I decide to go to the gym to have a workout and a swim. Maybe that will help my nervous energy and I can get back to my rewrite. I hesitate by my elevator because I think I'm starting to get agoraphobia. That would be a horrible psychological obstacle, crippling. So I force myself, will myself, to get in the elevator and go to the amenities wing.

When I enter, I nod to the receptionist. She immediately asks me if I'm feeling okay. I look puzzled. She says I look pale, so I head right to the locker room to look in the mirror. It's a brightly lit room and makes me squint because I'm not used to such a blinding glare. My darkened windows and one or two turned-on lamps give my apartment a cave-like blackness, a mood mirroring my own. I haven't really had a good look at myself in quite some time because I'm not interested in my appearance. Just being clean. My minimal grooming entails showering, washing my hair, putting on clean clothes. No makeup, no blow-dry hair styling. So now I take a good look and jump back horrified. *What the...?*

My skin tone borders on pale green. My eyes are puffy with red circles and the whites have a yellow look like I'm jaundiced. Pimples dot my chin and nose and are in flagrante delicto, blazing red, from my savage picking at them. My hair bushes out from my head in a wild mess. My natural curl becomes kinky when not tamed by a blow dryer and there are unwelcome gray strands peeking through the frizzy horror. Okay. I must stop this craziness and bring in more light to my home, literally and figuratively. Become my old self. Take charge of my life. I have a rewrite to do, deadlines to meet, and I must improve my personal appearance and my emotional stability. Got it.

The expanse of the room housing the pool makes my heart race and I begin to shake and hyperventilate. My first impulse is to run back out the door. Not good. Granted the huge room is imposing but my logical mind takes over and tells me there's nothing to fear. I take deep breaths and try to relax by staring at inconsequential and nonthreatening everyday sights. Like the swimming lanes defined by floating cables in the water, the other swimmers, my chipped toenail polish.

I slowly ease myself into the water staying in my consciously numbed state. As I swim on autopilot, I start to settle down and enjoy the sensation of weightlessness. After a few strokes, I begin to get into the rhythm and relax with each breath, with each kick, with each glide forward. My fear subsides as my blood rushes through my veins and arteries. My accelerated heart beat is from exertion, not from the panic that took over when I entered the room. I'm becoming normal in my assessment of my surroundings, of my reality. This is good. I make a vow to swim every day. Sanity is better than being nuts. Getting the blood flowing is better than being green.

When I'm done, I say goodbye to the receptionist in a rather loud and artificially happy voice. Must practice at feeling elated. Now it's her turn to look at me puzzled. My new self tells my old self that things are going to change, as I walk through the connecting bridge and take the elevator to my apartment. As soon as I get inside, I increase the light that comes through my windows. The bright sunlight washes over the entire loft and brings everything into focus. Pop, darkness becomes light. Cave world becomes my familiar and cozy loft. A flash of my paranoid self feels threatened but I push down the feeling and start humming to mask my unrest. Yes, it's good to see my furniture, dust that needs to be cleaned, the beautiful wood floors. And, of course, my fabulous view. When I look out, I get an unexplained flare-up of vertigo and my stomach tightens so I sit down and just look around inside.

I forgot how much I love my concrete countertops and colorful glass backsplash in my kitchen. Why did I hide everything in shadow? Looking around my kitchen with pleasure, I notice the red blinking light of my answering machine. There are two messages. How long they've been there? The machine answers my question with the first message. The first message came today, when I was swimming. It was from a Josh Hathaway, a composer of film soundtracks who works for a production company that's looking for new projects.

He said he had come two weeks ago with Margaret, his distant cousin. He wanted to talk about my trilogy but I seemed too emotional and not interested in anything but talking to Margaret, so he didn't bring it up. Oh yeah, I vaguely remember him. He was quite tall with thick, black curly hair. But I didn't pay much attention to him because I was just so glad to see Margaret. For some reason, I was in turmoil that something terrible had happened to her. I think I had a dream she was in a car accident and perhaps even cried in my sleep. He wants to make an appointment to try again to pitch his offer. I don't know…maybe.

The next message is from my agent. She has important news

about my publishing company, Jameson, that she doesn't want to tell me in a voicemail message. I'll call her back after I shower. Shuffling around in the kitchen making a sandwich, I turn on my kitchen counter TV. It's the news. *Wait, what?* Something about Jameson Publishing? I drop my sandwich on the floor when the news anchor says, "After decades as a traditional family run New York publisher, Jameson Publishing, has been sold to a relatively new company in media. Blakemore Media, a conglomerate, headed by CEO King Blakemore is gobbling up conservative television news networks, movie production companies, newspapers, magazines, internet-based media companies, and now foraying into print and electronic publishing with this latest acquisition. How this relatively unknown company came to have so much cash is anybody's guess. Company representatives are remaining silent, saying only that they're well-funded and have numerous wealthy investors. Stay tuned for updates on this breaking story."

King Blakemore! How strange Jameson would sell. What does that mean for me? I sit down at my computer to do a search on the internet to find out info on this Blakemore guy, when a new email from an unknown sender pops onto my screen. All it says is "Enjoy your second chance. Make wise choices in this rewrite of your life, *milaya moyna.*"

What the…?

And wham, my new book idea pops into my head. A very strong urge to begin it takes over. Pushes out any thoughts about the rewrite. I think I'm done with the *Darkside* trilogy rewrite anyway, and actually kind of bored with it. Let it stay as is and editorial can fool with it. Whoever the new editorial team will be. Strangely, any paranoia about handing my book over to the new publisher is gone. *What can they do to it?* It's all done except for some possible punctuation errors. My input is over; I have to let go. This is the time to start thinking of my next project. Acknowledging the fact that, in the past, I have not wanted to succumb to writing books about monsters and such, books that obviously sell, I'm very drawn to this story. Compulsively needing to write it, and right now. This idea has been sloshing around in my mind, interrupting my train of thought while working on *Darkside*. It keeps pushing its way into my consciousness. Words and sentences itching to be written. Who am I to fight this muse? So, I decide to jump in and start. I type my new title and just go with the flow.

When a Stranger Comes…
By Alexa Wainwright

In Loving Memory of Irene Isaacs
July 13, 1918—Nov 2, 2015

Made in the USA
Coppell, TX
16 January 2020